PENGUIN B

THE END
CROWNS
ALL

Praise for **THE END CROWNS ALL**

'This is a witty, sharp reimagining that overflows with heart. Bea Fitzgerald weaves ancient myth into a dazzling new story that is bold, compelling and a striking reflection on the power of storytelling. She is so very skilled in elevating the voices of women, giving them legends of their own that speak to a whole new generation of readers'

Jennifer Saint, *Sunday Times* bestselling author of *Ariadne*

'*The End Crowns All* is witty, romantic and a total joy. Bea completely flips the script, giving Cassandra and Helen agency to subvert their own destiny with dialogue that crackles with humour, love and fire! In short, this is the perfect summer read'

Elodie Harper, *Sunday Times* bestselling author of *The Wolf Den*

'Bea Fitzgerald's writing reminds me why I love reading so much – fresh, funny, smart, and full of wisdom and knowledge. The author expertly plays with the Greek myths, giving us a sexy, sapphic reimagining of the Trojan War that I couldn't put down'

Costanza Casati, *Sunday Times* bestselling author of *Clytemnestra*

'A snappy, sapphic reimagining of the Trojan War, *The End Crowns All* is a true epic about a love powerful enough to change fate'

Luna McNamara, author of *Psyche and Eros*

'*The End Crowns All* is an absolute delight from start to finish. Bea's incredible knowledge of Greek mythology shines throughout, allowing her to bring *The Iliad* to life in such a refreshingly unique and imaginative way. It's impossible not to fall head over heels for both Helen and Cassandra: they are both fierce, funny and fully fleshed-out characters with chemistry that sizzles off the page. This is a book with so much heart, centred around a beautiful love story that will leave you swooning'

Rosie Hewlett, *Sunday Times* bestselling author of *Medea*

'A poignant reimagining of the fall of Troy. Laced with rivals-to-lovers friction and so much slow-burn pining, *The End Crowns All* is a heartfelt depiction of an epic sapphic romance with the power to reweave fate itself'

Laura Steven, bestselling author of *The Society for Soulless Girls*

'*The End Crowns All* is epic in all senses of the word: a dazzling tapestry of threads thoughtfully plucked from the myth and twisted into something brand new and brilliant'

Sarah Underwood, *New York Times* bestselling author of *Lies We Sing To The Sea*

Praise for *GIRL, GODDESS, QUEEN*

'Reads like a breath of fresh air . . . a witty and touching story, with a heroine whose combination of idealism and misadventure will endear her to any reader'

Telegraph

'If you are a reader of fantasy, mythology and romance – the gods are on your side because your three favourite genres have collided . . . A YA feminist romance that is funny, easy to read and vibrant'

Glamour

'One of my favourite reads of 2023 so far, this debut novel from Bea Fitzgerald breathes fresh life into the oversaturated rom-com genre . . . 496 pages worth of brilliant banter and page-turning chemistry that you'll easily devour on a weekend'

You Magazine

'*Girl, Goddess, Queen* is simply divine. Bea has woven a classic myth with an electrifying romance and a witty, fiercely modern twist. Beautifully written, utterly glorious and fabulously powerful, this is a definite must-read that should be at the top of everyone's TBR pile!'

Beth Reekles, bestselling author of *The Kissing Booth*

'A captivating debut! *Girl, Goddess, Queen* is an incredibly fun and wonderfully crafted reimagining of a beloved myth – bringing to life timeless gods, the complex intimacy of family bonds, a fierce protagonist and a passionate slow-burn romance'

Sue Lynn Tan, *Sunday Times* bestselling author of *Daughter of the Moon Goddess*

'*Girl, Goddess, Queen* is a richly woven, gloriously funny and deeply swoony exploration of the Hades and Persephone myth and I'm so excited for everyone to discover the marvellous talent that is Bea Fitzgerald'

Lizzie Huxley-Jones, author of *Make You Mine This Christmas*

'What a triumph of a debut! This fierce and funny feminist take on a classic story weaves seamlessly from rage to romance and is an absolute joy!'

Bex Hogan, author of the Isles of Storm and Sorrow series

THE END CROWNS ALL

BEA FITZGERALD

PENGUIN BOOKS

PENGUIN BOOKS

UK | USA | Canada | Ireland | Australia
India | New Zealand | South Africa

Penguin Books is part of the Penguin Random House group of companies
whose addresses can be found at global.penguinrandomhouse.com.

www.penguin.co.uk
www.puffin.co.uk
www.ladybird.co.uk

First published 2024
This edition published 2025

001

Text copyright © Bea Fitzgerald, 2024
Illustrations copyright © Pablo Hurtado de Mendoza, 2024

The moral right of the author and illustrator has been asserted

No part of this book may be used or reproduced in any manner for the
purpose of training artificial intelligence technologies or systems. In accordance
with Article 4(3) of the DSM Directive 2019/790, Penguin Random House
expressly reserves this work from the text and data mining exception.

Typeset by Jouve (UK), Milton Keynes
Printed and bound in Great Britain by Clays Ltd, Elcograf S.p.A.

The authorized representative in the EEA is Penguin Random House Ireland,
Morrison Chambers, 32 Nassau Street, Dublin D02 YH68

A CIP catalogue record for this book is available from the British Library

ISBN: 978–0–241–62431–9

All correspondence to:
Penguin Books
Penguin Random House Children's
One Embassy Gardens, 8 Viaduct Gardens, London SW11 7BW

Penguin Random House is committed to a
sustainable future for our business, our readers
and our planet. This book is made from Forest
Stewardship Council® certified paper.

To Liberty Lees-Baker,
I'm glad you don't have to print my books off yourself any more.

LIST OF CHARACTERS

THE TROJANS

THE ROYAL FAMILY
PRIAM, king of Troy
HECABE, queen of Troy
HECTOR, the crown prince
ANDROMACHE, princess of Cilician Thebe, married to Hector
PARIS, a prince of Troy
ILIONE, a princess of Troy
LAODICE, a princess of Troy
DEIPHOBUS, a prince of Troy
CASSANDRA, a princess of Troy and priestess of Apollo
SCAMANDRIUS, a prince of Troy, twin of Cassandra
KREOUSA, a princess of Troy
POLYXENA, a princess of Troy
THYMOETES, brother of King Priam and one of his advisors

THE ROYAL HOUSEHOLD
ANTENOR, an advisor to Priam
AENEAS, son of Aphrodite
CLYMENE, a noble woman
ATHRAE, a noble woman
LIGEIA, a servant
AGATA, a servant

TROJAN CIVILIANS
LAOCOÖN, a high priest
HEROPHILE, the high priestess of Apollo
AESACUS, a seer

TROJAN ALLIES
SARPEDON, a son of Zeus and prince of Lycia
PENTHESILEA, queen of the Amazons
BRISEIS, princess of Lyrnessus
CHRYSEIS, daughter of a priest of Apollo

THE GREEKS

THE ACHAEAN ARMY

MENELAUS, king of Sparta, husband to Helen

AGAMEMNON, king of Mycenae, brother of Menelaus and leader of the Achaean army

ODYSSEUS, king of Ithaca

ACHILLES, king of the Myrmidons

PATROCLUS, companion of Achilles

DIOMEDES, king of Argos

TEUCER, prince of Salamis

AGAPENOR, king of Arcadia

EUMELUS, king of Pherae

IDOMENEUS, king of Crete

ANTICLUS, an Acahaean soldier

SINON, an Achaean soldier

THE FAMILIES OF THE SOLDIERS

HELEN, queen of Sparta

POLYDEUCES, brother of Helen and part of the constellation Gemini

CASTOR, brother of Helen and part of the constellation Gemini

CLYTEMNESTRA, queen of Mycenae, wife of Agamemnon and sister of Helen

IPHIGENIA, a princess of Mycenae, daughter of Agamemnon and Clytemnestra

TYMANDRA, sister of Helen

PHOEBE, sister of Helen

PHILONOE, sister of Helen

PENELOPE, queen of Ithaca and cousin of Helen

APIA, childhood friend of Helen's

THE GODS

INSTRUMENTAL IN THE TROJAN WAR

ZEUS, king of the gods and lord of the sky

HERA, queen of the gods and wife of Zeus

APOLLO, god of the sun, prophecy and music

ATHENA, goddess of wisdom and warfare

APHRODITE, goddess of love and beauty

ARES, god of war

ERIS, goddess of discord

TYCHE, goddess of luck and fortune

THE FATES, three women who measure the threads of mortal lives

IRIS, goddess of rainbows, a messenger of the gods

ADDITIONALLY MENTIONED

HADES, king of the underworld

PERSEPHONE, queen of the underworld and goddess of spring

HEPHAESTUS, god of blacksmiths

ARTEMIS, goddess of the hunt

POSEIDON, king of the oceans

DEMETER, goddess of the harvest

HESTIA, goddess of home and hearth

HERMES, god of travellers, a messenger of the gods

DIONYSUS, god of wine and revelry

EROS, god of desire, son of Aphrodite

A NOTE FROM THE AUTHOR

This book is a work of fantasy fiction, inspired by both ancient civilizations and contemporary society. My writing is, in part, a space for me to explore things that I find troubling, and my wish is that this is a space for them to be examined in a fictional setting, in a way that feels safe, reflective and ultimately hopeful. But everyone's lived experience is different, and some readers might find the topics in this book difficult to engage with. I've listed these below. If anything here resonates with you, then please be kind to yourself, and I encourage you to speak to a loved one, a trusted adult, a doctor or another resource as needed.

- This book features extensive conversation about and engagement with war. It also includes blood, gore, human and animal sacrifice, violence and main character deaths.
- This book discusses consent, rape, rape culture, sexual coercion and sexual assault. In terms of graphic or

explicit scenes of this nature, there are instances of forceful kissing.
- Ableism and misogyny are explored. There is a particular focus on mental health in this story, and, though critiqued and addressed, there is repeated use of words such as 'mad' and 'crazy'.
- There are specific mentions of suicide.
- This book features manipulative and abusive relationships.

I'd also like to take a quick moment to discuss the asexuality represented in this book. It's an authentic depiction, largely drawn from my own experience, but, given the lack of asexual representation in fiction, it's worth noting that it only represents a small sliver of the broad asexuality spectrum. Not all asexual people experience romantic attraction, nor do all experience sex-favourable asexuality as depicted here. Regardless of your orientation, I hope we can all resonate with learning to listen to ourselves and finding the strength to be true to all parts of ourselves.

PART ONE

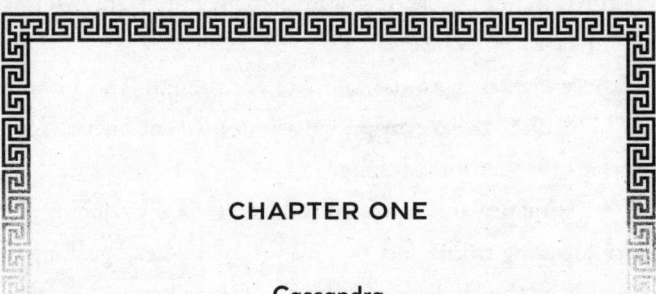

CHAPTER ONE

Cassandra

I NEVER ASKED FOR VISIONS, I was one. In my future, I see myself regal and glorious, luminescent with the glow of my god. The priesthood encourages simpler garbs of its high priestess, but I'll change that when I'm awarded the position, donning the finest silks, the largest jewels and the brightest gold. The people will love me like I am the closest thing to a goddess they'll ever see, and no one will be able to tell me what to do or where to go or anything at all because the voice of Apollo will be heard when I speak.

'Your presence has been requested in the throne hall.'

The interruption is like an insect buzzing in my vicinity – irritating but only enough to have me lazily swat in its vague direction.

'I'm busy.'

'You're sunbathing.'

'Apollo's god of the sun – this is worship.'

'*Cassandra.*'

I open one eye and see Ligeia anxiously wringing a cleaning

rag through her fingers. If it were actually important, Mother would have sent two servants.

'That's *Princess* Cassandra, if you don't mind. And I find it very difficult to believe my presence is needed anywhere. I have brothers for that sort of thing.'

'The issue pertains to your brother,' Ligeia says quietly, her voice lowering to the sort of whisper used when speaking of the gods of the Underworld. 'It's Paris. He's here – he's *alive*. Which means the prophecy . . .'

I lurch to my feet and run to the throne hall before she can even finish her sentence.

I know more about prophecy than most. I'm a priestess of Apollo, after all, and he's the god of it. Also poetry, music, art, truth, archery, plague, healing, sun, light and many more things I should probably have memorized. If you're only swearing yourself to a god because you want to keep your options open, he's a good one to pick.

In our training, we learn several key things about prophecies. Firstly, only select individuals at the temple can give them out. Apollo can't bless everyone – and why would he want to when the scarcity of prophecies allows us to charge a premium for them? Secondly, be vague and account for all outcomes so they cannot say you were wrong. For instance, with battle, say something like, '*You will go you will return never in war will you perish*,' and let the listener decide whether they want to place a break before or after 'never'. And finally, never engage with any matters that are *too* important – leave those to the oracles at the temples across the ocean. Anyone desperate and, crucially, wealthy enough will make the trip and declare the immense power of Apollo once they do.

Aesacus broke all those rules with *the prophecy* – because when you say 'the prophecy' in Troy, there's only one you could possibly be referring to.

Mother had dreamt of a flaming torch and Aesacus, who came from a long line of seers, claimed it was an omen that the child in her womb would be the downfall of Troy.

That's all I know. Everything else is hushed and quiet, rumours of the things they did – the way the prophecy and the baby were 'dealt with' and whether Aesacus really jumped from that cliff to his death, if maybe he wasn't pushed . . .

Mother never fell apart but she never quite recovered either – her smiles distant, her eyes sad.

Which is why I'm now storming towards the throne room, Ligeia begging me to slow down and shouting about propriety. My parents are the best king and queen this kingdom has seen but when it comes to Paris, they're still wrecked. The barest whisper of his name and their rationality dissipates.

So whoever this man is, claiming to be my brother, taking advantage of their greatest sorrow, he shall not live long enough to spin another lie.

I catch myself at the threshold.

I have seven siblings and dozens of cousins. This man could so easily be one of us.

He's got it all: Mother's slick black hair, Father's long nose, bronze skin like clay in a furnace and the same lanky build all my brothers share – like muscles are climbing ivy clinging to their slender frames. I'm fairly certain if I dragged him into the sun his brown eyes would glow amber like the rest of ours do.

But Paris is dead, no matter how much my parents might pray for a miracle. Which means whoever sent this man to pretend to be my brother has put time and effort into finding someone who might pass. Whatever they want, it must be worth all that.

'What is the meaning of this?' I demand, strutting into the room like I have every right to. It's empty, save for my other siblings, gathered in a watching mass, which explains why I was sent for – to bear witness, not to interrupt.

My parents sit on a plinth overlooking the expanse of the throne room. The same white stone of the palace, threaded through with glimmers of gold, curves and swirls into their thrones, like it has not been carved so much as enticed to form its new shape.

My parents are clutching one another's hands and before I spoke they both looked so hopeful.

Now they're glaring at me, Father even going so far as to stutter, at a loss for words.

'Cassandra,' my mother manages. 'This is not your place to speak.'

'A man claims to be the subject of a prophecy delivered by Apollo, where else should a priestess of Apollo speak?'

It's not the first time I've spoken out of turn but it's the first I've tried to boldly insist I have a right to, and the sheer audacity seems to still my parents.

'A prophecy brought me here,' the man says, a cocky smirk on his face that reminds me too much of my sister Kreousa. 'Your lord favours me.'

'You do not speak for my lord,' I hiss.

'Cassandra,' my father says. 'Perhaps you should gather the

other priests. If we are consulting Lord Apollo on the topic of prophecy, we should have the high priests in attendance.'

The dismissal grates on me. In the temple my royalty gains me prestige that the hierarchy of the priesthood does not technically allow.

But my family remember too well my indifference to the gods before I declared a sudden calling to join the temple the first time I was presented with a proposal for my hand in marriage. I have nowhere near the authority I'm pretending to, and unlike the rest of Troy they won't be awed into believing I do.

'What is there to consult? If this is Paris, then the prophecy comes true with him,' I push. 'If it is not, then he is a liar impersonating a dead Trojan prince. You should kill him regardless.'

Mother flinches. 'No!'

I suppose it's difficult to sentence your own son to death *twice*.

But the chances he is Paris are slim. The gods only deal in miracles when they have something to gain from it.

My brother Hector steps forward. As the crown prince, he shows no hesitation and clearly anticipates no scolding decree that it is not his place to speak.

'Cassandra makes a good point,' he says, and for a moment I'm relieved – this is what we do, the tandem we work in to protect our siblings from themselves. I'm ready to turn our efforts on our parents, but he continues: 'However, we must also consider the fact the gods do not take kindly to those who murder their own kin. Cassandra, you have studied the religious texts – do you not have numerous examples of the gods' wrath at filicide?'

Beside him, his wife, Andromache, presses her lips thin to suppress her entertainment at the suggestion I have studied anything at all – and she should know, given it was her I often skipped lessons with. I'm not exactly the most devout priestess.

'When the alternative is the prophesized fall of Troy?' I counter.

'My father would not order my death,' Paris – or whoever he is – says, like his supposed father hadn't arranged for his death the first time around.

'There is much to consider,' my father says. 'A curse for a curse. As Hector says, the gods do not take kindly to men who kill their own sons.'

I toss my hair back with a sullen huff. 'So send him out of the city and let the curse fall upon a different house.'

'That our efforts to do that twenty years ago failed suggest the gods also laugh at those who try to avoid their fates. Perhaps we simply interpreted the first prophecy incorrectly.'

I suppose my father is technically right, but I don't believe in prophecy, I don't care for the gods, and the hopeful look in my mother's eyes is breaking my heart because I can already imagine how thoroughly wounded she will be when 'Paris' vanishes with half the treasury of Troy or whatever it is this man has planned.

'Prophecy or not, we have no proof this man is who he claims to be.'

'We have no evidence to the contrary, either,' my mother says, her eyes not wavering from the man she desperately hopes is her son.

'Fine,' I say tersely. 'Then I'll pray for further guidance on the prophecy at the temple.'

By which I mean I'll make a big show of worship and then declare exactly what needs to happen.

Paris might not speak for my lord, but I sure do. And I have a feeling he's going to tell us to lock this man in the darkest cell of the dungeons.

CHAPTER TWO

Cassandra

My walk to the temple takes longer than it should with the way people stop in the streets to watch me pass. My accompanying guards try to hurry me along but I take the time to smile and nod, my assuredness growing with every step amongst the public. Troy's princess choosing not to marry a prince and live in a palace, waited on hand and foot, but instead joining the temple of the city's patron god, leading rites and rituals and serving the people? My brothers might have our people's loyalty but I have their love.

Of course, I do still live in a palace and am indeed waited on hand and foot, but that's beside the point.

It takes me ten minutes to reach Apollo's temple, winding through all the others that crowd the acropolis in a maze of white marble. Apollo's is one of our grandest – a huge structure of pale stone set round a wooden statue of him. At its southern edge, the temple's opisthodomos has been transformed – not the porch of other temples but a full terrace built into the side of the hill that overlooks the city, its terracotta roofs spilling down the mountainside like molten ore trickling to fill a mould.

I used to be so jealous when my brothers would set sail to neighbouring lands, while I was stuck at home waiting for an advantageous match. But since freeing myself of that, I've grown to love this city with a fierceness I never imagined myself capable of. It's beautiful, it loves me and it is the finest kingdom in all of Anatolia – why would I care to go elsewhere?

I leave my royal guard at the door. The temple is surprisingly empty for the middle of the day. Two new priestesses joined us this year and they scramble to rise as I enter, even though the only hierarchy that technically matters in here is that of the priesthood.

'Princess Cassandra!' they greet, their words quick in that excitable way people often use with me, like they're in awe of the fact I'm standing before them.

'Cassandra!' a far less excited voice snaps from the archway, preventing me from delighting in their adoration.

'Herophile,' I answer, allowing a second for the wince of displeasure to cross my face before turning to her. The new initiates see it and giggle into the jugs they hold, before scampering off to perform libations.

The high priestess is as willowy and lithe as the temple's columns, and with her sharp-edged features and ashen-white skin I could half believe she too is carved from marble. Everything about her is intentional: her sunset hair piled on top of her head to add even more height to her tall frame, always angling herself to best capture the light, even the way she moves like all eyes are on her. They're not – they're normally on me and she can't stand it. She is beautiful and she is awful and, as much as I enjoy looking at her, I would like far better to never see her again.

'Don't tell me you're actually here to perform a duty,' she says. 'The moon has yet to complete a cycle since you last graced us with your presence.'

'As always, I come and go at the behest of Apollo. And right now his voice urges me to prayer. Excuse me.' I push past her. As much as sparring with her might be fun, aloof indifference seems to aggravate her most. To be reminded that her appointment as high priestess gives her the right to give me orders in theory only – because what can she possibly do when I disobey?

I head straight into the cella, which is empty, and perhaps if I weren't rushing away from Herophile I might consider that I have never known it so quiet, that the marble busts of Apollo that ring this central hall all need polishing and I have never seen it without a priestess holding a rag.

I might wonder why that is. I might feel a touch of fear.

Instead I rush to the enormous wooden statue of Apollo in the cella's centre and fall to my knees before it.

The stone floor is cold and unyielding and it takes only a few moments for my knees to ache. I had to spend the solstice in here once as part of my initiation. I'd had Ligeia stitch padding into my tunic and my knees were still red for a week. Even the tops of my feet were bruised from pressing against the hard stone.

By the mercy of Zeus, this is hell. How do some of the priestesses do this every day?

The temperature soars, blistering heat that forces my eyes shut, protecting them from the shock of light that glazes a moment later, so bright that I have to throw my arm up to shield my face.

'You're not even trying to pray.'

I don't need the light to know no mortal speaks – mortal words don't ring off walls like that, and they don't wake some deep and primal part of yourself that tells you to flee, as if running could save you from the displeasure of a god.

Tentatively, I open my eyes and turn to him.

He is beautiful in the way the sun is beautiful – fiery and golden, imposing and impossible – and safest at a distance. With his golden hair threaded with laurel leaves and his whole being humming with a golden light, I don't have to ask which god stands before me.

'Lord Apollo.' I nod, staggering to my feet before I can think better of it.

'By all means, do rise,' he says with a flash of teeth. 'You've never venerated me in your life so I see no reason to start now.'

Something in my gut tightens. A god, here, in person. Confronting a priestess who never revered him, who's used his name for clout and prestige, with no other soul in sight . . .

Hubris fells heroes – what does it do to wayward princesses?

'Now, now,' he coos, enjoying my discomfort. He starts making slow steps which mock my racing heart. 'We'll get to all that. I'm going to show you exactly how to get down on your knees and worship me.'

'My lord, you honour us,' I say – my words rushed, voice high. 'Please allow me to gather the other priestesses, they'll be so –'

'If I wished to see them, I would,' he interrupts. 'No, my presence is a gift for my favourite priestess.'

'My lord?'

He laughs in a pointed way that makes clear I am the punchline. 'It's not every day a princess swears herself to you, especially not the world-renowned Cassandra, fairest woman in Troy. A princess so entitled she wouldn't know how to even begin with respecting a god, with lowering herself to anyone. No, no, don't protest. It's quite all right. I myself have been accused of having an ego larger than Mount Ida. I'm oddly fond of a kindred spirit.'

My fear is buffeted by all else that he stirs – bafflement, flattery, shame. But what sticks is the embarrassment – the way he is trying to put me so firmly in my place.

And in that moment, even the golden ichor in his veins doesn't erase a lifetime of people bowing before me.

I stand up straighter, raising my chin in defiance, and he claps with delight.

'There she is, my princess. You never lied, you know. All your claims you were my favoured priestess. It's absolute blasphemy, but it's also correct. This is my sacred city, after all. And its smug princess flitting around my temple, all her flippant prayers while everyone else prays for health and prosperity? My name has never felt so glorious than when uttered on your thoroughly spoilt lips.'

I can feel the heat radiating from him, a burn that reminds me he could take his true form at any moment, could incinerate me before I could blink.

A god. In front of me. No one I know has ever met one.

And slowly, my fear gives way to excitement.

I could leverage this – use it to rise in the temple's ranks. All that freeing power.

'So you came here to do what?' I ask, cocking my head to the side with an almost sly gleam, like we are in each other's confidence. 'Flatter me? You'd hardly be the first.'

'I came to meet my favourite priestess.' That light burns so bright in his eyes that I can't hold his gaze – but I have no doubt he's watching me intently. 'And to see if the rumours of your beauty are true. And to tell you to at least light a candle every once in a damn while.'

'Now that I've met you? I'll set the whole room ablaze.'

'Might it be too much to ask for the occasional sacrifice?'

'I'll slaughter a herd.'

'And a libation?'

'I'll drain the city's cellars.'

Apollo's eyes simmer with a gentle warmth now – like he does not wish to incinerate me but invite me to sit by his hearth.

'So tell me, Cassandra –' his tongue lingers on my name, elongating it in a way that makes my skin crawl – 'what ill omen befalls my sacred city?'

'The prophecy of Troy's fall at the hands of a son of Priam.' I had never actually considered the prophecy real, always assumed Aesacus was just manipulating court politics. Most prophecies are made with agendas. But if it's true, then Troy might really be in peril. 'Supposedly, that son has returned.'

'The Paris prophecy?' Apollo's brow creases. 'Yes, a tricky one. Some of my finest work, as prophecies go.'

'So it's real? We're in danger?'

'You're always in danger. The whims of fate are complex things, Tyche always weaving new strands where they don't belong, mortals veering to new cords altogether – your lives are such fragile things and threads can snap so easily.'

'So Troy isn't destined to fall?'

'All cities fall.'

'Answer the damn question,' I demand and my breath catches in my throat. Apollo stills, possibly startled, but possibly letting his rage settle into a collected and weaponizable thing.

Every word spoken with Apollo feels like a strong wind on a cliff edge, the fall always there, always waiting, and I traipse clumsily over as though oblivious to the threat.

His laughter bursts from him – only this time it does nothing to reassure me.

'Oh, Cassandra. I'm going to have such fun with you. I have so many devoted followers and what does it mean? When it's so freely given? Your devotion, sweet princess, will be a joy to wrest from you.'

It's risky, but letting him maintain the upper hand feels riskier. It's the only thought I have before I speak – that I've never found much opposition to my demands and Apollo seems to enjoy such boldness.

'Perhaps you should give me a reason to devote myself to you. Tell me the truth about the man calling himself Paris and the prophecy that claims he'll doom us all.'

'What is this obsession with prophecy? Are you –' He gasps, delighted. 'Oh, yes, I can see it now. My words through those lips. Delphi, Dodona, Trophonius, Menestheus and Troy – oh, Father will be furious, and that's almost reason enough to do it. How would you feel, Cassandra, about becoming my new oracle?'

What?

'Imagine it.' He steps towards me, circling me again, and laurel and hyacinth waft through the air. 'Power over the future itself, all yours to tell. People would flock to you. The whole city would bend. They might even summon you to distant lands – no more temple walls and palace guards. You'd have power.'

Power. Oh gods.

Apollo comes a little closer with each sentence and I hate to admit that I'm hanging off his every word. I feel caught. Enticed by the thing I've always craved and thought I would never get. The direction of my life was laid out for me before I took my first breath, and joining the priesthood felt like an urgent dive from a road I was hurtling down. It was an escape, not a dream. I don't even *want* to be high priestess one day, not really – it's just the only step up from here, the only thing worth reaching towards.

But this would be something else entirely. Nothing like the freedom my brothers have, but a third option beyond marriage or priesthood, one with so much more of the things I crave: attention, adoration, respect and authority. All packaged up in one glorious title: *oracle*.

'There are enough false prophets in this city, Cassandra – let me give them something real.'

'And what will it cost me?' I ask, before I can be persuaded by the soft lure of his bribe. 'I've never read a story where the gods gave a gift from the kindness of their heart.'

'Have I not been clear with what I want? What I should have been freely given. Prophecy is yours in exchange for your devotion, body and soul, for everything you have to give. As oracle, you'll bow before no king – but you'll prostrate yourself before me.'

My teeth grit, a bitter taste in my mouth at the thought of humbling myself so much. But the indignity of this morning still stings. If I were oracle, my family would not have hesitated to listen to me.

'If your issue is my lack of humility, granting me untold oracular powers is an interesting solution,' I say – partly because I suspect an ulterior motive and partly to buy myself time to consider.

He stops, his smile falls – his performance slips away. And he is just a man, waiting for his demands to be met.

'I've watched you, Cassandra. The things you do for attention, the way you flirt with visiting princes, their desire a game because you've sworn yourself to me. Why not elevate that? Why not make yourself truly untouchable to all but me? With the powers I'll grant you, you'll be utterly insufferable. And each night you'll go to bed and thank me. Profusely.'

'You mean . . .'

'You know damn well what I mean.'

I do.

I think part of me knew what he wanted from the moment he appeared, no matter how much I tried to convince myself otherwise.

'I want you to choose it, Cassandra. You may say no, and I'll offer the next intriguing girl in my temple the same bargain. But if you want to know what future is in store for your city, if you want to play any sort of role in the war that's coming, you'll lie with me.'

No.

It is not merely an abstract thought, it's a solidity in my bones, a certainty in my gut. It is the absolute dread that made me run here years ago.

'I'm a sworn virgin at this very temple.'

'You swore your virginity to me,' he corrects. 'But as I am a benevolent god, I won't hold you to oaths you took at twelve. And if you wish to see how very all-loving I can be, you'll agree to this.'

And if I refuse? Then what might he do?

'Wait, there's a war coming?' I startle, so distracted by the horror of what he's asking that I missed the much larger horror he's implied.

'Yes. And if you want to know more, you'll need my gift of prophecy.'

A war would be . . . I don't even know. I don't know enough about wars; they don't teach girls that sort of thing. But what I do know is that men fight and women are defended – until they're not – until their cities fall.

But if I had sight, I wouldn't have to be helpless. And beyond the war it would be freedom. My wonderful life shining even brighter – more people flocking, more lavish gifts, my voice actually *heard*.

I could do it, couldn't I? I could suffer him. Women do so every day, not all of them lucky enough to escape to a temple. I'm sure plenty of them aren't attracted to men either. I don't . . . I don't *want* to. But what would I sacrifice for the taste of a life beyond anything I could have dared hope for? I could bear it. Maybe I don't want him, but isn't it honour enough that a god wants me? I think myself capable of persevering for prestige like that.

I would like to say that I say yes because the fear of war is rooted deep inside me, deep enough that I would sacrifice myself and my wants and desires for my city.

Or that I thought it sacrilege to refuse a god, rather than lie with him and accept his gift. Or that I just wanted to find out the truth about the man standing in my throne hall, claiming to be my brother.

But I say yes because I can see myself as all that he describes me to be – powerful and singular. I have carved out a life for myself, a beautiful glimmering life, and it still has not been enough for me. I want renown and prestige and for attention to never waver from my side. I say yes because I am greedy and hungry – a princess who will always want more.

And I say yes because truly, in that moment, I think myself capable of doing as he asks.

'Once,' I suggest. 'I will lie with you just the once.'

He does not respond with the outrage I half expect – am perhaps even half hoping for – that he might retract his offer and take this horrific but tempting choice away from me.

'You know, Cassandra, I think you may be correct. I imagine I'd tire even of you, eventually. Perhaps once is enough.'

Oh gods, this is really happening. My heart is racing. I'm really agreeing to this.

'And no pregnancy. I'll never become Troy's oracle if there's proof of what we've done.'

'Very well.'

My lips are dry, my breath shaky, and the whole world feels as though it is rushing about me, disorienting and dizzying and slamming to an abrupt halt the moment I manage to speak: 'Then I agree.'

Apollo beams and steps forward, closing the gap between us.

I could choke on the sweet herby scent of all that laurel.

'Not right now,' I blurt. 'I want . . . I want to prepare. I've never done this, I'd like to bathe, to have a bed and –'

'Shh,' he soothes, pushing my hair from my face, and my world shifts, the nausea so strong I don't know how I remain standing. 'Prophecy is a powerful thing. I doubt you will remain conscious for long once I gift you with the sight of it. But when you revive, I'll come to you and take all that you offer.'

It is my first indication that I have made a terrible mistake – that I thrill at the thought of being unconscious rather than going to bed with him.

'I need you to swear it, properly,' he says. 'The vows, as you did once before.'

I take a deep, steadying breath and the words I spoke when I joined the temple rush to my tongue.

They felt like freedom when I said them last.

Now they feel like chains that bind me.

'I give myself wholly in dedication and service to the bright Lord Apollo. I pledge to lie with no man, so that I may give myself fully to my lord and remain pure in my worship of him. Lord Apollo, hear my dedication and know that I am your servant for evermore.'

By the time I finish, he is smiling a pompous, self-satisfied grin.

'Well, Cassandra, I hope this time you mean it.'

His smile twists until it is no longer a smile at all – it is a looming thing, the feral delight of victory.

'I bless you, Princess Cassandra of Troy,' he declares. 'I give you prophecy.'

The pain is instant, a blazing, devouring heat from within

my core. I keep my eyes open until they burn white. Agony serrates lines along my bones and sears deep beneath my flesh until I'm certain this whole thing must be a ruse, some sort of effort to trick me before he incinerates me.

'I'll see you soon,' Apollo promises.

Then it blazes hotter and I can't think of anything at all.

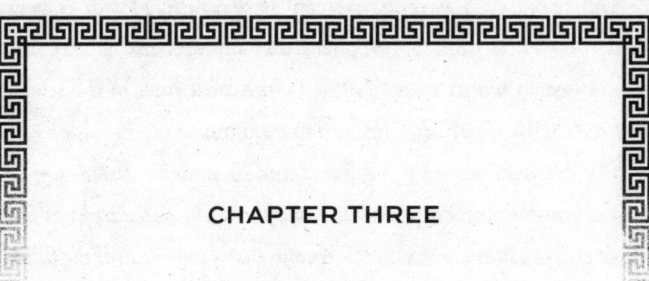

CHAPTER THREE

Cassandra

THE VISIONS START SLOWLY. AND then they hurtle through me, arrows shot through my skin, threaded like needles whose strands are knotting and coiling, stringing me up and wrenching me apart.

I see the Earth collide with the sky, fallen weapons coated in the golden ichor of the gods, monsters clawing free from the ground – everything that has ever happened in snatches as the threads constrict around me.

Images of distant lands are replaced by lands I know well: the oceans and mountains of Anatolia. I see a statue – the Palladium of Athena – fall from the Heavens and an eagle snatch up a shepherd and then, with a start, I see Apollo and a god who must be Poseidon by his side, layering stones too heavy for mortals to lift – building the walls of Troy, a punishment from his father, Zeus, the king of the gods, for an attempted uprising. But the city loves Apollo and Apollo loves it back and the strands drawing ever tighter through me hum as though in recognition of this god who reads their shapes.

And then – my parents, glowing with youth. Hector is born. And then Paris and the prophecy and the decision to slaughter him. I hear a baby's cries muffled by the thick trees of the woods, and see the shepherd who hears them and rushes to his side.

More visions, my own childhood and then, as the threads of the universe entwine themselves with the Fates-cut thread of my own life, it crashes into the present – Apollo in his temple and me falling to the floor.

I see Paris – who really is my brother – surrounded by impossible beings, too incredible to look at for long – and I pick out the things that matter – the peacock feathers and the plumed helmet and the features I recognize from every beautiful woman I've ever met. Hera, queen of the Heavens; Athena, goddess of war and reason; and Aphrodite, goddess of love and beauty. They stand around Paris and demand to know which among them is the fairest, and the strands now strung through my body like sinew whisper their first breath of the war to come.

My eyes shoot open.

A canopy of viridian and teal, soft sheepskins tangled round me and a moist rag pressed to my forehead, scented with some herbal paste that reminds me too much of Apollo. I lurch from my bed and vomit on the stone floor.

The servants squeal and scatter, apart from one who holds my hair back – and when I look up I see it's not a servant at all but my mother.

'Thank you,' I mutter but the words are weary, the visions overworking my tired brain.

'Cassie! You've been in a feverish slumber for days. When they found you on the temple floor, I . . . we were so worried! Did something happen?'

She looks tired from her vigil by my bedside – and I find myself oddly touched in the way I always do when we're alone together, like I should be thankful for her time. I stopped being given much of it once I escaped the prospect of any marriage for her to arrange.

For a moment, I think she's so exhausted that I can count the veins beneath her paled skin – but then I realize the greyish lines are twitching together, and when they collide they shine in bright bursts of gold. I am watching fate weave itself together. I am seeing the potential become the immutable.

I reach for a cup on the side. I need to rinse out my mouth – and I need a moment to think. This is it – my big announcement, my opportunity to change my life.

But not if they find out how I got these visions.

Oracle or not, if rumour makes it through the city that I exchanged sex for power, I'll be ruined.

'I visited the temple to pray for guidance,' I say. 'But when I entered it was filled with golden light and I heard Apollo's voice.'

My mother doesn't look particularly convinced but I press on.

'He said he wished to honour his city by gifting his favoured priestess. He would like to establish an oracle in Troy, and he has blessed me with prophetic visions.' I try my best to look profound. 'Ever since then, I have been witnessing the past, so I might better guide the future.'

'Cassandra,' my mother says carefully. 'Did you hit your head? We could find no injury –'

'I'm sorry about Paris, Mother,' I interrupt. 'What a tremendously difficult decision for you and Father. I can but commend you for taking so seriously the word of Lord Apollo and the will of the people. And you yourselves, unable to perform the act, so sending him into the woods with a herdsman – Agelaus, wasn't it? But he could not do it either, so presented a dog's tongue as proof –'

'Stop it,' my mother snaps, blinking away the tears gathering in her eyes. 'That's enough, I . . . You saw this?'

'Paris is gone now, isn't he? How could I know that if I were not speaking the truth? He is on a hillside –'

'He returned to sort some affairs, he ought to be back soon.' Mother's voice is quiet. I let her contemplate all that I have said, all the things I have suggested. 'And the future?'

'I believe so, though I'm yet to see it. It aches to show me, though – I can feel it.'

I'm hesitant to mention the war – in part because I would like to know more of the details, but mostly because I would like my visions to be a glorious gift for the city, not something to be feared. At least for today.

'Apollo wishes to host an oracle here, in Troy? And he wants *you* to become it?' Mother's brows draw together in a way that is too familiar – the edge of concern that my behaviour is troubling, that I might bring disrepute upon the family.

That I can see her point doesn't lessen my irritation – who cares if I'm not the most devout priestess, when I hold both a tiara and the love of the people?

'You expect Apollo to gift one of the other priestesses, when the princess of his city is sworn to him? Whatever your thoughts on the matter, Mother, I trust you understand the importance of appearances and prestige.'

I know before she speaks that she's sold. I've seen that look of resignation several times before – that awareness that they stopped holding control over my life from the moment I swore myself to the temple.

'I'll tell your father. We'll have to announce this properly – some sort of ritual, a banquet, perhaps with invites to the neighbouring nations. I'll confer with him but I expect that tonight we will celebrate Apollo and the gift he has bestowed.'

Tonight.

The floor beneath me vanishes and I am falling, tearing at cords of prophecy as I go, until two twinning ropes stretch before me. I cannot trace their threads, cannot see where they lead because that heaviness in my gut is anchoring me too strongly to the present. But in the hazy distance of both, I see Apollo – and it terrifies me.

My mother's hand is on my shoulder and she's wearing an expression I have never seen directed my way: a slight smile and eyes soft with something that might be admiration.

'This is a great deal of responsibility, Cassie. It's an honour awarded to our family and I'm sure you will make us incredibly proud.'

'I –'

'And Paris?' she asks almost hesitantly, hope trembling in her voice. 'That's what you said, yes? That Paris is gone. So you admit it, then: that Apollo guided you to the truth that he is truly your brother. An oracle and a returned prince. What a thrilling new age for our city this will be.'

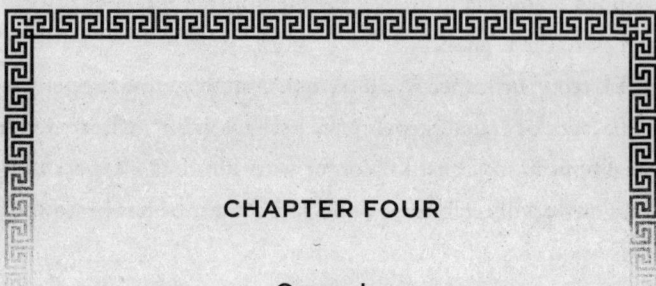

CHAPTER FOUR

Cassandra

I TRY PLUCKING AT THE PROPHETIC threads, desperate to see something – *anything* – that will truly strike the citizens with awe – to make it all that much more thrilling, my newfound talents all the more admirable.

At this point I'd take a party trick – a vase I might save from falling, or a chariot race I might successfully predict. But the most I can do is focus enough to see the golden threads flittering beneath my own skin, or shimmering in the world around me.

I sit down on the edge of my bed, ready to try following the strands again, but they stick firm in the present, refusing to let me know where they lead. I fear reading them may have something to do with hard work, practice and patience, none of which I feel particularly confident about achieving.

My door is thrown open – and I don't need prophecy to know the only people who wouldn't knock are Andromache and my sister Kreousa.

'Are you all right?' Andromache hurries towards me and clasps my face in a warm, gentle hand. It must be one of the days when her joints ache more than most, because her other holds the walking stick she sometimes uses and her eyes dart across me like she might read the answer on my face. Her careful touch, her face so close I could count every pore nestled in her dark-brown skin – I try to pretend it doesn't make something in my chest take flight like a startled beast.

Thankfully, despite both Kreousa and Andromache knowing I favour girls, neither seems to have realized I was once quite besotted with Andromache – before she married my brother, of course. I might not pine for her any more, but I'm not sure anyone could think straight with someone so beautiful so close, and looking at them like that.

'Obviously she's fine,' Kreousa snaps. 'Honestly, Cassandra, lingering on your deathbed then awaking to declare yourself an oracle is eccentric even for you. What were you thinking? You know, Mother actually believes you!'

'She should, because it's true.' I turn to my sister, drawing myself up with a petulance that only comes out around my siblings. 'And I've already proved it to our parents so I don't know why I should have to prove it to you too.'

Kreousa hesitates. 'Scamandrius says it's just because attention wasn't on you for two minutes.'

I scoff. 'You're the last person I thought would be stupid enough to listen to anything Scamandrius says.'

My twin brother tends to only open his mouth to say something foolish or cruel – or, more often, both. The womb must have been an unfair place: I took all the brains, looks and talent and he took all the freedom, respect and opportunity.

Kreousa deflates and falls on to my bed. 'In my defence, I'm somewhat rattled. The tailors delivered another trunk to my room this morning. They're all suitably hideous.'

'I'll fix it,' Andromache promises.

Kreousa spent the first decade of her life being given things fit for princes and Mother seems to be making up for those lost years by sending her every embroidered cloth and glittering pin she can find – the sort of thing she might have loved as a child but decidedly doesn't at sixteen.

'These were the only decent things and they don't even fit me, so they're yours if you want them.' Kreousa draws out a bundle wrapped in twine and tosses it my way. I manage to catch it and unwrap a pair of finely crafted sandals. 'I don't know why Mother thinks pretty shoes will secure my hand in marriage.'

I run my finger over the patterned leather. 'Enjoy it while you can – I stopped getting pretty things when I gave up my hand.'

Kreousa has a sort of allergy to sincerity, and any reassurances I've given her – that she's beautiful, that she'll have her pick of suitors, that they are lucky to even be considered by her – tend only to result in more disgruntlement. She seems to be all right with the thought of marriage, but the pomp and ceremony of the arrangements and the wedding itself make her anxiety soar to such a place that I've often had to hold her while she hyperventilates.

'You know, it's phrases like "gave up my hand" that have everyone struggling to believe Apollo would choose you to be his new oracle,' Andromache says with a wry shake of her head. 'Most people would say something like "since I devoted myself to eternal virginhood in service of the great god Apollo". So, come on, what happened?'

I have to turn away – if I look at them both, I'll tell them. I'm not sure I've ever kept anything from them before.

But I can't ... Well, I never wanted to marry and I was so relieved when I escaped the prospect of it, but when I *did* think of the wedding night and all those marriage duties, I imagined my older sisters, Laodice and Ilione, talking me through it, Andromache giggling with me about it the next day and Kreousa wrinkling her nose with distaste for the whole affair.

But Ilione and Laodice are in far-off nations, married to husbands from other lands, and I can't risk telling anyone what I have agreed to do. I face this alone – and I cannot speak to the panic constricting me even as I know that voicing it might give me some small reprieve.

'Tell us while we get you ready,' Kreousa suggests. 'You'll be expected to lead tonight's celebrations and I imagine you'll want to look your best.'

I breathe a sigh of relief – back on stable ground, anticipating the whole city celebrating me and what Apollo has gifted me. With my head high and a smile on my lips, I might even manage to forget the bargain I've struck long enough to enjoy it.

'Did you say a package from the tailors?' I ask Kreousa with a sly smile.

'No, absolutely not, I already gave you the shoes.' She manages to both pout and glower at the same time.

'I thought you said they were hideous,' I challenge, though I already know the answer because I'd say the same. Hideous or not, if there's a thing to be had, we both want it.

'Come on, stop stealing things from your sister. Or are you saying my designs aren't worthy?' Andromache crosses to the large wooden chest where most of my chitons – several of them made by her – lie folded. 'You have plenty here, we'll be able to make you the fairest –'

Paris, anxiously turning a golden apple in his hands, running a thumb over words he cannot read. Around him, the goddesses bicker, insisting he choose from among them, to determine which of them is the fairest and worthy of the apple.

The scene is embedded with twisting coiled strands that wrap into three ropes, connecting Paris to each of these goddesses and shooting beyond into some distance I cannot quite see.

The cords that bind me to my own present loosen and it is so easy to reach out to the nearest. I glimpse a new picture, the fate Hera offers when she promises to make Paris king of Europe and Asia, lands that swallow and consume even Greece and Anatolia . . . and when I touch the golden light of the future I see long, bloody battles, citizens dying in mud, villages on fire, corpses rotting in rivers and – I choke, releasing the thread.

I move to Athena, the fate spinning and shining, and she speaks, offering Paris wisdom and skill in war, and I do not need to see this future to know it looks much the same, but I touch it anyway and see Paris leading battles across Anatolia – alliances formed through marriages and trade pacts turned into cities to be conquered, into land to be stolen.

And then Aphrodite, offering the most beautiful woman in the world. Relieved, I rush to this strand and let out a strangled sob when boats charge towards my own city, when snatches of battle clash outside my own walls and funeral pyres can be seen burning from the palace windows.

And it strikes me that someone sent these goddesses here. Someone declared Paris the judge. And that someone clearly wants blood to run and cities to fall.

I blink and I'm in my room – Andromache holding up two chitons for my selection, Kreousa staring with a distinctly academic curiosity.

'Did you see something?' she asks excitedly. 'Was that a vision?'

But I'm already out of the door, running for my father.

I need to tell him to assemble the war council.

CHAPTER FIVE

Cassandra

'**WAR IS COMING,**' **I FINISH**, my explanation rushed with panic, words tumbling one after the other – like if I just kept talking, the dread would not consume me. I knew war approached and knew too that Paris would place all of Troy at risk – but it is very different to see it with my own eyes. 'Combined with Aesacus's prophecy about the downfall of Troy, I suspect he chooses Aphrodite and war comes to this city and –'

'Any war brought to the shore of Troy would be swiftly dealt with, girl,' Antenor rebuffs me.

'I think what my sister is trying to say is that she has had a prophetic dream, likely some sort of meaning in there, but of course she does not believe it literally.'

'I think what I was trying to say was quite clear, actually, Scamandrius.'

My uncle Thymoetes waves a dismissive hand. 'You're likely confused. Even if you had seen such things, you have no way of understanding the nature of war.'

I'd found my father locked in conversation with two of his

advisors and my brother Scamandrius. Foolishly, I'd thought that better – that half the war council was already assembled. But now as I look round Father's study – the scrolls slid into shelves, the plush chairs set round the enormous wooden table, and the dark, heavy fabrics musty with the scent of decades' worth of plummy wine – I realize this is their space and I am as much of an intruder in it as I am on this topic of conversation: I have no right to their games of dice and none to speak of war.

'This is a good point.' Antenor nods. 'Clearly, the girl's temperament is not well suited to oracular pursuits. Apollo has supposedly made his choice, but at Delphi they carefully select the Pythia and train her accordingly – Cassandra, if you're to share your prophecies, you cannot allow yourself to become alarmed by them. A pity prophecy suits women well, when the emotional tenacity required would be better served by a man.'

I can barely hold my tongue long enough to let him finish. 'Yes, well, thankfully Apollo chose, not you.'

'This is precisely what I mean, Priam: the girl has no respect for her elders.'

My father shakes an amused head. 'And you have no respect for the oracle of Troy, Antenor.' For a moment I'm relieved. 'There is a point here, though, Cassandra. Oracles hold power because they are a bridge to the gods – you cannot allow yourself to be too human in your delivery. Detach yourself, perhaps.'

'Will you please stop advising me on how to speak and actually listen to what I'm saying? We need to . . . I don't know, go after Paris and reach him before the goddesses do, or at the very least prepare for the futures he's bringing.'

'You saw three potential futures, yes?' my father asks.

'We can't have that.' Thymoetes shakes his head. 'Oracles must be sure of the futures they read, not offer options.'

'She probably doesn't understand them anyway,' Scamandrius mutters, shooting a glare in my direction. 'Antenor's right; Apollo should have gifted someone more in control of their emotions.'

'Like you, you mean? Because you seem quite emotional right now. Jealous, perhaps?'

'Don't be crazy, Cass, what would I –'

'My point,' my father speaks louder, 'is that this is your first prophecy, Cassandra. I must admit, much of this feels far-fetched – Paris chosen by the gods? Three such noble goddesses bickering over an apple? And I cannot see the goddess of wisdom being drawn into a contest to be labelled the fairest. Many foolish men have been led astray by misinterpreting a prophecy. You have yet to spend time getting to know your gift. It may not be factual, but a lesson to be learnt, derived from what you see.'

'But –'

'As I said.' Scamandrius practically preens.

'Wars are not caused by beauty competitions, Cassandra. In time, if you prove yourself as oracle, perhaps we might ask you to advise on war, just as the oracles at Delphi do. But for now, please leave such matters to the men with experience in them. And Antenor does have a point about the decorum expected of an oracle – perhaps your time would be better spent considering your role and how you shall behave within it.'

I leave before I can cry in front of them. These threads of

fate are wound round – *through!* – my very bones and it's in them that I know the truth of what I've seen. Changeable though it may be, it's the future, not a fable to be told!

I force myself to my room, where Andromache and Kreousa are waiting for me to explain my sudden disappearance. My chitons are scattered across my bed, my gold jewels piled next to them in matching sets.

Looking at them, I have an idea.

If my father wishes for me to consider decorum and appearances, then I'll put on one hell of a show.

I am resplendent.

Kreousa and Andromache have outdone themselves, Andromache managing to work magic with the ropes and cords we bind our chitons with, layering them beneath my dress so that it flares out in a delightful circle, my purple cloak knotted at my throat, a gold necklace twisted through the tie – it's perfect, not too much jewellery as to be ostentatious, nothing that would imply *I* want attention rather than to give it to Apollo, and nothing that might be a flash of wealth in poor taste, but something to catch and bind the light all the same.

Kreousa's drawn my hair into spiralling curls, pinned up to show off a delicate gold laurel leaf at the nape of my neck, gifted to me by my parents the day I joined the temple. My skin looks radiant, my jaw harsh, and, combined with my own skill with a brush – my eyelashes longer, my eyebrows thicker, shiny glossy lines cut sharp across my cheeks – I look as though I would not need a crown to make people stop and stare.

I've been called the most beautiful woman in Troy for so long I'd forgotten what it meant. But right now, it feels like it means power.

Crowds overflow from the temples, lining the broad streets of the acropolis, and I refuse the carriage my parents offer to take me from the palace gates to the temple. I want the whole city to see me.

I want all of Troy to believe not that I have been gifted, but that I am the gift.

I keep a somewhat aloof distance from the people. My popularity is based on assumptions and impressions, after all – that I selflessly joined the temple, that I would waste my pretty face on an oath of virginity out of love for the gods, that I am single-handedly responsible for every good and gracious thing the temple does.

Up close, that all cracks.

But now I swan among them, not only smiling and waving but calling greetings and wishing good fortunes, shaking hands with small children and even going so far as to distribute sesame honey sweets and hard olive loaves.

My father will be livid at the extravagance and will see it for what it is – about me and not about Apollo. But he'll know, too, that I know exactly how to wield power as an oracle and I do not need his lectures, just his listening ear. With the way these strands twist in a dozen different directions, I might be able to lead us down a different thread, away from Paris's war. Listening to me might save us from all that bloodshed.

So this public debut has to convince everyone I'm worth hearing.

As I approach the temple, a priestess passes me a length of rope, looped round a goat's neck. I used to struggle so much with this part, my hand shaking on the knife, my fingers slipping on the rope, like letting the animal run free might have given it a chance. It didn't. The sacrifice is the most essential aspect of the priesthood – and certainly the most public. When I realized it was the cold edge of a blade or wedding vows, I gripped the knife tight and shoved my repulsion and despair down so deep I no longer feel anything at all as I take the rope and draw the animal behind me, leading it up the stone steps to Apollo's temple.

It is swollen with people, so busy I struggle to squeeze through. And at an altar in the centre, I slash my blade across the creature's throat, unable to look, even now. I just see its blood spray in a fierce arc across the tiles as I turn to face the crowd.

Herophile is practically biting the words out when she declares me an oracle, chosen by Apollo. But, unlike me, she's used to covering her real feelings, especially in front of the watching royal family – and she beams when the crowds of people begin cheering, the smell of roasting goat meat a heavy backdrop. Performers enter the temple with lyres and as the ceremony shifts to a party I see threads unfurl – tiny woven coils wrapped round people – and I try to follow them, like I did in the vision with Paris, but the strands flicker under my touch. It feels like reaching for a mirage.

Out on the temple's balcony, I'm locked in conversation with a combination of priestesses and nobility. Troy is a windy city and on the balcony it normally howls so loudly it would be impossible to converse. But tonight it's still and the people ask me about meeting Apollo, and I'm feigning a smile, throwing compliments, and he must know – because the prophecy that strikes is so strongly scented of him that I stumble backwards, gasping: *'Look now to the Heavens, Apollo shows his favour to Troy.'*

For a moment, there is nothing. And then, even though it is late and the sun set hours ago, its rays jolt across the night sky like stars shooting through the air – flickering out again as cheers and applause erupt.

Apollo is proving my power – and more so, he is proving his.

This is what I wanted, is it not? This irrefutable proof that my power is divine and worthy of attention.

But instead panic surges at this palpable reminder of just how invested this god is in my person – and all that he will soon be coming to claim.

Back at the palace, the threads tease round me – drunken people flirting and new people meeting, all these potential futures weaving together. Sometimes I watch threads draw people together, meetings already determined to happen. I keep trying to read them until my head pulses.

So I make them up instead, introducing people whose threads link them. Perhaps they'll be a love for the ages or perhaps they'll hurt one another so deeply it will change the course of their destiny, but all I need them to believe for tonight is that they might matter – and I know it. I stare off into the distance like I'm seeing something that's not there, and at one point I even proclaim to my mother that my little sister should definitely be allowed to stay up past her bedtime, to which

Polyxena claps her hands gleefully and dashes off before anyone can say otherwise.

I take a candle from the side and nearly burn Hector, who appears right behind me.

'Does that topple over at some point?' my brother asks.

No, I'm just making a show of moving it so people think that's what happens and that I have saved them all from a fiery death.

'Yes, you're very welcome.' I give a saccharine smile.

Hector laughs. 'You're enjoying this far too much.'

'Wouldn't you?'

'Honestly, I have no idea. But a word to the wise –'

'From you?'

'The tale of Icarus, Cass. Be careful of flying too close to the sun.'

'Ahh, but Apollo is the god of the sun, dear brother. I couldn't possibly fly close enough,' I joke, half hoping that making light of it all might ease some of my anxiety. It doesn't – Apollo's very name on my lips makes my heart race with fright.

'I'm serious, Cass.'

'What, you, Hector?' My favourite brother, Deiphobus, appears behind him and claps him on the shoulder. 'That's unlike you. We should alert the temples that more change is afoot in the house of Priam: one son returned, one oracle gifted and the crown prince turned serious.'

Hector gives an incredibly weary sigh. 'Do you know what it's like to have to put up with you lot? You think that life is just one big joke and consequences don't apply to us.'

I flutter my lashes in baffled innocence. 'They don't, do they?'

Deiphobus feigns a look of shock. 'Do you see this, Cassandra? The poor little prince who will one day take the crown curses his responsibility. He berates his younger siblings for . . . what's that? Not taking the crown?'

'It must be so hard.' I nod. 'So he has to make sure we know how burdened with responsibility he is, that he suffers even despite the . . . what was it again?'

'The throne that he's going to take.'

'Ah, yes, poor little throne-taking, crown-wearing princeling.'

Hector doesn't even offer us the decent sort of glower, he just looks thoroughly bored with us both. 'Don't make me set Andromache on you. You know she hates it when people are mean to her perfect husband.'

That's true – as much as Andromache teases Hector, she gets vicious when other people do.

'Very well, princeling.' I bow. 'We shall behave, for fear of the future queen.'

Hector wanders away, shaking his head and muttering things I don't think are complimentary.

'So,' Deiphobus starts, 'this is all incredibly well done. I never knew you had such gravitas.'

'I'm a royal oracle – it comes with the territory.'

'Apparently. Have you seen Scamandrius?'

'A little. I believe he's sulking.'

'Of course he is. Once again, his twin sister is upstaging him.'

'And Paris returned, pushing him further away from the throne,' I point out.

Deiphobus shudders. 'I do wonder if he'd like my head on a platter to bump him up in the line of succession, but I think he rather enjoys resenting us all too much to actually want me dead.'

'He doesn't have to be fourth in line – he could go court the only daughter of some king if he wants a throne so badly. Or if he just wants renown, he could join a temple or make a name for himself as a hero.'

He has so many bloody options. I had two and he's still jealous of them.

'But then he couldn't moan. And he's not the best fighter.'

'Wait!' I exclaim, turning to my brother. 'That makes me think.'

'Oh, don't go trying something new like that when you're fresh off your deathbed – you might faint again.'

I ignore him and push on. 'I told Father about a vision I saw earlier, a war that's coming. He was with his advisors and they all felt I was misinterpreting it, that I couldn't understand what I was seeing when it came to war.'

'That's ridiculous, war is the main thing people go to oracles for consultation on.'

'Yes, but apparently I don't have the training and my visions are too new. I just don't think they wanted a woman telling them something they didn't already feel they knew. So I could use someone they actually will listen to. A man. A brother, perhaps . . .'

'Urgh.' Deiphobus takes a long sip of his wine. 'Fine, but let's do this in the morning, yes? I should probably be sober for so serious a subject.'

I think that's as good as I'm going to get, so I nod and Deiphobus returns to the party, probably seeking out another sibling to tease or some strapping nobleman to audaciously flirt with.

The party winds down and I find it harder and harder to distract myself from what might possibly await me. I consider staying later, never letting myself wind up alone.

But I'm worried — or perhaps I'm hoping — that the anticipation will be worse than the reality.

So I say my farewells and head to my room, knowing in my gut that Apollo will meet me there.

This is what they will not write: that I never avoided it, never planned it from the off, never scrounged for loopholes and escape routes to trick a god out of powers, that I was not some malicious bitch who thought she could outwit a god, just a girl who thought she could until the moment she couldn't.

And as *they* are not writing this but I am, let me say something true, because soon they will not believe a single word that crosses my lips: it would not have mattered if I had.

I had every right to do what I did.

CHAPTER SIX

Cassandra

HE'S NOT THERE – BUT THAT tension in my gut doesn't uncoil and nor do the golden strands of prophecy anchoring me to this moment, no matter how much I push against them, straining until my skull could split in two and my frustrated demands to see what lies ahead morph to desperate pleas and back again.

I sit at a small dressing table in the corner of my room – an ornate looking-glass twisted over a surface still littered with the cosmetic efforts of the evening. I am almost done plucking out the pins holding up my hair when that light blazes again, and I'm yet to open my burning eyes when Apollo speaks.

'You dressed up for me.'

I expected apprehension – not this riotous thunder in my heart and the whispering burn in my veins begging me to flee. I have survived him and I know the parameters of him – or, at least, of what he wants – so why do I still feel like prey skittering about in the undergrowth?

I turn to Apollo and, to my surprise, see that he holds two chalices of wine. He offers one to me and I hesitate before I take it and surreptitiously place it on the side. I may have already consented to what we are about to do, but I'm not taking a drink from this man.

'Are you enjoying your gift?' he asks.

'Yes, my lord.' I nod, hiding my anxiously curling hands within the folds of my dress. 'Although I'm not sure it has taken as well as I hoped it might. The threads are reluctant to show me where they lead.'

'Why, yes, you're not the god of prophecy, able to seamlessly navigate its waters and control its tides,' he says, taking a sip of his wine. The dark stain of it clings to his lips and it's enough to make me shudder. 'As oracle, you may occasionally divine its truths. You do not control the drops of rain that hit you, and so too the power of prophecy will decide what you are privy to.'

I nod slowly, not wanting him to think I'm not appreciative of the powers he has given me.

'The city is pleased,' Apollo says, letting his eyes run over me. 'I ought to have found you long ago. Did you see the way I set the sky on fire for you?'

'Could we just do it, please?' I ask, my voice strangely high.

I expect him to laugh or smile – it seems to be his response to everything I do, but he merely arches a slender eyebrow and sets his drink aside. 'And here I thought to make this romantic.'

'This isn't a romance, it's a negotiation.' I shouldn't provoke him but I'm so tightly wound that his words could crack me apart. And this one touches a nerve. Often, romantic sensibilities are all I've had – daydreams about soft hands in mine, about the ability to stare unabashedly into lovely faces which might gaze fondly back upon my own, longing so much for something so intangible that I thought it might break me. I'll give him my body, but he's not taking romance from me too.

His jaw twitches, teeth grinding before he barks: 'Get on the bed.'

That I can do – so I do, and the moment I perch upon its edge his mouth is on mine.

His lips are smooth, his breath scented with peppermint and, despite his rage, his movements are oddly gentle.

But I don't like it. It's not an instinctive lurch away from him, no voice screaming no, just something crawling on my skin and a desire to put a little more distance between us.

I keep going. I can do this – I can tolerate this discomfort.

Then his fingers fumble at the clasp of my cloak and my breath freezes before coming in short, sharp pants and he must mistake my panic for excitement because he sighs against my lips. My stomach churns.

But I don't pull away until his hand grazes my waist – still clothed, barely a touch.

I launch myself back, scrambling up and away from him until my back hits the stone wall.

'Cassandra,' he warns, voice low.

'I know, please,' I gasp, clutching my arms to my sides. 'Please just give me a moment.'

'It's natural to be nervous the first time you lie with a man. Trust me when I tell you that you will enjoy it.'

I try to tune him out but with every passing moment more things surface: nausea frothing in my gut, a slight spin to the room, every breath shaking in my lungs.

I could still swallow it down – I believe that. I could close my eyes and ignore it or even keep going and focus my attention on his pleasure rather than my own.

There is no screaming demand to refuse him or irrefutable terror at the thought of his touch. It's all quieter than that, skin deep, slight, a whisper and not a shout.

But ignoring it feels like a betrayal of something too deep to name – too deep to *know*. I have spent the whole evening twisting my every thought and action towards making myself grandiose, to give everyone a reason to *hear* me when I speak. I can't not listen to myself now.

'I can't do this,' I say quietly, like that might possibly soften the rejection.

Apollo's head snaps to face me but everything else is slow as he rises from my bed to tower over me once more.

'Say that again.'

'I'm sorry, I really am,' I say quickly. 'I thought I could but I can't.'

I know what I risk – and I half expect him to incinerate me where I stand. But even with such a threat, my resolve holds firm. So I take a deep breath and prepare for the consequences of refusing a god.

'I'm sure you know better than to renege on a deal made with me.'

'I do. Which is why I pray you'll trust I really, truly cannot do this.'

'Your prayers mean nothing, little priestess,' he spits, his eyes actually flashing – embers sparking with his rage. 'Are you truly so audacious as to believe you can lie to a god? To take all that he offers and refuse your end of the bargain?'

'I didn't . . .' I've never felt chaos like this: my swirling fear, all those feelings of failure and confusion, not knowing why I cannot do something so simple, my indignation that he would speak to me this way, accuse me of this, and in my own home too . . . 'I'm sorry, my lord. But please know how much I appreciate all that you have offered me. I truly wish it were otherwise, but please take it back.'

It appears that's the wrong thing to say. Something in him snaps, his irritation becoming full-blown fury.

'You dare reject my gift? Reject me?'

It suddenly occurs to me that my permission might mean little – he is a god and besides that he is a man and I am alone. I glance at the door. I'd never make it. The heroic women struggle, they fight, they are rewarded with a quick, clean death, bodies bending like boughs in the wind. My eye catches on the laurel leaves in Apollo's hair and revulsion has me stumbling back again – Daphne was transformed into a laurel tree while trying to escape this man's pursuits, and now she's a symbol sacred to him.

'I'm not going to force you,' he sneers, like he knows exactly what I'm thinking. 'What do you take me for? A common rapist?'

'No, of course not,' I lie. But, from the stories, he likes to consider the girls his lovers. He wants them to choose him – even if he has to coerce them into it. So maybe the only threat I face is more of his efforts to persuade me.

'You parade around this city, showing off my gift, making yourself holier than half the gods whose temples adorn these streets. And you expect me to believe that your refusal was not always your plan.'

'It wasn't, I swear – I am risking ruin, my lord. If you take these powers back, everyone will ask why. I just declared myself an oracle to the entire city.' Oh gods, this will ruin me. But at least it will not break me in the way persisting might. 'But I understand the deal I made and, being unable to follow through, I offer you your gift back.'

Apollo's anger has been contained to flashing eyes and tense, rigid movements – but at this his curling lip twitches and his voice shakes, like the hold he has on his anger is slipping. 'You stupid girl, do you think that's how it works? Prophecy is bound to the very core of your being. It would destroy you to tear it from you, which is no concern of mine, but it would damage the cords of prophecy too, to have its outlet torn asunder.'

'I . . . Can I do something else instead?'

'You can lie on that bed and earn my forgiveness.'

'I can't.'

'You promised.'

But I'm starting to think this isn't the sort of thing you can agree to in advance.

'No.'

'You do not wish to make an enemy of a god.'

'And I do not wish to make a lover of one either.'

He falls silent at my retort – vicious and ripped from my lips. Pushed beyond the edge of my fear and humility, right back to the very entitlement he is accusing me of. But I don't care – I'm a princess of Troy and no one is forcing me into anything.

If these are my final moments, I'll die as the spoilt princess he wished to humble.

'You will regret this.'

'I don't see that in my future.'

'Terrible things happen to those who deny the gods.'

'Worse than sleeping with you?'

He snarls, rushing forward and curling my dress in his fist, his voice a whisper that chills me to my core.

'You have your prophecy, Cassandra. But you have betrayed the god who granted you such gifts – and for that I curse you.'

He kisses me – but, unlike before, it's little more than a press of lips, and the shiver that runs through my body is not through *me* at all, but through the threads that have bound me, fraying as he pushes this curse into me.

When he releases me he does not even offer a final glare before vanishing.

And – despite the miracle of my continued survival – I feel myself fraying too.

CHAPTER SEVEN

Cassandra

I DON'T SLEEP UNTIL THE LATE morning, when my exhaustion finally pushes past the fear that Apollo will return to enact a more specific revenge. I have not felt anxiety like it since my mother presented the first proposal for my hand. A third prince of some craggy island off the Peloponnese. We didn't even consider it. But it still troubled me, still felt unshakable. More would come. One would finally be agreed.

Apollo was supposed to be my salvation.

And now my head screams of war and curses and Apollo's lips crushing my own.

Even when I wake, it's with a jolt.

I run in search of Deiphobus. If I can put just one of those fears to rest, perhaps the rest will follow. I can't handle another night like that – full of haunting memories of futures yet to pass.

My brother is returning from the city's gymnasium when I find him – and I contemplate waiting for him to bathe first. But this can't wait so I'll simply have to ignore the foul, sweaty stench of him.

'Outside, please,' I ask. 'I need the ventilation to survive you.'

'You know I'm doing you a favour, right?' he grumbles but follows me into one of the courtyards. 'So, war. Tell me what you've seen.'

'Paris is going to be elected to decide a competition of the gods.'

'Don't be ridiculous.'

'Oh, believe me, I question the decision too – blame some previous matter with Ares. It doesn't matter. But every option leads to war, either by design or by the anger of the losing gods.'

'The gods wouldn't set a trial with only failure as an outcome.'

'Of course they would.'

Deiphobus laughs. 'Yeah, sure.'

He's hardly even paying attention, blinking something out of his eye and glancing back the way we came like he's wondering how much longer this conversation will last.

My throat tightens like I might choke on my own disappointment. I did not think Deiphobus would dismiss me like all the other men have.

'Well, I can certainly see why no one believed any of this.' He sighs and rises to his feet. 'Let me know if you actually see anything.'

'Please, listen to me.' I start to explain the particulars of what happens if each goddess wins – but Deiphobus interrupts me.

'I've heard enough. Olympus above, Cass – did you lie about it all?' He shakes his head with disgust. 'I have no idea how you're going to get yourself out of this – but the whole city thinks you're an oracle. So you might want to work on making your tales more believable.'

I stay put as he leaves, staring into the distance, trying to work out what went wrong.

Embarrassingly, it takes me days before I begin to understand – days spent in my new role of oracle. Every new prophecy feels like a fragile gift, cradled in my hands and offered to people who snatch it and fling it back. All I have are broken fragments anyway, each vision a struggle to obtain, or else something I stumble into so completely I nearly put myself at risk – staggering to a halt in the middle of the road or on a precarious step of the palace.

So I invent tales, spin vague lines like we were always taught to deliver.

It is ironic, when Apollo is the god of truth, that it is only through lying that I recognize his curse.

Because the lies get cursory nods, hesitant belief and thanks for my time.

The truth gets swift rebuttals and sneering disdain, spoken from glazed-eyed patrons who blink their dazed confusion at me, uncertain of all they have heard.

Apollo has cursed my prophecies not to be believed.

I could applaud his cleverness if it weren't so troublesome for me – because I cannot keep clinging to the lies and covering my lack of sight with more words. I'm not very good at making up lines and what do I do when they find me out? Claim I lied? That I did it all for attention? That I took Apollo's name and used it for my own advancement? The truth is somehow worse – that I agreed to sleep with him *and* changed my mind? They'd call me a whore who couldn't even keep her word.

I'm on borrowed time before my reputation shatters like a

cheap glass pendant – and after a lifetime living like some precious jewel, I'm not sure what it will do to me.

But as visions of war mount, I cannot shake the infuriating futility of it all. The men of this city did not believe me long before Apollo forced their hand. No one listens to a woman on matters of war and, even gifted and chosen by a god, how many times would I have had to prove myself before they believed my words as worthy of note as their own? Delphi has had centuries to prove their oracle is worth paying attention to – I'd need years for them to even consider it.

The only hope I have is that one of those other lines will lure us to a different path. That maybe war is not the only thread we may follow.

But one evening I'm on my way home from the temple, exhausted and second-guessing why I wanted such responsibility in the first place. It's only been a few weeks of recounting invented prophecies and I'm already tired from the long hours and the lying and the visions that seem only ever to strike me at inopportune moments. For the sake of Olympus, I'm even tired of my own voice!

I had no idea such a thing was possible.

My knees crash into the cobblestones, agony shooting up into my spine, and it's that which I register first – the collapse – not the darkness or the chill piercing ever colder, just the pain. The ground shifts beneath me and the golden cords that wrap round this world shriek as they realign, as something shifts into place.

Paris sails – or, rather, men around him do, his life in the mountainous farmlands not having familiarized him with the ropes and mechanics, leaving him looking on, lost but hopeful. The

Spartan palace looms enormous as his boat pulls towards it, the yellow stone painted red.

When Zeus, the king of the gods, took the throne from his father, it was in a bloody, gruesome war that lasted a decade. His father before him had taken the throne with one quick cut: Ouranos's blood had fallen to Earth, forming creatures where it landed, forming monsters.

That's what the pillars of the palace look like: blood raining from the Heavens.

A beautiful woman appears: Andromache's dark brown skin and full lips; the emerald eyes of my first crush, Briseis; Herophile's tumbling waves of sunset-orange hair; and Kreousa's sweeping curves and dimpled smile. I even recognize some of myself: my high cheekbones, my thick brows, the slope of my nose. It's not a surprise. I'm the most beautiful girl in Troy, after all. Her presence means Paris declared a winner: Aphrodite, goddess of love and beauty.

The visions flicker, a thousand reels in a single second.

Distantly, I feel my fingers claw into a burning skull. I think it's mine.

In some visions Aphrodite climbs the crimson steps of the Spartan palace, in some she turns to mist and floats through a window, in some she lies in wait in a garden. In some it's Paris himself that makes the journey: knocking at the front door, heralded in and honoured as an emissary, disguising himself as a servant.

She speaks. He speaks.

The same eventuality: a girl. Led in by a procession, raising her cup at a banquet, jolting in surprise, perhaps even terror – every vision leads to her, one way or another.

She's beautiful, but that word pales beside her, feels so false, so disingenuous that, if applied to her, the letters might fall apart.

Honey-gold curls frame a freckled face, like lily-pollen peppered across her ivory skin. Eros's bow is drawn in her lips. And her eyes are a changing ocean – midnight blue when Paris meets her in the dining room, aqua under the bright sun when he climbs her balcony, cold as frosted waves when dragged to the throne room to meet the ambassador of Troy or bow to the goddess of beauty.

In some Aphrodite and Paris are honest, and in some they lie, and in some they don't use words at all. In some this woman nods her head and says yes, of course she'll come, and in some she backs away, yelling for guards, and in some she wakes up bound on the ship, eyes wide, and begins snarling and spitting and fighting with everything she's got.

Paris chose his prize – the fairest woman in the land. But she's another man's wife. And he's going to launch a long and bloody battle for her at our very walls.

She's going to start a war.

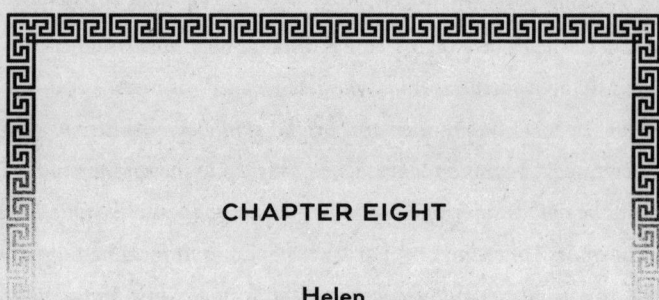

CHAPTER EIGHT

Helen

THE FIRST TIME I SEE Paris I think: *This man could be a fast ship out of Sparta.*

He's in our throne hall, mumbling through trade proposals as a translator twists his hesitancy into polished and assured statements. I'm the only one in the room who notices. My father insisted I learn the language of Troy – but what sort of prince is taught neither Greek nor the matters of trade he is so clumsily attempting to speak of? And why have I never heard of Paris of Troy when I've had all the princes of every kingdom memorized since childhood?

What a mystery this man is – and how delightfully interesting. A laugh bubbles from my lips as the translator spins poetry from Paris's foibles – cut short as my husband hisses for my silence. Paris's eyes meet mine – shock, a hint of rage – and it cements what I had considered from the start: this man is not loyal to my husband. He could be an ally. He could be my way out.

The second time I see him, he is a vague outline in the dim moonlight filtering through my bedroom window. But he's standing in the doorway beside a patchwork goddess of love and I do not need her to command us to elope, because I'm already taking his hand and running.

As we sail to Troy, I still look upon him like I did that first time, trying to make sense of him. I have never met a prince so bashful, nor one so utterly clueless yet optimistic. Is it an act? Does he mean to disarm me? I dissect his sentences like they are riddles with hidden depths and run myself in circles trying to scout out an agenda.

Everything about Paris is beautiful, though just as hesitant as the rest of him: thick eyelashes that flutter in nervous blinks, long graceful limbs that arch to make himself smaller, his tawny-brown skin often flushed with a rose tinge.

And then he smiles – and *oh, that smile*.

It lights something in me – something I didn't know still had fuel to burn.

Straight white teeth, dimples in his cheeks, eyes sparkling – a grin so thoroughly contagious that I cannot help but answer it with my own.

Unlike every smile I've ever drawn from people, Paris's are not turned outwards towards a smug audience, bragging about my existence and their right to be in it. These are for me. And little by little, with every curve of his lips, I stop doubting his innocence and his unapologetic, uncomplicated joy. I start to feel shadows of it myself – like if I bask in it enough, I might feel that happiness too.

And for that, I'd follow him anywhere – even across an ocean.

We spend our days on the ship in each other's arms in his quarters or curled against the masts, out of the way of the sailors, staring at the blue horizon and regaling each other with stories. Or, rather, he tells me them – because he doesn't ask for mine and I have few cheerful ones to give. And his are all so adorably quaint – a prince raised as a shepherd, stealing the heart of the queen of Sparta with stories about petty grain thefts and escaped cows running amok.

But then his stories shift: he tells me about his parentage and the prophecy that would have had him killed. He mentions a river nymph who told him never to go to Troy and how he decided to find out why. He shares how nervous he was to return and how welcoming his parents have been – and how vitriolic one of the princesses was, wielding the power of Apollo to try to have him cast out.

I make a note of the name. *Cassandra*. There's only one reason royalty would join the priesthood: power. And a power-hungry princess is the sort of thing I should be wary of when marrying one of the princes.

'She fell ill at the temple,' Paris adds. 'I didn't see her again before I left, and Aphrodite sent me to Sparta before I could return –'

'I did wonder why Aphrodite was with you. What happened?'

We're sitting against the bow of Paris's ship, our legs entangled and the waves rocking beneath us.

My fingers trail a lazy circle across his thigh, my eyes locked on to his with a keenness I've long since perfected – like I'm ready to hang off his every word.

I am truly curious, but my question is pointed too, as though I am saying: *Talk to me, look at me, love me.*

'She came to me with Hera and Athena,' he explains. 'They held a golden apple in their hands, inscribed with dangerous and deadly symbols they said meant *ti kallisti* – that means "for the fairest".'

The translation isn't necessary, given that it is my language he translates from, but he's smiling softly as he says it and I let him have this moment of pride.

'They wished for me to judge which of them the apple belonged to,' he continues, but his fingers have looped through mine as he speaks and his eyes track the way my skirt has hiked up, revealing a sliver more skin than when I stand. He glances away quickly like he does not wish to be caught looking. It's quite adorable given that he has seen far more of me.

We're yet to settle into the rhythms of each other, but moments spent writhing around in bed have certainly been a pleasant enough way to pass the time.

'And you chose Aphrodite?' I prompt.

'How could I possibly choose between them? When I couldn't, they tried bribing me: Hera offered kingdoms and Athena glory in war. Aphrodite presented love. She offered you.'

The moment between us cracks, though Paris keeps beaming at me like he has no idea I'm plummeting.

I should be used to this by now. I was a prize at ten when two men kidnapped me, intending to raise me into the perfect bride; a prize when my brothers won a war to get me back mere days later; a prize the men of Greece came to compete for the day I turned sixteen. The husband I foolishly chose saw me as one too, and spent the whole year of our marriage trying to make me his own personal Galatea – a statue modelled by his own hands into the shape of something he might love, waiting for Aphrodite to make me whole.

But instead she sent Paris, who never stops looking at me like he can't believe how lucky he is to be by my side, stroking my hair and telling me how beautiful I am, how wonderful – how perfect.

I realize that I'm doing it again – expecting the worst of him because the worst is all I've ever been shown. I might factually be Paris's prize but that does not mean he sees me as such.

'You chose me,' I say quietly – trying to find the beauty in that rather than all there is to doubt.

'Of course. Now that I've seen you, I can't imagine another option.' And there it is again, one of those earnest smiles so bright it feels like a promise.

At night, I sneak from the small chambers we share, past the men pulling at ropes, and stand by the prow. The sky burns brightly among all this wine-dark water. I glance up at the stars and find them quickly: my brothers.

Four years. They've been gone four years.

Not quite dead, not quite alive – one immortal life split between the two, their days in the Underworld, their nights in the Heavens as the constellation Gemini. No time spent here, with me.

'I can't believe you bastards left me alone,' I whisper at the sky, though I don't mean it, not really. All right, maybe there's an edge of bitterness, but mostly I'm just ... sad. I think I might have been sad for a while, actually.

I don't realize, at first, that I'm crying. I think the salt on my lips is the spray from the waves.

'Please let this work,' I whisper, clinging to the hope that Aphrodite has brought. A prince delivered by the goddess of love – this should be the sort of love they tell stories about, that legends are built around.

I have given up everything for one last attempt at a joyful life. With Paris I feel that might really be possible – that love, which feels so within reach, might save me.

But sometimes I fear I may be too broken to let something so good happen to me.

I glance at the sky again. My brothers hover over the horizon, like they're leading me there. Like they're telling me I'm right to make this decision, that happiness lies in Troy and it's waiting for me to find it.

The next day, birds fly overhead and it's clear we're close to land. Paris and I are speaking on the deck. Or, rather, he's speaking and I'm flirting. I can't help it – forcing it all, like our courtship is a game I have to win. I'll hope for a love that's pure and simple when I'm safe; for now, I'll do what I always do and become whoever I need to be to make Paris fight for me in this city where we are both newcomers.

Because those city walls drawing nearer make it all feel real. Menelaus must know I left with Paris. When I'm behind those walls, he'll know exactly where to find me. And I'll need Paris to refuse to send me back, no matter what Menelaus offers for my return.

'You know,' I say quietly so Paris has to lean in close, 'men from every nation in Greece vied for my hand. How funny that a handsome prince from a far-off realm would come and snatch me away from them all.'

He frowns, confused. 'Troy is only across the ocean. It's not that far.'

My fragile heart squeezes. Is this a sign? Ordinarily such denseness would infuriate me, so is the fact that my fondness for Paris grows indicative that I am indeed falling in love with this man?

'Yes, I'm simply romanticizing, as I'm sure the poets will. Sparta and Troy, Greece and Anatolia. They might as well be other sides of the world.'

Which is when the horns blare and Troy comes into view. It's just a speck on the horizon, but every inch we draw closer takes my breath away. This isn't like Greece: city states made of bundled homes and small palaces, fortified against their neighbours' armies, not daring to build too high lest the gods take offence at their hubris, or their neighbours believe there might be something to claim. I can see the palace from here, nestled up the mountain that rises behind, white stone and a dozen turrets. The city trickles down in a haze of colour, the roofs orange stone but everything else glowing in soft pastel shades, growing bolder as we approach.

But where I'm busy finding my breath, Paris groans.

'I never should have done this,' he says. 'Gods, they don't even know me. They have no allegiance to me. And now here I am, not only saying, "I am your prince," but I've also got a wife. And I stole her from the king of Sparta.'

'Paris,' I start, but he doesn't let me get far.

'I should turn this ship round. I should take you back.'

Something in my gut gives a sharp heave and, after a moment, I realize I do not have to hide the pain. I let the cracks surface, the distress spilling across my face, a strangled cry shouting before the tears glisten in my eyes.

What exactly does he imagine will happen? That he can

just say: *Ah, yes, here you are, Menelaus, your woman returned. Don't worry, I didn't do anything to her; you haven't been cuckolded.* Menelaus would divorce me for sullying myself with another man. And he sits on the throne my stepfather abdicated for him. My brothers are half dead and my sisters are scattered – Phoebe and Timandra in cities beyond the mountains and Philonoe wherever Artemis leads the hunt. My eldest sister, Clytemnestra, is closer, but her husband is Menelaus's brother and I doubt she'd help me anyway. I'd have nowhere to go, no home, no protection and, with no husband to defend me, nothing but my pretty face to claim as a prize.

But, of course, Paris has thought of none of this; he has thrown his anxieties out carelessly without thinking them through a dozen times first, as any sensible person might.

'Paris,' I say, blinking back tears and pretending the hurt is only for him. Whatever real things had been budding are hidden now. I will say whatever I need to. 'How can you say that? I could not bear to let you go. I know we've only been married a handful of weeks, but I love you.'

It's instant, as I knew it would be. His face falls, he stutters, he stares at me.

'I love you too!' he finally declares, emboldened. He clutches at me with sudden thirst, hands tangling in my hair. 'Of course I do.'

I kiss him, closed lips against his, and he clutches me like I'm all he's ever wanted. It hurts – to be so desperate for the truth of a thing and to say it in an agonizing, manipulative plea instead. I feel robbed, and whatever hope there is for Paris and me flickers like a flame on a short wick.

Lips still pressed to his, I open an eye and look out at Troy.

Surely here our love can flourish – on solid ground, when I am no longer fleeing all that I left behind. I could build something every bit as stable as those famed walls.

Maybe, in Troy, love will endure.

CHAPTER NINE

Cassandra

I'M CLINGING TO MY DIGNITY but each scowl of doubt and whisper of disbelief has me clutching ever tighter to something I know – even without my gift – is destined to slip through my fingers.

It's been weeks, and despite a handful of prophecies a day, none have shown me much of the war beyond a few scenes so chaotic I've struggled to decipher them. If war does come to our shore, then my first request is that we colour-code the Greek and Trojan forces, perhaps even paint names on to the armour so that I can keep track of who everyone is and what foolish choices they're going to make. Face down in the dust, they all look the same.

Most visions have been thoroughly mundane – the future full of many more boring things than those worthy of note – and still, when they burst free in public, people disbelieve me and mock an oracle who might believe the coming of something as foolish and impossible as sunshine or breakfast.

My nails have pierced skin, my jaw clenched so tight it hurts. I am not used to holding back my retorts or hiding my displeasure and it's taking everything I have not to begin forming curses of my own.

Instead I'm lying through my teeth. The main risk, aside from people growing suspicious of prophecies whose metre I just can't seem to get right, is that an actual vision comes when I'm in public. I have no control over what shape they take – sometimes they're lines bursting from my lips, or I'm thrown into a scene or, worst of all, I am wrapped in the future's strands while my present self speaks – and I revive to a crowd of people sneering at words I don't remember saying.

Now I'm pacing the temple's cella, waiting for visitors to arrive, trying to encourage the prophecies to come while I'm alone. It works, occasionally, though mostly they just show me the face of that woman again – sometimes she is crying and sometimes she laughs in a clear, high chirp, she smiles serenely or her eyes widen in worry, but it is always, always her.

I am beginning to believe no other path exists. There is only the girl and the destruction she brings.

'*When guests draw near, seeking allies' embrace strong,*' I whisper. '*Is the voice that persuades –*'

'There's no one here, you don't need to perform,' Herophile scolds, her footsteps hidden by the sound of clashing blades still ringing in my ears.

'Is that what you think is happening?'

'I've heard enough nonsensical prophecies or shoddy imitations of the lines every seer in this temple has churned out to know one of two things. You're either lying – and attempting, quite badly, I might add, to act the part.'

I fold my arms across my chest and try to look haughty enough that she might fear some sort of repercussion.

'Or?'

'Or you truly were blessed by Apollo. He even sent lights through the sky to commemorate it. But you weren't strong enough. All that power has addled your brain and you're confused by what you're seeing.'

'The princess of Troy is either a liar or a madwoman – is that what you're saying? Just so I can be clear on what accusation is being made.'

'Oh, please, Cassandra, let's not bandy your title about like the rumours are not circulating within the very palace of Troy. I'm merely repeating what others – the council, even – have said.'

Is that true? I'd thought the public the greatest risk to my reputation. I had not realized those in my very home were whispering too. Am I not even safe within the soft-blue palace walls? Do the servants talk over my sheets as they make my bed? Do my siblings gather together and air their concerns? Or worse, do they laugh too?

'Why would you try to discredit a priestess of your own temple?' I hiss, my fear transforming to lashing fury – a reminder that I am powerful too, that whispers are nothing against a princess's rage. 'I know you don't like me, Herophile, but does having an oracle under your roof not bolster your reputation too?'

'If you were any good, perhaps. But we both know you're a fraud and you're not smart enough to avoid being found out. I'm not letting you bring more shame on Apollo or this temple, so if it's all of us or just you, then I'll make damn sure you take the blame.'

A man clutching a wound at his side, stumbling back and

staring into the distance with eyes that are already unseeing before he hits the floor. I watch his blood stain the earth beneath him.

The vision vanishes and my anger bleeds out with it, a familiar guilt settling heavily into my gut instead. No one believed me when I warned them of war before the curse, but if I'd been able to prove myself with smaller prophecies, would I have been able to stop this? Can I still?

'Help me, then,' I say. 'If you fear I'll damage the temple's reputation, help me escape it now. I'll step back. I won't play the oracle any more. Whatever you want, please.'

She must know what it costs me to say those words – to plead for her mercy.

And she laughs anyway.

It rings off the temple walls just like Apollo's did.

'Oh, no, Cassandra. You've brought this on yourself. I've waited years to watch you fall – and I can't wait to see all that you have coming for you.'

I try to prepare us for war without triggering the curse – offering prophecies to store grain or encouraging men to train with a blade. But I'm lost – despite the visions of clashing swords and broken spears, I have no clue what might help other than sending that woman back the moment she arrives.

I ask Kreousa what might be useful preparations to make before a war – she knows so much more than I do. But she's irritable, demanding to know particulars I cannot share.

'You can't just ask that without giving some context – how big are the armies and what fortifications does the city have? There's no universal trick to winning.'

I tell her not to worry. I'm still feeling out the limits of the curse and what it classes as a prophecy. So far it discredits any attempt to explain what I've seen or to paraphrase a line. If I gave too close a description of Troy, would it trigger it too?

My dread of the people turning against me has me stumbling over my words and keeping me up at night.

But ever since Herophile suggested it, the thought of my own family growing to despise me too has taken root. The fear strikes me at every quiet moment and it's a despair I struggle to hold within myself, one that needs to be emptied into bundled fists striking my mattress, or loud crashing doors swinging shut and screams muffled in pillows.

It's also starting to seem increasingly inevitable.

On the afternoon it all changes, I deal with three different people asking about their fortunes and how to improve them, and I'm struggling not to recycle advice and prophecies. There are only four compass points to say their destiny lies in, only so much treasure I can promise awaits them, and I learnt the hard way that they don't enjoy being told their suffering is unavoidable.

'My lands are failing,' some member of the minor nobility tells me. 'Nothing will grow.'

'Poseidon is angry,' I lie. 'You have not honoured him in your prayers – too focused on the land rather than the ocean – and so he causes storms that keep your land barren. Scatter seawater across your crops and they will bloom.'

The man blinks. 'You want me to salt my fields?'

'Yes,' I confirm. 'I see that will solve the problem you face.'

He tenses, teeth gritted as he offers a curt nod and leaves without even thanking me.

Beside me, a priestess stares before shaking her head.

'He should not doubt the gods,' she says. 'It is a test of faith – scatter saltwater in the name of Poseidon and know he will not allow it to make the land infertile.'

Well, how am I supposed to know that salting the land stops things from growing? Why are people coming to me with farming nonsense? Is an oracle not too important to be consulted on every little thing?

I need to get out, need a way to abdicate my position before I embarrass myself beyond redemption.

I don't realize it's real when the bells start ringing – I have heard them so many times, both in visions and in the echoes of them that bleed through to reality.

But the next visitor jolts at their chimes, and the other priestesses glance about with mild curiosity.

I rush to the temple's edge, its thick winding terrace that overlooks the city. I know what I'll see before the railing presses against my ribs – I've seen it a dozen times.

The sun is high.

And a ship is on the horizon.

CHAPTER TEN

Cassandra

'M NOT ALLOWED TO LEAVE the city without a guard and I've never been stupid enough to try.

It's never bothered me all that much. This city is everything to me, crawling up the mountainside like we're climbing closer to the gods themselves. At the very top rises the palace and past its walls, down a long gradual slope, is the half-circle of the acropolis where the temples and scholars' halls are, each interspersed with the other. They all model themselves after the palace, white marble veined with gold or other, cheaper stones painted to look the same.

Beyond all that white, the city bursts with colour. Every shutter is slicked with a bright burst of paint, every wagon shining in a dozen different hues, every market stall tented in bold fabrics. It's beautiful, a place where art and music are celebrated more than war, and you can *see* it, the famed wooden statues that litter the streets, the performers spilling from taverns, the very palace itself perched on a mountain but a palace nonetheless, not a castle, not a fortress, not designed for strategy but for the view of the city it loves.

I wander the city whenever I can. But this time I don't wait for a royal guard.

I need to see it, even as I dread it – like a horrific fable enacted, the threads of fate drawing me on, begging me to watch what they have already shown me.

I need it to feel real. I need everyone else to see it too – to watch as my visions become their reality.

After weeks of people denying the things in my head, I am not even hopeful I can change this moment. I just need the validation.

Because I think I'm starting to doubt myself too.

And if I'm right in the face of all that resistance, I need to let the truth of it fuel whatever I try next to save us.

Without guards and among all the movement the ringing bells have triggered, I manage to weave invisibly through the streets and past the outer city walls which tower above at impossible heights, a thing no man could build. And no man did build them – they are the work of Poseidon and Apollo.

I follow the dirt paths beyond to the ocean, shining like a thousand jewels in the sun.

I arrive when the boat is drawing near, lines cast to pull it closer.

Hector stands at the edge of the crowd, watching it all with the same stoic expression that's often etched on his face.

The people see me and my stomach turns, the reaction half what I have always expected – nudging elbows and excited whispers, quick bows and generous smiles – and half stifled snickers, judging sneers and rolling eyes.

But they part, forming a path for me to reach my brother,

though Hector's so focused on the ship that he doesn't see me until I'm beside him.

He greets me with a teasing smile. 'Do you think Paris will have Aphrodite with him?'

I glance away, face burning with anger. Deiphobus didn't believe me and nor did anyone else I warned before I figured out the curse, and now this is one of their favourite jokes – that Paris is favoured by Aphrodite. So ridiculous it must have been said in jest.

'Come on, Cass, I'm just joking –'

'Stick to pompous refrains, you're better at them,' Deiphobus says, appearing abruptly through the crowd. 'Mother's going to be livid when she finds you here without a guard in sight.'

'I don't know what you're talking about. We clearly came together.'

'Sure, for twenty silver.'

'You're a prince – what do you need silver pieces for?'

'Thirty.'

'Fine, yes, whatever.' I refrain from rolling my eyes solely because I know it's what he wants. I sometimes think Deiphobus needs to irritate us in the way the rest of us need food and water.

'Paris isn't alone,' Hector says, staring at the ship. 'Is that a woman?'

I turn and time slows enough that I wonder if this is some new type of prophecy, but no, it's her, hair fluttering in the ocean wind, clutching Paris and, even at this distance, even in the shadows of the ship, I know it's the woman who's haunted me for weeks.

Then Paris takes her hand and guides her into the light.

I've seen her image a dozen times but there's something different about seeing her in person – like growing up on tales of natural wonders and finally seeing one only as you take your final breath. She is a lifetime of awe, a myth that could sustain you.

'She's beautiful,' I say, because it feels like the simplest translation of the riptide I feel caught in.

The crowd murmurs, snatches of conversation reaching me about how stunning this woman is. Even with the horrors I know she brings, I cannot disagree with them. But I've always been weak when it comes to girls who look like works of art – unattainable, aesthetically pleasing women are what half my daydreams consist of.

As they dock and prepare to disembark, their wedding bands glint in the sun.

'Wait,' Hector says. 'He's married her? Who is that?'

Would it count as a prophecy? I'm not sure. So instead of saying, *Queen Helen of Sparta*, I say: 'Is that a crown?'

Because it's not – it's the tiniest circlet of metal, but that's what passes for a crown in Sparta and Hector knows that as well as I do.

She's wearing a purple dress – a colour only royalty could afford – and it's clearly Spartan: short with slits up the sides. Who else would bare that much skin? As though her face alone were not enough of a trophy, she had to show every inch of her legs, tightly corded in muscle and tanned by the sun.

'Helen of Sparta?' Hector stares with dawning horror.

'Idiot,' Deiphobus hisses, eyes narrowed at our new brother like he might rectify Paris's existence himself.

'He can't do this,' Hector says. 'So many men went to Sparta to vie for her hand that they had to make a pledge to respect the marriage she chose. They agreed that no man would try to take her from her rightful husband and if one tried, they'd all unite to get her back.'

'You mean this . . .' I have to let him get there by himself.

'Is war.' He doesn't even say it like it's a question.

'What do we do?' Deiphobus asks. 'We can't send her back and we can't fight every bloody polis in Greece.'

'We need to gather the war council, now,' Hector says, turning towards the city where the huge arched gates have been wrenched open, carriages beginning to roll out from the walls towards us. My mother is in the first, and she sees me before I can duck, her bright smile darkening.

I'd better pay Deiphobus quickly, or I'll be in a great deal of trouble.

But, oh, who cares? Because my brothers believe me. And if they think Helen is a problem, others will too. The threads flitting through the air don't even twitch but I'm so convinced the future might be shifting, a new picture about to be shaped, that I forget I'm in public and do a happy little jump complete with clapping hands.

'Adorable.'

I turn not towards the voice but my brothers – like they might protect me from a god. But they're gone, racing towards our parents. And, even though I'm surrounded by people, I feel alone with him once more.

'You've done well, little princess,' Apollo says.

'My lord,' I start, but I don't know where I go from there. When I saw him last, I was convinced he would destroy me and was ready to go out with as many insults as I could muster. But I'm feeling a little less ready to face my inevitable doom today, and the thought that he might be here in front of everyone to make an example of my death instils a terror so deep I feel the ice of it crystallizing down my spine.

He reaches out as though to trace my silent lips, but I step back out of his reach, a cold glare burning in my eyes before I can think to temper the expression. How many times must I play this out, so aware of the danger of him and still unable to behave as I should?

'It's been thoroughly entertaining, you know,' Apollo continues. 'Watching you navigate the curse. A clever idea too – all the lies. It's a shame you never cared enough about your worship of me to apply yourself – if you were better at crafting lines of poetry, they might even have believed your false prophecies.'

Paris is helping Helen down the gangplank now, and I don't know what scares me more – Apollo standing beside me or the thought of her setting foot on our land.

'Carry on as you are and they might turn against you in a year.' He opens his hands, palms wide, and I'm given the distinct impression he's rehearsed this speech. 'But I can't wait that long. War is coming, Cassandra. And one day you're going to stop fighting me in this little game of ours and realize how thoroughly helpless you are.' He meets my gaze, his eyes burning with desire and hatred in equal measure. He drops his voice to a low whisper, a growling promise that if he cannot find satisfaction in one, he will take the other. 'I hope it breaks you.'

He presses his hand to my forehead and I am violently

thrown into a vision. The strands around me tighten their hold, and everything flickers before me so quickly I can barely keep track.

The red halls of Sparta again, and the king sits on the throne, shouting, screaming, demanding an oracle be sent for, missives sent to every prince of Greece who ever swore a pact, telling them the time has come to fight for their words, for their honour, for the riches of the vaults of Troy.

It cuts to the gathering forces at our city walls, boats piling into this very spot, all here to tear my home apart in search of this woman.

And then I'm on the battlefield where I have been so many times before, only this time I can feel it, can feel that it will be so much worse than I can possibly imagine, and the vision spins, shifting my focus over, and I see Hector's body, tied to a chariot. I've seen so many bodies in my visions, so many of them battered and bloody and barely recognizable. But this is something else: flesh little more than a minced pulp, flesh I wouldn't recognize as my own brother's were it not for the wedding band on his finger, an unmistakable ruby stone clinging to torn and shredded skin.

I blink as reality shifts back into place before me. My gaze locks on the woman taking her first steps in the city she threatens.

Hector's corpse, if it can be called that, blood clinging to the earth, eyes torn by jagged rocks, the chariot stampeding on.

I'm screaming – not even words, just horror scraping my throat as it wrenches free.

She does this. This woman creates the futures that have raced through my mind for weeks. This woman is going to get my brother killed, his corpse defiled, and, by the gods, how many more? How much red will stain these lands?

I don't think – can barely even see past the blood before me. I just move.

She blurs, those golden curls merging until they're all I can see, and I think that if I can just reach her, I can save us.

My arm is wrenched back with such force I hear something crack.

It doesn't stop me; I'm still leaning towards her. She has so much hair it's obscene. I want to wrap it round her throat.

Another person, arms round my waist, lifts me off my feet, and I clutch something metal and I hurl it towards her.

Someone else screams and I think: *Good, good, they should be screaming*.

But I'm surrounded now and my arms are pinned behind me and it's all I can do to spit at the ground by her feet.

There's a split second of uncertainty on her face before she turns to Paris, leaning into his side.

I can still see my brother's beaten, bloody face, and the prophecies are howling too. '*For Helen's sake, the Achaeans and Trojans will clash, in years of war, where countless lives will pay the toll, and sorrows weigh on both sides, heavy and –*'

The guard holding me finally claps a hand over my mouth and I never thought I could be grateful for so humiliating an action.

There must be hundreds of citizens gathered at the shore – all are blinking, their eyes glazed over as the curse settles in their ears. Then smiles twitch on to faces and everywhere I look I am met with a condescending smirk.

'Cassandra!' my mother shouts, so angry she's shaking. Father is speechless.

The guard lowers his hand as my family draw closer.

'Hector, Deiphobus,' I beg. 'Please, you know she's dangerous.'

But Deiphobus looks at his feet, embarrassed, kicks at the dust and shrugs. 'Cassandra, please stop. How could she possibly be anything of the sort?'

No.

Hector turns, a thread wrapped tight round his throat, and the visions still cling to him, his flesh flaking from his skull, muscle and tendon stretching as he nods at Paris and the woman who damns us. 'We're delighted to have you here, Helen of Sparta. Although, I suppose we ought to call you Helen of Troy.'

Hector smiles through torn lips, blood staining his teeth.

In the distance, I hear a Keres shriek as the demons of violent deaths flock to our walls and wait for it all to begin.

CHAPTER ELEVEN

Cassandra

THE ROYAL GUARDS THROW ME into one of the carriages and race me back home, where they proceed to ignore every one of my protests and manhandle me to my room, pausing only to summon a doctor to rather unceremoniously shove my arm back into its socket.

My shoulder throbs with pain and I screw my eyes shut as tears well. Is it worth this? If I told my parents the truth – confessed to what I did, told them about the curse – would they find some way round it? It can't be worse than this slow unravelling.

A dozen visions of the future flash at once: my mother glancing round the room like someone might hear my words, my father's scowl deepening the grooves on his forehead, Kreousa's inferno of fury, Deiphobus's stone-cold rage, Hector's disappointment shifting quickly to pragmatism, Andromache's arms wrapping round me, and even Scamandrius, nostrils flaring, declaring that only he gets to make my life hell.

I see tumbles down flights of stairs, choking poisons, falls from horses, mythic beasts, mysterious illnesses and stray arrows – and always, always Apollo's laughter, his threats tangled up in the prophecy.

I fall to the floor, shrieking in agony. It's too much, too many possibilities, all terrible and all tearing through my mind at once. I am used to suffering a handful of lines each day or glimpsing a few snatches of visions. This is a torrent. This is a burst dam threatening to shatter my fragile, aching skull.

Whatever Apollo did to show me that vision of Hector, the prophecy and its binding hold on me has changed.

But the message of them all is clear. In any future where I tell someone of the curse, Apollo ensures their tragic, untimely end.

The door flies open and my mother storms into my room in a swirling tempest of rich green silk, bundles of it curled into her hands like she can't move quickly enough.

'Start talking,' she commands, and I startle back so hard that I fall on to my bed. Ghostly grey apparitions rise from the floor behind my mother, clanging swords. I recognize their shields – I've seen this before. It's not wholly a vision because I'm still in my bedroom but as I focus on the threads of fate – always lingering, easily tuned out – I see they're practically sparking.

The future is bleeding into the present.

'Cassandra!' my mother snaps.

'Sorry.' I wince. This is exactly what Apollo wants: me muttering prophecies, tracking invisible figures and spacing out in conversations, distracted by things I cannot explain in any believable way.

He's expediting my fall from grace.

I could cry – all these things I'm seeing, all the horrors I am burdened with, and that's not even the punishment. I thought he just wanted me to feel powerless to stop the terrifying things I'm seeing from happening. But it's more than that. Apollo doesn't just want me helpless, he wants me isolated and desperate.

Does he really hate me so much? But then his words echo in my mind and it all becomes clear: *This little game of ours.*

He wants to break me down, an opponent to beat, a girl with no choice but to turn to him and pray for his mercy. This is a game to him, and the only game these men know how to play is one of chase and conquer.

I was wrong; he's not satisfying his hatred in lieu of his desire – they're one and the same to him. He's hoping I'll have only him to turn to, that I'll come crawling back and beg him to take me.

'Well?' My mother pushes once more.

I need something to get me out of this, but these last few weeks have shown me how atrocious a liar I am – which isn't a surprise. My whole life I've only ever blurted exactly what I'm thinking. Why would I temper my thoughts when no one can do anything about them? A princess of Troy has no need to lie – she could get away with murder.

Unless she attempts it in broad daylight, screaming unbelievable prophecies in front of subjects.

'I . . . I can't do this,' I say, letting my anguish break. 'The prophecies are so confusing, spiralling through my head, never telling me when they'll happen or whether they even will, or if they depend on something else. I can't control them.'

It's not exactly a lie – more a very mild frustration against everything else. But it nearly works. Mother is halfway towards reaching for me before thinking better of it.

'I'm yet to hear why you attacked Helen.'

I shake my head. 'I saw something and it . . . I was wrong. I thought she was going to do something to –'

'And that's an excuse?'

'No! I was an idiot and I'm sorry.'

She doesn't break her gaze and I try to cling to my sorrow – the emotion is right, even if Mother reads it wrong. But thinking about hurting Helen has my distress shifting to anger – because I didn't think at all, I just reacted to my brother's corpse. And even if I should be relieved it didn't work – because surely the Achaeans would simply come to avenge her if it had – part of me is livid I couldn't at least hurt her, because look how much she's going to hurt us all.

'All right.' Mother nods. 'Until you get a handle on your prophecies, no more assemblies. You can offer your oracular prophecies in private, and let the other priestesses deliver them.'

I'm so relieved I nearly forget to look humble and apologetic.

'Apollo gifted our nation when he gave you this sight, Cassandra, but if you're not capable of discerning what's real and what's not, then you need to pray to Apollo for guidance. Make offerings, hold vigils, ensure you're honouring him properly.'

Great. I'm sure that will delight him.

'Yes, Mother,' I say, managing to get the words out without spitting them.

'And you'll apologize to Helen.'

That one somehow angers me more. I've spent weeks seeing her face bringing about our ruin and now I have to seek her forgiveness?

It should be easy to at least fake, but the very thought makes bile rise.

'Fine,' I snap. 'But what I did aside, why is she here?'

Mother pierces me with a shrewd, suspicious look that lets me know I am walking a very narrow line right now.

'She married your brother.'

'But why?' I push. 'She was a queen of Sparta and she gave that up to marry a prince who's not even the heir? Why would she do that?'

'We provided you with plenty of offers for heirs and kings. Sometimes it's not persuasive.'

'What if Paris took her against her will?'

She turns to me so sharply it's like the mere suggestion is a blow. 'Your brother would never do that.'

'We don't know him!'

'Not this.' She shakes her head. 'I can't do this again.'

'Cassie.' Her voice taut, heartbroken – laden with regret. She stares at me with wide, pleading eyes. She's done something awful, something unforgivable – to me. 'What choice did I have?'

I blink and my anger wilts.

'Look, I'm not saying that something's definitely happening,' I manage, my voice choked, 'just that there's plenty about this that doesn't make sense. We should consider it.'

I see a flicker on her face – doubt. But she steels herself.

'They are young and they're in love. And when we make their marriage official tonight you'll apologize to Helen and make her feel at home. And you'll be nice to your brother.'

Oh, absolutely not.

But I don't want to make this worse for myself.

'Of course,' I agree. And then, because I can't help myself: 'Will Helen need to borrow a gown? It doesn't appear like the sort of clothes she owns will be appropriate.'

Mother glares, catching the insult – but she can't deny its truth. So she sighs and says: 'Most likely, yes. Bring some along with you later. And I mean it, Cassandra: you'll be a delight as far as Helen is concerned. I want you to make her feel like all of Troy has been waiting for her.'

Minutes after my mother leaves, Andromache and Kreousa pile into my room and throw themselves on to my bed like we're gossiping before a banquet.

'Are the rumours true?' Andromache asks. 'That Paris is married?'

I said this, I want to scream. But I know that's not how this works.

So I simply nod.

'To the Spartan queen?' Kreousa frowns. 'Why does she sound familiar?'

'Because you've read every book in the library,' Andromache suggests, sitting at my dressing table and propping her walking stick against the wall. 'Probably some record of royal marriages. Cassandra, can you do my make-up?'

My stomach flips, as it normally does.

This is our routine: Andromache arranging the dresses, me applying our make-up, and Kreousa styling her hair and mine – Andromache's is set by maids she brought over with her from Cilician Thebe and it's currently twisted into a hundred tiny braids, each threaded with shells that clink together as she moves.

I've run brushes across Andromache's skin a hundred times, and there's always something about being so close to her, about my fingers dipping into pigments and reaching back towards her, that makes me feel ever so slightly on edge.

I move to sit in front of her anyway. If nothing else, it's a relief to be here with them and pretend everything is normal.

'I feel sorry for her,' Andromache says, while I set about powders and gels. 'You're a terrifying family to marry into.'

'Why, thank you.' Kreousa fakes a flattered swoon before gasping. 'The queen of Sparta! Helen, right? I remember now, she was mentioned in some religious volume I read.'

'I thought you went more in for history and war,' Andromache says.

'Yes, well, Aeneas stole the scroll I had reserved, so I decided to steal his.'

Andromache meets my eye in the mirror.

'Just marry him already, Kreousa,' Andromache deadpans.

'Don't be disgusting. Besides, his mother's Aphrodite and everyone knows she hates the daughters-in-law.'

'And is that the only reason you won't?'

'Well, he's also an arsehole that steals scrolls. Now, do you want to know what I know about Helen or not?'

'Do you want to tell us?' I smirk. Kreousa can't resist an opportunity to brag about all the things she's read.

'She's a daughter of Zeus.'

'We know.'

'Yeah, well, did you know he apparently came to her mother, Leda, as a swan? Leda laid eggs and Helen hatched from one of them.'

I miss the pot with the brush and scatter black powder across the table. 'Sorry, what?'

'Helen hatched from an egg. Apparently there were four children, and because Leda was sleeping with her husband at the same time, two of them were his and mortal, and two of them were Zeus's semi-divine offspring. There were whole years – decades, even – between the eggs hatching, so I'm not sure who is who, but I think Helen's Zeus's daughter.'

'That's ridiculous,' Andromache says. 'Honestly, the things Greeks come up with to try to pretend they have divine heritage.'

'Yeah, probably.' Kreousa nods. 'I guess if she starts clucking we know why.'

'Did she have a beak, Cass?'

'No,' I say, not wanting to linger too long on her face. It turns out it doesn't actually matter if it starts a war or not – a lovely face is enough to fluster me.

'Do you think we'll get along?' Andromache asks.

'Well, I tried to kill her, so I don't think she'll be my biggest fan.'

'Yes, we'll get to that. Olympus above, what were you possibly thinking?' Andromache scoffs. 'But I was actually asking if we'll like her or want her back on the first ship out of Troy.'

By Zeus, Andromache's a genius. I do not need to convince anyone of a prophecy to encourage the Fates to weave a future away from war. I just need to get rid of Helen. And I have spent years in a court ... There are so many ways I could do that without bringing prophecy into it.

If they found she was using Paris, for instance, or stealing from the vaults of Troy, or – I smile – some sort of sacrilegious offence, claims against a god that were simply unforgivable, because she's not a princess of Troy with a free pass.

Or I could drive her out, make her beg to leave this city – maybe even take Paris with her and let the Achaean forces chase her to another town.

Apollo could make me scream a prophecy about the ways she'd destroy us, and they wouldn't even care, because they'd be sending her away for other reasons altogether.

Very well, Apollo, if you want this to be a game, then you've designed your own undoing.

You've created an opponent with nothing to lose.

CHAPTER TWELVE

Helen

THEY DRAG CASSANDRA AWAY, QUITE literally. Dust kicked up by her heels trailing in the dirt, hand over her mouth, arms pinned behind her even though one is clearly dislocated. It's like they don't care. But she's a princess. How could they not care?

Everyone looks away, like if they don't watch, it can't be happening, but the golden-haired man who had stood behind her is laughing like he's enjoying a show at the Dionysia.

Paris asks me again if I'm okay, if I need to sit down or want a skin of water, and it's only when someone clutches smelling salts in my vicinity that I realize I should be distressed by the apparent attempt on my life, if a lot of screaming and a clumsy throw can be considered that.

But everyone is acting like I just narrowly escaped death by coin toss, so I clutch Paris anyway and thank him for protecting me, which he didn't, but it puffs his ego, which he needs in front of a family he's still uncertain of.

When I look back, the laughing man is gone.

We pile into a carriage filled with royals – three princes and the king. Paris falls quiet and my heart tugs with every glance of anticipation he casts towards his family.

I've grown used to categorizing men quickly and knowing how to sway each one. King Priam, intensely proud of his city and his people, shines as I show interest in a topic he so clearly adores – asking a dozen questions about Troy and how it came to be this shining jewel on the edge of the Aegean. As the princes bicker, I slot them all into their places: Hector, who wishes for affirmation of his decisions and person; Scamandrius, who wants attention and needs a fine line between flirting and encouragement; and Deiphobus, who might treat any woman like a sister if she laughs at enough of his jokes.

When we reach the palace, Paris draws me aside.

'Thank you,' he says, taking my hand. 'I couldn't . . . I thought I was prepared and then I found I could not speak at all.'

'Oh, my love.' He looks so utterly vulnerable that I want to pull him into a corner and soothe him with tender kisses and longing caresses.

'You were wonderful. They adore you,' he says, a little enviously. Then he seems to shake the jealousy because when his eyes meet mine they're back to their usual doe-eyed purity. 'And, more importantly, so do I. Everything is so much easier with you by my side. I feel like . . . like a sheep.'

I had been leaning in, preparing for a moment, and maybe I should have pretended still, but I jolt back. 'A sheep?'

'Yes.' He nods seriously, though a tinge of pink touches his cheeks and I feel awful for putting it there. 'Contented. The family is my flock and you are the dog come to herd us along – and, happily, I at least follow.'

I try to work out if my husband just called me a bitch.

'How sweet,' I say, offering a small smile in return. 'But I am happy to take that role to give you a rest before you become the hunting hound I know at heart you are.'

By Zeus, what are we even talking about?

I kiss him before we can say more things – and it's sweet and reassuring and I didn't even register my own nerves until he settled them in a single press of his lips against mine.

'I'll see you soon,' I promise, breaking away. The statement is underwhelming – and he must realize it too, because he is serious once more as he nods and returns to the men.

We will see each other again at our wedding.

Technically, we are already married. Aphrodite herself oversaw the ceremony – but there are records to keep and an official way of doing things, although the official way of doing things rarely involves a woman who is already married to a distant king.

But I'm not the first. When I was young, word of my sister Timandra came on the lips of travellers: *She has vanished in the night. She has left her husband.*

And then the reports that she had been found – that she was married to another.

When Menelaus learnt of the incident, years after it happened, he tightened his leash on me – hardly ever leaving me without a maidservant he'd appointed or some other spy he'd placed nearby.

I wonder if he realizes that the idea that I could leave was always in my head, even when he squashed it to a vague, distant and impossible dream.

And I wonder if Timandra was as nervous as I am about starting all over again in a new land.

A servant leads me through the palace and I try not to stare, but I can't help it and soon I'm outright gawking. The walls are threaded with gold – white marble veined with a metallic sheen that makes me think of ichor bleeding from the gods. Chandeliers glisten high above my head, strung with jewels that shine bright drops of colour into the halls, lights dancing in emerald and ruby and sapphire. Plush carpets line the floors, or else patterned tiles, art painted on to the walls themselves.

A deep, woody scent lingers in the air, mixed with something that, miraculously, reminds me of home, until I recognize it as the smell of clean laundry, of the lavender soap the servants use. We walk up a staircase whose banister is nicer than anything in the palace of Sparta, twisting metal wrought with ivy. And when I'm shown to a room, it features a large window, filled with tiny, colourful panes of glass that look out on to the steep mountainside.

I slip the coin Cassandra hurled at me from my pocket – thin, hammered copper with a rough etching of their walls. Clearly, the Trojans treasure their defences.

The door swings open and in walks the queen, a few women following close behind. At first I think they must be her ladies-in-waiting, until I recognize the girl at the back. It takes me a moment, her thick black hair braided into a neat crown round her head, cheeks dusted with a shimmering powder – hardly the crazed woman who attacked me. But it's clearly her – her arm's even in a sling. And she's smiling a little too saccharinely in my direction for me to relax.

'Helen.' The queen comes to take my hands in hers. 'How lovely to meet you.'

I rush to curtsey but she waves me away.

'Nonsense, you're family,' she says. 'Is the room to your liking? We will of course begin construction on a separate home for the two of you, but I hope this will do for now.'

'I've never seen anything like it. It's beautiful.'

'Wonderful! In that case, we thought we might help you ready yourself for the wedding.'

'How kind.' I beam, trying to act like this isn't a ridiculous suggestion. Why would the queen and the princess help me get dressed? Do they not have servants? 'I must confess I'm a little nervous. So silly, really, when we're already married.'

'That's perfectly natural,' one of the other girls says, as I'd hoped they would. Show weakness first and they'll rush to comfort me, be so caught up with doing so that they won't even stop to consider whether they want me comforted at all. 'I'm Andromache, wife of Prince Hector.'

Ah, yes, I can see that – Hector shouldering the burden of the crown, and here is his wife, beautiful and polished; her dark brown skin is free of blemishes, her dress neatly pinned, wooden jewellery in the exact same shade of mahogany as the cane she leans against, stepping forward first to help the new princess settle into life in Troy. Andromache smiles encouragingly, as if to say, *Here is a helping hand*. Well, sorry, Andromache, but I don't trust it.

'Lovely to meet you. Have you been married long?'

'I brought dresses.' Cassandra pushes forward before Andromache can answer, raising a pile of chitons in her arms. 'So you won't have to wear . . .' Her eyes trail down me in an attempt to be sneering that only manages to be endearing – how quaint. '*That*.'

The queen coughs rather pointedly.

'Oh, of course,' she rushes on. 'Helen, I'm so sorry about what happened earlier.'

I assume by 'what happened' she means her frenzied attack. She's not particularly convincing but I don't get the impression she's trying to be – it feels more like going through the motions in front of her mother.

'My daughter is an oracle. She was gifted visions by Apollo himself, though there is sometimes little sense to be made of them,' Queen Hecabe explains. 'They overwhelm her sometimes.'

'Right,' Cassandra says, a little tersely. 'So I hope you can forgive me. I bring my own gowns as a peace offering – though I'm not sure they'll suit you.'

Hecabe looks to the final girl, a little younger than the other two and clearly Cassandra's sister – she has the same warm bronze complexion, the same thick black hair and sharp brown eyes. Cassandra is taller and lacking her sister's generous curves, but the main difference is the way they stand, Cassandra with her shoulders back, one hip cocked like she's bored of this already, this girl shifting nervously and potentially on the verge of shuffling back behind Andromache.

'Kreousa.' She nods, glancing up only briefly before ducking her head down again.

My door bursts open once more and a younger girl storms through, arms folded tight across her chest.

'Father said you were in here. I want to help too.'

Hecabe looks at her pointedly. 'Then what do you say and how do you ask?'

The girl turns to me, her eyes big and pleading. 'Can I please help? They never let me join these things.'

Hecabe coughs.

'I'm Princess Polyxena, daughter of Priam, King of Troy in the land of Anatolia.'

'We don't need the full title,' Kreousa mutters, but I offer the young girl my hand.

'Lovely to meet you, Princess Polyxena.' I consider which title to give, *Queen of Sparta* rolling to the tip of my tongue. 'I'm Princess Helen and, now that I'm marrying your brother, I'll be part of the kingdom of Troy too. I'd love for you to help me get ready for my wedding.'

'We'll appoint you some handmaidens,' the queen says, a smile on her face, and already I can tell my response to Polyxena has ingratiated me with her more than anything else I could have done. 'But the girls enjoy forgoing them for banquets and getting ready together instead. In that tradition, we thought we might help you prepare.'

I am not changing clothes in front of my mother-in-law.

'How kind, I'd be delighted.' I nod, smiling at all of them. 'You all look wonderful – did you ready yourselves tonight?'

'Andromache is a very talented weaver and her dresses tend to make up for our lack of skill,' Cassandra says and Andromache smiles warmly in response.

Cassandra lays out said dresses on the bed. I wonder which are Andromache's, unable to believe a princess would weave so many and then give them away to use as clothes. They're so fine in quality, the patterns so intricate that we might save them for wall hangings and tapestries in Sparta. Apparently, in Troy even the people adorn themselves like art.

But they're also long, with so much fabric to be wrapped and tied I'm not sure I'll be able to move.

I consider the options – the simplest might imply I don't care, while the more intricate might suggest I am here solely for what they have to offer. I choose a chiton that's somewhere in the middle, a dark navy blue with golden rope-like cords to tie it round the neck and waist. I duck behind a screen to throw the bulk of it on, before Hecabe and Andromache start draping it round me. Polyxena watches, delighted to simply be here.

'*It's buying what we most detest with what we hold most dear!*' Cassandra mutters.

'Pardon?'

'Ignore her,' Hecabe says. 'She's struggling with the prophecies, but we pray to Apollo that they will be within her grasp once more.'

Cassandra isn't quick enough to cull the murderous glare she sends her mother before I can see it.

They ask how Paris and I met and I don't know what to say or whether to mention Aphrodite at all, so I skirt close to the truth while avoiding that crucial detail.

Kreousa is quiet and I can't work out if it's hostility or nervousness, before catching her rolling her eyes in the mirror and realizing it's both.

Cassandra continues to whisper things under her breath and, like everyone else, I try to ignore it. Every so often I catch snatches like '*trenches*' and '*ships*' and something suspiciously like the names of those I know: '*Agamemnon, Odysseus, Menelaus*'. She's a princess, I remind myself, and probably memorized the names of the world's royal families just as I once did. It doesn't mean anything other than some insidious attempt to unnerve me.

'Cassandra, do you need to excuse yourself?' her mother finally asks.

I expect her to look offended by the question but she presses her lips together and shakes her head.

'Paris is so excited to be back,' I say, trying to spare her the embarrassment, but this she does look offended by – like she does not wish to owe me a thing. I continue, gushing about the journey here, spinning a tale of Paris comforting me while I was seasick into his heroic efforts to calm the boat and impressive skill with a rope and sail.

'You seem to truly love my son,' Hecabe comments with a warmth I pocket away for later – Paris will be pleased to know his mother cares. Surprising, given she agreed to send him to his death twenty years ago.

'I do.'

'And when can we expect chicks?' Cassandra asks so innocently I don't catch the meaning until Kreousa snorts, dropping the strand of my hair she'd been braiding, and Andromache barks a sharp laugh that she smothers behind a cough.

Ah, so the swan story has made its way to Troy.

'Sorry,' I say, fluttering my eyelashes in an attempt at bafflement. 'I'm not sure I understand the joke.'

Cassandra had been tidying away the cosmetics and she glances up now with a challenging gleam to her eye. She's not subtle. She'd never survive a day in a Greek court.

'Oh,' she says, feigning naivety. 'I didn't mean to ruffle any feathers.'

'Girls,' Hecabe snaps. It's clear she doesn't understand what they're laughing about but she's worked out it's something at my expense. She's glaring at Cassandra like she's realizing the same thing I am – that this is a clique of cruel girls and Cassandra is their leader.

If only Cassandra knew how many groups like that I've destroyed in my time – whispers and rumour, planted evidence – shipped off to temples or neighbouring courts. Or, better yet, twisted over to my side. At most Cassandra might be an irritation, with her snide jokes and mean comments. Because there's no bite to it – it's all petty, surface-level effort.

And when I mean to hurt someone, I do it with the decisiveness of a final blow.

So my thoughts on the matter shift quickly. The menacing promise of *You're going down* shifting to the delighted excitement of *This could be fun.*

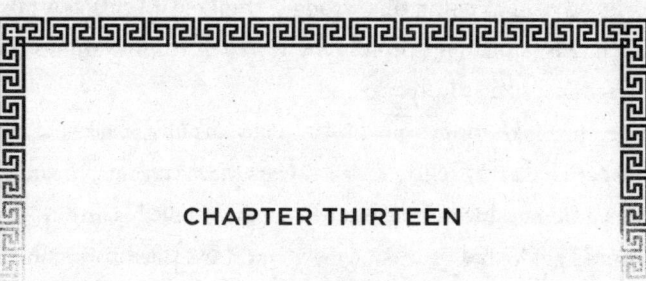

CHAPTER THIRTEEN

Helen

ATHENA'S TEMPLE IS ENORMOUS, RINGED with dozens of friezes telling her stories: Athena in her chariot, Cyclopes emerging from the ocean, giants falling. In the centre is a large courtyard where a wooden statue stands, Pallas Athene, so tall her head towers above the temple's roof. It is incredible, like liquid poured into a mould, wood so smooth it shines.

At her feet, Paris stands, nervous as ever. I want that lurch in my heart, that time-slowing feeling I sometimes get around him.

But a spike of rage shoots through me instead. I am in a foreign land, speaking their language, building alliances, all to settle him. And even now he gets to be anxious while I offer reassuring smiles.

He *does* ask if I'm all right but it's in a careless sort of way. He believes every nod, and never thinks to question if that might be a lie, or if I'm even in a position to tell the truth. All I do is worry about how he feels, and how often does he stop to seriously consider my happiness?

By Zeus, I'm doing this wrong – thinking all this as I take his hands, smile and profess my love. I'm ruining things for myself just like I always do and –

'*For the sake of one woman! And one man's love of her have lost a countless host in seeking Helen –*' Cassandra screams, breaking my panic, and Hector rushes to her side, places his arm round her and guides her out. I imagine it's more out of embarrassment than concern for his sister, but when they pass me I hear him whispering soothing refrains to calm her. I expect everyone else to awkwardly ignore her but a gentle murmur ripples through the crowd – ringed with the echo of hissing laughter, quickly smothered.

Interesting. It seems that the princess of Troy has more pressing concerns than some vendetta against me. Does she think she can convince the people to turn on me instead of her? Does she not realize that the public do not have to choose which of us they despise, they are quite capable of both?

Dissecting Cassandra's motivations distracts me from my spiralling mind long enough to marry Paris. Water is poured, fruit consumed, veils lifted, offers made to Athena and rings re-exchanged.

Then we return to the palace to begin celebrations.

I do not know where to start when we take our seats in the Great Hall. Before me, olives are placed like art in gradating spirals of green, clinging with lemon peel and dried flaked herbs. Baskets of bread beckon, roped into decorative shapes and studded with huge flakes of salt. There are turrets of olive oil, and I could ignore everything else – the stewed vegetables, the glazed meats, the crispy chickpeas and soured yogurts – to simply tear chunks of bread and dip them in the different infusions.

I spend the whole meal smiling so brightly I might shatter.

In the evening musicians strike up a beat, food is set aside and the Trojans dance.

Paris and I take the first chance we have to escape into the shadowy hallway outside the Great Hall.

'How are you?' I ask. 'I know this might be a bit much.'

I run my hand down his arm and he leans closer, reaching to absently toy with a strand of my hair like it brings him comfort. 'They're more welcoming than I feared, but I miss the peace of the boat, just the two of us together. Hopefully we will be able to slip out of this limelight soon.'

'Paris,' I start carefully. 'You're a prince of Troy, you'll never –'

'Oh, I know.' He nods. 'I know. I didn't expect the quiet of the fields I left. But I'd like to prove myself a prince of Troy, to find my place here through the work I might offer or heroics I might achieve. Not this theatrical performance of a love that should be private and intimate.'

'Well, we can be private and intimate soon,' I promise, my voice warm with a suggestive hum, leaning forward like I'm inviting him in. Honestly, I'd like nothing more than to be by myself for an evening. But if I ever want the future to allow for what I want, then I need to be all Paris needs me to be – and if that's a reassuring ear or a pair of arms to hold him, then that's not all that difficult a mould to fill. I practically broke myself to fit into the one Menelaus demanded. Paris's at least sounds pleasant.

He glances back to the hall where music pulses and people talk, and even to me it all suddenly feels a bit too much. 'I wish . . . never mind.'

'My love?'

Paris sighs and something about it feels like a sigh drawn from my own lips, resonating with that deep heaviness in my soul, and I wonder if he too carries such sadness inside him.

'I wish we'd just met,' he says. 'At a banquet or a temple. And I wish we had spoken and felt something and wanted to speak again. I am so incredibly grateful I was brought to you, Helen, but I wish we had fallen in love quietly. That we weren't some orchestration of the gods, ready to prove their might with all this extravagance. I wish we were simple.'

'I love you simply, might that be enough?'

He takes a shaky breath and smiles in a bashful, self-conscious way that makes my heart warm. 'I think it might.'

He lifts my hand to his lips, pressing a chaste kiss there before he returns to the party. I have had so many men fawn over me, but how few have sought tender romance rather than the satisfaction of their own lustful egos? I contemplate this, enjoying a moment to myself in this dimly lit hall. But it is too dimly lit, apparently, even for my sharp gaze.

'Ohh, she won't like that.' Her voice first – scathing – and then she steps from the shadows. Has she been there the whole time? How horrifying – the powers of prophecy in the hands of an apparent voyeur.

'Cassandra.' I smile like this is a pleasant encounter. I've seen her wandering round the banquet hall, whispering to whoever will listen. I assume her words are about me.

I'm not worried. In one day I've made the king and queen like me, and throughout our evening meal I've made good headway with the princes. I have weeks and years to make everyone else love me – and I will.

'Married in Athena's temple *and* he's regretting her involvement entirely? She'll be livid.'

'Who?'

'Aphrodite.'

A violent chill strikes me.

'How do you know about her?'

As far as I'm aware, Paris hasn't told anyone. And he certainly wouldn't have chosen Cassandra to confide in. So is he leaking information more freely than I'd realized? Or did someone overhear us? Does Cassandra have a spy among the ranks of Paris's companions?

She arches an eyebrow. 'Is it still a prophecy if it's come to pass?'

Is that all this is? A lucky guess?

'Spew enough nonsense and I'm sure you'll hit the mark once or twice.'

'I really don't care for your opinion on the matter.'

'Yes, I believe you've made that quite clear. Would you care to discuss your aversion to me, or shall we continue to pretend it doesn't exist?'

'Have you heard the stories of Athena and Aglauros? Auge? Ismene? And where do we begin with Hera?'

I tense a little more with each name, each one a marker, a woman turned into a warning tale of the retribution of the gods. Aphrodite cannot merely be a lucky guess if she also knows about Athena and Hera. She has a source, likely multiple – and listening ears working on her behalf are dangerous.

I may have underestimated the threat of Cassandra.

'Your point?'

'Athena and Hera are vengeful goddesses,' she says, leaning against the wall, arms crossed. It's such a different image from the woman who first greeted me: hair pristine, eyes artfully smudged, dim lamplight casting long shadows in the hollows of her cheeks, her collarbones, thick eyelashes fluttering attention to her burnt-gold eyes every time she blinks.

'Vengeance is the nature of the gods,' I say simply.

'Precisely. So do you think they'll take kindly to Paris choosing Aphrodite? And do you think Aphrodite will protect you when they come for you?'

The music and chatter of the party dims, all my focus locked on her. I did not imagine she might have a legitimate reason for wanting me gone. I thought it was petty jealousy, protected territory, a wariness of strangers – not a fear of the gods' retribution.

'And do you really think your ex-husband will let you leave so easily?'

No, no, I don't.

I've been trying to convince myself that the worst he will do is send missives and bargain for my return – that all I need to do is get the Trojans to want to keep me and I'm safe. But if I'm truly honest with myself, I know Menelaus would rather see me dead than suffer the humiliation of my abandonment.

Assassins are a very real possibility.

'I had no idea you cared about my well-being.'

'I care about Troy. You don't have to believe my prophecies – are spurned gods and kings not enough to worry about?'

She could be a real threat, with such drive behind her. I need the loyalty of guards, the ear of the king, the layers of walls encircling me and an armed husband by my side – all the things that the gossip Cassandra has been spreading all evening could take from me.

Already I'm running through scenarios – ways to depose her before she acts. The prophecies seem too cruel to leverage, too beneath me to manipulate a thing like that. But there will be ways. There always are.

'Paris has connections outside this city. If you love him so much, you should be happy to be a farmer's wife.'

Of course not – Troy's fortifications are the best protection I have.

'Certainly, but I have no need to.'

'Or I have cousins who might take you in.'

'And bring ruin to them instead, if that is your fear?'

'Leave,' she hisses. 'This is the only warning I'm giving you. Get out now. Before you are thrown out, exiled, not a penny to your name. I'll give you jewels, clothes, enough to set yourself up somewhere. Away from here.'

'You know perfectly well that's not going to happen,' I say, examining her closely. 'And how exactly do you plan to make the people of Troy cast me out when your position is so much more precarious than mine? I'm the wife to the long-lost prince. Second in line to the throne. You're a fallen priestess, a soothsayer no one believes – and if that weren't bad enough, a surplus princess.'

'I'm Trojan,' she says, with such fierce assuredness that this is all the leverage she needs that I nearly forget the whispers following her and believe it myself. 'I know this court and these people.'

'It sounds as though you are issuing a challenge.'

She narrows her eyes and steps forward, reaching to readjust my clothes, to tighten the binds. We've drifted in our conversation, no longer standing in the shadows but lit by the doorway to the hall. I do not think she even does it for appearances – so that if anyone looks over, they'll think she is helping me with my dress. I think she just wishes for an excuse to stand threateningly close. So close I could count her eyelashes, identify notes of cardamom and redwood in her perfume. 'If that's how you would take this, then you're a fool. Did I not list goddesses who might wish you more harm than I do?'

'I can handle myself.' I flash a smile – just in case anyone does look our way. And to unnerve her. 'And my husband adores me. And Aphrodite. I've been here mere hours and, after your little display at the shore earlier, I dare say more people here would rush to my side than yours.'

'This wasn't personal,' she says coolly, but she tugs sharply on a cord of my dress, my waist cinching so tight my breath hitches. Then she steps away. 'But if you would care to make it so, then yes, Helen. Consider this a challenge.'

She spins, her crimson dress flaring around her, and stalks back to the banquet hall.

I find myself smiling in earnest. I can't resist a challenge. And where's the fun in destroying her reputation before she can ruin mine? No, there's a trickier game here, and one I determine to win.

I'm going to make her do the one thing she'd hate the most.

I'm going to get Cassandra to like me.

CHAPTER FOURTEEN

Cassandra

IT BEGINS WITH WHISPERS, AS it often does. Last night's rumours echo and by the time morning crests above the mountains, Helen is all anyone can talk about.

She's radiant. Sure, but she's Spartan – how could we let so barbarous a girl marry our prince? And he was only a prince for a matter of days before she swept right in – clearly she saw her moment. Paris looked besotted, though. Of course he did, have you seen her?

I've grown used to listening at doorways, waiting for someone to mention my name. The paranoia Herophile instilled was at least good for something, I suppose. I never had to learn the subtle manipulations of court – I threw myself clumsily and brashly from palace to temple and made myself so grandiose that being *Princess Cassandra* was its own sort of protection. I could say anything, do anything and nothing anyone said against me could stick.

But Helen was right – my position is precarious now. I'm not too untouchable to be toppled. My slow descent has at least given me a head start, a few weeks to wrap my head around the power of rumour and sabotage and start the mills running. Maybe it won't be enough, but women can be felled with a single word.

In my case, it's *crazy*.

I just need to find Helen's.

As I walk the halls of the palace, I collect snatches of conversation like trophies and round the corner to find Hector and Andromache, hesitating at the door to their chambers like Hector has paused before they part.

'I feel like I've hardly seen you in all this chaos,' Hector says, voice soft in a way I've certainly never heard it. 'Do you want to do something tonight? We could go into the city and find a show, or sneak into one of the taverns.'

'Can we just dine alone? Or take a pouch of wine and watch the stars? I want an evening with only you.'

'Absolutely,' Hector says, grasping her hands and pulling her forward as he takes a step, like he needs that gap between them to close as quickly as possible. He draws her close, into his arms, practically enveloping her.

I step back so that I can make an entrance without intruding. I feel hollow, like the visions have carved out the pieces of myself that might ache. If you cut me open, you'd find ragged scraped edges but nothing left to bleed.

It's so far from how I normally feel around Hector and Andromache, on edge and hyper-aware, like I might think the wrong thing and take something precious from them. Once, I could have sworn myself in love with her. But they were so well suited together that when they first began seeing one another it was never quite jealousy I felt and more a vague sort of longing, that I wanted something *like* that rather than *exactly* that, because 'that' was theirs and it was beautiful. Still I unpick myself, piece by piece, around them, like I need to ensure nothing poisonous creeps in.

But there's nothing now, and that's so much worse.

He could die. I could lose him. She could lose him. I could lose her.

There's so much to fear, so why am I wrestling with this awful numbness?

An idea strikes so suddenly I half wonder if it's Apollo again, pushing thoughts into my head. But I can't blame him; this malice is all mine.

Other options first, I promise myself.

But this unspeakable one if I have to.

And later, when Andromache pours tea into my and Kreousa's cups, it becomes clear other options are still available.

'I didn't really think of it before,' Andromache says. 'But that swan story – it must mean the old king of Sparta never claimed Helen was his child. Leda must have had an affair. Call Helen the child of Zeus and no one will say what she really is: illegitimate.'

Because that's my own whisper circling back to me. And 'illegitimate' is a very good word to fell Helen with. I don't imagine it will be enough by itself – we hardly care about that sort of thing, but other cities do, so if I can pair it with something else . . .

I've been making up stories for the last month.

I hope I've become quite adept at it.

That night I fall into bed, satisfied with a day well spent and thoroughly exhausted from the night before, when I'd been too distracted strategizing rumours to sleep. The visions have been incessant, but tolerable – no other corpses I recognize, and scenes of battle are almost a relief because it's too chaotic to tell who's falling.

But I haven't slept since Apollo forced that vision on me and opened the valve to so many more. And the moment I finally shut my eyes, I get to add another torture to my long, growing list: visions, prophecies, apparitions and now nightmares.

I wake wearier than I was when I fell asleep and stumble on my way through the palace – a murmur from a group of girls that catches me unawares.

'Did you hear the mad princess screaming last night?'

It hurts in a way such whispers never have before.

These things I'm seeing are more than scarring. They are gutting. They are debilitating. Even now, memories of the visions I've seen will flash like an echo at the slightest heavy door shutting or loud voice shouting.

No one needs to believe I'm seeing the future to believe I'm seeing *this*, do they?

They know I spend my days trapped in terrible visions, even if they don't believe they're true.

They know I'm suffering and they're laughing.

And now I'm not sure what terrifies me more: spiralling into lunacy – and would I even call it that? Because it feels a very rational thing to react to all this by running as far from my own mind as I can – or the fear of needing their help if I do.

Which means making Helen leave is self-preservation. The city might survive a war. But I'm not sure I'll survive the constant glimpses of it.

*

At midday Helen dines with us and afterwards my mother insists that we show Helen the acropolis, and as we wander past its empire of glistening marble I'm reminded of what all this is for.

I'm used to the public stopping to stare at me in the streets – so I hardly notice when they do it now. But then I realize it's not me they're looking at – and not me they're whispering to one another about.

I wonder if my rumours have made it out of the palace yet.

'Your doing, I assume?' Helen asks, sidling up to me and looping her arm through mine before I can resist – and then, of course, I can't, because we're in public and my mother is a few feet ahead of us. I'm supposed to be pretending to welcome Helen to the city, after all.

'Oh, I assume they're just thrilled to catch sight of the woman the whole city is talking about.'

'I'm sure,' she says, waving at a few women muttering into each other's ears – and they flush and hurry to bow. 'You do realize that the whole city talking about me is not the terrible thing you seem to think it is.'

'It depends what they're saying.'

'It really doesn't, actually.'

I turn to her and she's smirking – smugness oozing from her every pore. Irritation creeps beneath my skin and I can hardly believe I manage to stay, arm looped in her vile arm. But breaking free and walking away from her would be exactly what she wants. Or is this what she wants – me to stay put and hear her provocations? Helen has an infuriating air of careless glee to her, like any action I take will result in her amusement, like it's all just petty entertainment.

'Gossip swirls for any new arrival to the city. And there's plenty about me to discuss. What you've very kindly done with your meddling –' she gives my arm a squeeze, like she really is thanking me for a gift – 'is give me a larger platform upon which to right the record.'

She turns to one of the attendants accompanying us and nods.

They're all carrying baskets. I assumed they contained offerings for the temples or scraps of our morning meal or . . . no, I hadn't really assumed anything at all, because I hardly pay much attention to what servants carry.

And now Helen lets go, the sudden loss of the heat of her skin against mine its own lingering impression.

'People of Troy,' she calls, stepping forward, and it's mesmerizing. I thought I knew how to control a crowd but, by the gods, it's nothing compared to the way Helen's every movement whips up and snatches attention, like Charybdis pulling sailors to the ocean's depths. 'You've all been so welcoming. I wanted to thank you for your generosity, and share the joy I feel at being here.'

The maids pull the cloth from the baskets, revealing small rounded honey-cakes piled high. The energy switches, curiosity to joviality, laughter filling the air as the cakes are passed out.

By Zeus, how do they not see this for the bribe it is?

I should know – I did the exact same thing when I declared myself oracle.

'Oh, isn't that lovely?' Mother says to her companions, who nod their agreement. I'm livid: nails-in-skin, bone-crushingly, jaw-achingly furious.

When she's done, she walks right up to me and throws an

arm across my shoulders even as I try to duck away. People are watching us so I don't push her, just draw my arms tight across my chest and set my eyes dead ahead, looking anywhere but at her taunting face.

'See, I don't really care what they say,' she says, voice low and warm against my ear. 'So long as I'm the one they're talking about.'

Helen is winning over the people of Troy, but that's fine. There are other cities – ones with just as much influence.

So I write letters, though that's a mission in and of itself: hardly midway through a sentence before my eyes blur and I'm on a battlefield, swords clashing, the *stench* of it all – things no one should be exposed to, like the smell of a man's innards trodden into the dirt by a stampeding army – and then back at my desk, seeing that in my haze I've scrawled things from the vision, and I toss the parchment aside and contemplate quitting. But then I think of Helen flitting through the city or her smug smile or the echo of soldiers cursing her as they die, and I pick up the stylus and start again. Round and round I go – the writing, the visions, *her* – until I finally have four letters written.

I hope I will not need a fifth.

I send them to the handful of people I know outside these walls: my sisters, Laodice and Ilione; Briseis, a queen who visited briefly when still a princess; and Chryseis, the daughter of a priest to Apollo who occasionally journeys with her father from their town's temple to ours.

The latter replies with the sort of invaluable thing I didn't even know to hope for.

It's the strangest thing. The man you describe sounds so like a Paris I met a few years ago. The first and last time my father ever presided over the wedding of an immortal. The woman was a nymph named Oenone, daughter of a river god. And the man, Paris, was a mere shepherd. I heard a rumour he abandoned her – no one could work out why a man who was so lucky as to marry divinity would walk away from it all.

I think about taking the news to my parents. But they've made it quite clear that they think if Apollo's not responsible for the sun, then Paris is, and it's shining out of his every orifice. I doubt they'd hear a word against him. No, I have to convince Helen herself – upset her with the information so that she flees back to Greece.

I traded a bracelet to have the letters delivered and I'd give every ring, necklace, hairclip and brooch I own to get her on a ship to Sparta. She could be there in a week.

But I don't stop to think about the possibility she might believe me and simply not care – laughing in the face of my vicious, smug declaration.

'My dear, I left a husband for that man. What does it matter if he left a wife for me?'

My smile falls.

'Oh, no, did you think I would be devastated?'

'Did he tell you?' I manage to grind out.

She hesitates for a short second, which she covers with a condescending laugh, like she had been trying to stifle it. But I'm starting to see through my adversary enough to know the answer to that question is not one she wants to truthfully give. 'Men don't have to tell their wives things like that, Cassandra.

Now, when will you give up this attempt to drive me from the city? Even if you made me despise him, where would I go? I'm lucky to survive leaving one husband, I doubt I could leave two.'

'I'd rather not wait to find out who will and won't survive you leaving your husband,' I snap. I'm so used to hiding what the future holds that it's almost a relief to bite it out like this, to so disregard Helen's opinion of me that I don't care in the slightest whether she believes me or not.

But it's not a prophecy and there's no curse swirling in her eyes, just a tilt of her head and a coy smile. 'You're so obsessed with me. It's cute.'

She reaches to pat my shoulder but I'm already turning away, already trying to think of something else, and already letting the creeping sound of battle cries smother her laughter.

As the visions escalate and the days trawl on, I start to believe that the reason I've seen no potential future with Helen gone is because that possibility doesn't exist.

Which might mean there's no possibility without war.

Or without Hector's death – which I'm starting to see with disturbing regularity: his eyes staring blankly, cord torn through the flesh of his heels, the chariot racing before the walls, his dead body drawn behind it by the rope that pierces him.

And all the while Helen is smiling and laughing, batting away any attempts to be free of her like they're amateur efforts – which they are.

I claim she has none of the decorum that befits a princess of Troy. And there she is, hosting the ladies of the court in a glittering afternoon party, spinning round and seeding herself among them, every head in the room turning to her.

I say she is not as devout as she should be, and suddenly she's ingratiated herself with a dozen temples where she now spends a portion of her days, even charming the other priestesses of Apollo over to her side.

I say she's a snob and she begins conversing with the servants, and I see what I had not noted in my scheming: that Helen is good with people and I am decidedly not. She is not merely charismatic, she is thoughtful. She asks questions about them – their lives, their customs.

She's collecting allies. She's winning hearts.

And throughout it, every time I close my eyes, there is death, destruction and pain. I'm tired of feeling helpless. I can't stop this – I can't even control what I'm seeing. I'm fighting against a force I do not even understand, fooling myself into believing it might matter, and even my unshakable defiance is wearing thin.

Part of me doesn't even want to stop it any more. I just wish I could walk into it as oblivious as everyone else.

One last chance, I promise. There are games being held for the messenger god, Hermes, soon and a small banquet afterwards where many of the city's most influential nobles will be gathered. A final opportunity to weaponize those rumours before I resort to the last option.

At the party, I fly from group to group, eventually ending up in a small huddle with Deiphobus, Aeneas and a few other men I don't know particularly well.

'Helen abandoned her husband to marry Paris. It's a disgrace to Hera, and I fear we have angered the goddess of marriage,' I start, preparing to dive in deep – but considering the gods first gives this all a moralistic angle that enables me to 'advocate on behalf of the pantheon' and not merely 'gossip'.

'Official vows have been taken,' Aeneas says. 'It would be just as much an offence to Hera to send her away when we have all witnessed their union.'

'That's true,' I concede. 'But if she would leave one husband, who is to say she would not leave another? Perhaps she already has – it is clear that loyalty and fidelity are not something she is particularly concerned with.'

'Cassandra,' Deiphobus starts, a warning in his voice that would better suit Hector.

A shadowy figure spills out of the wall beside us – a woman clutching an empty, bloodied swaddling cloth. She opens her mouth and screams and wails and I cannot comfort a ghost of a future yet to come but I want to, and I feel aching guilt for not running to her side. When such pain is truly real, will I even care? Or will that numbness take over?

'Excuse me,' I manage before rushing from the room.

I collapse against the stone wall on the hall's other side, wondering how I can possibly outrun visions that exist in my own head.

I try to get my breath but the strands around me sense my weakness and tighten, squeezing words from my lips.

I let them, hoping they might run their course and be silent – but by the time a figure appears through the doors, it is all I can do to quiet them to a whisper.

'Cassandra,' Helen says – and of course it's her. *Of course.* 'You need to stop. Look at you – do you even realize it's the kindness of my heart that stops me annihilating you? It would be so easy.'

'So do it,' I manage to gasp. The prophecies subside a little with the distraction. 'I don't care.'

I am used to Helen parading about this city in a manner that stings in a vicious, acidic sort of way. I used to do that: walk these streets like art to be admired. Now I scurry with my head low, like I might slip from sight altogether. Maybe it's time I stopped worrying – maybe I'm too preoccupied with my own social standing to really, truly prevent this war.

Out here, in the lofty corridor and dim light, Helen is not the prim, imposing figure she sometimes appears. Instead she looks slight and small and unbearably human. It is a dangerous thing for her to become – better to see her as the monster who brings all that I have seen. 'Don't be ridiculous. We're women of the court, Cassandra, reputation is all we have.'

'So destroy mine. I don't care! Just leave! Make me a name too shameful to mutter, if you must. If that's what it takes to get you out of this city, then so be it.'

'You truly hate me that much? When all I have done is exist within these walls?'

'It's what you're going to do.'

She takes a breath. 'You have my sympathy, you do. But if anyone believed any of the things you're saying, they could cast me out with nothing. People could be killed, Cassandra. You accuse some poor man of having an affair with me and Paris would have the right to slaughter him.'

How dare she claim some moral high ground with all the destruction she's bringing? 'We don't do that in Troy,' I snap, like it would stop me even if we did. One person's blood is a small price to pay to save the lives of thousands.

'Princes evade the law, Cassandra. Words hold a terrible

power and, given how clumsily you wield them, I can only assume you are not particularly accustomed to such games. Now, I've let you run your lies about town and foiled you at every turn. Give it up.'

One person's blood. I wince. It appears I've finally talked myself round to it.

Because I'm under no illusions about the sort of future waiting for Helen back in Sparta. Returning willingly might save her, but selling her out? I might as well sign her execution order myself. I might as well volunteer to be the one wielding the blade.

And despite trying to strangle her on her arrival, I'm not actually all that comfortable with causing this woman's death.

'So this is my final warning,' Helen continues, and her whole demeanour shifts. Her voice – always so light – now glimmers with cutting iron, her eyes narrow, her chin a sharp slash as she angles it up to face me. 'Enough. Accept that I am here, that the citizens love me – in fact, why not accept that there's a new fairest woman in Troy? Accept it all. Maybe you don't care about your reputation, but I'm willing to do awful things for the sake of mine.'

She doesn't wait for me to reply. She simply turns on her heel and slips back into the party, ready to dazzle and schmooze and pretend she wasn't just making threats to the kingdom's princess.

I go straight to my room.

And I write a final letter.

CHAPTER FIFTEEN

Helen

SHE DESERVES MY IRE BUT I'm still angry that she broke me so quickly.

'Helen, are you all right?'

It's not Paris's voice but for just a moment I let myself think it might be.

Instead, I look up to find Aeneas. He's tall, broad-shouldered and well muscled, like every other Trojan trained to wield a sword. Beyond the brawn, his features are delicate and slight. His nose slopes like an upside-down psi, his chin is dimpled and a slight scar cuts across his forehead, a deep line drawn through his warm brown skin that only serves to highlight the eternity of his eyes, almost black and so dark they might go on forever.

His beauty is a threat. It comes straight from his mother, Aphrodite.

He claims she directed him to look out for me in Troy. But I suspect 'report back on me' might be more apt – though admittedly he's given me no reason to distrust him beyond 'Troy is a court like any other and trust has no place here'.

'Please don't let them get to you, it's just idle chat,' he says – which is when I realize I must be wearing my displeasure on my face.

I really thought I could rise above Cassandra's efforts to obliterate my social standing, appear unfazed and let her slowly realize her own shortcomings. Then, just when she was on the cusp of despairing at her powerlessness, I'd swoop in and show her how to really spin a story. I'd repair Cassandra's crumbling reputation and build her back up – with me by her side.

But there's one glaring flaw in that plan: Cassandra will never acknowledge her own flaws. She'll never see her limitations, never think herself incapable. It's almost admirable.

But it's going to be the cause of her own ruin if she keeps pushing me like this.

Then I realize what Aeneas has said – and it's worrying it took me so long.

Cassandra's a distraction in a time when I can hardly afford one.

Not when Menelaus is yet to make any effort to get me back – no letter, no retinue of diplomats, no trade missives. Every day of silence winds my fear tighter – especially when everyone else begins to relax. They do not know Menelaus like I do. If he's not going through official routes, it's because he's planning something underhanded and every boat that docks in the port has me patting my thigh to ensure the dagger I've begun carrying is still in place.

'What are they saying?' I try to focus.

'It doesn't matter, it's nonsense. Besides, it looks like you dealt with the source.'

I give my head a soft shake, and clutch my arms to my sides. I want to look like something to save, and hope he leaps to the rescue. 'If anything, I worry I just exacerbated things.'

'They're just words.'

As though there could be anything more damaging in a royal court.

'What if they aren't, though? What if that's only the part we can see? Can you ... can you please just keep an eye on her? Maybe ask someone to follow her?'

'Follow her? That's a bit extreme, isn't it? Look, Cassandra is ... she's had a rough go of things recently. The gift of prophecy without any training or support? It's a lot. And she's taking it out on you and that's not fair either, but it's petty, not a real threat.'

'Please, Aeneas. Can you just do it for a few days, for my own peace of mind?'

Pleading like this is a risk but I don't have enough of my own contacts in this city to have someone shadow her. Many other men would roll their eyes, say it's not worth their time and tell me to stop being so hysterical.

But Aeneas offers a wry smile. 'I ask my mother for help landing *one* date with Kreousa and this is the sort of trouble she drags me into? All right, Helen. I'll help.'

The men who competed earlier in games to honour Hermes are becoming drunk and rowdy and it's starting to unsettle me to be in the same room as them. Besides, the advisors I'd been ingratiating myself with have already retired and I don't want to interrupt Paris in the corner, bonding with Hector and Deiphobus.

'I might make my excuses soon,' I say to the two girls in the palace whom I've begun to consider my companions.

I thought I might be more likable if I had friends – but I wasn't actually expecting the friendship to be real. I can feel myself holding back from them, flinching every time I smile and catching myself every time I laugh. Friends – Menelaus took those from me. I don't want to risk it again.

But they make it hard to resist.

Athrae draws me close when I return, hugging me tight. 'I was going to follow you but Aeneas got there first.'

Ludicrous, really. I can think of dozens of reasons to choose a friend – and Clymene and Athrae certainly fit what I would have looked for. They're daughters of Queen Hecabe's companions, which means they might overhear something important. Athrae's beautiful, with full lips and a splattering of freckles across her golden-brown skin. She can disarm men and get them to let slip all sorts of things with a slight scowl of confusion they just love to explain things to. And Clymene's husband oversees the city's import of fine goods – which means he knows every ship coming in and out of port. She's also quiet and observant, with quick, dark eyes that dart round the room and catch things even I don't.

But none of that is why I've kept them close. It's this – Athrae's arms round me.

Comfort. Someone who notices when I leave a room. Someone who cares.

'Leaving early might be a good idea,' Athrae says as she draws away. 'You've had an exhausting couple of weeks. Are you sure you're okay?'

'That entirely depends on what Clymene says.' I turn to

the other woman, who has been avoiding my gaze and now offers an apologetic smile. 'Go on, what are they saying? I can handle it.'

Clymene lowers her voice to speak. 'I've had numerous conversations tonight where people questioned your loyalty to Paris, your general fidelity and, ah, forgive me, a few lewd comments on your sexual history. Everyone's intrigued by such a beautiful woman who was *not* a virgin when she married our prince, which, combined with certain rumours about Sparta's debauchery . . .'

'Right.' I nod – not exactly surprised. I've been waiting for this one. I've already listed all the ways I would target myself, to predict Cassandra's next move – although if I were her, I'd be trying to get Paris out of the city. There are so many more opportunities for men to be called away on trade or diplomatic pursuits, and he might even take his wife with him. But she seems to think it easier to force me from the city – and Paris might be a touch gormless, but I don't think he'd let me just run off because some gossip upset me.

Like I've summoned him, he appears at my side, hand round my waist and drawing me in close.

'I might retire,' I say.

'No, stay!'

'I'm getting a headache, I need to lie down.'

'Oh, okay, but listen, I was talking to this man over there who monitors the city's livestock,' Paris starts excitedly – and dread settles like a dark cloud shading the sun. Every gathering, every meal, every contact – my focus has been sharp. Establish Paris in the city, build the respect they hold for him, look for opportunities for him to gain prominence and power. Hector is active in the council, advising Priam on strategy and intelligence. Deiphobus leads the city's armies. I thought Paris might monitor the treasury or trade or the temples.

But no, he's going to take sheep.

'Paris, my love, I'm really not feeling well,' I finally interrupt, letting my hand flutter to my forehead with a wince.

'Oh, okay. I guess go rest then, if you have to.' He leans closer with a strange mix of expectancy and hesitancy – like, even knowing I will kiss him back, there's still something about kissing me in front of a room full of people that makes him nervous.

When his lips do press mine, it's a chaste and quick farewell.

He never, not then, nor in the days that follow, asks me how my evening was.

In fact, I start to notice that he doesn't ask me much at all.

Days pass without me seeing Aeneas so I decide to find him. I know he practises his sword work every other morning. But my maid, Agata, has noticed some sort of tension between Paris and me – though I'm not sure it exists apart from my own feeling of hesitancy, like I'm waiting for Paris to show any sort of interest in me beyond all that I do for him. Now Agata has taken it upon herself to offer advice on a problem I'm not sure either of us understands.

She could be an excellent source, with ears all over the palace, so I don't want to interrupt her well-intentioned monologue, but she's taking so long giving it that I'm worried I'll miss Aeneas altogether.

'My husband does the same. Keeps all his stress inside him

and only tells me about it once it's resolved. He thinks he's protecting me.'

'I'm sure that's it.' I nod, though that's decidedly not it at all. Paris shares his woes like they are a leaking pithos and my only purpose is to stopper them. Agata finally pins the last part of my dress in place. I watch her carefully as she does it, where she tucks each section of fabric. I don't understand how it all stays together. 'Thank you.'

I practically run.

In one of the courtyards, boys train under Aeneas's instruction – and from the looks of it, it's their first time trying to wield both a sword and shield at once. The Trojan fighting style is different from Sparta's, almost a dance with its light footwork.

I draw closer slowly, a longing so fierce I don't know what to do with it other than follow its call. Maybe it's the way Aeneas is so clearly enjoying it, or the way my mind leapt like a retired horse into sudden gallop, dissecting form and posture, or the way those boys keep picking up their fallen swords, ready to try again. But it awakens something I thought I'd suffocated when I was forbidden from training myself. Not that Menelaus would ever have classed it as such.

No, he simply said he didn't like it.

And when I did it anyway, he punished me with foul moods, insults and keeping me from gatherings with snide comments about how tired I must be. Menelaus would take my hands in his own as he told me he loved me, his fingers running over my skin in search of calluses that might indicate hidden swordplay.

Aeneas glances my way and hurriedly instructs the boys to pair off.

'You're uncanny,' he says when he's by my side. 'I only heard word from the docks this morning and here you are.'

'The docks?'

'Cassandra.'

'What? What was she doing there?'

Aeneas sighs, and draws something from his pocket.

It's not what I'm expecting – a long chain unfurls, a large amber gem hanging from it, and from the sun-shaped setting it's clear who it belongs to.

'She traded it to send a letter.'

'Has she not heard of gold?'

Quite the overpayment too, which would have raised eyebrows even if she hadn't chosen something so obviously hers. It's sloppy.

And I think she'd know that too.

So did she mean what she said? That she didn't care if I obliterated her reputation? She's making messy, desperate strokes in the hope they hit.

'Where was the letter sent?'

'They weren't sure. The man gave the necklace to his brother and set sail. But the ship he boarded was bound for Gytheion and Cranae.'

I snatch the necklace.

'Check every incoming vessel. *Every single one*. If he writes back, I need to know. We need to intercept it.'

'It might not be . . .' It's a weak protest, and he trails off as he realizes that.

Cranae is the island where Paris and I spent our first night together. Which is to say, it's the first place ships to and from Sparta dock.

I don't let my panic hit until Aeneas rounds the corner, and then it comes in such a fierce swoop that I'm nearly doubled over, clutching at the railing to stay standing.

For all my talk of not really believing Menelaus would just let me go, I was still clinging to the hope he might.

And now this. They're colluding. What's her plan? To let men into the city to take me? To lure me out to him? To wield the dagger herself?

I'm so stupid. Why did I think there were rules she might abide by? Unspoken ones? Ones like: don't send a woman to a man who wants to hurt her.

Ones like: don't weaponize the things they would damn us all for to tear each other down.

I'm going to annihilate her. I'm going to raze her to the ground. And I want her to know. I want to place this fear back on her, to make her terrified of all I might do.

I drape the necklace over my head so that the pendant settles between my collarbones, over my clothes and on full display.

Then I find her.

She's in the dining hall, tearing chunks of bread into shreds in her nervous hands, letting them fall on to her plate.

I slam my hand down on the table before her and she startles, dropping the roll and glancing up at me. She's already alarmed – and then her eyes settle on the necklace.

I wish I could capture this moment in fine linen threads and weave it into anything as satisfying as the look that crosses her face: terror, guilt, regret.

But she knows nothing of regret – not yet.

'Cassandra,' I squeal as heads turn in our direction. My fingers flutter to the jewel. 'Thank you so much for so kind a gift. Oh, how blessed I am to have found such kinship so far away from home. You're too generous.'

Gasps and murmurs run through the room.

'Of course,' Cassandra says, forcing a smile, though she must see the unspoken threat. Her hands are curling on the table edge, her jaw clenched tight. 'It suits you well.'

Her tension is not enough. I want to push her further, tease her more, see what depths of anger can be drawn out.

When I first saw her, she was flying at me, blood on her hands, hair in wild matted strands across her face as guards held her, spitting and snarling, hatred like I've never seen burning in her eyes. Then at my wedding, sleek and demure, back straight and shoulders high. Throughout the palace I've seen her hiss words then double over, clutching her chest like she has no idea where they burst from, avoiding eye contact, making herself smaller, like she'd disappear altogether if she could, before drawing herself up once more.

I've always been drawn to angry girls – I think I see myself in them.

If she weren't so focused on hurting me, she might find me the only person in this palace willing to give her the time of day. Gods, I was even planning on saving her.

Now she's going to lose spectacularly.

I've been watching Cassandra, practically studying her. She's spent an awful lot of time in the temple, putting on a rather good show of devout worship of Apollo.

A handful of people believe her visions have brought her closer to Apollo. Most believe she's confused by the prophecy and is praying for some sort of guidance, a view first professed by her mother and repeated every time she says something ridiculous out loud in public.

Confused is not mad, but it is a precursor to it. Menelaus used it with me, normally when he lied about what had happened and said I was misremembering, that I was confused, that I was his crazy wife.

So there are some lines I won't cross. And I do not need to perpetuate such gossip when I can weaponize the people sharing it instead.

The high priestess of the temple accosts me every time I visit — which, thanks to Cassandra's rumours that I do not care for the gods, is every few days.

'Helen,' Herophile coos. 'You honour us yet again.'

There's nothing wrong with trying to court favour with the royals, but I prefer a more subtle approach to this outright flattery.

It doesn't take long for our idle chat to turn to Cassandra — the woman is obsessed. I understand — I'm getting there myself.

'I worry her mind was not strong enough for the prophecies our lord gifted her. It's a tragedy.' She rounds off her rant with a solemn and thoroughly disingenuous shake of her head.

'Herophile, may I speak candidly?'

'Certainly,' she says at once. 'I trust your opinion.'

'Oracle or not, this is your temple and you deserve some peace of mind. She's clearly causing you a great deal of stress. Is this a burden you are expected to carry forever?'

'I can't expel her, she's a princess — and an oracle.'

'No, but it is perfectly reasonable for the high priestess to assign chores, is it not? Have her watch the temple overnight.

You won't see her and she can issue her prophecies as she leaves in the morning.'

'Apollo is god of the sun – we don't tend to occupy the temple at night.'

I shrug. 'Having a priestess – and such an important one – say farewell to Apollo as he draws the sun away at night and to greet him as he returns each morning would say much about this city's dedication to the lord of the sun. But I'm sure you –'

'No, no,' she rushes. 'It's an excellent point.'

'And if all else fails, a vow of silence so that only Apollo's prophecies may pass her lips is always an option.'

A slow smile begins to unfurl on Herophile's lips. 'I believe you and I, Helen, are quite alike.'

I have more planned – so much more. Discord to sow among her and her friends. I could create jealousy between her and Kreousa by placing Aeneas with Cassandra at the right time, or wrench Andromache away from her with a handful of well-crafted lies. Maybe even something with Deiphobus.

But I have plenty of time for that, time when I'm not distracted by shifting shadows and strange noises – the sort of things I have grown sharply aware of, never relaxing even for a moment.

And it turns out this little nudge is more than enough, like knocking a single brick out of those famed Trojan walls and seeing the whole thing come tumbling down.

Cassandra is exhausted from the long nights at the temple, sleeping through the days and leaving little time or opportunity to scheme against me or send any more letters.

Her tiredness seems to make the prophecies worse, so she's yelling them loudly and often. No one believes her and the courtiers are growing exasperated. The kindest think she's doing it for attention. The cruellest think she should be locked up until she learns to keep her mouth shut.

Then one day she looks at me with eyes that feel pale despite their dark hue, like any life has been drawn right from them. There is no hatred, no resentment, just tiredness.

I smile right back, bright and bold and so smug it rivals the gods themselves.

I win.

CHAPTER SIXTEEN

Cassandra

WITH THE BATTLES IN MY head, I never thought that my own future could scare me just as much. But I don't know how much more of this misery I can take – the constant churning of it from loneliness to fear to desperation and right back round again.

I return from the temple when everyone else is gathering for the first meal of the day and for a moment I consider joining them.

But the hall shakes, and visions swarm through it. I jolt back, avoiding a chariot that isn't really there, and a servant hisses a sound of displeasure.

A *servant* hisses at me.

I feel myself like a memory, a viewer in abstract. I see her draw herself up, turn with her head high and a reprimand on her lips.

Spoilt. Entitled. Selfish. Stubborn. Foolish. I hear the words that have been whispered about her.

But I miss her. I think she was wonderful.

That numbness feels like a thick fog now, settling low across my foundations. It should upset me, shouldn't it? I used to be loved once. Adoration was all I had.

But that feels like another life. A life before Helen.

A gold thread spins out before me, one of those ones strung through my body like I'm a bead on its chain, like I'm little more than an adornment on the future: unimportant and expendable but a nice detail to the whole.

Helen might have pushed me to the brink but I think I stepped up to it when I sent that letter. It was more than a necklace I traded away. I think I gave away some part of myself. And Menelaus never even replied.

I crawl into bed just to stop feeling this dreadful nothingness, waking up after a nightmare-filled sleep to the sun setting and the fog creeping back in. I trudge to the temple, tired and drained and, finally, defeated. The cella is quiet and I pick up a rag and begin the services I spend every night performing.

The hours wear on. These chores make my shoulders ache and my spine groan under its own weight. My thoughts chase each other like they're circling me, trapping me in their tumbling vortex.

'You win,' I finally whisper into the marble bust I'm scrubbing. 'Please, just let me warn them.'

Scavenging through bodies, searching for weapons or armour or anything of use. The slick resistance of the flesh as hands tug an arrow back through the chest and feel it scrape against bone.

I stumble backwards and there on the floor next to the statue I've just cleaned is my brother's body: pale grey, half-translucent and recognizable, for once – not the battered corpse I am accustomed to seeing – but now I'm not sure this isn't worse, to look at Hector's eyes, staring and unseeing.

'Apollo, please,' I shout – because I can shout. It's the early hours of the morning and the only people to hear me are the guards stationed at the temple entrances. 'You can't let this happen!'

The bright flash comes, as I hoped it might.

'I can do whatever I please, actually. I think this might be good for you. A pampered princess masquerading as a priestess – to be reminded that, despite your tiaras and your beauty, you are powerless against the wrath of a god.'

Apollo's perching on the altar, lazily regarding me. He glows, a golden, pulsing aura that clings to his radiant, sun-kissed skin. His hair is perfectly curled round crisp leaves, his robes draped almost recklessly, flashing skin along his chest, sloping off his muscular shoulders. He is so other-worldly it makes me feel half formed.

'I know. You are impossibly powerful, my lord. And I'm nothing. And I'll continue to be nothing, I'll spend the rest of my life scrubbing this temple and professing your might if you'll just let me warn them of what's going to come. Your curse has worked. But please don't punish this city for the things I've done.'

'You don't lie to a god, apologize and have your punishment removed,' he scoffs. 'You live it. You become a lesson for every other mortal on this planet. And you, Cassandra, are going to be a glorious lesson. You're going to have a very long downfall in the middle of a war.'

'I've already fallen! Please, my lord. I have nothing more to give.'

'You have yourself,' he muses, flashing me a glittering, dangerous smile. 'You claim you care so much about this city and not once have you offered the one thing you know might change your future.'

I was wrong – I do have more to give. That smug expectation on his face is etched in the same grotesque entitlement I've seen a hundred times in visiting dignitaries and foreign princes. Boys who have everything being shown a thing they cannot even touch, certain they will be the exception.

She comes back to me then – my former self. Apollo's demands snap me right back into a girl who would never entertain the idea of herself as a thing to be sacrificed. A girl who thinks the very fact she *cannot* consider it is answer enough.

'A war is coming to this city,' I hiss, all humility vanishing. 'Thousands are going to die gruesome, thoroughly avoidable deaths. And you care only for your own sexual conquests. Do you just want someone to punish for refusing you? Am I paying for the rejections of Daphne, Marpessa, Coronis, Cyrene –'

Anger flares in Apollo's eyes and he leaps to his feet, pacing before me, his robes flecked with blood from the altar. 'You don't know your place. That is what you are being punished for. And as you are so wonderfully a case in point – what better way to get even the most reluctant mortals begging at the altar of their lords? Do you know what happens in war, little priestess? People become more devout. Look at what the mere thought of it has done to you.'

My nostrils flare but I manage to keep to the points that might persuade him.

'But war against *your* sacred city?'

'I have others.'

'Did you build their walls too? What will the other gods say if they fall?'

He eyes me warily. 'They won't.' But he doesn't sound certain.

'Maybe, maybe not. But there's a chance. And the other gods will cause it. It's not just mortals attacking your city.'

He smiles but I think his confidence might be a reflex. 'You know, darling, that they're praying to me on that side of the Aegean too? I have options.'

'Pick the Achaeans, they're a safer choice. We could have spent the last month preparing. Now our soldiers will head to battle convinced they'll win because I shouted about our loss at the breakfast table.'

'Then leave. If you're so convinced that you will be Troy's downfall, then pack your bags and leave the city. Go get yourself captured by the Achaeans and sing your broken tales to them. Or fling yourself off a tower. Or cut out your tongue. You have options too, little priestess – don't pretend I've left you with none.'

I stare at him, though I shouldn't be shocked that a god has demanded blood.

'If you want your city to survive, you need all the advantages you can get,' I push, thinking of how I've seen Helen play the court – all those appeals to egos who just can't help themselves. 'Just think of how useful a girl with prophecy could be if she was believed.'

He laughs with such mirth I flinch.

'How self-aggrandizing. And here I was thinking I'd whittled that out of you. You should count yourself lucky all I did was curse you. Worse things have happened to entirely innocent girls. When they tell the stories of this war, do you think they'll mention that the first blood spilt was that of a teenage girl? Iphigenia thought she was marrying Achilles and instead she was sacrificed for the wind to sail, yet you think you are suffering most with this war?'

'Who cares who will suffer most, when we will all suffer? And I can help!'

'Wars are won by men on the battlefield, not by girls spinning tales. We'll win this war without you, and you can rave in the tower they'll shut you in when they tire of your lies. You claim gods will join the Achaeans. Very well – do you really think your prophecies could be what makes the difference between winning and losing, when gods join the fray?'

He stands before me, reaches for my cheek, and I step away, jaw clenching.

He leans in anyway and speaks softly: 'You're lying to yourself – saying you're here for the good of the city. You have never prayed for salvation, for your soldiers to have courage in battle, for conflict to keep the Greek nations from forming the Achaean army or storms to keep them away. You've not asked for anything that might truly help – all you've asked is that I remove your curse. You're selfish, Cassandra. And you know what the final proof of that is?'

I stare at him, not knowing how this conversation got away from me so quickly. It's clear where he's going with this but I am clinging on to something as intangible as the threads strung through the air – something I'm certain would be destroyed by agreeing to the demands I know he's about to make. I'm not even sure it would be the act of it that would break me, but of knowing that when the whole city refused to hear the words I spoke, I stopped listening to myself too. 'You say you'd do anything for your family, for your city to win the war. And still you deny me the one thing I have shown any interest in – a thing you yourself once vowed to give. You could end this, Cassandra.' He takes another step, so close that his robes flutter against my skin. 'Give yourself to me and save your city.'

'Never,' I hiss, and before I can think better of it, I reach behind me for a weapon, clutching his own statue – a marble bust of his head, each golden curl finely chiselled – and I heave it at him.

It sails straight through him and smashes to the floor.

He glances down at the shards and laughs.

'I believe you. And what a brilliant idea.'

Every single bust and statue in the room shatters, shards of marble spraying out, and I flinch, hunching over to protect myself from sharp edges, the horrible clatter ringing off the walls.

I look up as the guards rush in.

Apollo is nowhere in sight and they stare at me, then at the demolished statues, and finally at each other like they're deciding whether to restrain me again.

They don't get a chance – because bells ring through the city.

I should have realized Apollo would never visit me in the middle of the night. He is the god of the sun. He brings the dawn.

And right now, that pink sky and weakly burning daylight are illuminating something on the horizon.

Ships.

A thousand of them.

PART TWO

CHAPTER SEVENTEEN

Helen

THE WOMEN GATHER IN THE Great Hall and wait for the scraps of information that leak into our hands. We huddle in groups, gathered anxiously, sharing whispers like secrets.

'Boats on the horizon, we're not sure who or why.'

Menelaus.

'Greeks – they can see their insignias.'

Zeus above, please.

'Dozens of city states united to form one Achaean army. No one's ever seen anything like it.'

How is that even possible?

'I heard something about a pact. They all agreed to fight for whoever won Helen's hand.'

'They're requesting an audience.'

'They want Helen back, her ex-husband is here.'

Fuck.

I collapse into a hard wooden chair and try to pretend I don't see their cutting glances or the way my name sounds more and more disdainful with each repetition of it.

Athrae takes my hand.

'It will be all right,' she promises, by which I think she means: *I hope it will. I hope you'll get to stay. I hope they'll sort it all out and nothing will change.*

But with Menelaus so close, I don't see much room for hope.

Beyond my terror, there's an odd haziness to my thoughts, something that keeps bringing me back to Cassandra though I can't work out why – like every time I get close, my thoughts rearrange themselves.

They're here for me. The guilt is white-hot – a physical ache. Menelaus would tear this city apart for me – I always knew that. I just didn't know he had the manpower to actually accomplish it.

There's nothing I can do – and I wonder if he's picturing me here, powerless and scared. I imagine he'd think all those ships worth it just for that – but I don't think the men at the helm of them would. And they're not going to come all this way and be happy if I'm all they get out of it. But will the Trojans send me back, arms laden with treasure as an offering?

I worry Menelaus would simply fill my pockets with the gold and throw me overboard.

We're there for hours, until conversation turns from what the Achaeans want to the fact we're actually sitting down to negotiate with them.

They're discussing this. They're considering it.

I squeeze Athrae's hand – have I been holding it all this time? – and slip from the hall. There are some things even I cannot mask and this fear is one of them.

Every girl in the palace must be in the hall so I run to the women's quarters, ready to hide in the gynaeceum until I calm down – but it's not empty.

Past the looms and the long, low sofas, in an alcove beneath the window, Cassandra sits with her eyes screwed shut and her knees drawn to her chest, rocking back and forth as words fall from her trembling lips.

I hesitate, wondering if I should leave her. I'm sure I'm the last person she wants to see. And she should *certainly* be the last person I want to encounter. But between my fear and guilt I can't seem to find the hatred I ought to hold for her.

And more than anything, it's a distraction. A way to lock my horror away and hope it withers in the darkness.

'Are you quite all right?' I ask, with the lightest tap of her shoulder.

She flinches violently, her eyes snapping to me.

'Don't touch me,' she snarls, pulling back and leaping to her feet.

'All right, I won't. But are you okay?'

'Imagine being okay at a time like this,' she says, shaking her head as though to clear the things she sees – the things she thinks will become true. I take it from the way the visions haunt her that she doesn't imagine a good tomorrow. 'How can you stand there and ask that when you've caused all this?'

My concern vanishes. How *dare* she?

'I'm not the one who sent Menelaus letters,' I say coldly, tossing my hair back not with my usual practised flick but with a huff of annoyance. 'How do I know you didn't invite him here?'

'I regret that.'

I snort – is that what she considers an apology?

The tendons in her neck become rigid lines. 'The biggest army ever seen just arrived at our gates – do you not understand why that might push me to offer you back before their ships could launch?'

'Oh, and I take it he turned down your kind offer. Were you going to at least tie a bow round my waist? Or tuck a letter of well wishes behind my ear?'

It feels better, actually, than locking it all away – to push it out at her like this.

'I told you, I regret it! But you knew this might happen and –'

'How could I possibly imagine a thing like this? I had no idea Menelaus had the means to amass an army of this size, and I certainly didn't make him do it.' I feel split by it – the guilt I feel versus the logic I know is true. But I'll be damned if she makes me feel worse than I already do.

'It's your name they're crying, isn't it?'

'It's not my honour they defend but my husband's. And their own – you think they're here for me and not for glory?'

Cassandra takes several hurried steps back as though scrambling to put distance between us.

'And you'd let my home burn to prove a point? Or because you're too busy debating the semantics of blame? If you had any honour at all, you'd go to them right now.'

I lean against the table and regard her with a calm disdain. I shouldn't be doing this, I should be trying to win her over to my side. But there's something exhilarating about not having to package my words up into some persuasive ruse – about the rawness of it all.

'You know as well as I do that men don't go to war for love. Do you really think me going back will soothe their egos? Women leave their husbands every day and no battles are fought – but leave your husband to go to a city as rich as Troy and suddenly there's an army assembled. Do you actually think it's me they want?'

She hesitates and I seize my chance. 'And do you really think that Paris will let me just walk out of the city? I'm his prize as much as I was Menelaus's.'

There it is. That truth I've been holding tight to my chest, a thing I thought I'd never dare utter in these halls – that I am not Paris's love, I'm his reward.

Her wild eyes snap around the room as though checking we're alone. When she turns back to me she's more the biting princess than the crazed priestess, lip curling, chin up.

'You're clever, Helen, I'll grant you that –'

'Generous of you.'

'– but you won't convince me as easily as you convinced everyone else. Not when you've started a war, just as I warned.'

'*I* didn't start a war. Menelaus did. Which none of us could have predicted, not even you –'

'Did I not make myself clear at your wedding?'

A sharp pain lances through my skull. I remember her snarling threats, yanking tight the cords of my dress, promising to do all she could to get me to leave – but not why. Something about jealous goddesses? I bring my hand to my head, pressing my palm sharply against it, and the pressure relieves some of the sudden, throbbing pain.

Cassandra stares at me, fascinated. 'Did you forget?'

I scoff. 'I don't remember every sentence of our every conversation, Cassandra, but I think I'd recall you saying an army would be on its way.'

'So this is how the curse works in retrospect,' she muses, as though I'm not even there. 'It warps your memories. Of course I can't be proved right – you'd have to contend with the fact my prophecies are true.'

More nonsense. But I indulge her.

'A curse?'

She shakes herself, blinking tired eyes as though she had forgotten I was there.

Then she smiles with cruel victory.

'Yes, Helen, a curse. Apollo gifted me with oracular sight if I slept with him. But when I couldn't uphold my end of the bargain, he cursed me so that no one would believe my prophecies.' She turns her head skywards and shouts: 'Go on, Apollo! She knows now! Do your worst!'

'Be quiet!' I hiss, checking that we really are alone. The last thing I can afford to do is be seen with someone cursing out our patron gods while armed men gather at the walls.

But then I remember something else – a golden aura, a laughing man. 'Apollo was at the docks the day I arrived,' I say slowly, as it all comes back. 'When you screamed that prophecy and attacked me.'

Cassandra's delighted grin falls. 'You saw him? How? No one else ever has.'

It's happened a handful of times before: people no one else could see. A broad-shouldered giant of a man rushing through the Spartan training fields, sudden skill in the deft sword strokes of the people he touched. A being with winged sandals shooting across the sky. A woman lurking at the edge of the forest, bow poised.

'My father is Zeus. Gods have a harder time hiding themselves from their offspring than from other mortals.'

'Olympus above, don't tell me the swan story is actually true,' she mutters, collapsing against the wall and looking at me with an expression I can't place. 'Do you believe me?'

I consider – because what would that mean? That she really did see this and no one believed her? That's why she tried to drive me from this city? All my fear of the army outside and the death that will surely follow – is this what Cassandra has been carrying around in her for months?

Fury sears in my veins. Cassandra did awful, thoroughly unforgivable things to me. I don't *want* her to have a good reason for it. I don't want to understand it or contemplate whether I'd have done the same, because . . .

Because hating her was a distraction – a thing to cling to when I couldn't face the mystery of what Menelaus was planning or my growing frustrations with Paris or the fact this place might be better than my last but it's not the happy ending I thought I was reaching for. I'm the daughter of Zeus but, damn it, this is exactly the sort of bullshit the gods would pull – and it makes far more sense than a girl breaking under the weight of prophecy.

'Yes, I believe you.'

She draws her arms in close. 'Are you just saying you believe me to manipulate me, like you've manipulated everyone else?'

I look at her, really look at her. I've been analysing her for weeks – the way those prophecies have been slipping out more and more, her whispered threats, the way everything she's done felt so pitiable, so desperate . . . Now she's here, abandoned, disbelieved – looking at a woman she hates with more hope than I've ever seen.

I think: *She's broken.*

And then: *She might be more inclined to like me now.*

'I believe you, Cassandra.'

She shuts her eyes, like she's savouring the moment – like she's preparing for it to shatter.

I wait a moment, realizing I'm indulging it too. 'Does Apollo not understand how much it also damages his reputation? To curse his own priestess like this? His own oracle, even?'

'I'm not his priestess any more, or his oracle,' she says, with a bitterness I'm not sure I understand. 'While everyone else was panicking about the ships in the docks, my mother was informing me my priesthood has been rescinded. She thinks it's for the best, that I shouldn't have to bear the public humiliation of uncontrollable prophecies and frenzies that apparently break statues. She thinks she's protecting me.'

Ah. That I do understand: *Trust me, I know best, I'm just looking out for you.*

Does Menelaus even need to cross these walls when his voice lives in my head like this?

Being removed from public life isn't protection, it's a form of control – once again I find myself righteously indignant on behalf of a girl whose fall I facilitated.

'The irony is, of course, that I've spent the last two months trying to protect everyone else in this city.' She laughs with a self-deprecating groan. 'I don't even know if the prophecies *can* change. But sometimes they feel like fragile threads and sometimes like forged iron, so I thought I'd try.'

'But surely there won't be a war. They're negotiating right now, they'll come to a solution.'

'I told you there'd be a war,' Cassandra says, resigned. 'You can't believe me.'

Oh. And still it seems ridiculous, like knowing the ocean stretches wide and still not conceiving its depths – to believe and disbelieve a thing at once.

'It doesn't sound like the threads are fixed. You already found one alternative strand. No one needed to believe your prophecies if you convinced me to leave.'

'But I couldn't and you didn't.'

'Because you were terrible at it. But I'm not. I could help. We could work together to influence the decisions of men, based on the things you're seeing. I hardly have to believe your prophecies to do that, do I?'

We could be a weapon against Menelaus.

She stares into the distance again and I wonder if it's visions of a future or simply memories of the past distracting her.

'I'm not interested in an alliance with you, Helen,' she finally declares, eyes flashing with an almost violent hatred. 'Because of you, I've lost everything. People I love are going to die. So I don't care how helpful you might be. You can throw yourself from the city walls and let them fight over the memory of you.'

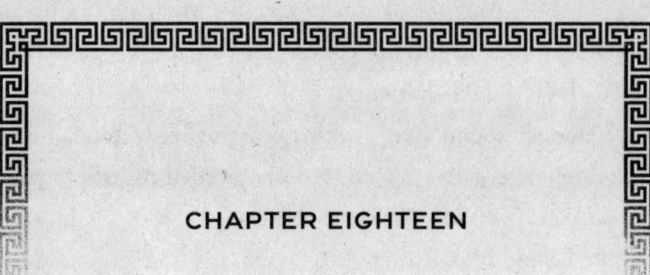

CHAPTER EIGHTEEN

Helen

I SIT BEFORE MY MIRROR, TRYING to reckon with the fact that the face staring back at me might possibly be worth all this. I get stuck smearing rouge on to my cheeks, sudden doubt stilling the brush in my hand. Is it better to look like a trophy they'd fight to keep? Or worse, perhaps, like all this fuss is over someone of no consequence?

When I glance down, I see I've been gnawing at the end of the brush.

I curse, throwing it aside. Girls worth fighting for can't do that.

I'm distracted by a knock at the door and, even if he doesn't wait for me to answer before poking his head round it, I'm pleased for the moment of notice, for being married to a man who at least knocks.

'My love,' I greet him excitedly, rushing to his side like I cannot bear another second apart.

If they send me back to Menelaus, I'll have to cry at his feet, pretend I was taken against my will, that all I wanted was to get back to him – and throw as many compliments in as I can.

I doubt he'll take me back as his queen, sullied as I am, but I might live – if I'm lucky, he'll put me up in a house somewhere isolated, living in exile as a story to warn other girls. Or he might make me a handmaiden to his new bride, or a server in his court, or marry me off to a distant cousin.

He'll probably just kill me, but it's reassuring to consider the things I might persuade him of instead. A future spent fighting for the least horrific scenario is still better than one spent suffering the worst.

Paris clutches me so tightly he runs the risk of breaking something.

'How lovely!'

We turn as one to face the woman who has appeared in the door frame. She shimmers as her features fall into place, and there is so much Cassandra: her prominent cheekbones, her slight smirk, the cocky tilt of her hip and her sleek black hair, tied back in the same hasty plait Cassandra often throws hers into. I finger my own curls – the part of me that's always held the most value – and wonder what it means that Aphrodite chose Cassandra's hair instead.

Does she really think it better? Or is beauty simply insecurity?

Paris and I practically fall over one another in an effort to bow.

'Well?' Aphrodite demands. 'What do they say?'

'Everyone's in shock,' Paris says. 'Nearly every nation of Greece, united under one Achaean banner.'

'Yes, and? Are they leaving?'

Paris gnaws on his lip, like he does not know how to deliver such news – and I know then the answer.

Should I be relieved? I'm not sure. But I take his hand to help him find the words.

And I think, as his warm hand, clammy with nerves, slips into mine and grips a little tighter than necessary, that maybe I do love him.

I care about him and his happiness. I want him to be safe and protected. I want to soothe his anxieties and stand by his side when he needs someone there. I've spent so much time waiting to fall in love with him that maybe I wasn't recognizing the love I already held.

It's just not the kind I crossed an ocean to find.

'It is war,' he says at last, and dread settles in my stomach.

How many will die because I fear a life of misery with Menelaus? Am I lying to myself that they would fight anyway if I returned to him? Should I not at least try? Would a war make even the Trojans turn on –

Aphrodite is a flurry of movement as she shrieks with delight. 'Oh, yes! Oh, this is perfect!'

She claps each of our shoulders and draws us closer together – as though we need more manhandling. As though our entire marriage isn't the result of her forcing our hands.

'Imagine it,' she says, turning us towards the mirror and watching her own glorious reflection revel in her words. 'A love to fight for – a love to die for! A whole war in my name!'

I am horrified – but I at least am nodding, smiling right back at the reflection of the goddess. Paris looks terrified.

'You might die too,' she says, forcing some sadness into her voice, but it's at odds with her beaming smile. 'Perhaps this is a tragedy, young lovers falling with the weight of their effort to be together. Oh, they'll never forget it!'

'My lady,' Paris mutters, 'I'd really –'

'Oh, I wouldn't worry,' she says, finally letting us go. 'You are my champion, Paris. I would much prefer you to heroically defeat those who would steal your love from you. Besides, there are some who are forgetting my affiliation with war in their worship. I should like to remind them of it. I'll be beside you on the battlefield in a quest for love to prove victorious.'

'Battlefield,' Paris repeats, glancing at his own reflection doubtfully.

'You have told me much about your prowess with a bow,' I remind him, hoping desperately that he was not making such a thing up to impress me.

'You should go, my champion, and tell your people that many gods will side with you when the war comes,' Aphrodite says – but she places her hand back on my shoulder to root me to the spot. Apparently, I'm not going anywhere.

Paris doesn't seem to notice – he's already nodding. 'Yes, of course. I . . . thank you. Thank you so very much.'

His hand slips from mine.

'I love you,' I promise. I need to. I do not have the luxury of figuring out how exactly I feel and certainly not of speaking honestly about it. In every conversation about this war that Paris enters, he must have our love at the forefront of his mind.

Aphrodite's grip tightens.

The moment Paris leaves she releases me, her glee giving way to unbridled fury.

'You lie to him,' she snarls. 'You speak my power in falsehood – how dare you?'

'My lady?' I suspect I know exactly what she means but I'm not admitting anything until I'm forced to.

'You do not love him.'

My mind whirs – excuses and apologies rolling to my tongue.

'No,' I admit. 'But I will. You yourself delivered me to him – how could I not?'

I used to believe that. Now I'm not so sure.

Evidently Aphrodite expects only one answer and I don't want to discover the consequences if I don't give it, so I press on. 'What harm is there in comforting him before a war when I know I'm close? Matters of the heart take time.'

I try to hide my trepidation. Saying whatever I must is second nature. I can lie with such fervour the truth itself can change shape – but Aphrodite can see into my very heart and she isn't buying a second of it.

'Not if I say they don't. Would you like me to have my son shoot you with an arrow?'

'No.' I jump. Eros's arrows are not the love I seek – they're obsession, the kind of relentless pursuit that makes you forget yourself. 'I . . . I want to fall in love with him. Not have that forced upon me.'

'Fall quicker,' she says, stalking closer. 'Because I tell you to.'

She reaches me and this time, when she grasps my shoulders, my skin burns beneath the thin fabric. She spins me and pushes down, forcing me to sit at the dressing table I'd been at moments before, taking a lock of my hair in her fingers under the guise of arranging it for me, though I take the threat she so clearly intends – that she could hurt me at any moment, tear out the hair that marks me, snatch my beauty or my life.

'Because pretty girls like you, Helen, do exactly what I tell them to. You know that, yes?'

'Yes,' I say quietly. Because Paris might be her champion, but I'm simply the mark of her favour, a piece she has moved, a decision she has made. And she's a jealous goddess. Better she sees you as a lovely face under her thumb than competition to be reckoned with. Myth is littered with beautiful corpses. She's not responsible for anywhere near all of them, but several scream her name as they stalk the halls of the Underworld.

'You need to realize what story you're in, Helen. If you're going to survive it, you'll take the role I offer you. I have a lot to prove on that battlefield – and I task you with just one thing. Make my champion happy, give him cause to fight, give him love to defend. Do you understand?'

Of course I do. My words aren't enough. I need to not merely pretend but to become a lie incarnate. I've done it before and it's not all that difficult. It's amazing what you can believe and who you can become with the right circumstances. And the right motivation.

I'll do whatever I need – *be* whoever I need – to be loved, to make my husband happy, to live.

So perhaps it doesn't really matter which side of the walls I'm on, after all.

CHAPTER NINETEEN

Cassandra

'IT'S A BIT MORBID, ISN'T it, calling this "one last night"?' Deiphobus asks, glancing round the 'banquet' we're supposedly hosting. But it's unlike any banquet I've ever been to. It's enormous and chaotic and messy, the people are drunk before we even sit down to dine, and everyone's talking too loudly, like if they make enough noise they can drown out the fear. The food is pushed aside – mountains of breads and fruits, tureens of stews and soups and platters of smoked meats and salted fish. No one is touching a thing – they're all too focused on the people and the music and the amphorae of wine.

Everyone seems desperate for a distraction but I've already found one – the prophecies are silent. I haven't had a vision or felt the need to shout a line of the future since the ships arrived.

Or, rather, since Helen said she believed me.

I'm huddled at a table with Deiphobus, Scamandrius and Kreousa. There's a lump in my throat that's too big, and now is not the time for tears but for forced smiles: to pretend we have no doubt we will be victorious, to not let anyone question the royal family's faith in our soldiers.

'It shouldn't be our last night,' Kreousa seethes. She's been livid all day – no one studies war like she does, and now it's on our doorstep she's barred from every room she should be in. 'We're a walled city. We should be gathering as many crops as we can and hunkering down to wait it out.'

Scamandrius snorts. 'What honour is there in a city under siege? We fight for glory.'

'You'll perish for glory. Fight for victory instead.'

She folds her arms across her chest and glares into the distance. There is one, tiny glimmering thread that coils round her. I can just about make out its shape, though I cannot see its full picture – a future where that is what we do, holed up in the city, hungry and angry but alive. The thread frays before it can reveal whether Kreousa's plan would work. It's not a real future. It's not a real possibility.

Still, I can't help but feel like it could be – that the men bar Kreousa from their talks because she has all their knowledge and none of their ego, and none of them wish to be shown up by a young girl with a library at her fingertips rather than a blade.

'You should be in those talks, Kreousa,' Deiphobus says, like he's thinking along similar lines. My jealousy unfurls with corrosive acidity. Deiphobus was the first person I turned to for help and the first person the curse filled with doubt. I wanted him to support me like this. 'Are you sure you don't want me to talk to Father? I think he could be persuaded.'

I take a sip of my wine like it might stop the envy. Kreousa deserves this. She picked up a scroll at four years old and refused to ever put it down – even when she moved from the boys' classes to the girls' and all the tutors suggested she might like to learn the lyre or loom instead of burying herself in tomes inappropriate for a princess. Maybe that's why I became closer to her than my elder sisters – we were both determined to be princesses however we damn well pleased.

'No,' she says, already flushing at the thought. 'I couldn't . . . I wouldn't be able to talk in front of that many people.'

Scamandrius rocks back in his chair, huffing a laugh. Part of me had hoped he and the council might have realized there was some truth to my prophecies – after all, I told them of the war before Apollo laid down his curse. But it's either worked in retrospect or they've conveniently forgotten about it. 'Right. Who needs one crazy sister when you can have two?'

Before either of us can say anything, Deiphobus is hauling Scamandrius up by the collar of his chiton. 'Okay, you and I are going outside to have a little chat.'

'Piss off, Deiphobus.'

'That's "Piss off, sir." We're at war, baby brother, and I'm your superior officer. So let's go talk about the behaviour I expect of my soldiers.'

Scamandrius continues to grumble but leaves with Deiphobus and I turn to my sister. 'Are you all right?'

She laughs but it doesn't quite sound right. 'Please, I'm not going to let an arsehole like Scamandrius ruin a lovely last night before a merciless war. Besides, Father might listen but the council wouldn't. They don't care for knowledge, just experience.'

Aeneas appears behind us. 'Yes, experience is very different. But we –'

'Well, Aeneas, maybe you should try for both.' Kreousa flushes a deep red and I think it's her usual shyness before she turns on him and I realize it's anger. 'Perhaps you shouldn't be shooting down valuable intelligence when we're literally at war.'

'Yes, I was going to say we have more than enough experience in the room and some knowledge would be useful.'

'You know, maybe if you pulled your head out of your arse for one second, you might be able to see that there are other people who could help. It's not just men waving swords that win wars.'

'I agree.'

'And I am so sick and tired of you all being so very mediocre and then, in the moment of need, you're suddenly all that matters, like battle strategy isn't just a combination of history and – What the hell do you mean, you agree?'

'I think shutting you out of strategic planning is idiotic.'

She stares at him, unblinking, possibly not even breathing.

He smiles a little hesitantly. 'I know we've never exactly got on, but I do know that every time I've requested a scroll from the library you've already got it checked out. And I know you'd save us a lot of time making clear the flaws in plans we all know are terrible but don't want to cause offence by pointing it out.'

'I . . . Well, if you aren't coming over here to annoy me, then what *do* you want?'

'I came to ask if you wanted to dance.'

Her eyes widen and she seems to suddenly remember I'm sitting here. I meet her panicked glance with an encouraging smile.

'Oh, all right, but don't step on my toes.'

His eyes shine with the smile he's trying to hide. 'I wouldn't dare.'

Kreousa takes his hand and drags him over to the other dancers with enthusiasm that verges on aggression. She dances with him as though she's not even thinking about all the people watching her or the stares that would normally have her cowering in the corner.

Behind them, Hector spins Andromache in effortless twirls. Under any other circumstances I'd be teasing her. I'd say she's showing off and taking advantage of the fact I can't prove myself the better dancer when I have no partner to dance with, and she'd scoff at the very idea and make some joke about her flexibility being good for something other than dislocated joints, as though her skill weren't a matter of grace and rhythm and some thoroughly mesmerizing, intuitive connection to music. She dances like the notes hum through her bones, like her pulse pounds to the beat.

But when she and Hector finally collapse into chairs, laughing and breathless, I don't go up to them and I don't say anything. Because these aren't other circumstances and my dress is still damp with tears from where Andromache clung to me as we dressed for tonight.

'I begged him not to fight but he insists on leading the charge and I . . . What if he doesn't come back?'

It was all she managed to choke before she broke down, burying her head in my shoulder, and I didn't have to pretend I don't see his death every time I look at him, that its fated thread is yoked round his throat like a noose ready to pull tight.

I turn, because watching them is too painful, and nearly collide with Apollo.

'No, gods, why? What do you want?' I demand.

Every single time I've seen him he's made my life inexorably worse. Every time I think I cannot fall further, he proves me wrong.

Is he why the prophecies have been silent? Is he changing them somehow? Pausing them so something horrible can happen without forewarning and then he can send them hurtling back?

I watch as he takes me in, eyes tracing the contours of my olive-green chiton, and a different kind of adrenaline races through my veins – a different sort of horror dawns.

'Don't worry, darling,' he soothes, clearly enjoying my panic. 'I'm not here for you. I'm enjoying the party.'

He looks around the room like he's perusing fruit at a market stall – searching for the ripest offering.

'Who knows how much opportunity for revelry we'll have in the coming months? Well –' he offers an intimate smile, like we are both bonded by the things no one else can believe – 'I suppose we do.'

'So you're not . . .' I glance at Helen – who moments ago was spinning round the dance floor but is now watching me. Talking to myself, I suppose – only, no, she can see Apollo too, can't she?

'Sorry to disappoint, love. I will do it, you know. Tell anyone of the curse and I'll ensure they do not live long enough to do anything about it. But Helen is under Aphrodite's protection. It hardly matters anyway – they're going to hate her as much as they ever hated you.'

I nod, relieved. After all the guilt of writing to Menelaus, I've done it again by throwing Helen to the mercy of Apollo.

Was this horrible part of me in here all along, or have the prophecies pushed me to this?

'Now, you have a twin, don't you?' Apollo says with a leer that makes me feel like my skin is recoiling from the very fabric against it. 'Perhaps I'll spend this evening with him.'

'By all means,' I reply curtly. If he hopes to draw my envy, he's more arrogant than I suspected, and if he wishes to make me concerned by pursuing a member of my family, then he chose the wrong sibling. 'Excuse me.'

For the first time in all our encounters, I turn my back and walk away.

CHAPTER TWENTY

Cassandra

I FIND A NEARBY ROOM, ITS furniture pushed to the sides to form a dance floor, soft candlelight revealing the near-empty space. Later, perhaps, it will be a more intimate area for the party to break away. But for now it's vacant and my footsteps echo as I cross the room.

I hardly have a moment to relax into the quiet before Helen bursts through the door. She looks harried – hair flying about in her haste, dress bundled in her hands to move quicker.

'There you are,' she cries with relief – a sound I never thought I'd hear from her. 'Are you okay?'

I wince, and in doing so let my eyes linger shut, like I might block her out too. I want to be alone. I want the world to stop spinning, for everything to grind to a halt like the prophecies have. I feel like I have been hyperventilating into still-empty lungs and I just, desperately, want to breathe.

'Do you actually care, Helen?'

I expect flippancy or an immediate lie but she stills, her head tilting as she considers. 'I'm still trying to work that out, I think. But I'm not sure I could wish any girl alone with a god.

Even if that girl is you. I think *especially* if that girl is you, and that god is Apollo. He disguised himself as a courtier and flickered into existence the moment you left, and the fact he keeps wanting to speak to you without anyone else knowing... that's terrifying, Cassandra.'

'It is rather, yes.'

'But you're all right?'

'I'm all right.'

I watch the tension fade from her taut body and she throws herself into the nearest armchair. I'm oddly entranced by the way her limbs have fallen so haphazardly. Her dress is Trojan but it rides up as she sits and her toned legs stretch out across the chair like they might go on forever. There's so much freedom in her movements, so much carelessness and power twinned.

I realize part of what has me enraptured is the casualness of it all. I've seen her be a thousand different things for a thousand different people but I've never seen her relaxed – it's always careful poise and deliberate steps. And here she is, slung sideways across the chair, unguarded, like I alone am in her confidence.

At least I recognize it now: the way everything she does, right down to the way she presents herself, is an effort to win people over. Even this – following me, checking on me, performing relaxation like she hopes to invoke some false sense of intimacy – it's all part of her need to be liked by all. And I refuse to let it work.

'Did he say anything awful?' she asks.

I should leave – just walk right out of that door and determine not to engage with her. But my traitorous feet take me to the chair opposite and I perch on its edge, like I'm ready to run.

'No, but after everything he's done, he doesn't have to say anything to make me feel . . .'

She nods like I don't need to name it, like she might understand anyway.

My heart soars with that nod. She knows. She believes me. And she doesn't think I should be thankful or relieved or consider myself lucky.

So I tell the truth. 'The reason they stripped me of my priesthood is because Apollo appeared in the temple this morning. He said I deserved the curse and if I was that concerned I could hurt myself to prevent it. Then he heavily implied the curse would be lifted if I slept with him, so I threw a statue at him.'

With every word her scowl deepens. 'No wonder so many men are terrible, when these are our gods.'

I don't want to owe her a warm, bright feeling like this. It's one thing to tell her, knowing she'll believe me, and another to have her indignant on my behalf.

The glimmering golden threads shine brighter – and, as I pay them a little more attention, a strand comes loose, twisting and stretching in another direction before it too fades and fizzles . . . Like Kreousa's, it is no future at all.

Then it coils up and lashes at me, striking me hard.

Helen – although she's different: a sword in her hand, her hair cut short, laughing in a strange sort of cackle that speaks of something unrestrained. A glimmer, a flickering glimpse, before she fades and the thread runs out.

I'm almost relieved by the vision – that they are not gone. I'd worried their sudden absence meant Apollo had something even worse waiting for me. But no, they simply needed the right trigger. They needed Helen.

'I'm sorry,' I blurt – the truth rushing out of me now I've started. 'Apollo threatened the life of anyone I told about the curse and so, when I told you, I think part of me hoped ... well, if you were dead, maybe there'd be nothing to fight over.'

Silence falls. Her gaze sharpens and I feel like spun wool pinned and stretched, weighed down by the intensity of those azure eyes.

'You know that's foolish. If I die behind Trojan walls, I'll become a thing for the Achaeans to avenge. They'd have no mercy.'

I chafe against her lecture-like tone but I can't fault her – this is certainly a lesson she needs me to understand.

'I know. I was shaken and desperate and stupid. And I'm sorry.'

Her carelessness returns and she is relaxed in her chair once more, picking at a chipped nail. 'Well, so long as that's agreed. But please do stop trying to deliver me to men who would like to kill me – it's getting quite tedious.' She looks up at me with a wry smile but, perhaps seeing the disbelief on my face, she continues. 'I'm still angry, Cassandra. But I understand why you did what you did.'

'I ...' I trail off. Am I really so desperate to be believed that I'd crawl back to her after so soundly rejecting her?

'Go on.'

'I saw ... well, what you just said about terrible men, I ...'

'Spit it out.'

The phrase startles me. It's not one that I, a princess who must be protected from even the evils of foul language and acknowledgements of bodily fluids, have ever heard.

'I saw Paris and Aphrodite in my visions. I saw a hundred different scenarios. Did they ... I mean, did you come here willingly?'

She snorts a laugh, more undignified behaviour she's never shown in these halls. 'You thought I might have been here against my will and you still tried to kill me several times over? By Zeus, Cassandra, you don't do things by halves.'

She sounds almost begrudgingly respectful.

'I was about as willing as I could be. Paris came to the court and bartered with my husband – ex-husband – somehow, and then he came to my room that night with Aphrodite by his side. I thought maybe we really might fall in love but, if not, at least he would get me away from Menelaus.'

The way she says his name feels heavy with a wariness that endures in every woman I've ever met – the very fear that had me joining the temple.

'I'm sorry,' I say, and it feels both too much and not enough, a weak sentiment, but a resonant one, one I imagine anyone faced with this truth of hers might feel.

'I blamed myself for a long time,' she says, looking at her hands curled in her lap. 'I chose Menelaus from a long list of options. He'd lived with us for a while – we were allied with him and his brother against their uncle. He was charming, I suppose. And a war hero – which, in Sparta ... well, that's everything. So I thought, if I did this to myself, I could get myself out of it. I could run away with Paris.'

I'm not sure what to say. I have no experience with marriage, and what I ask surprises me: 'Do you still blame yourself?'

She thinks about it for a moment. 'No, I made a sensible choice with the information I had. I thought we could be good for the kingdom – a Spartan queen with all her freedom and fortitude and a man from beyond the mountains who might bring kindness as well as strength. He made so many promises. It's only after we married that everything changed. He didn't try to improve Sparta, he tried to remould it. Starting with me. I wasn't his princess any more, I was his wife and he wanted every part of me to hinge upon him.'

'Yes, I've heard they do that.'

'And the sex was terrible. He's gorgeous so I thought he'd know what he was doing, but at one point I even thought about drawing him a map. Oh gods, I forgot you Trojans are all prudes – you're bright red, are you okay?'

'Fine, fine, just . . . um . . . ew?'

'Aphrodite above,' she curses with a shake of her head. 'Remind me to find you a nice boy to show you what you're missing.'

'Oh, absolutely not.'

She waves her hand. 'Nice girl, then.'

'Can we go back to you running away with Paris?' I can't even look at her, scared that if I do, I'll see something knowing there.

She chuckles, enjoying my discomfort, before finally continuing. 'Well, after a year of Menelaus trying to condition me into his version of perfect, always feeling like I was doing something wrong and never quite living up to what he wanted, along comes Paris. Aphrodite was with him and I just thought, well, what if this is it?'

'But it's not?'

She takes a breath. 'I . . . I hope so. I really do.'

Which is as close as I'll get to a confession that it's not.

I remind myself that she's saying whatever it takes to manipulate me into siding with her. But it's still an awfully brave thing to say – or not say – in a palace where anyone might hear. 'Why are you telling me this?'

She gives a sad and apologetic smile. 'No one would believe you, Cassandra. You're safe.'

I think I surprise her by laughing. But she's right. With me, Helen can take risks she would never consider taking with anyone else. And she's the only person I can talk to about any of this. Despite everything we've done to one another, we're also each other's only reprieve.

How thoroughly detestable. *The face that launched a thousand ships, and burns the topless towers of Troy, sweet Helen, make me immortal with a kiss –'* I force the words into silence, finally, gasping for air, my cheeks burning with a blush I hope she can't see in the dim candlelight. 'Sorry.'

'Don't be – I'm flattered, though, at the risk of complicating this situation further, I think I'll keep my lips to myself.'

'I want your kiss about as much as I want Troy's towers to burn,' I snap.

'I simply don't believe it.' She grins and it soothes something in my chest that I didn't know was hurting. A joke, an inside one. A flirtatious one, though I suspect that's all Helen knows.

But it's an intimate joke all the same, and how glorious to be on the inside of something again.

'Helen, I have to ask. Is it worth it? Dooming my city?'

She narrows her eyes. 'You said in some of your visions I was taken. It sounds like your city was doomed regardless of any choice I made.'

'I just need to know.'

'Why?'

'Because you're proving yourself rather likeable and I'm not sure whether to trust it.'

She regards me for a while – and what is it about her gaze? When she lets that intensity linger I feel like I can't look away until she breaks it – which she finally does with an exhausted sigh.

'You're a real bitch, you know?'

'First I've been informed of it, but good to know.'

'Cassandra,' she says seriously, leaning forward a little. 'If I could stop this war by going back to Menelaus, I would. Even if we win, even if the Achaeans leave, if a single life is lost, I'd rather have never left. But Paris told me the men who vied for my hand made a pact – not just to steal me back if someone took me, but to burn the offending city down. There's no room to negotiate – they're bound by their oath. Send me back and they'll still fight to destroy Troy. After coming all this way, they'll see it through.'

Her voice shakes and she toys with the ring on her finger. She's staring at me with wide eyes, like she's begging me to believe her. Like she's begging me to forgive her.

I nod without thinking because I don't like this vulnerability. I don't want to see her as a real person in the middle of this. So much easier to see her as the cause of our destruction.

So much easier to see her as a prize that has exchanged hands.

'What would you do?' I ask quietly. 'If you didn't need to align yourself with a man? If you could just leave and know you would be safe?'

Her eyebrows furrow and I recoil against it – because Helen does not show her confusion, she weaponizes it. I've seen her, batting her eyelashes with quizzical smiles, waiting for men to explain themselves further, drawing more information from them than they're willing to give.

That this expression is softer, less exaggerated – less of an *act* – does not prevent me from believing it is one, because then I'd have to contend with the fact that Helen really is showing me something true.

'What do you mean? How would that work?'

'It doesn't matter,' I say quickly.

All this time spent railing against Helen and she's a better person than I am – because if she could go back, she'd change the choice she made. And I'm not sure I can say the same.

Even if the threaded futures told me that lying with Apollo would save the city, I'm still not sure I could do it.

I should just have suffered him. But even now I stubbornly refuse the act.

Guilt churns so turbulently I might be sick. In that moment, I hate Helen more than I've ever done for reflecting the worst of myself back at me.

'I need to get back.' I climb to my feet and brush down the creased fabric of my chiton.

'I should return too. It's reckless, leaving Paris's side for so long when Achaeans abound.'

A crowd of disgruntled Achaean soldiers – tired, injured, calling to go home.

One of their elders, weathered skin crossed with aged battle scars and a nose that has clearly been broken several times, calling for them to stop. 'Do not rush to set sail before you can snatch the wife of some Trojan and avenge on her the pain, effort and misery that we have suffered for the sake of Helen.'

I jolt, eyes locked on Helen, all that anxiety and regret etched into her face.

Here it is, the cold honest truth: Helen's name is bandied about to justify the thing these men want. Victory, treasure – the women of the city. How could I possibly argue it is Helen's fault and not merely her name on the lips of men, who will do what men will always do and always have done: whatever they damn well please.

I can't condemn her for this.

'Blame me,' I say. 'If he asks where you were. Say you were helping calm me down after a vision or something.'

'Are you sure?'

'It would aggravate Apollo, I imagine, to know we're using it as an excuse.'

'And is that the only reason you'd do this?'

I don't answer her. I don't know how I feel about her or why I'm doing this or where we've landed. So I leave her waiting for an answer and return to the banquet, trying to avoid watching her every time my attention wanders.

I dance with my family, so many of us linking arms that my parents join too, Father spinning with as much dignity as he can. I hold Kreousa's hair back when the gallon of wine she's drunk hits her and I put Scamandrius to bed when he slumps in the corner. I'm the body an embarrassed Andromache hides behind when Hector – *Hector!* Who I have only ever seen drink one carefully measured glass of wine at dinner! – climbs on to a chair and yells 'I love my wife!' followed by a barely audible monologue on her best traits.

And I ignore Helen's high-pitched laugh every time Paris speaks, her graceful twirls around the dance floor, her holding court with gathered circles.

I enjoy the night, and I don't think of her at all.

CHAPTER TWENTY-ONE

Helen

PARIS'S HANDS ARE ALL OVER me – at my waist, grazing the small of my back, brushing my face, toying with my hair – like he could keep me here by visibly loving me enough.

We retire early, desperate to spend our last night taking each other's mind off the weight of the impending future.

I wrap my body round his and hold him close. I don't want him to leave. Paris is the only person fully committed to me. He's been my only constant since leaving Sparta.

I fear it will be lonely without him.

'It will be over soon,' he promises. 'And then a long lifetime of happiness bestowed by the goddess of love herself.'

'A long lifetime and I still find myself impatient to spend every day by your side,' I reply, and it's not a complete lie but it's not the sweet hum of true longing either, so I weave my fingers through his and pull him on top of me before I can think much more about it.

He should rest. Going to war sleep-deprived is a foolish thing.

But we stay up most of the night anyway, savouring each other before it's all gone.

I feel like an imposter saying our farewells the next morning. It's so . . . loud. Gathered at the gates of the palace, hordes of people are sobbing, clutching one another, shouting for friends and family lost in the crowd.

I watch as Cassandra rolls her eyes then pulls her twin brother close with shaking hands. Andromache grasps Hector's hand like it truly would take an army to prise them apart, and Polyxena laughs through her tears as Deiphobus desperately tries to keep them from falling. Next to them, Paris and I are on the fringes.

A few people cast glances in our direction but not as many as I feared – if anything, there's an air of excitement. They're convinced the men will return victorious in mere days.

I hope they're right.

King Priam claps a hand on Paris's shoulder and I'm expecting words of encouragement or of rallying strength. Instead he says: 'I am sorry to ask you to fight for a city you have not had a chance to feel is your own.'

Paris nods, as though he – *we* – did not bring this war here.

'I'm so sorry,' I blurt. 'I wish I'd never come here and caused all this.'

'You?' Priam eyes me with surprise. 'Helen, this is hardly your fault. You are not the army at our shore. While your guilt says a great deal about the kindness of your heart, please trust that no one here blames you.'

He offers a smile and turns to one of his other sons.

I burst into tears and clutch at Paris, letting everyone on the field think my tears are for him rather than the fact not everyone believes me responsible for this.

And then the men are gone.

And the joy vanishes with them.

For days, the palace feels desolate, even emptier for the way the remaining women and girls huddle in corners and whisper conversations until they finally resign themselves to the fact this might be a longer campaign than we'd hoped.

Rooms fall silent when I enter – even people I know well.

'No one's said anything, have they?' I ask my companions as we walk through the palace garden. 'Do they blame me? Does the city curse my name?'

'For the sake of Olympus, Helen, this isn't about you,' Athrae snaps.

I pause, and in a second all three of us are laughing.

'Okay, all right, I suppose very technically it is,' Athrae says, tucking a strand of her hair behind her ear as she turns sombre once more. 'I'm sorry, I didn't mean to take this out on you. It's more that, well . . .' She glances at Clymene, who picks up the cue to explain it.

'It's not anger, it's awkwardness. You don't have as much at stake as the rest of us.'

I try not to immediately leap to my own defence. 'How so?'

'You have Paris,' Athrae says. 'And that's horrible and dreadful, but it's not every man you've ever met and loved – your father, your brother, your sons. People are terrified and in a weird way it's uniting us all. But you don't have as much of your heart on the line so no one knows how to behave around you.'

'Paris is my whole heart,' I say. Because I must. Aphrodite wants a war for love, so I must never stop pushing that our love is so much more than everyone else's.

'We adore you, Helen,' Athrae says, squeezing my shoulder affectionately. 'But that's why people are avoiding you. Not because they hate you but because they're jealous.'

'Andromache gets to actually see Hector and no one is treating her like this,' I retort. He returns to the council so regularly to discuss strategy that women have begun gathering at the small Scaean Gate in the south of the city, begging for news of their loved ones every time Hector slips through.

Athrae hesitates before finally shaking her head and offering a small shrug, like she does not understand it either.

I turn to Clymene. Athrae has a tendency to put comfort above truth whereas Clymene treats fact like a gift respectfully bestowed. Now she shrugs. 'The only way we survive this is to convince ourselves it's not happening, to pretend we can't hear the screams beyond the walls. But your mere presence is a reminder of everything we're ignoring. You're the war embodied and no one can bear it.'

If I can do nothing but remind people of the war, I might as well do all I can for it.

Queen Hecabe is leading efforts in the city while King Priam and his advisors strategize at the walls. She organizes the things the men don't think of – the leather armour that needs repairing, underclothes slashed by swords needing to be stitched back together, food packaged and parcelled and sent to the camps, medical supplies and, most essentially, prayers and sacrifices at every temple in the city. I help her, and in the process tell her everything I can of the Greeks and the politics of their courts. There is more than one way to fight a war, after all. And that army is made up of several divided poleis that would never have united of their own volition.

There are other things to sort too, long boring conversations and tricky arrangements to pick over the details of, especially around how we get things from one side of the walls to the other without constantly opening the gates. And there's something thrilling in working through these problems, in looking round a room and seeing wives of advisors given licence to offer advice of their own.

And once I see it, I never stop noticing it: the shift in the women of the city.

It starts with the almost uncanny sight of women after dark: gathering to chat amicably rather than hastening home, like the night is no longer the threat it once was. Then I see the other things the women are doing: mending wagon wheels, playing raucous games, hauling goods, manning forges abandoned by those repairing weapons at the front, and building shelters for the steady influx of farmers coming to the city to escape the Achaeans, who are razing their fields and raiding their villages.

It takes me weeks of watching the other girls, my awe and my fascination building, until I'm brave enough to try it for myself.

I go to the armoury. All the best weapons are gone, of course. There is a war to be fought and always more bodies than arms. But I find training swords and, in the back, a rusty sword – short, sleek and likely designed for a youth's hand. A few years ago, I would have scoffed at such a blade. Now I scrub and oil it, sharpening its edge and re-holstering its handle with strands I spend a whole evening weaving.

In a shady, craggy corner of one of the palace's courtyards, away from prying eyes, I practise swinging this precious thing. I am awful, fumbling manoeuvres I once managed instinctively, out of breath after a few laps of the courtyard, shoulders aching with heaving even this light blade.

It feels miraculous.

So miraculous that soon my every morning begins with a sword in my hand. Every day I feel my muscles return to me, the glorious push and pull of them, the power within my own skin.

This. This is the freedom I wanted.

Alone, in the courtyard, sword in hand – I start laughing. This is worth crossing an ocean for.

CHAPTER TWENTY-TWO

Cassandra

WEEKS PASS AND THE LONGER the war rages, the more hostility I find in the palace. People who once may not have even dared to look at me now glare as we cross paths. They make comments they pretend I can't hear – comments I would once have done something about.

I tell myself I don't care, but the remnants of the respected princess buried inside myself ache, and my tears fall just as freely when I turn from thoughts of war to thoughts of how much disdain everyone seems to hold for me.

The visions are worse than ever, taking hold of me whenever they please and refusing to let go even when the things I'm seeing leave me sobbing and shaking.

The prophecies are another matter – I can stop them for a little while now, if I concentrate, but then they come louder and more forcefully while my head pounds.

Whispering works best – with the additional benefit that no one will hear a prophecy they'll immediately disbelieve. But wandering around whispering things beneath my breath seems to disconcert everyone even more than speaking them aloud.

Kreousa and Andromache are the only ones who still speak to me as though I'm a person and not a hindrance. Actually, that's not true – Mother pretends nothing has changed at all and ignores all signs of my anguish.

Polyxena has taken to asking questions I can't answer: *Why are you saying you're seeing things? Why aren't you a priestess any more? Are we going to be okay?* And I can't cope – I can feel myself close to shouting at her and she hasn't done anything wrong, so I start avoiding her and then I start avoiding everyone. I wish I could hide in the city but Mother prohibited me from leaving the palace when she rescinded my priesthood, like I might smash statues wherever I go. So I lock myself in my room, or scurry down servants' staircases, and cling to the shadowy courtyards where the rocky mountain rises sharply above. I even avoid Kreousa and Andromache because it feels like a matter of time until they tire of me too.

And when I can't quiet the prophecies, when my lips form words I'm refusing to say or when they whisper under my breath so that people only catch the occasional word, like *'die'* or *'perish'* or *'ruin'*, or when a prophecy comes that shakes me, that overwhelms me, that uses me as a vessel to scream its will, it's enough to wish I could have a break from myself too.

Maybe I'm not the only one who needs to escape the stares because one day, a month into the war, Helen stumbles across one of my hiding places, the shady nook between the east wing and the shrine to Hestia, goddess of home and hearth.

She's not the goddess we're praying to most right now.

'So this is where you've been hiding,' she says.

I haven't spoken to her since the banquet – unsure where I stand and terrified her belief in me will cloud my judgement.

Besides, I've been spending far more time locked in prophecy than I have within these palace walls.

'One of the places,' I answer.

'You'll have to show me the others.'

'That would ruin the concept of a hiding place.'

She smiles and it's earth-shattering. She must know it too because there's something self-mocking about it, and then she tilts her head and says: 'You wouldn't want me finding you?'

'I don't know, Helen,' I sigh, because I'm too tired to spend another moment trying to work her out. 'Are you going to look for me?'

'Who says I haven't?' she asks then tuts at my glare. 'You're no fun today.'

'And to think I came out here because I'm too much fun to be around. Did you want something?'

She crosses to the alcove opposite me and climbs on to the ledge. I shouldn't be so consistently surprised at seeing her like this, so careless, climbing the dirty brick without hesitation. She runs her finger along the edge of it, tracing the little vines etched into the windowsill. 'Is every part of this city a work of art?'

'What do you want, Helen?'

'Well, I'm reluctant to admit it now, but I wasn't actually looking for you. I just wanted to get out of the palace and be somewhere people wouldn't find me.'

Perhaps I'd feel guilty if I hadn't just watched a dying man curse her name on a dusty battlefield.

'You're not the only one getting dirty looks,' she explains. 'I'm the girl who started a war and you're the one who won't stop talking about it.'

'Yes, and one of us was cursed by a god and one of us made a mistake we're all paying for. We're not the same, even if we're being treated like it.'

'Pariahs can't be choosers.'

'You wanted to be alone, right? I'll leave you to it. I have a hundred more places to hide.'

'Cassandra, wait, what's wrong?'

'What's wrong?' I whirl on her. 'There's a war outside our walls that half the people I love are fighting in, I can't stop seeing death, and every day I watch my family distance themselves a little more from me because of it.'

'Are they? Because from here it looks like you're distancing yourself.'

My jaw tightens and she shrugs.

'Oh, I'm sorry, did you want empty reassurances?'

'Both can be true. The same way most people seem to like you but every so often catch themselves remembering what you being here means.'

'That's hardly my problem.'

'Fine, whatever, goodbye.'

I turn to leave just as a vision hits, and it's so sudden it throws my equilibrium off. I'm plummeting, falling down as the vision claims me.

Men in the camps, gossiping, trading rumours I've heard before – Agamemnon sacrificing a young girl, Iphigenia, on her wedding day, just as Apollo mentioned. But then one of them says something that staggers me: 'What kind of bastard slaughters his own daughter? No wonder this whole bloody war feels cursed.'

I come back to reality and see those blue eyes hovering above me. For a moment I wonder if I am still falling – because the ground beneath me has surely vanished.

Agamemnon killed his daughter. Agamemnon, who is brother of Menelaus and husband of Helen's sister Clytemnestra. Which would make Iphigenia Helen's niece.

I can't tell her this – can I? But surely she'd want to know. And apparently I now care about what Helen wants . . .

'Are you all right?' she asks, reaching a hand to help me up that I decidedly ignore as I stand.

'Iphigenia,' I start – and Helen is clearly surprised. I suppose, with a battlefield of men, her niece back in Mycenae is probably not who she thought I would mention. 'The Achaeans couldn't get the wind they needed to sail to Troy.' I pause, waiting to see if she doesn't believe it. But this isn't a prophecy, is it? Just something I learnt from them that had already happened. Helen nods, urging me on. 'Agamemnon killed a deer in Artemis's sacred grove and she cursed the winds to halt. The only way to lift the curse was to kill Iphigenia. He told her she would marry Achilles, summoned her to Aulis and sacrificed her.'

For a moment I think she's going to scream that she doesn't believe me.

Then she gasps, covering her mouth with trembling fingers. '*What?*'

'Oh, Helen, I'm so sorry.'

I can see her wrestling to get her feelings under control, to package something more presentable for me.

'I hardly knew her, but that poor girl –' She breaks off with a choking gasp. 'How am I worth that to them? Their own daughter? For what – to reunite me with Menelaus? Or to bury me to restore his honour? Whatever they want to do to me, how is it worth *that*?'

A prophetic man twists before my eyes, hovering over Helen's shoulder like he's mocking her. I've seen enough visions for that over-confident stance and sneering brow to be disturbingly familiar – Menelaus. *'It was not for her I came,'* this image of his future self says. *'It was for the man – the con man, the thief who dined with me and then stole my wife away.'*

Helen continues to cry as the man disappears.

For the first time in all of this, I feel sorry for her. Menelaus does not want Helen back because he loves and misses her. She's not even the reason he's here. If she were hidden away somewhere, if she'd left the city like I'd wanted – would he have attacked us anyway, for the sake of killing Paris?

I don't know what to say so I clutch her hands a little tighter.

'It's not going to be enough for them, is it?' Helen says once her tears subside. 'Artemis would never demand the sacrifice of a young girl – she's their sworn protector. Agamemnon did it to prove his dedication to this war. And he must have run because Clytemnestra is a woman of Sparta and she would have sooner disembowelled him herself than have allowed him to touch their daughter.'

'There's a lot of judgement from the Achaeans,' I say, relieved to be able to say anything at all. 'Some fear that rather than getting the gods on their side, it might have damned them.'

'Let us hope so,' Helen says, her nostrils flaring. 'Because Agamemnon just declared to the whole Achaean army what he is willing to give for this war. They'll stop at nothing until they raze this city.'

She's right. And I can't believe I fell for the lies they're telling themselves. The justifications they churn out like it might mask their own hunger for glory.

Helen stills – or rather, she tries to still. But her hands shake and her lashes flutter in quick blinks that whisk her tears away before they can dare to fall again. 'Please excuse me,' she says, her voice taut. 'I must pray for my niece's safe journey to the Underworld.'

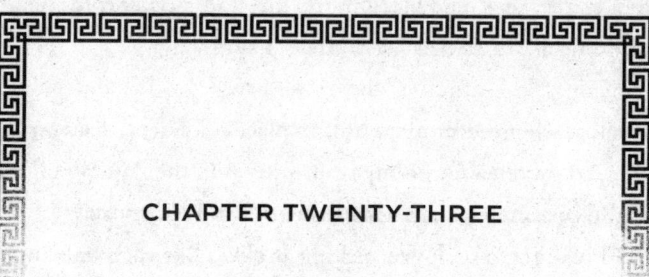

CHAPTER TWENTY-THREE

Helen

I STAY UP LATE, EYES ACHING with the weak candlelight I have been writing by, a dozen scraps of notes and nothing close to a complete letter.

My dear sister, word has reached me of your loss and –
　Please know I would sooner have faced the blade myself than have Iphigenia –
　I'm sorry –
　I know you must hate me. I hate myself –

I clutch the stylus until the reed cracks. Writing any form of letter to Greece would be considered treason. The Trojans would execute me themselves.

So I feed the letters one by one into the fire, ensuring no fragment remains. Two nations fight over me and I still feel worthless, little more than a pleasant face staggering under the weight of the blood on my hands.

It feels a far more treacherous thing than letters to my sister, in a land where men bleed in the dirt and girls' corpses lie on wedding altars, to be so very tired of surviving.

I wake early, needing extra time to place cold metal discs on my eyes, to rub cream into my skin – to undo the damage of last night, to erase my pain with cosmetics and old tricks.

I break my fast slowly, picking at olives like each one might give me the jolt of energy I need after such an exhausting night. But with all that time sitting in the hall, chatting with Athrae and Clymene, I notice Cassandra doesn't appear.

And then I am caught in a whirlwind of thoughts that is becoming far too familiar. Cassandra never merely crosses my mind, she consumes me. Any thought of her spirals into the next – all her schemes, all her machinations and all her cruel demands. Is it possible her resolve has hardened, that once again she seeks to expel me from this city?

Is Iphigenia really dead or is it simply the next step in another ill-conceived plan?

I've had more than enough and, marching to her room, I plan to tell her just that.

There's no response when I knock but I can hear her, speaking more lines of nonsensical poetry, so I push the door open.

She's in a flurry of parchment, ink on her fingers and splattered across her clothes, eyes rolled back in her head while her hand continues to trace the page so frantically that the nib of her stylus has torn straight through and is now scratching at the table below.

It's clear that whatever she's working towards, I am no longer the crux of it, and the irritation that drove me here fades.

I take the stylus from her, her hand still moving in the air, and I'm not sure what she's trying to do but I write down what she's saying because it's clearly important to her – something about the wrong armour, about a weak spot.

My eyes slide across the page and it reads like just another fable – something instinctive telling me it's false, a fiction she's crafting.

But it's true. Yet it *feels* false. A disconnect between what I know and what I believe – but that's not something I'm unfamiliar with.

How often have I doubted stories? Men tell tales of valour I'm sure they're exaggerating; we are told legends of the gods that I'm sure priests have invented so we all fall into line – and we do fall into line. We pretend we believe them. And even if in our hearts we don't think they're true, we act as though they are. Disbelief is a luxury afforded to many – if Menelaus gives a decree, we all follow it whether we believe it or not; we do not even think to question it, his will supplanting our own. Men speak like our belief is assured, women like we are doubting it in our own minds before we give it voice – and I wonder, would Cassandra's curse have been so damning if we weren't already powerless? When even the prestige of royalty and priesthood means little if men say it's nothing?

'Helen?' she whispers, voice a scratch.

She seems present, not locked in a vision.

'I think you should take a break.'

She shakes her head rapidly. 'I can't – there must be something here, right? The prophecies were supposed to be a gift, so if I can work out what they mean, what it is I'm seeing, I might – *Breathe in your hearts, and string your arms to fight –*'

They take her so suddenly she nearly falls from her chair and I rush to write what she's saying, one hand on her shoulder to keep her still.

'Sorry,' she gasps when she comes to.

'It's okay, you lie down and I'll write what you say.'

'But you don't believe them.'

'That doesn't mean I can't write. And afterwards, when we decipher them, I can work out what I'm not believing in.'

She seems too tired to argue, stumbling to her bed, and I take her seat – guessing at the spellings of names I've never heard of and faltering every time there's one I know far, far too well.

After an hour, she burns herself out and lies, panting, on the bed.

'It's okay,' she says. 'You can stop now.'

'Are you sure? I don't mind.'

'Yeah.' She can barely talk, her throat is so raw.

I duck my head out of the door and summon a passing servant, requesting something soothing for her. With all this paper, she must have been yelling prophecies all night.

I cross to her bed and perch at its foot with her sprawled on the sheets before me – trying not to think about how arresting she looks like that, ink-smeared and unkempt. But it's difficult to ignore when what's always been enticing about her is some wild edge that even royalty hasn't been able to smooth out.

'So,' I say, 'they were bad today?'

'They're all bad, every day.' She takes up a pillow and clutches it tight. 'The future is not a happy place.'

'That's not what I meant.'

She sighs and pulls herself up so that we're sitting facing each other. 'I know. Today was a bad day, but it's not the first day like that I've had.'

'Days like . . .' I look at the pages. Days where she throws herself into it all?

'Days where the prophecies take over,' she says quietly. 'Days where I become exactly what they think I am – frenzied.'

'You've been writing these prophecies down for days,' I say, crossing back to the desk and examining sheaves of carefully piled paper. 'You think there's something here?'

'I have to,' she says, staring at the pages. 'Apollo gifted me these visions. Not being believed is the final stumbling block, but I can't get past the first, can't work out what it is I'm supposedly seeing. Maybe if I did, there would be some way round – to say the opposite or advise without revealing or –'

'Or I could pass them on,' I say, lighting on the idea. 'I could suffer the curse of not believing you without handing it to others. I've parroted enough of Menelaus's nonsense to give a convincing enough performance, I should imagine.'

'Helen, that won't –'

'No, you're right,' I realize. 'If no one else believes you a viable source, they'll think I have some insider – maybe even that I'm in contact with the Achaean army. No, we'll have to be smarter than that. To find something that won't incriminate either of us.'

'Helen!'

'Cassandra, if you're going to ask me why I'm doing this or argue against us working with each other, then I'm simply going to scream. You have a gift from the gods that could help us in this war and I'm the only person in the palace who believes that, overall, what you're saying is the truth. Even if I can't believe the particulars. We have to work together. And frankly, we've wasted enough time.'

She stares at me, still clinging to the pillow, though now it feels more like she just wants a barrier between us.

My eyes keep dropping to her hands clutching the fabric – I've always had a thing for hands, and the way she's twisting hers into the silk is distracting, long delicate fingers and nails short and ragged from scraping against stone when the visions knock her to the ground. I wonder how they'd feel –

I'd like to slap myself, but it's hardly my fault that gorgeous princesses clambering on to beds throw my mind into free fall.

'I'll consider it,' Cassandra says finally – and it's clear that while I've been ogling her she's been considering the important matter of the war and our role within it. What a brilliant start to my proposed partnership. 'But I can't think about it right now. And you don't get to take advantage of these visions to manipulate me.'

For the sake of Olympus, she's so intent on clinging to this antagonism between us.

'Iphigenia,' I say, refusing to dignify her attempts to push me away with a response. 'That was the truth?'

It takes her longer than I expect to answer, so long that for a moment I begin to hope the answer might be no.

'I've really been so awful that you believe I'd lie to you about that,' she says – eyes downcast. 'Yes, that was true.'

'Yes, well. Let's review those other prophecies.'

I cross to the table and take up a sheet of paper. This is fairly clear – a detailed description of blows and sweeps. But I see what she means: there are no identifying features of anyone involved, just two nameless people fighting to the death. And even then, I find myself thinking that no one would really fight that way, that it could not possibly last so long, that this couldn't really be a killing blow.

'And you have no way of controlling what you see?'

It's a gamble, to push her right now. This close to the edge, she might snap and refuse to talk to me again. But I'm certain she's desperate to talk about these things, and she's right – I'm manipulative enough to have no scruples about reminding her I'm the only one she *can* talk to about this.

I'm not sure she's going to answer, but when she does it's quiet and quick, like she doesn't want to think too much about it. 'No. I'm the stylus, not the writer. I'm just the outlet.'

'And when you're in visions, can you look around?'

She glances away. 'Sometimes. Occasionally I'll see it from someone else's eyes, but most of the time I can scan my surroundings, even move around – try to find some clue to when it's going to happen or who it is I'm seeing.'

'So there's a degree to which you *are* reading them,' I say. 'You're not a passive vessel, and if you can do that with visions, maybe you could do that with prophecy. We should experiment –'

'Helen.' She winces, raising her hands to her temples. 'Can we not do this now? My mind is fried from all those visions.'

There's a knock at the door and I rush to answer, returning with two mugs.

'What is it?' she asks as I pass one to her.

'Honeyed milk,' I say, unable to look at her. It's my comfort drink. Just a drink, but also revealing, another small part of me handed over to her like it's not an enormous thing to do. 'I thought the sugar might help.'

She takes it, and just the one sip seems to restore some colour to her face.

A thought occurs to me.

'When was the last time you did anything fun?'

'What do you mean?' she asks. There's something stripped back about her – her exhaustion maybe, or the intimacy of our conversation – the pretence and snobbery fallen away, and she's looking up over the top of her cup, her eyes quizzical.

'Have you even been into the city since all this began?'

'I'm not allowed to, not since they stripped my priesthood.'

I try to hide how incredulous I find this. 'Cassandra, you've been through too much to bind yourself within these walls. Come now, a war is no time for abiding by the rules.'

CHAPTER TWENTY-FOUR

Helen

THE PALACE IS EERILY QUIET and I am incredibly conscious of Cassandra walking by my side. It feels more intimate than when we were alone in her room. There, we were two people observing each other, separate and apart; and here, where we might be seen, we're an *us*.

I've spent so long watching her sweep through these halls like they were lucky to bear her within them. Now Cassandra scurries nervously and when a servant walks past, eyes tracking us, she grasps my arm and pulls me into a storeroom.

'I'm flattered,' I say as my back presses against the wall. 'But I'm married to your brother.'

She ignores me and even though I'm joking it turns out that sitting on a bed is nothing to her dragging me into a cupboard. I try very desperately not to let my eyes fall to her lips.

She's taller than me.

Has she always been taller than me?

'Do you want to go on without me?'

'What?' I ask, thrown as much as I am flustered. 'No, the whole point of this is that I'm going with you.'

'I was honest. I'm not outright saying no to working together, I just need time to think. Going into town with you isn't going to make up my mind.'

'We're going into town because you need a break and if I don't force you, I don't think you're going to take one.'

'And you're fine with being seen with me?'

'We've been seen together plenty of times.'

'In quick conversation. You want to be seen spending time with me? In the city with me? I'm disgraced, Helen, and you once made quite clear how important your reputation is to you. And that was before war was declared in your name.'

Ah. I struggle to parse the right response – how honest to be, how revealing.

It's Cassandra, after all. It doesn't really matter what she thinks. I'm sure she'll realize that, regardless of how she feels about me, working together is her best chance of using the prophecies somehow. But I want her to like me, for some strange reason. It's not the usual sort – not because she might be useful or she might be a threat. Between her lack of credibility and her appalling attempts to get rid of me, she's proved neither of those things. I want her to like me because I need her to – because her hatred so far has cut me surprisingly deep.

'Well?' she pushes.

'Give me a moment, I'm trying to decide how nice I should be.'

'You're not nice, Helen.'

'Sure I am, but I don't see being nice getting me anywhere with you.' Which is not a lie. Cassandra wants my truth – which is a terrifying thing and something I've never given anyone a lot of.

She watches me carefully in the dim light like she might see the moment I choose to lie to her. Or perhaps she's not expecting a lie but a confession. Or maybe she's waiting on a moment when I decide she's not worthy of anything at all.

'All right, fine,' I say because I can't take those desperate eyes of hers a second longer. 'First of all, I don't think as many people actually dislike you as you think.'

'And the others?'

'Well, you won't damage my reputation. If anyone sees me with you, then I'm just the loving, caring princess taking pity on the crazy girl who tried to kill her.'

'Okay, first of all, I'm the princess in this equation.' She draws herself up with a haughty air.

'That's what bothers you most about what I just said?'

'Well, you're not wrong,' she relents. 'Though I'm not happy about how quickly you devised such a plot.'

'I'm in a foreign land while a war rages in my name. If I didn't devise quick plots, then I'd be dead.'

'Again,' Cassandra says tersely, 'you're not wrong. But there are plenty of ways for me to take a break that don't involve being in public, so why are you so intent on actually going out in the city together?'

Because I want her to like me, and even though I want everyone to like me, this feels different.

And because she went to such extreme lengths to save this city that I want to see the place through her eyes, to see a thing worth destroying yourself for.

But I can't speak before she continues. 'Do – *The earth will rot your bones as you lie here at Troy* – Sorry.'

She jolts, hand clutching her head.

'Ah, I don't think I'm going to be able to keep them back today. I'm still weak from yesterday and I don't need to make this headache worse.'

'The prophecies hurt you?' I ask. I hadn't realized that.

'Sometimes.' She shrugs. 'They're tolerable if I keep them to a whisper, but if I hold them back entirely for too long, then it feels like my skull is cleaving apart.'

'Oh. Well, don't be quiet at all, then, not with me. I don't want being around me to be draining for you.'

Her breath actually catches.

'It's not like it's just me muttering nonsense, Helen. It's all gruesome and horrendous and nothing you want to be hearing non-stop.'

'Yes, and I'd rather hear it than have you need to lie down every time we spend a day together.'

'But –'

'Why don't you try it and I'll let you know if it gets too much?'

She stares at me, and I get the impression she might continue arguing just for the sake of it, but she stops herself with a quick shake of her head. 'Fine. Now, I think we've had quite enough of this cupboard.'

'Oh, I don't know, I was growing to quite enjoy it.'

'Why do I get the feeling you'd flirt with the broom if I left you alone together?'

'It's a fine-looking broom, I think I could sweep it off its feet.'

What am I doing? What am I saying?

More importantly, when did I lose all ability to flirt well and start resorting to such cumbersome, heavy efforts that leave me far more flustered than my mark?

Cassandra narrows her eyes, then shudders with a glorious sort of surrender. 'This is going to be a long day, isn't it?'

CHAPTER TWENTY-FIVE

Cassandra

I CAN'T SHAKE THE BELIEF THAT I will only get one chance to do this. If something happens – a prophecy leaves me screaming in the middle of the street or a vision startles me at the wrong moment – and my parents find out I ventured into the city without a guard, they'll take what few freedoms I have left.

It's almost too much to risk.

So why am I?

I keep glancing at Helen from the corner of my eye, like the answer might be writ across her face.

But I know why – she believes me. And it is one thing to say it – I can argue with that, push it away and pretend it doesn't matter. But to *see* it, to wake up to Helen, who can't believe the things I'm saying, writing them down anyway because she knows they matter to me . . . that's something else entirely.

It's probably intentional. Helen is more strategic than most men fighting at our walls – she will have clocked the way shoulders turn when I whisper prophecies, the way eyes narrow and doors close. She'll know exactly how to demand my loyalty.

That's fine – I don't care. I'm tired and I'm lonely and losing hope with each passing day. If Helen wants to exploit me, she can use me all she likes. If she wants to bend me to her side, she can break me.

And if she wants to drag me to the city and force some joy into my exhausted body and pre-emptively grieving heart, I suppose she can do that too.

Women glance in our direction as we pass through the acropolis. I can't get a read on their expressions but there's little of the usual hostility that has begun to follow me around.

And then, moments later, we're out in the cobbled streets of Troy.

I'm not sure I'll ever be used to this city – and it may just be that visits to it were always exciting, prepared for days in advance even though it was mere footsteps away. But I think it's more than that, because Troy is the sort of place that would take even the gods' breath away.

There is one long road that stretches to the city gates with tall white houses on either side, coloured window shutters and the red-orange roofs that spill down the street towards the ocean, all of them overflowing with life. There are clothes lines, market stalls, carts, dogs darting through crowds, paper lanterns strung across buildings, small wooden decorations and so much more. It's so loud, too, with chatter and bartering, taverns where songs float out, children playing in the street.

I turn, curious to see how it appears to someone unaccustomed to it – but Helen isn't looking at it; she's watching me with a smile playing on her face.

For a moment I bristle, reluctant to be scrutinized. But I force myself to relax, to surrender myself to her.

'What now?' I ask.

Helen shrugs. 'This is your city, show me around.'

'You've probably been here more than I have.'

'Yes, on all those glorious sanctioned trips to the textile merchants and jewellers – Come on, there must be things you always wanted to do but weren't allowed to on official visits.'

I . . .

Yes, yes, there were.

I turn back to her. From a distance, Helen is everything the legends detail – graceful and beautiful, a thing to admire. But up close, she is expectant and urgent, her attention a bright light exposing all that you are – and I have no doubt that while everyone is busy admiring her, she is busy staring right back.

This feels like a challenge, like she has brought me here to prove what she has seen of me – this city, my longing for it, all on show.

Suddenly I want to challenge her too, to say: *Yes, you're right, I love this city, but you are going to come with me and you are going to love it too.*

I slip my hand into hers, and I draw her down one of the side streets, away from the well-worn paths that I have walked before.

'What are all these?' Helen asks, gesturing to the wooden sculptures that stand on street corners, stretching to the sky. 'They're in the temples too, aren't they?'

So I begin telling her our history – relaying classes I haven't had in years, stepping down cobbled streets, recounting how it came to be – and revelling in the opportunity to talk about, to even *think* about, something that's not the future.

I start with Athena depositing the Palladium on a hill, indicating to Tros where the city was to be built. And how when Poseidon and Apollo were sent to the city, the citizens built more statues in their honour.

'Apollo liked them so much he declared them sacred and every year since we've had a festival to build more, inspired by the gods and their stories.'

'They're beautiful,' Helen says, stopping at one in the form of a bear – the myth of Callisto, who was transformed into the animal after sleeping with Zeus. It's taller than one of the houses, carved from the trees that grow up the slopes of the mountains. There's a whole guild of craftsmen who can work with such large materials, and they spend all year creating them, each one worth a fortune to a city outside Troy where such skills are hard to come by.

The statues continue as we work our way around the city.

We sample food at market stalls, tossing copper pieces for the sellers' time. We browse wares displayed on carts outside shops. It's not quite as it was, but it's a new kind of thrilling: instead of performers begging coins for magic tricks, women gather to repair clothing for the front and take it in turns telling stories more gripping than any play I've seen at the Dionysia, and the people who have fled to the city from nearby towns share songs that gather small crowds excited for lyrics they've never heard.

Helen shines. Her eyes glitter with excitement, her smile so deep it carves creases in her cheeks, her every movement careless.

By mid-afternoon, we collapse on the banks of the River Scamander and look up at the sky.

'I'm not pressing you to reconsider a potential alliance,' Helen says. 'But I need you to know that I want to save this city. And I think we might be able to if we try.'

'I've been trying!'

'Yes, but together.'

I expect more – a return to her earlier pitch, perhaps. But she leaves it at that.

I think of her writing my visions down, of her insistence that I do not suffocate the prophecies in her presence – even of today, walking around this city.

And I realize I cannot imagine even trying without her.

'Yes, all right, then. Together.'

The golden weave of the world staggers, strands cut, others strengthening, the whole thing shaking at the sudden change.

I gasp as the cords round me tighten, pulling me in a dozen different directions – it is like when Helen said she believed me and the whole world felt like it was holding its breath, only now it feels like there is no air at all. It is unravelling, it is fraying at its every end, a quake throughout existence.

And then, all at once, calm – as some delicate strand winds into being and slots into place.

Something monumental has changed.

I look at Helen, at that bright, shiny new strand strung about her oblivious frame. She is the root of our destruction, but, if that cord can be believed, she might also be the path to our salvation.

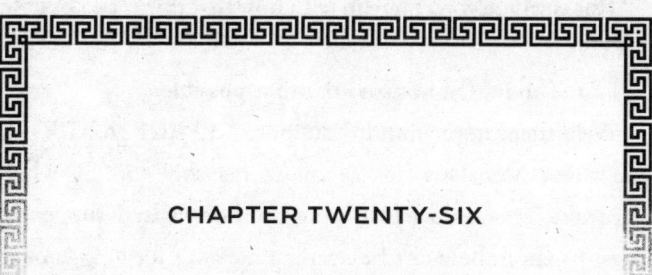

CHAPTER TWENTY-SIX

Cassandra

THE NEXT DAY, HELEN TAKES me to the courtyard she's been training in. There's an edge to her that I've seen only when she threatened me – a fearless determination. I'm so used to her efforts to appear unassuming that this fierceness takes me by surprise.

'It seems to me that we have three main areas of focus,' she says, pacing the courtyard with long steps that have the hem of her chiton flicking up around her ankles. 'We need to control the prophecies, decipher them and convey them without triggering the curse.'

Three impossible tasks that she has turned into items to be checked off a list.

'That first one is going to be the most mentally taxing, I imagine. So I thought that's where we might start.'

I nod, though I'm not really listening – I'm staring at the strands around Helen, trying to see them twitch. But Helen is so intrinsically tied to the future of this city that her strands are a jumbled knot, tangled with other cords stretching through the air and even with my own.

'This is where you chime in with how that might be possible,' she says.

'I don't know. I'm not sure that it *is* possible.'

'Well, then, never mind. I suppose I'd better go pack. Do you think Menelaus has room on his ship for my whole wardrobe, or should I just bring the essentials? I suppose it doesn't matter, he won't be keeping me alive for long enough to –'

'Helen,' I growl, with the pained annoyance that accompanies my headaches. I don't have one at the moment but I'm not sure being around Helen is all that different. 'The prophecies just happen. Apollo said I couldn't pick and choose what they show because that's not the power of an oracle but of a god.'

'That's bullshit – kings consult with oracles all the time, they don't just sit and hope the right prophecy lands in their lap.'

'That's because most of them are making it up. We were literally taught how to deliver prophecies in the temple. No one ever made any mention of the differences between prophecies and visions, or the way they bleed through – they never even mentioned the fact the threads shift sometimes, reweave themselves right in front of you. They made it sound like the future is certain.'

The path ahead might have a fixed core running through years of war, something I'm not sure can be bent and reset, but the threads around the edges are constantly flicking back and forth as different choices are made on the battlefield or as different weapons strike true.

Helen is staring at me intently but I recognize the sudden hollowness in her gaze that implies she's too busy thinking of her response, or her next step, or her latest move, to truly hear the words being said.

'Threads?' she asks. 'Weave? The future is a tapestry, then?'

'I suppose. But the threads are all around us. If I focus, then every person is a chaotic mess of pulsing strands – they stretch out, link people, push onwards to the future or back to the past. And that's only what exists with us now. I always got the impression that what I can see is just one surface of a many-sided thing.'

'Can you read those threads? Just walk right up to someone and divine their future.'

I shake my head. 'No, I've tried.'

'Try again,' she says. 'I want to see.'

I consider protesting more but trying and failing seems the quickest way to prove my point. I focus on the glittering threads, spiderweb-thin, shot through the air around me, until they're all I can see, shining and molten.

'Try one of mine,' she suggests. 'It might be easier to work out a timeline or to change it if we must.'

It won't work anyway, so it hardly matters.

I focus on a strand running through her wrist, stripping it away from those it is braided with, reaching for it, pleading for it to reveal itself to me.

Nothing happens – except a slight pulse in my head that I might be imagining, like the prophecies are rebuking me for my attempt.

'See?' I hiss. Knowing it wouldn't work doesn't change how much I despise failing in front of her.

'That's what I thought.' She worries at her lip – slightly, the barest brush of her teeth, but I catch it along with all the times

I've seen it before: the look she makes while she figures out how to parse something she knows I won't like.

'Whatever you're going to say, say it.'

She sighs. 'You're frustrated, quick to anger and impatient.'

'And you're self-righteous, arrogant –'

'In battle, irritation is where you make mistakes – your javelin misses, you fall for a feint, you grow clumsy.'

'Prophecy isn't battle.'

'No, it's a tapestry, you just said. And weaving needs a calm mind too. You don't strike me as someone with an eye for precision, and if these are threads as you claim, then precision is what you need. But if we're going to work on your discipline, then I thought you might be more receptive to sword work than weaving.'

'I know how to weave, Helen,' I snap – not giving her the additional caveat that I was never very good at it and used to spend most of my classes pining after Andromache and thoroughly incapable of working the loom. 'And I'm not waving a sword around in some cruel imitation of the men dying outside our walls.'

'It's not a cruel imitation, it's a valuable skill most women are shut off from. Not to mention, it's fun.'

'Jogging round a courtyard is not my idea of fun.'

'What about waving a sharp pointy thing?'

'No.'

'Why not?'

Because the thought of holding a sword brings up too many memories of the future, of visions seen through the eyes of the men who wield them.

'Let's not give the angry thoughts in my head any opportunity to become real.'

'Oh,' she says gently – too gently. 'All right, then, let's go on without it.'

I take the distraction – and soon she has me trying a dozen things: trigger words, methods of cleansing my mind, of directing my thoughts, begging, asking, demanding, screaming for a prophecy to come.

Nothing works – just the occasional random line with little relevance and certainly no clarity.

Eventually we exhaust ourselves, and we sit on the dusty ground beneath a tall pine tree whose leaves shade us from the hot midday sun.

'Thank you for trying,' Helen says. 'I know I've probably been a nightmare, pushing you to the brink. But I appreciate you bearing with me.'

'Honestly, it's kind of a relief to have someone else come up with ideas. I'd exhausted my own.'

'I can't believe you've been doing all this by yourself for months. It's only a day and I'm already despairing. If I could go back – Wait. Apollo gifted you visions constrained by the power he wants to give an oracle. Maybe he was so focused on only allowing glimpses of the future that he left the past wide open. Did you say you could see that too?'

'Sort of.' I stare at the threads ensnaring Helen's arm, focusing past those golden strands to beneath, where duller cords still gleam. 'I've only ever grasped them by accident while reaching for the future, but everyone contains the strands of their past. Though I don't see what help reading them would be in preventing what's to come.'

'It might help your control. Or to become more familiar with how the threads work.'

Helen reaches her arm towards me, and the network of threads embedded in her skin.

'Do you want to try?'

By now, I am so used to trying anything she suggests that I don't really think about what she's offering – not a future to be avoided but a piece of her carefully masked past. I just reach in and grab it.

Terror, confusion – a tall man dragging her forward. The air is tinged with meadow flowers and heavy with sulphur – which is when I see the lava, the heavy heat of it scalding the hairs on my arms – and then I realize it is not lava but actual flame, trickling like water. A river of fire. The Phlegethon. The Underworld.

CHAPTER TWENTY-SEVEN

Cassandra

I GASP, LETTING THE STRAND GO.

'What did you see?' Helen demands – excited rather than anxious, and I wonder if she realizes what monumental things she gave me to experiment with.

'It was the past but . . . you were in the Underworld.'

'Oh,' she laughs, relieved. 'That.'

'That? Did I miss the part where you died? Or is there a third lover in your past, some Orpheus type that rescued you?'

'There are at least five lovers, Cassandra, dear. I haven't married all of them. This wasn't one of them.' She goes to say something else but stops herself.

'You don't have to explain. I don't want to pry into something I shouldn't have seen at all.'

'No, I want to tell you. It's more that . . . well, do you know anything of my brothers?'

'You have brothers? But Menelaus sits on the throne of your father.'

'Yes, they're not with us any longer,' she says, her voice thick with something more complicated but just as heavy as sadness. 'Zeus only met with our mother once. Zeus was a swan, as you know, and, no, I'd rather not think about any of that further. But there were two eggs from the union. My mother and her husband, Tyndareus, already had four nearly grown daughters. My brothers' egg hatched almost immediately – both of them in one, identical, though Castor was glowing, bright shards of light with the clear blessing of Zeus. And my egg remained cold to the touch. They thought it empty, as though one brother had escaped into the other's shell. But a few years later . . . well, the egg cracked and there I was.'

'I . . .'

'Yeah, try having this explained to you when you're fourteen and your brothers half die and half become immortal. I'm told there was a great deal of fuss when I was born –'

'Hatched,' I correct.

'Hatched, yes,' she confirms, then picks at the clasp of her dress. I suspect it's to avoid looking at me. 'When I was seven I was wrestling at the palaestra and I was abducted.'

'What?'

'It's fine, they were dealt with, and frankly they were perfectly decent to me while I was with them. You know Theseus?'

'Theseus the legendary hero who killed the Minotaur? Yes, I've heard of him.'

'Yeah, *hero*,' she scoffs. 'He kidnapped me. He and his friend Pirithous decided they were such noble heroes and great men that they deserved to have daughters of gods for wives.'

'Wives?' I yelp. 'You were seven.'

'Exactly, and in seven more years I would have been a perfectly marriageable fourteen. He was going to take me to his mother to raise the Spartan out of me, but Pirithous got ambitious. He wanted Persephone.'

'I . . . what?'

'He wanted Persephone. No demi-god for him but a full goddess, the very much already married queen of the Underworld. So that's where we went. Hades agreed to see them and even invited us all to dine with him, and I remember when Persephone entered because tiny little flowers bloomed where she stepped. Hades was watching her and I thought it was funny, because he didn't look at her the way other men looked at their wives. I think I've been searching for that look ever since – adoring, admiring, but mostly intimate, like a thousand words were being said in a glance between the two of them.'

'Helen,' I prompt. 'I really don't care about how much the king and queen of Hell love each other when you were literally an abducted seven-year-old.'

'Right,' she continues. 'Then Hades turned on Theseus and Pirithous and smiled, and that was a look I did recognize because I loved going to the fighting pits.'

'Of course you did.'

'Theseus and Pirithous were oblivious. They didn't catch the edge to it at all and carried on chatting and sharing stories and spinning some tale about why they were there, and the moment they finished Hades just looked at them, stone-cold and murderous, and snakes sprang up along their arms and legs, holding them in place.'

'I guess it's only okay when *he* kidnaps his wife.'

'Yeah, a bit hypocritical – but then he did the weirdest thing.'

Helen doesn't seem uncomfortable now she's at this part of the story – she seems almost excited, swept up in the thrill of it, and I find myself leaning in, not sure if I want to know what happens next or if I just want to keep her enthusiasm churning.

'What?'

'He turned to Persephone and said something like, "Do you want to handle this one?" and she smiled, and it was a hundred times more terrifying than Hades, and said, "Absolutely." Then Hades crouched in front of me and asked my name and he took my hand and led me out of there before she could do whatever she did to them.'

'He . . . what?'

Helen nods. 'I know, few people even believe I went to the Underworld, but *no one* believes me on that point.'

'It's just . . . he's the king of the Underworld.'

'Yeah, and good with kids, apparently. I don't think I realized he was the same Hades as the one from the stories. I'm not even sure I knew I was in the Underworld until I left. But Hades took me into another room and asked me things. Like I say, I was seven, I mostly remember that at some point an automaton served honeyed milk and it was delicious.'

My breath hitches. Helen brought me honeyed milk when the prophecies incapacitated me. Was that a coincidence, or was she sharing the comfort it once brought her with me?

'Hades asked me who my father was, said he could sense some divine presence, and he wasn't happy when I said it was Zeus. He said he was going to try to make him come and get me. Zeus must have ignored him, which isn't surprising, as I'd never met him, but it annoyed Hades. A few hours later he managed to get a message to my brothers instead. They'd been waging war on Athens to get me back at the time.'

'Ah. So this isn't the first war declared in your name?'

Her smile falls. 'They declared a war in a seven-year-old's name and still tried to blame me for it.'

For a moment, we stare at each other as the full weight of that settles between us.

'Anyway,' Helen chirps, trying for that joviality again. 'Hades took me to the gates and we waited and I played with his dog for a bit – you know, the giant three-headed one that guards it. Complete softy. Then Castor and Polydeuces arrived and took me home. I heard later that Heracles broke Theseus out but Pirithous is still down there.'

'Helen, that is such a wild story.'

'Yes. It's fine if you don't believe me. Most people think I made it up to deal with the trauma, and I was waiting with Theseus's mother the whole time.'

'I believe you, I just believe it could only happen to you.'

Helen considers. 'You know what the worst thing was?'

'About being abducted as a child?'

'That's what started it all. Everyone said that for them to have taken me I would have to grow up to be a great beauty, and then it was practically a prophecy, and then it was just a fact. I mean, it's stupid, isn't it? I was beautiful because a man picked me and decided I was.'

'Of course it's stupid. We're currently fighting a war because Paris chose beauty over glory and power.'

Helen turns to me, her eyes guarded. 'Beauty? I thought it was love?'

'No,' I correct her, nowhere near as gently as I'll later wish I had. 'I think that's what makes me saddest of all. Aphrodite offered him the most beautiful woman in the world. Love was never a part of the equation.'

Helen considers this, her face growing taut as she stares. 'That's not . . . not how he made it sound to me.'

She blinks rapidly and I look away, not knowing how to comfort her and feeling like I'm intruding.

And then she is rustling through the folds of her skirts and pulling out an ornate dagger.

'Helen, what the –'

'Awfully convenient, your Trojan clothes, for hiding things. All those layers.'

'For covering modesty, not weapons.'

'I know – a travesty, really, when they hold such potential.'

Before I can do anything she grabs a chunk of her hair and raises the dagger to it.

'For the sake of Olympus, what are you doing?' I jolt to my feet and turn to see the gold curls fall to the dirt.

'What I always wanted to do,' she says, hacking at another piece. 'It's annoying and gets in the way all the damn time. You know we're supposed to cut our hair short on our wedding night? Menelaus wouldn't hear of it. He called my hair the "gold of Sparta". And Paris too, the way he strokes my hair when he says how much he loves me. Aren't I famous for these curls?'

'You're famous for being the most beautiful woman in the world. I hate to break it to you, but you're going to be beautiful with short hair too.'

'Yes, but I'll be beautiful the way I want to be, not the way they want me to.' She hacks off another clump. 'Give me a hand, will you? I don't think I can do the back well.'

'Oh, yes, whereas I will, of course, give you a brilliant style with a dagger.' I shake my head softly and turn my eyes skywards, like the gods themselves might be laughing at how ridiculous this is. 'So many people saw us come out here together. They're going to think I'm responsible somehow.'

Helen shrugs. 'Well, your reputation can't fall much further.'

'Stop using that as a free pass.'

'Are you going to help me or not?'

'Fine, but you really don't want me with a blade, of all things, near your neck.'

'I'll take the risk.'

I snatch the dagger before she can pass it to me, in part because I'm a little worried about her wielding something so sharp while clearly in turmoil over Paris. But when it touches my hand all I can imagine is the feel of it piercing flesh and I nearly drop it with the way my stomach roils.

'You know, I could show you how to actually use one, if you wanted?' she offers as I divide her hair into sections. The back of her neck, the way she bows her head forward – it all feels so exposed, so vulnerable. Helen handed me a dagger and presented her neck, mere weeks after I last tried to have her killed.

My fingers tremble as I shear the blonde locks, and I try to convince myself it's only the thought of all her sudden trust that has me nervous, and not the sheer closeness or the need to pay attention to every detail of her, down to the very last strand.

'If the thought of a sword is too much,' she continues, 'a dagger might be more manageable. I could show you how to wield it.'

'You mean this isn't its intended use?' I ask, rather than what I want to say, which is that I don't want to know how to use one. I don't want to be a part of anything so violent.

Or, rather, I'm scared of the part of me that might want to be.

It takes only a few moments and Helen beams with her lopsided look. The ends are uneven, the curls flying in different directions.

And I was right, because she's still beautiful, impossibly so. This close I can see the freckles across her ivory cheeks and I think of how lucky they are, these boys, to have free rein to look at them, to memorize their patterns, find the constellations.

There's something else, too, and it takes me a moment to realize it.

Her smile. It's slightly crooked and her right incisor is chipped. And sometimes, when she laughs it gets stuck in her throat and, as she gasps, it slips higher, like a cackle of glee.

I've seen her smile a thousand times. I've heard her laughter ring through the halls of the palace. It's not like this. It's usually practised, polished and perfect. And this is real.

I look away, turn back to that city because I don't know how I'll ever cope with the truth of her.

'Right, shall we get back to it?' she asks. 'Let's try that again – I think we might learn more about the threads that way. But I hope you're prepared for this, Cassandra. If you're plumbing the depths of my past, you're going to know me awfully well. You might even mistake that for friendship.'

We spend hours tempting the strands to reveal themselves, running through memories and mundane instances. I expect some sort of headache by the time we're done but it never comes.

The prophecies do, though. They're practically a constant stream throughout dinner, so that I'm picking at what is already very little food. We're saving up as much as we can in case the Achaeans cut off our supplies. I should probably leave. But something keeps me there – and I have the uncomfortable feeling it's Helen. She's sitting with Athrae and Clymene at another table but it's her voice I hear: *Don't be quiet* and *I don't think as many people actually dislike you as you think.*

I think she might actually be right. There are certainly a few dirty looks but most people seem used to my rambling by now. Kreousa and Andromache barely pause in their conversation, even as a prophecy shrieks loudly out, the usual sort – blood and guts and death. But my mother appears before me, hand on my shoulder.

'Cassie, are you okay?'

I nod, struggling to hold back the poetic lines long enough to answer.

She takes the empty seat beside me and, even though we're in a room full of people, it feels as though we're alone.

'How are you feeling?' she asks, her voice low. 'From what I've heard – from what we've all heard – well, I can't imagine how terrible it must be having such things churning through your head.'

I shrug. 'We are at war – I suppose it makes sense that the visions are horrific.'

'And so confusing too, showing in such a jumble as they do.' She nods sagely, like she understands. Then she hesitates.

I hate when she does that. It's never good, it just means she feels guilty.

'This isn't easy, Cassandra, but, as you say, the visions are horrific. And I am doing everything I can to keep spirits in the city high. Look at this room, everyone together for unity. But then you shout a prophecy about someone's loved one dying... We can't risk morale like this – we don't need people turning on us within the walls before we can deal with the threat outside them.'

My nails are biting into my palms. 'So what are you saying?'

'Yes, I'd really love to know that too,' Kreousa adds. She and Andromache have turned in their seats, decidedly becoming a part of this.

Andromache's clearly trying to temper herself, but Kreousa's making no such effort to hide her fury.

'Girls, you have to understand that as queen I have the people to think of. And as your mother, Cassie, I hate seeing you like this.' She places her hand on my shoulder again. It feels like a dead weight. 'I hate hearing what people say about you and I just don't think we should give them more ammunition.'

'Cassandra existing is not ammunition,' Kreousa seethes. 'You're the queen – if they're talking about your daughter, then do something about them, not Cass.'

It should be comforting that she's fighting for me.

But I feel like I'm not even there, like they're all just talking about me and I'm somewhere else. The strands flicker, gleaming brightly, the hall transformed with their light, and maybe I really am living in a different world to theirs, maybe that distance is this.

'I am supporting Cassandra,' my mother snaps. 'You can all pretend this isn't happening but it is, and that means making adjustments. You may not like it, you may resent me for it, but I *do* know what's best for you all. So for now, I think a separate, quieter space might be best until Cassie has more control over her prophecies. It's far kinder to her than keeping her here and perpetuating the whispers.'

'She's right,' I say, rising to my feet. I don't know if she is – I have no idea what I think – but my throat feels thick and my cheeks are warm, and this feels like the quickest way to end the conversation.

Andromache slips her hand into mine before I can leave – on her feet too.

'Very well,' she says. 'If we need to go elsewhere, then let's go.'

I leave with them both beside me but it doesn't halt that cavernous ache of loneliness in my gut. Maybe this is what Helen meant when she said people don't dislike me like I think they do. Look, here I am with people by my side. But the fact of that doesn't change that I still *feel* alone, that still these prophecies are mine to bear.

Kreousa's ranting as we leave, and Andromache's holding me tight.

But this isn't the sort of loneliness their love can fix.

And going somewhere quieter doesn't stop this horrible, churning feeling inside me, and the wish that I could simply vanish for the sake of everyone's convenience.

CHAPTER TWENTY-EIGHT

Helen

I ACCOMPANY AGATA INTO THE CITY to collect bolts of fabric, which is highly inappropriate – women unchaperoned, a servant and princess acting the role of courier. But so much of the war has become doing whatever needs doing and helping where you can.

That I strategically placed myself where I might be most seen to be helping is neither here nor there.

But after weeks of sneaking off with Cassandra to explore prophecies, I need to make the most of my time in public. And, frankly, I could do with the distraction. I didn't even hesitate when I offered up my own past for her experiments, but now I wonder if I should have. Every day, in a handful of memories, I give up pieces of myself. It's what I do, what I've always done.

But my fingers toy with the rough edges of my hair, thinking about the city we're trying so desperately to save, wondering why. It's certainly more than Paris, more even than it being a city away from Menelaus. It's this – Agata by my side and Cassandra reaching for yet more threads and Clymene and

Athrae moving the weights on my loom each evening as I weave.

I want to save Troy because I want to save myself. They could have sent me back but they didn't. They didn't sacrifice me.

So why do I keep sacrificing myself?

I tune back into Agata's rant.

'The usual girls were called away from the kitchens to help in the forges – I suppose they know how to heat a consistent fire – so I was asked to wait on the council. I'd forgotten what they could be like, and the fact we're losing ground isn't helping their foul moods. I was relieved when the priestesses of Athena were summoned and stopped it being a room full of men.'

My impression of the council has mostly been men too old to fight boldly declaring just how quickly the war would be won if they were on the field. They talk in their chamber in the palace, talk as they dine, talk on the walls of the city as they watch the war, and talk each evening with the men who have been fighting. It all seems a great deal of talking.

They're also who I need to get to listen to us and, unfortunately, all my early efforts in getting them to like me enough to not send me away were centred on how very harmless I was – so innocent and sweet. Certainly not the kind of person you'd let advise on war.

I might have convinced Cassandra that the most pressing matter is to control her visions. But the truth is I have no idea where to start with converting those prophecies into advice and getting people to actually heed it.

'It's priestesses from Artemis's temple tomorrow,' Agata continues. 'The council are desperate for any sort of omen, and they'll take it from whatever god is willing to give it.'

Olympus above, it's obvious – and I know one member of the priesthood desperate to build bridges with me.

I can't tell Cassandra what I'm doing, of course – she'd hate it. And if Herophile realizes where such information is coming from, she could turn the whole city against me.

But I start visiting the temple of Apollo and seeking out the high priestess. I begin with small talk and build up to sharing the occasional anxiety.

It is jarring to spend so long giving real things over to Cassandra and then share these falsehoods as though they mean something.

Cassandra cannot always read the past – in fact, at times it appears just as difficult for her as the future. And she's so quickly frustrated.

'I hate this,' she fumes one morning on only her third try that day. 'I didn't need to not be believed. Is the ineffectual nature of prophecy not curse enough?'

I try not to smile – but her irritation is equal parts adorable and enticing. Her slight scowl, her flushed cheeks – and the volatile nature of it all, the beauty of a woman who feels so deeply and cares so much.

'I still maintain that something to hone and focus your mind would be useful. And if you're still resisting all forms of physical exercise –'

'I very much am.'

'Which is fine, but I think you should try something else to . . .' I trail off, realizing that 'to build patience' will likely not go over well. 'Enhance your concentration. Weave. Paint. Make dresses with Andromache. Something.'

'We don't have time for that!' she protests. 'People are dying with every minute we waste.'

So we continue as we are.

It's strange, I never see anything when she does manage to read one of my cords. But I watch her see it – which is its own sort of vision.

This time her lip curls with the strength of her disgust.

When she comes to, she fumes: 'I saw the men fighting over you. All the bartering? Offering livestock and land for your hand, like a trade.'

'No,' I say – but, unlike her, I'm smiling. 'My stepfather didn't like it much either. Tyndareus asked me who I wanted. A shame I chose so wrong.'

'Do you mind . . . you don't have to answer –'

'And you don't have to start every question like that,' I say. 'I promise, if I don't want to answer, I won't, but I don't actually mind sharing with you, Cassandra.'

At least this way it feels like a choice to tell her. And I revel in the way a touch of colour tinges her light brown cheeks.

'Why him?' She practically spits it, like she can't say his name. 'I know you knew him but, from what I've seen, he's just so awful.'

I consider – trying to think deeper than my usual answer of: *I made a mistake. His promises were lies. I was a fool.*

But what is there to say about Menelaus? Our relationship was a game of petteia – tokens running across a board, racing to capture one another. And he won and won and won – convinced me he loved me, convinced me I'd be safe with him – and, once the victory was his, he upturned the board.

He took my blades from me. He barred me from assemblies of the court. He took things in ways so insidious they never felt like the punishments they were: cancelling my sister Phoebe's visit because of poor conditions on the roads between us – after an argument; asking me to spend less at the merchants' because it was poor form after increasing the taxes – after I'd questioned him in front of his council; arranging an honourable marriage between my childhood companion, Apia, and a foreign dignitary that would send her to live in Argos – after catching us sparring together.

Menelaus is not merely upset that I ran away with another man. He's upset that he never considered it a potential move, like I changed the rules of the game he had created.

'I chose him because I had no idea what he'd do to me.'

'I'm sorry,' she says – hesitating only a little before she continues. 'I'm happy you got away. I'm glad you're here. Even with all this.'

I imagine those threads inside me unspooling, something tightly wound easing. She sounds so sincere I do not even let myself question it – her words mean too much to taint with my disbelief.

'Thank you. And for what it's worth – I would have made the same deal you did. I think any woman would – the opportunity to see what's coming? We've all had moments when that would have saved us a lot of pain.'

She draws her arms close to her chest. 'You'd have seen it through, though. You wouldn't have got yourself into this mess. You wouldn't have been so useless.'

'Cassandra.' I step closer to her almost instinctively – only just stopping myself from reaching for her. 'What do your prophecies have to do with your value? You are so much without them — the comfort you've brought your sister, Andromache, your brothers . . . even me.'

'I could be more, Helen. I could have saved lives.'

So could I. If I'd never come here.

How long have I been out here? How many hours spent with Cassandra in the dusty shade of the mountain, churning through my own past and trying to unpick threads — never once realizing that she was carrying the same guilt that weighed me down when war was first declared.

'Maybe. But it's not your fault you were cursed.'

'Of course it is — I'm the one that couldn't fulfil my end.'

She is toying anxiously with her hands, her fingers writhing so tightly her knuckles have paled. I resist the urge to take them in my own.

'Cassandra, you know you're allowed to change your mind, right?'

'Yes, and then you deal with the consequences. And if I could go back, I still don't think I could do it. How foolish is that? Women do it all the time and I still couldn't just get through it. I'm just as selfish as Apollo accused me of being.'

'No, no, you're not,' I insist. 'Look, those are two different things. I've stopped sex before! Because it hurt or I was distracted, or I just didn't want to any more. That option is part of sex, and if Apollo took that away, then he's the one who reneged on your deal. As for feeling like you could never do it, even for Troy, that's fine! Why are you yelling at yourself over a hypothetical? It's a big thing — and to some of us it doesn't mean very much and to some it does, and all that really matters is that you're listening to yourself.'

'That doesn't *actually* matter, though, certainly not as much as the city.'

'It matters,' I insist. 'And if the city matters more, then ask why your patron god isn't able to get his dick wet elsewhere. However much you're blaming yourself, I'd argue that's the actual problem – the one trying to coerce a girl into sex rather than the girl saying no.'

'No one in this city would agree with that.'

'I don't care about that, I care about what you think,' I push – my voice edged with the anger I'm trying to hold back. I would like to find everyone who has put these ideas in her head and made her feel this way and treat them to the sharp edge of my blade. Aside from anything else, it's too reminiscent of a man who decides that a wife saying no to their marriage is a reason to go to war. If Troy has taught me anything, it's that 'no' is a precious and sacred thing. 'He put you in a position where that wasn't an option that could go unpunished. He's the bastard dooming this city.'

'I . . . I suppose.' She reluctantly agrees.

I leave it there. But I am determined to keep reminding her that she did nothing wrong until she starts to believe it.

'And on the subject of changing your mind, I'd like to stop looking at the strands of my past. I suspect if it was going to make reading the future easier, it would have led to some improvement by now, and I . . . I don't think I can keep running through it all.'

'Of course,' Cassandra promises. 'Are you okay with me trying to read your strands of the future? Because I can try the ones that lead elsewhere – those in the air, even.'

'No, use mine – it'll be easier to test whether they're changeable. Besides, the future doesn't feel as invasive as the past. It's something we're still creating.'

She nods and starts plucking at strings.

Our days shift. We spend our mornings training her ability to read the future and our afternoons trying to decipher vague prophecies.

She's getting better. It's marginal, so slight she refuses to acknowledge the improvement. But we rarely pass a day without her reading *something*.

Deciphering the prophecies is strange. Some are easy to interpret – even if they do not give us the vital clues we need about time, location and the people involved. They seem fictional; it's like knowing Apollo draws the sun across the sky even if you can never truly wrap your head round a chariot hauling it through the air.

Then one day it happens – something specific. Something we can't ignore.

'On the morn of Olympieia, prayers futilely drift, Zeus, preoccupied with Diomedes, grants him might, Scamandrius, alas, shall bear the pain that fate bestows.'

Cassandra clutches at my arm. 'We need to do something. That's my brother!'

I try to think, to see it as nothing more than a game of strategy. What hypothetical advice might I offer?

'The Olympieia – that's an Athenian festival, I think. That's what it means, right? That while they're praying in Athens, Zeus won't be listening because he'll be on the field. And Scamandrius will be, um, injured, by Diomedes.'

'I think so,' Cassandra says, looking at me with frantic desperation but, perhaps, a twinge of hope. 'We have to stop it.'

Herophile is delighted to see me. We take tea at the temple, on the wide terrace that overlooks the city.

I let her speak about the new priestesses, occasionally nibbling on my lip, or blinking a bit too quickly before letting my gaze get caught on the distance.

'Helen, may I ask . . . I hate to pry,' she says, in a tone that implies she very much does not hate to pry. 'You seem distressed.'

I laugh, making it a choking sound. 'I should have known you'd realize. You're too clever. But yes, I wanted to speak to you. Sometimes I feel you're the only person in this city I can trust.'

She's practically glowing. 'Of course you can trust me!'

'I did something,' I say quickly. 'I thought to help, so I sent a letter to a man I know.'

She gives a confused sort of smile, so I continue.

'A man on the Achaean side.'

'Oh, Helen!' she exclaims.

'I know, but that's the issue! I was trying to glean information from him and it worked! He's practically agreed to spy for us. But I don't have any way of getting that information to the people who need it without them asking how I came by it. Speaking to another man, even so innocently, could damn me. But speaking to an Achaean, even on behalf of Troy, could convict me of treason. But how could I not? How could I not do all that I could to save this city and its people?'

I bury my head in my hands, letting my shoulders heave as I sob.

Herophile's arms are round me at once and I know then that I've got her – not because she'll care to comfort me nor even that she'll want to help Troy. She'll do it because she's thrilled I've made myself vulnerable to her, that I apparently trust her so much. The illusion of being in my confidence will be a high she'll chase.

'Helen, it will be fine. Your secret is safe with me. What was possibly in this letter?'

'He said that on the morning of the Olympieia there would be a targeted effort on one of the princes. They're seeking to pick them off, I believe. And they're starting with Scamandrius. I was thinking, maybe if they pulled Scamandrius back from the front and got him to advise on strategy on that side instead, then the Achaeans might not be able to fulfil their plans.'

Herophile considers. 'What if I told the council to summon Scamandrius instead of Hector that week? I could say the signs from Apollo indicated his advice was more invaluable than his efforts on the field?'

She's practically glowing with delight – to have a source, to deliver such information, to take up a position of such importance.

'You'd do that?'

'Yes,' she says, smiling, head a little higher already. 'And you're right to use every tool at your disposal. You should keep writing to this Greek man. I can deliver the warnings as omens from Apollo and no one will ever know you're the source.'

I jump to my feet, squealing with real excitement – even if the thing I'm truly excited for is to tell Cassandra the next day that it's all in hand, that Scamandrius will be in a stuffy room in the palace rather than on the field.

But I don't get a chance – I come down to our quiet, barren courtyard and she's already there waiting for me, bloodshot eyes ringed with dark purple shadows, and a shaky grip on a blade far too heavy for her.

She thrusts the sword into my arms.

'Teach me how to use this.'

CHAPTER TWENTY-NINE

Cassandra

'TELL ME WHAT HAPPENED.' HELEN tries to push the sword back on me but I won't let her.

'Nothing happened.' I can barely stand; I can hear my own pulse pounding, have already been sick so many times and might double over again at any moment.

'Tell me what is *going* to happen, then.'

We're going to lose the war.

I'm going to –

We are ensnared in the ropes of ruin.

I shake my head so vigorously Helen looks alarmed.

I can't. I can't tell her and have her not believe me. I can't tell her and have her pretend she does, reassuring me with platitudes she thinks are false. I'd rather keep it to myself than force her to lie to me then resent her for doing so.

'Why, my dear brother,' I mutter, 'are you arming yourself? Are you going to send any of our comrades to exploit the Trojans?'

'Okay, yes, fine.' She shakes her head and examines me with such shrewdness that it cuts through my worry and I feel my cheeks go red. 'All right, let's start with a lap around the courtyard.'

'I asked you to show me how to wield a sword.'

'And without warming up your muscles you won't be able to do so for long.'

'But –'

'Two laps.'

'Helen.'

'Three.'

I run.

At least if I'm thinking about how much I hate running then I'm not thinking about what the future holds.

I've seen Helen train every day, because why not admit that I watch her most mornings, as the sun bleeds across the horizon, and I see her cropped hair and her rippling muscles and her short dresses that are more like men's chitons than women's, and I think of what she said about being beautiful in the way she wants to be beautiful and I hope she is, I hope she's happy, because I recognize two things: that she is, of course, impossibly beautiful; and that the men, when they return, will not be pleased.

The way my muscles burn would have me screaming under any other circumstances but here it reminds me my body is my own – *not the property of the Greek king who captures me* – that I am here – *in a Troy not yet on fire* – in the present – *not in a future too horrible to name.*

She has me stretching and pushing and straining for an hour before she gives me my sword back. She closes my fingers round the hilt, tells me how to hold it in a standard pose, tells me not to let my arm move that much, that it's how I'll end up breaking my wrist rather than their skin when I bring it smashing down.

She kicks at my feet until I move them into the right position, nudges my elbow until I tuck it in, my hips until they're square, my knees until they're bent. She's so close and my heart is still racing from the laps I ran and everything feels so much more intense.

She turns my chin, forces me to look at her, those cold blue eyes more unforgiving than the ocean that delivered armies to our shore. She's so close I can feel her breath on my skin.

'You look a man in the eyes when you kill him.'

She lets go and I laugh a little derisively. 'What use is honour in a war like this?'

'It's not honour; if you follow his blade, you'll watch as it pierces you. You look up, you see movement in the corner of your eye, you feel the wind cut across you and you react to what you can sense.'

She flips her own sword in her hand and smiles, a grin that tells me she knows precisely how she looks, knows exactly what it is she's doing to me and can she tell me, please, because I feel at once deeply uncomfortable and also like I might never catch my breath again.

I grit my teeth, level my own blade at her and focus.

Iron clashes and I don't think any more, just lift my blade again and swing.

I'm exhausted when we finish and even she is gasping for breath. I am too weary even for my own despair, my hopelessness a distant echo in my skull compared to more immediate needs: food, rest, to peel these sticky clothes from my skin.

Helen and I sit in the shade of the palace walls, stretching our legs out, our swords abandoned next to us.

'I take it we lose the war,' she says.

And I don't know how to react to that. Is it convincing her of a prophecy if I don't say it, simply let my actions speak for me?

She hums softly. 'Yes, I thought as much.'

It shouldn't surprise me. Haven't I been screaming for months that Paris dooms us all? I just hoped it was somewhat hyperbolic. But there it was, all laid out for me: the city on fire, the men and boys dead, the women and girls in chains on the beach, being distributed with the rest of the treasure to men who hate us for keeping them from home for so long.

And the worst part: how unyielding it was. These weeks of honing my ability to read the strands have sharpened my awareness of which are flexible, which could yet weave a new shape, and which form that iron core, unbreaking stone, as strong as the very walls themselves – which still stand even in my visions, ringing a city of flames. This future is the foundation for all the other futures to come, the solid, enduring strand at the heart of it all.

And no amount of plucking threads or swinging a sword can change it.

'So what do you want to do?' she asks.

I try to envisage any form of 'want' that isn't my city safe, my family by my side or my head quiet. What drove me here, of all places? *Want?* Helen stretching each morning in the golden sun, sharp edge of a blade catching its light. And here I was, weapon in hand.

'I want to hurt someone,' I confess – and why does everything with Helen feel like a confession? 'I want to make someone else bleed before I do.'

Helen doesn't seem alarmed – does not laugh or scold. She considers. 'Well, I don't know about making him bleed, but if you want to make someone hurt, what about getting revenge on Apollo?'

'Apollo's not the one who kills me.' I don't think about it, the words just rush out as quickly as any prophecy ever has.

'Who –'

'It doesn't matter.'

Because how do I even begin to put that into words? How do I say: *It's your sister?* And *Yes, yes, that does mean I'm dragged across the ocean by your husband's brother, torn from my family, forced into servitude*, and *No, that's not the worst thing that happens to me*, and *Your sister, yes, Clytemnestra* – and *Don't worry, Helen, because they can try to squash the Sparta from you both, but it's a war axe she wields when she buries it in my neck, and it's your eyes I see when she does.*

How do I say that, by that point, it feels like a mercy?

'I could run you through with this blade right now,' she says.

'I'd rather you didn't.'

'What I'm saying is, no future is definite.'

But parts of it are. Parts are immutable. Parts like *Troy will fall*, which still rings through my ears.

'It doesn't matter,' I say. 'What's another horrific prophecy in a long line of them?'

'One too many, I'm guessing. I'm here, Cassandra, talk to –'

'For the sake of Olympus, is this where you've been hiding?'

Kreousa appears from the shaded portico that lines the palace, her expression rapidly shifting from shock to delight as she spies the swords lying in the dirt.

'You're training Cassandra? Can I join?'

Everything I saw last night – that long, churning nightmare – spins through my mind once more. And I realize that I didn't see Kreousa.

Maybe she makes it out of here.

It's a slim hope, but I grasp it.

'You want to spar?' I ask her. She always hated the wooden training swords forced on her when she was young, before they led her to dance classes instead. Though she never really liked that either, or anything, really, that kept her from the library.

She glances down. 'It's foolish, I suppose. I spoke to Father, hoping I could help, but he told me that waiting in this palace giving the men something to defend was more helpful than any other strategy I could offer, and I can't just sit here. Maybe if I feel I could defend myself if the Achaeans get past the walls, I'll be less terrified of every loud noise and sudden movement.'

Kreousa toys with the fabric of her dress before wringing it so tightly it creases beneath her fingers. I realize how awful these last weeks must have been. To have the very thought of war on her mind at all times, and her brothers fighting in it . . . Well, it doesn't sound all that different from my prophecies.

'You should train everyone,' I suggest. 'I'm sure Kreousa isn't the only one who could use the reassurance of knowing how to fight back.'

Is that part of why I came here too? In the hope my future might feel less terrifying if I at least think I have a chance?

Helen worries a nail between her teeth. 'I don't know. I wouldn't be a match for half the men on that field. I don't know what I could teach that would be valuable or worth the time.'

'It would be good for morale,' I insist. And I think it would make her feel better. She's found such purpose in helping me with the prophecies that I imagine this might really make her feel at home. And I want that – for her to think of Troy as home. I really do.

Her shrewd eyes pin me in place. 'Do you think it would help the direction of the war?'

Nothing will remould that very horrific future waiting for us.

But could smaller tweaks be possible? Maybe we can't stop it, but could we postpone it? Could we enable a few people to get out and survive?

'I don't know,' I say honestly.

'I'll think about it,' Helen says. 'I can just about get away with practising out here by myself. If I start offering classes to every woman in the palace, the king or the council might not be so forgiving.'

'You're not planning full Spartan agoge, are you?' Kreousa asks. 'I read you all wrestle naked. That you're cast out and encouraged to steal to survive, to –'

'I was thinking simple combat,' Helen says, flushed.

'Why don't you just start with Kreousa?' I suggest. 'You two have fun, I'm going to head in.'

'Are you sure?' Helen asks quickly. 'We can begin tomorrow, if you want me to –'

'I'm all right, honestly,' I say, eyes locked on her.

Because I didn't see Helen in that carnage either.

Maybe I can't change my own fate, but there's hope for everyone else – and if I spend every second I have left trying to save them, then perhaps it will be worth all the pain I'm going to endure.

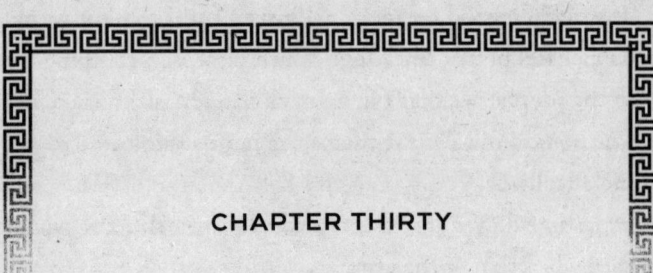

CHAPTER THIRTY

Cassandra

AFTER CLASHING SWORDS WITH HELEN, I am disgustingly sweaty and ready to collapse in a hot bath. I'm so focused on the soreness of my muscles and the promise of warm, soothing water that I do not even see my brother until I nearly collide with him.

Scamandrius's laugh is cruel and loud, a boisterous thing that I have not heard much in these halls in recent months. I always forget how unafraid men are to take up space – with noise, with their bodies, with anything that pushes us aside.

'Well, I'd heard you were a pitiful thing now, Cass, but to wander the palace in such a state is taking it a bit far. Your hair! Your clothes! What happened to the sister who couldn't leave her room without a dozen jewels?'

My relief is short-lived, flickering to annoyance before he's even finished laughing. 'Scamandrius, I should have known you'd be the brother to retreat first. What are you doing here?'

It must be Helen – but how? How did she possibly do this? And will it keep him here long enough to save him?

'I was summoned to advise the council, actually. I was just pouring libations for the gods before I meet with them.'

How did she possibly manage that? I look past reality to the flickering strands. Scamandrius's are different somehow. I reach out, mentally filtering through the strands, each one burning as I flick to ... yes, there it is. The spun threads of prophecy – I do not need to read it to see that it is already fraying at its edges.

It's working. By Zeus, it's actually working.

Helen is a genius. She's brilliant. She's everything they'll never give her credit for.

But I will.

For now, I turn back to my brother with a withering sneer, knowing it will wind him up – Scamandrius can throw out insults quicker than arrows from the parapets but he can't cope with being hit by them himself. 'Do the council know what they're letting themselves in for?'

'Yes, actually,' he snaps. 'They must have heard the rumours circulating around the camps. They want to speak with the city's new seer.'

I'm so baffled that for a moment I think he's talking about me, that the council want *my* opinion.

Then I catch the cruel shine in his eye.

'We're at war! Now is not the time for you to lie your way into a position of prominence. And you could at least be a bit more inventive than to steal my –'

'Deal with Apollo?'

My words catch so suddenly my lips tremble on the vacant air. I can't fault Scamandrius for his snorting chuckle – I'm sure my floundering is quite the comedic sight.

He pushes open a nearby door. 'Let's not do this in the hall. Shall we? I'm sure the council can wait a moment longer.'

I follow him wordlessly into the small room – clearly the study of some councillor. We definitely should not be in here, but I fall into the rough-hewn wooden chair beside the long low desk still scattered with parchment and ink.

'What did you do?' I ask as Scamandrius settles opposite me, no longer trying to stop the satisfied grin that he has managed until now to keep at bay.

'Apollo is fighting down there with us. We've spent a great deal of time shoulder to shoulder. And, after some discussion, I made the deal you reneged on.'

'I didn't renege on anything – is that what he told you?'

'Yes, yes, he did.' The corners of his lips twitch in smug amusement. 'And given he honoured our deal, I'm going to believe him on this one.'

'Yes, I think not believing me was part of the curse he levelled. So you don't care that he did that to me?'

Olympus above, I . . . I can't tell anyone what happened to me, and here's my brother, finding out of his own volition and siding with the man who did it.

I'm saving him right now because I love him, even if I can't stand him. And he's contemptuous. Hateful. And breaking my bloody heart.

'Don't sulk, Cass. I'm here. I'm providing the prophecy, so you don't need to.'

'You fucked Apollo for prophecy, then?'

He laughs, shakes his head and sighs to himself. 'Darling sister.' I wince because those are Apollo's cadences and I don't like what that implies. 'Have you seen him? I would have fucked him for nothing. But sure, I'll happily take prophecy if he's offering it.'

So this is Apollo's move. I was a fool to think he would be focused on the war – of course he would do something like this.

'So what have you seen? Can you help?'

Scamandrius shrugs. 'It's coming slowly but surely. I suppose the main thing is that Paris isn't going to survive the war. So I'd like to spend some time with Helen while I'm back.'

If it were anyone else, I might ask what they meant.

But with Scamandrius, it's fairly obvious what he intends.

'You're repulsive.'

'If Paris dies, she'll go to one of us. I can't imagine Deiphobus will want her, but he is older, so he'd be offered her first. If I seduce her now, then I might be able to claim her before he can.'

'She's not an item to be inherited!'

He shrugs. 'We're fighting a war over her – of course we will have to keep her if Paris dies.'

Keep her. Like she's a pet.

I stand so abruptly the chair falls behind me.

'You're an idiot, and Helen will destroy you. Stay away from her.'

'Calm down, you crazy –'

I laugh almost hysterically. 'You know, I am so sick and tired of everyone calling me crazy. You know Apollo cursed me. You're seeing the same things I am. How long until people call you crazy too?'

'They'll call me a seer. You, on the other hand, are a mad hag who always thought she was better than everyone else.'

'Not everyone, just you,' I say, which is untrue. I thought I was magnificent. Looking back, maybe I was.

'I don't even think they believed you *were* crazy at the start. I think they just wanted to see you fall. Not now, though. Now they're waiting for an opportunity to lock you up. And, unlike you, I have the self-control not to scream the prophecies every time a room falls quiet.'

'Do you think it's news to me that "crazy" is little more than an excuse to sideline the women they don't like? But I'm still loved by the people who matter and I'm still trying to save this city rather than serve myself. Whereas you? Scrounging other people's gifts, other people's wives – what a repulsively desperate effort to achieve power.'

Power he could have had by simply being clever or brave or working hard. All my life I've wanted to shake him until he realizes he's a prince – male and royal and with the whole world before him. But he was too busy looking at the rest of us, trying to work out what we had that he had been denied.

Scamandrius stands calmly, but his eye is twitching.

'I don't even know why I'm wasting my time with you. Apollo is right – it's going to be fun to watch you drive yourself into ruin.'

CHAPTER THIRTY-ONE

Helen

I HAVE BECOME MORE OBSESSED WITH the prophecies than Cassandra – even as I bristle at each word I read. Every spare moment, snatched between war efforts and visits to the people and greeting the occasional visiting dignitary, is spent poring over these pages.

As I skim one now, I don't realize I'm not alone until Clymene leans over my shoulder.

'What are these? Riddles?'

'Um, of a sort.'

She plucks it from my fingers. 'I wish I hadn't seen this. I can't stand an unsolved puzzle. I won't be able to sleep until it's answered.'

'My cousin Penelope is the same,' I say, hit with a sudden wave of homesickness so strong I could double over.

But Penelope is married to Odysseus and lives on Ithaca now.

And my sisters left home long ago.

And Polydeuces and Castor are constellations in the sky.

And Sparta is . . .

It's not homesickness, it's grief. Longing for something non-existent, something practically buried.

'What's she like, Penelope?' Clymene asks. 'You never talk about home.'

Because any talk of Sparta could be seen as a betrayal of Troy.

And Penelope is an especially dangerous topic – her husband is one of those kings on the field, leading armies against us. And, knowing Odysseus, he's probably leading on strategy too.

But I want to talk – and, as much as I've loved sharing with Cassandra, I think speaking of it only in whispers in the shade of the palace is making it feel more secret than it needs to be.

'She was the cleverest person I've ever met. When the men gathered to bid for my hand there were a number of schemes afoot to secure it. One time we intercepted a coded message, written on a beeswax tablet. There were strange symbols carved into the wax and my father assembled the smartest men fighting over me to decode it. They had it for days and they couldn't – then Penelope went right up and wiped the wax away. They were furious. But there it was – the real message carved into the wood beneath. Odysseus proposed to her on the spot.'

And if I had to bet, I'd say she created the tablet for that sole reason – let it be found, let it give her the opportunity to impress the man she'd been fawning over since he arrived.

'That's actually rather sweet. My husband proposed six times – I kept turning him down. Of course, it doesn't help that the first time he tried, we were seven and he offered my father a jar of pretty shells he'd found at the beach.' Clymene's hand flutters to the chain at her throat, and I realize what I always took for beads are crushed shells, a pearlescent scallop dangling from its centre.

She smiles, but it's sad and wistful – filled with all the fear she doesn't want to give voice to about her husband on a battlefield. I offer one of my own – sympathetic but not without its own deep sorrow, something that goes beyond jealousy, like watching a tragedy but still hoping the end might differ this time. Like I know I'll never have love like that, but I can't help but hope for it anyway. And my hope rising just gives that little bit further for my disappointment to fall.

'Now.' She swallows thickly and nudges the page closer. 'Let me try to work this out.'

She stares intently at the paper for minutes – not even looking up when Athrae arrives.

'What are we doing?' she asks.

'Solving a riddle.'

'Why?'

I think of Penelope.

'We think they're coded messages from the Achaeans. But we can't break the code.'

I don't enjoy lying to my friends, but Cassandra's secrets are not mine to tell.

'One of your sources, I assume?' Athrae says with an amused shake of her head. 'I can't believe you've been here a handful of months and already have a network of spies at your disposal. Let me have a look, then, pass it here.'

Clymene shows her.

Athrae barely glances at it. 'What do you mean? It's quite clear. Look: "As Selene blinks" – it means on a new moon.'

'Yes, but it's the "Medea rises fierce" part that's throwing me,' Clymene says.

'That doesn't say "Medea", it's "Medeon". It's a Boeotian fortress. This is saying the Boeotians will raid the camps on the next new moon. Which sort of makes sense – the night will be dark and they can take our army by surprise. But they couldn't actually get close enough to do that, so I don't think your source is accurate.'

Clymene stares at Athrae.

'Helen,' she says, not looking away from her. 'Please pass me one of the other riddles. I'm not having her beat me on this.'

Athrae's eyes light up. 'Oh, accurate or not, I love a challenge. I'll take another too.'

So we spend the evening decoding them, unconvinced of the prophecies we unravel even as we make sense of them, a constant shift from sharp excitement at understanding, to doubt as the curse takes hold. But we push through in the name of competition and the next morning I take the advice yielded to Herophile, who heads straight to the council to relay it.

I tell Cassandra in a breathless yelp – and I'm so thrilled, so happy – but I'm not expecting her to be too. I am too familiar with my intent optimism and her jadedness to hope otherwise.

But she throws her arms round my neck and we jump up and down and I hold her waist, lift her, spin her.

I don't want to let go.

Not when she leans back and looks at me with the sort of smile I'd like to immortalize in stone.

And, in that moment, I become cruel.

I send a prayer to the Heavens that the war will never end.

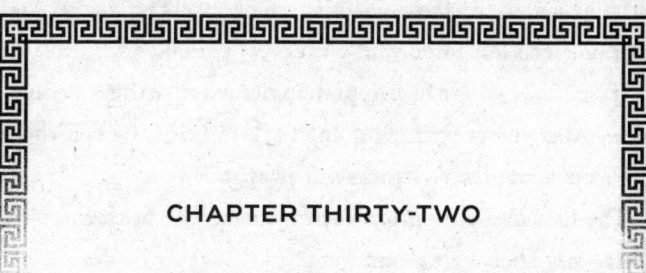

CHAPTER THIRTY-TWO

Helen

CLYMENE AND ATHRAE BRING FRIENDS, and soon there is a covert network of ten women decoding Cassandra's prophecies – or, rather, the messages my supposed contacts are apparently intercepting from the Achaeans. Herophile's advice proves so effective the council are calling her in every day. And though Cassandra's prophecies still grab her unawares, she grows better at navigating their revelations with every morning spent in the shady courtyard plucking at threads.

It's working, it must be. True, there are no reports that we are winning, but there are certainly fewer that we are losing, and for now that feels like a win.

Among the women working through the prophecies is Kreousa – and she mentions the fact she's spent the last few weeks training with me and now all the women are clamouring to learn. I protest but they combat my every excuse: finding temples we can practise in, unlocking the gymnasiums where the men no longer train, and gathering crude weapons for us to use. Finally, I run out of reasons to refuse them – except for that most important one: *it might make the men angry*. And that one feels less important with every passing day.

If we are weaving a future, perhaps it looks like this – because I can't imagine everything going back to normal when those gates open and the Achaeans sail away.

The first day, I train fourteen women. The next, there are thirty-six. Then eighty-one.

Polyxena arrives with one of the maids – Ligeia, I think – and demands to be allowed to learn too. Ligeia looks apologetic, like she's already tried to dissuade the eight-year-old princess from a thing like this. But why should she? Spartans wrestle and Trojan boys wield wooden swords at just as young an age.

'Let's find you something to fight with, then,' I say, and she joins more than a hundred others who are gathered and waiting for class to begin.

It's exhilarating and purposeful and awful because Cassandra isn't there.

Andromache seems to feel the same way – though at first she wasn't interested in learning how to fight.

Then her city fell. News reached us a few days ago. Andromache told me she'd been warded here since she was a child, so I don't know how close she still is to her family back in Cilician Thebe, but she spent days locked in her room, only letting Cassandra see her, before arriving at a class one day with a spear in hand.

'Where in all of Troy did you get that from?' I asked. Most women were clutching broom handles and loom weights, the few lucky ones with wooden training swords or rusty, broken weapons from discarded piles in the barren armouries.

'I asked Hector for it. He didn't hesitate, although he did request that I learn how to wield it properly – something about my coordination paired with a weapon being more terrifying than our invaders.'

The joke fell flat, her eyes downcast but edged with a steely determination. I saw what Cassandra meant, about the reassurance – to know that if the Achaeans make it past our walls like they did Cilician Thebe's, Andromache might stand a chance where her family did not.

Now she's easily my best student, having picked up manoeuvres like steps in a dance. One day, she lingers after a class.

'We need to do something,' she says. 'Every woman in the palace is here but not Cassandra.'

'I'd love nothing more than for Cassandra to be here. But she doesn't want to. That's her choice.' She's kept jogging, saying she likes the way it makes her thoughts quiet. But she's refused every invite to join us and fight.

'Is it? It's every woman in the palace – half of them have made it very clear she's not wanted wherever they are. Her own mother asked her to leave the dining hall. I just don't even think it's a case of giving her the option any more, we have to actively undo all that and make her feel welcome.'

She has a point. So a few mornings later, as we explore the threads – no longer mine, moving on to those running through the air itself, drawing the weave of the world – I clear my throat.

'So, I know you don't want to learn combat,' I start hesitantly, in part because I'm so distracted by the work she's doing.

Her fingers flitter out in front of her like she is detangling the invisible threads.

She's majestic – her eyes shut, reaching out for things few will ever see. To hold such incredible power, to demand it yield to her will . . . there are times she seems more god than mortal.

Her eyes open and I glance away, as though I do not want her to know I have been looking.

'I didn't mind the combat,' she admits. 'It's the classes – they're too loud and busy and, well, it doesn't matter. My time is better spent in prophecy anyway.'

'It's your choice,' I say. 'And if you want to learn, but not attend the classes, I'm happy to teach you. But if you do want to join us, I went to the temple of Demeter. Since the grain was rerouted in case of a siege, they've brought cushions and sofas into their storerooms – so if you needed to rest, or step aside for prophecies, there's a space for you. And I've adjusted some of the drapes in the room so that there's a section where sound doesn't carry far, where you could run the risk of saying something without worrying about being overheard and disbelieved. And I'm not particularly tolerant – if someone is an arse to you, then they can learn how to use a sword elsewhere. They can leave. Not you.'

'You don't have to do all that.'

'All what? Hang a curtain?'

'I . . . All right. I'll try.'

Cassandra looks vulnerable in a way she so rarely does – her slight frame curling inwards, her eyes downcast, her arms clutched tight to her sides.

'I'm sorry,' I rush. 'I've done this wrong – look, you shouldn't say yes just because you feel like you have to and you think I've gone to such trouble. I really haven't – and I don't want you to come just because . . . well, no, I mean . . . Look.'

Cassandra chokes out a watery laugh. 'Olympus above, I've never known you lost for words. I thought you were silver-tongued.'

'Rumours of my sexual prowess aren't what we're discussing right now.'

Cassandra flushes and I look away. It is excruciating – this growing awareness of the parts of her I would like to hold close. Her hesitant laugh, her flustered blush, the wry arch of her brow, the exasperated ring of my name on her lips . . .

I swallow hard, like I could force such feelings down too.

'I just want to make sure you have a choice. And Andromache brought it to my attention that, without such efforts, maybe it wasn't really a choice at all. If there's anything else you can think of that would help, then let me know – and if you still don't want to, that's truly fine.'

She nods but she's not looking me in the eye. 'It would mean more time with you, I suppose, but I'm sure I can cope.'

There's something about the way she says it that makes me wonder if maybe that's the real reason she says yes.

And there it is, the same feeling as when Clymene showed me her necklace of shells: long-smothered hope surging to the surface, just waiting to be dashed against the shore.

Cassandra insists on walking 'the long way' back from training, often taking us on hour-long detours through parts of the city. It's beautiful, but it's nothing compared to her joy at seeing it all, at showing it to me.

One day she takes me to an orchard on the edge of the acropolis, where the stone floor runs into natural mountain rock and, where they meet, grass grows. It's small, more symbolic than anything. But I insist on climbing the largest tree for the juiciest figs, bringing armfuls back down for us, dusting the dirt from my hands on to my dress. When we sit beneath its boughs, I turn to Cassandra. Juice clings to her lips.

It's terribly distracting.

For a second, just a moment, I imagine what it might be like to taste it, my lips against hers, heady and sweet, protected from prying eyes by the boughs of the trees. A perfect secret.

But I shake myself. My mind is slotting Cassandra in where she doesn't – where she *can't* – belong.

No one can. Not when the love between Paris and me fuels a war outside those walls.

'What do we need to do next?' Cassandra asks. 'To change things?'

'I suppose that depends on what you've seen.'

She nods. 'There's something – but it's more what I can't see. Kreousa's threads are a knot so tangled I can't find the trailing ends to even begin to pick them apart.'

'So that means . . .'

'Possibly nothing. But I think it means she's important – and I think we need to get the council to listen to her.'

'We'd have greater luck convincing my father to remain faithful. But maybe we can get her advice through the same way as your prophecies?'

'It's worth trying.'

It has always been the real tragedy of Cassandra's curse: she would have struggled to get the men to listen to her anyway – and they never would have valued her truth above their own egos and bravado.

Every woman in this city might as well carry a part of that curse in her: that we will always have to fight to be believed, to matter, to be heard.

And maybe, together, we're getting a little louder.

CHAPTER THIRTY-THREE

Cassandra

'GOOD EVENING, LITTLE PRIESTESS.'

Apollo's voice cracks across my calm like thunder, a violent intrusion.

I should have known something was wrong. Every single night since the war began, my dreams have been filled with clashing violence and bloodied corpses. But here I am, sitting on the beach, staring at the ocean, not a ship in sight.

'I'm getting home visits now?' I don't turn. I don't indicate that I care. But I can feel my body straining to wake me up.

'It's a dream, dear.'

'Yes, I gathered from the lack of war.' In my visions, the beach is crowded with Achaean camps, bonfires mixing with funeral pyres in a stomach-churning haze of sickening, choking smoke. I rise to my feet and turn to face him. 'Dream visits. Should I be honoured that you chose me and not whichever nymph you're currently chasing?'

'Yes, darling, you should. You're all the talk in the camps – the mad princess, the fallen priestess. You should hear the things they'd like to do to you. I have to admit, it's making me rather jealous, hearing your name on their unworthy lips.'

I know he's trying to rile me, to repulse me – that everything he does is for a reaction and the joy he takes in hurting me.

But that doesn't change the fact that it's working – that my disgust is so strong I could be persuaded to abandon all my efforts to save those repulsive men.

I manage not to show that he's getting to me only because my rage is tempered by my relief.

He's here to annoy me, not hurt me. Which means he is not here to punish me for navigating prophecy despite his best efforts to expel me from it. He might not even know.

'Are you lonely, Apollo? Is that why you're here? Most of your family side against you in this war. Is a former priestess the closest thing to a confidante you have left?'

He laughs, but from the glint to his eye I'm sure I've hit close to the mark. 'You are no former priestess.'

'I've been stripped of my station.'

He tuts, waving a dismissive hand. 'Please, those people don't speak for me, however much they might claim to. You didn't pledge yourself to the temple, you pledged yourself to me.' He steps towards me and I move back instinctively, hating myself for doing it, for the way he smiles at my retreat. 'It will take more than breaking a statue to get out of your vow. You belong to me, Cassandra.'

'I have no interest in my brother's sloppy seconds.'

He laughs uproariously. 'I have half a mind to haul you to Olympus, sometimes, to drag you down an aisle and make you mine forever.'

'First you try to coerce me into bed, now you appear in my

dreams threatening marriage vows and a place on Olympus. What's next? Or are you out of cards to play?'

'You can't tell me you don't feel this draw between us – the way we inflame one another. You're not just some – what was it you said? – *nymph I'm chasing*. You run circles through my mind. You spark fury like I've never tasted. What is that but the madness of love?'

Is this what his time on the field has done? Expanded his desire to possess me beyond my body and into my mind and heart? Like his conquest will only be complete when I am the sun drawn across his sky, locked in his orbit.

'I only feel things for other women,' I say as matter-of-factly as I can, like I'm not outing myself to the enemy.

'I'm not a mortal man, Cassandra. I'm a god. I'm the exception. I can take you to the very Heavens themselves.'

'Very well, Apollo,' I say. 'Let us say that I forgive you, that I accept the curse and do not beg for its removal, that you haul me to Olympus and you give oversight of prophecy to me, make me the goddess of the oracles for evermore. And I will love you in the only way I possibly can: with fierce platonic adoration. Would you be happy?'

'I don't want your friendship.'

'Then you don't love me at all.'

'If I did not love you, I would not grow so angry every time I hear the men in the camps speak your name. To think of them, envisioning you the way only I can? I've never felt rage like it.'

'Love isn't proven by jealousy, it's corrupted by it.'

He smirks. 'Poetic words – and I the god of poetry. Tell me more about how we do not belong together.'

'By that logic, you should sleep with every poet in Anatolia.'

'I have and I will,' he dismisses. 'But you are more than that.' He reaches to brush my hair out of my face and I lurch away from him.

'Can I go back to visions of horror and gore now?'

He quirks an eyebrow – still no anger, like this is just another stage of courtship. Like he can wear me down. 'Very well.'

With a flick of his wrist I am thrown into a vision.

My youngest sister, Polyxena, now about my age, reassuring our frantic mother. I've seen one of the Achaean men in enough visions to know his name is Odysseus. He tells my mother not to cause a fuss, that it would be smarter to accept this fate.

They cut Polyxena's throat on Achilles' grave, declaring that her spirit will serve him in the afterlife. Even dead men get a share of the spoils of Troy.

I jolt awake, thoroughly disoriented – expecting the still and silent night and meeting the bright midday sun. But of course – Apollo would not visit unless the sun had crested.

I think of those golden threads strumming through Kreousa. Maybe she can guide us to a future where Polyxena lives. Maybe I don't need to solve it all myself, just identify the people who might do a better job of it.

It's normally easy to locate Kreousa, and, indeed, as soon as I set foot in the library, I see her belongings on a table, her careful scrolls and quills laid out. She must be in the stacks somewhere, so I wander the shelves until her voice filters out.

'. . . absolute idiot, you cannot be serious, I thought you were smarter than to –'

She spots me and flushes deep red.

Aeneas leans against the shelves, smirking at her tirade. His arm is in a sling that pulls his chiton down a little, the dark brown skin at his shoulder marked with angry lines, chafed by his own armour.

'Can I help you?' I demand. I can't imagine what he's done to deserve it but my fists curl, knowing it must be terrible to have Kreousa shouting like this — especially in a place as sacred to her as a library.

'No, no, it's fine,' Kreousa says. 'Come on, let's go.'

'I'll be seeing you later, then,' he says dryly but still with that stupid smile on his face. 'A pleasure, as always.'

'Oh, go to the crows.'

He chuckles as he walks away.

Kreousa turns back to the books and I get the feeling it's to avoid looking at me. She's still flushed, her hands clenching at her sides.

'So,' I start.

'Oh gods,' she groans.

'Do you want to tell me what that was about? What did he do?'

'He got injured,' she says quietly.

I'm confused for a moment, and then I get it.

'Oh.'

'Yeah.'

'So that means . . .'

'Yes, Cassandra,' she snaps, clearly furious with herself and not with me. 'I'm fully aware of what that means.'

'Okay, well, um, I'm here if you want to talk about it.'

'Like you'd get it. What do you know about love?'

I flinch.

'I didn't mean it like that,' she says with a frustrated sigh. 'But you've never been in a relationship. Have you ever even liked anyone?'

Andromache – but now I'm doubting myself. The things I wanted with her – time together, soft touches, longing gazes meeting across a dance floor – I'm aware there's something missing from that equation.

I am drawn to a pretty face in the way of art – a wish to look, to admire, to revere – not to ruin with a touch. And if I think of touch ... I simply wonder why. No repulsion, no desire, just a strange sense of bafflement.

Like when the temple first preached about keeping our virginity intact and I couldn't understand why they were harping on about something so easy to accomplish – like if we were not constantly vigilant, we might trip and land on a phallus. Celibate relationships were banned too, like it was naive to believe they were even possible. Everyone seemed to think that the moment we were alone with the object of our affections, the allure of their genitals would overcome us and we'd be ravenous beasts, stripping off robes and coming to in a daze once it was all over.

Who am I to give advice when I don't even know if what I've felt is what everyone else means when they speak of things like love?

'So you love him,' I say instead of answering.

She deflates, wilting like autumn leaves curling as they fall.

'There's no place for love in a war,' she whispers and grasps the shelves like she can't hold her body up without them.

Love caused this war. At least, that's what the stories will say.

'Love is the only thing that makes war bearable.'

It's certainly the only thing holding me together – the only thing I still have to fight for. If I didn't have people in my life who I cared for, what would be the point of it all?

Kreousa nods, slowly, more to herself than to me.

'Damn it,' she whispers. 'What did you want, anyway?'

I don't know whether to let her move on so quickly but suspect she might need some time to sit with the revelation that she's in love with the boy we've all been saying she's in love with for the last four years.

So I get to the point. 'We might have a way of getting the council to listen to us, but it involves a very obscure back channel. I wanted to know what advice you'd give them.'

She perks up. 'Allies – our biggest issue is that our allies aren't coming through in the way we need them to. The Achaeans have most of Greece on their side. So let's get more of Anatolia to come to our aid.'

'They've tried –'

'I know. But what if we could get the Amazons to side with us? Once men find out an elite tribe of warrior women are joining the fray, they're not going to want to be shown up as cowards who did not fight. We might even get allies from far further afield – Thrace, Paeonia, maybe even Ethiopia. Few will wish to miss the glory of partaking in so legendary a war.'

'So how do we get the Amazons?'

'The men are framing the war as some macho defence of who has a right to Helen. The Amazons won't care for that – but they might care to defend a woman who made a decision to leave her husband. The idea a man is waging a war over a woman making her own choice? Well, hopefully they'll come running.'

'You're a genius.'

'Yes, yes, I am. Now, if you'll excuse me, I need to go bash my head against the wall for a little while. At least until I forget Aeneas's name.'

Helen catches me as I leave the library and I swear there's something about her turning the corner, all her radiance and the excited smile on her face, the way she gleefully yells my name, that makes it difficult to breathe.

'Outside?' I suggest.

We find the shady corner by Hestia's shrine and I climb on to one windowsill, she the other. I explain Kreousa's plan with such enthusiasm I'm surprised the words are even comprehensible.

'That's so easy,' she says, just as thrilled, and the excitement feels like a current between us, taut and irresistible. 'We don't even need the council to get in touch with the Amazons – the letter would be better coming from me.'

'Do you have a way of getting it out of the city?'

'No, but . . .'

'But?'

'Well, you do, don't you? You sent that letter to Menelaus.'

The air chills to a vacuous chasm.

'I'm so sorry about that.'

'I know.'

'Really, I –'

'Cassandra, please. I forgave you for that long ago. Besides, I thought you just wanted me gone for some petty reason. But to stop a war? I might even have done the same.'

My eyes meet hers, the intensity too much, and I glance away quickly, locking instead on the glimmering threads strung between us. There are so many now, and not one of them has let me divine the futures they weave. But one glows now, and I feel it in my skin, in my veins – how deeply touched I am. Not only absolution but understanding.

Sometimes I still think of myself as that perfect, shining princess – and when I reckon with my new reality I feel lost. I've done such terrible things. I don't know who I am any more. But Helen? She sees me more clearly than I do, I think.

She makes me feel found. Like I was never really lost at all.

It takes me a moment to realize she's expecting a reply. 'There's a ship captain who readily takes bribes but he's probably been called to the army.'

'Sailors are useful – especially in securing allies. I'm sure some are still under the council's employ. Give me his name and I'll find him.'

'Perfect.'

'And have you . . . I mean, have you seen anything change? It must, right – getting the prophecies through and training the women to fight, it has to . . .?'

She trails off when I don't answer.

I might be able to direct prophecy a little better, but it's still overwhelming. I am still beaten by its efforts to smother me. But what I do see, with piercing regularity, is a city on fire.

'So that's a no.'

'It's a *not yet*. Come on, don't make me be the optimist here – that's your role.'

'Maybe I'm rubbing off on you,' she teases. 'Just a shame it's not in the fun way.'

'*Helen!*'

She laughs and I can't look away, her smile a captive beacon. Out of the sun, her hair goes from blinding gold to bronze, glistening like a monument to the gods. Her blue eyes take on a tinge of grey but the colour is no longer the most fascinating thing about them, and then I'm gasping as a vision overtakes me.

We're sitting on the roof of the palace, overlooking the city, and she's smiling, framed by the sunset, and she yawns, and her eyes flutter closed. She sighs contentedly, rests her head against my shoulder, and even in the vision I feel its weight.

'*Maybe we should just stay here forever.*'

And then I'm back in the present and Helen is laughing.

'It's a bit dirty for forever,' she says, holding up a tarnished finger.

'Sorry – vision,' I say, fumbling for words.

'Yes, I know. It didn't sound . . .'

'It was good.' I'm not sure I've had anything good before.

'What was it about?'

I shake my head.

I want to keep this one to myself for a little while.

CHAPTER THIRTY-FOUR

Cassandra

I FALL TO THE GROUND, SAND grains piercing my skin, sudden tension released from my body. The vision was brutal – Achaeans sacking the city and me locked in the body of a man hiding his family in their small home. The Achaeans found me – *him* – beat him and dragged him from the house, slitting his throat as he watched the building catch alight.

'We lose the war,' Apollo says, his voice almost soothing against the violent cacophony in my head. I can't help the way I lean into it now, after so many intrusions into my dreams when he has come to brag about plagues sent to the Achaeans or his prowess on the field, or, most startling of all, to simply talk. But his visits are the only thing that pulls me from the worst visions that cross my mind when I sleep. Apollo ends the violence, for a brief while. Which means, despite my every effort not to, I long for his visits to quiet it all.

'Yes,' I say, rising and brushing the sand from my knees.

'You've seen it?'

I nod, short and sharp. He is the last person I want to discuss this with.

'It's fated,' he says, kicking a stone across the beach. He stares at the ocean like it's personally wronged him. 'Some strands of fate are more flexible than others, some threads more ready to be cut. This might as well be iron.'

'Iron can be warped.'

'Don't tell me you still have hope.' He turns and the moonlight casts his face in a glow that softens his usual harshness. He looks younger. He looks desperate.

I don't want to provide him with ammo but I want to know what he knows.

'Yes. I'm only mortal. Hope is all we can do when the gods demand war.'

'Nearly all the gods have sided with the Achaeans, but it's entertainment to them. It's entertainment to the ones on our side too: Ares, Aphrodite, Artemis, when she bothers to join.' He paces angrily, glaring out across the ocean.

'Does it shock you,' I ask, 'to remember we are on the same side of this?'

He stares at me intently but there's none of his usual joy. 'I don't see you as the enemy, Cassandra, I never have.'

No, just something to be conquered.

'Frustrating, though, isn't it? When people make games out of something that means so much to you.'

He stares and stares.

'Tell me about prophecy,' I suggest – realizing that if Helen met a god every time she closed her eyes, she'd have been manipulating answers out of them from the first blink. 'How is it set?'

Apollo's despair shifts. 'That's not for you to know.'

'What am I going to do with the information? If you're

going to visit me every night and share your despair, I would understand it well enough to ease it.'

The words stick in my mouth – but then it occurs to me that they would delight Helen to say, and then they come a little more easily.

'The Fates measure and cut the first threads,' he says, staring at the horizon like if he doesn't look at me, he doesn't have to acknowledge what he's saying – or who he's saying it to. 'Then they fray, smaller threads flying out with every decision made, every brush with Tyche, goddess of luck, who weaves small patches of tapestry whenever she sees fit – otherwise different threads collide, different people meet and the threads knot, continue knotting and weaving, and you're left with the quilt, occasional glimpses of which might be considered prophecy.'

'So an inevitable thread like the fall of Troy is just random?'

His eyes cut to me. 'It is the collective effort of dozens of gods: the Fates, Tyche, Eros, Ananke, Eris and on and on – human will, yes, but how many gods influence that, pushing love and hate into their hearts? And above all else, little princess, above everything else in this damn world – Zeus.'

'Zeus?' I repeat, startled by his sudden vitriol.

'Yes. He loves Troy but he loves power more. He'll bring pain and grief and remind you all just how thoroughly mortal you are. He's been playing both sides, trying to force as much death on to the field as possible, but the end result, the one he's marching us all towards . . .' He trails off, swallowing his words, and when he speaks again, it's with the edge of something malevolent. 'I never asked for prophecy, do you know that? I declared that I would read the will of Zeus for mankind. Those stark, unyielding threads? That's a dozen gods working in tandem to cement *his* will – the scales of fate are his to measure. So when I look into the woven strands and see something so immutable, and it's *my city* falling – that's the grief of my own father working against me. So how would you comfort *that* despair?'

I don't say anything. He is not angry, but something close to it – some indignation that could spark at any moment – and I do not wish to be caught in its crossfire.

'Goodbye, little priestess.'

In the morning, I seek out Helen in the usual places – the courtyard she trains in, the quiet places we hide in and the gynaeceum. Helen isn't there but Andromache is, and when she sees me she drops the linen threads she'd been weaving and runs out after me.

'Looking for Helen?' she asks, not bothering to greet me, and there's a smile on her face I don't particularly like.

'Yes?' I say carefully, but my stomach tightens like it knows where this is going – which means that I, possibly, know something I'm not ready to face.

'You're spending a lot of time with her. And you did spend a good long time hating her, so I have to ask.'

Oh gods, this is the way we used to tease Kreousa, and I . . . This isn't that. It might be. But I'm not sure – Olympus above, I'm not sure and I thought I'd have more time to figure it out before I ever gave it voice.

'Please don't,' I say, but in the quiet whine of the plea it's clear I've already resigned myself to whatever she's about to say.

'Come on, Cass, this is exciting – please don't try to sap the fun out of it. I've never seen you like anyone before and frankly it's hilarious, like you're so used to getting what you want you don't know how to cope with –'

'With my friend who's married to my brother?'

The problem is, I'm not sure how I actually feel because I enjoy convincing myself I'm half in love with people. It's practically a hobby, and certainly a habit. I love longing for someone, ruminating on them. Briseis, Andromache – gods, even, *very* occasionally, Herophile. Beautiful girls for me to idolize and wonder if one day, maybe, in some tangled thread of the future, there might be space for us to . . . well, what exactly, I'm not sure. And that's the problem: I've never really got beyond that very start, my fantasies ending with trembling confessions of love before looping back to the beginning again.

It's almost cruel. I'm not really sure it's even *them* I like but the version of them I romanticize, and I don't want to treat Helen like another amphora for me to pour my affections into.

'You'd make such an adorable couple, though,' Andromache says – which feels absurd, *adorable* a word that applies to neither one of us.

I can't bear to think of this a moment longer so I say: 'Just because you can't cope with Helen and Paris becoming Troy's new favourite couple doesn't mean you can –'

'Excuse me, they are not even in the same league as Hector and me.' Andromache glowers, then seems to realize she fell into my blatantly obvious trap to change the topic. 'I'm not going to drop this, Cass. It's the most exciting thing to happen in weeks. Besides, there's only so long you're even capable of keeping a secret from me.'

*

THE END CROWNS ALL

I almost don't want to see Helen after that, but I need to recount everything Apollo said on prophecy before it twists in my mind and I get something wrong. When I finally find her, I relay it in one continuous stream. Neither of us is uncertain of where it leaves us – if Zeus's will is at the core, we'll never be able to persuade the varied gods who control the future.

So while we wait for a response from the Amazons, we continue in our efforts to shape the tapestry ourselves: training women to fight, decoding prophecy and using Helen's secretive channels to get things to the temples.

Whenever I have a spare moment, I am with Helen. Some days we spar and some we're too tired to do that and sit exhausted, doing little more than talk. Sometimes I can see why Andromache asked me if there was something more, but I'm starting to wonder what could possibly be more about this. Different, maybe, but this friendship is so fiercely acute that it quiets any questions Andromache placed in my mind – because I like whatever this is and it's certainly enough for me.

One day I take her to a bakery in the city and buy her a marbled cake, swirls of colour meeting in the middle, my favourite as a child. Something about that feels unbearably close, like I am sharing too much of myself. In return, she chooses for me a pastry drizzled in honey and nuts, sticky and delicious but not as sweet as the closeness of knowing she'd choose it from the moment I saw it, that honey is her favourite, that I can hold knowledge about her that's only useful in making her happy.

We spend hours in the gardens of the palace, and she tells me about her brothers while we pluck flowers and thread them into crowns that we adorn each other with.

'One of your brothers was immortal. Does that mean you are?'

'No, not all children of the gods have gifts, and immortality is rare even for those who do.'

'I'd be livid if my brother had a divine power and I didn't.'

'I didn't say I had no powers,' she says in the voice of my father. I start and she continues. 'It's quite useful' – Kreousa's voice. 'Mainly for telling people I'm not in when they come asking for me' – my mother's. All of them perfect imitations.

I might be gaping.

'I can do this one too.'

It takes me a moment. 'That is not what I sound like.'

'It is. It's exactly how I, Princess Cassandra, sound. Especially when I tell Helen how utterly brilliant she is, the prettiest, smartest and absolute best princess Troy has ever seen, and how lost we all were without –'

I clap a hand over her mouth, laughing too hard to even tell her to stop. Her breath is warm against my palm. I'm leaning close, and have to jerk away with sudden concern for a thing I can't quite name.

Later, in the library, Helen plucks poetry off shelves and we dramatically read it to each other. Helen particularly loves the erotic ones – telling me that this man has clearly never seen a woman, clearly never spoken to one, clearly never made one happy, and she laughs as I flush, as she calls me a 'Trojan prude'.

We stumble down the wrong aisle. There's Kreousa in Aeneas's arms, their lips pressed together, and frankly I can't believe she'd desecrate a library like that. We rush out before we can ruin the moment for them, slamming the door shut behind us before collapsing against it in hysterical laughter.

*

It takes weeks until the rumours begin – messengers racing ahead to declare that the Amazons are on their way. The council are certain the rumours must be false, but soon there are plans for the princes to return, for a banquet to be held to greet our guests – and for missives to be sent to more allies, should they wish to join and meet the legendary Amazons, perhaps to bring armies to fight alongside them.

The idea of the palace swarming with men again is unsettling.

So, on the night before the life I have become too accustomed to is disrupted, while it's still just us and a city that feels like it is ours, I take Helen to the roof and we watch the lights of the city flicker to life.

'Can I give you a reason to hate me?' she asks.

'I'm sure you can try.'

'I don't regret it.'

'Coming here?'

'Yes. If I could go back, I'd choose to do it all over again.'

She's right. I should hate her.

I reach for her, though I can't look at her while I do it. She jolts as my fingers brush hers and from the corner of my eye I catch the way she turns to face me.

'If I could go back and stop it, I wouldn't,' I say.

She squeezes my hand. I'd expected smoothness, delicate princess hands, which is foolish. There's nothing delicate about her, and she's spent years wielding swords. Her hands are chapped and creased, lined and weathered.

'We're terrible people.'

'Yes.'

'I'd cause a war on purpose to be here.'

But it feels like she's saying something else – or, rather, feels like she's *not* saying something else – and it strikes my core.

I let go, unable to touch her a second longer. Whatever it is I feel, it hurts. It's a physical pain in my stomach, like something I need has been taken.

She yawns and her eyes flutter closed. She sighs contentedly, and rests her head against my shoulder. Its weight is warm, uncomfortable and too close. I can smell her hair, the jasmine soap she uses, and it all hurts more.

The sun is setting over Troy.

'Maybe we should just stay here forever.'

CHAPTER THIRTY-FIVE

Helen

I SET MYSELF UP AT THE loom, surrounded by the other women of the palace and where I will remain until Paris returns.

'I can't wait, can you?' Clymene squeals.

I would wait a century more if I could. I have avoided thinking about Paris, staying too busy to reckon with the confusing mass of feelings knotted inside my chest. I'm scared that once I start unpicking them, they might altogether unravel.

I focus on the threads before me, another distraction for me to cling to.

Athrae works my loom with me, lining the left while I draw the right, both of us walking short paths before the threads. Clymene stands by to retie any weights that come loose.

Without battle, this might be all we do. If we succeed in ending the war in victory, is this the life we are winning for ourselves? I like weaving but it seems such a singular part of who I am to wed myself to.

'The princes have returned and await you in their chambers,' Agata declares.

We rush, putting on a very good show of excitedly returning to our husbands.

Paris is lying on a bed that is definitely *ours* but which for the last few months I've been thinking of as *mine*.

'Helen.' He jolts to his feet, snapping my name with alarm. I struggle to take him in – the finer cords of muscle, the wind-chapped skin, the dark bruise at his collar. And he's staring at me with just as much curiosity. 'For the sake of Olympus, what have you done?'

He rushes to me then, fingers reaching to the tips of my hair – shorn shorter than I'm sure he'd like.

Of course. I should have known that would be the first thing he would notice. But to speak of it before any declarations of love and longing is unexpectedly wounding.

Beauty is what Paris chose, not love. It should not surprise me that he comments on it first.

He looks at me with sudden pity before drawing me into his arms. 'Oh, Helen, I know you must be scared, but it won't work, trying to make yourself less beautiful.'

It shouldn't matter but my gut lurches. I cut my hair to control my beauty – this was intentional. But if it's *less* beauty, then it's *less* value and power.

He presses his lips to mine.

I don't move.

'The thought of you is all that has got me through these last few months,' he says, still holding me close.

'My love,' I say – but it's difficult.

These last few months have made me too comfortable, have

had me lowering my guard and finding out who I am without all the pretence. Now it appears my mask is a difficult thing to wear.

'Helen, come, sit.' He draws me to the edge of the bed – my footsteps dragging. 'I need to talk to you about the things I've heard.'

He is uncharacteristically serious and suddenly I'm running through the things he might be unhappy about. 'You're teaching the women how to fight? Do you not realize how that looks to those of us out on the field? Like you don't trust us to defend you.'

They aren't his words – they never are. When Paris has a thought it's one he's borrowing from someone else – and it turns out I like it less when it's not me filling his mind with ideas.

Clearly the men at our walls are unhappy.

And what would happen if they started to say I was not worth it, that Paris should give me up?

'I love you,' he says softly.

'I love you too,' I say, though it takes me a moment.

I don't know who to be any more. Whether to slot myself into the image of myself Paris is creating – scared, meek and desperate – or to fight against it and hope he likes a different version enough to defend her too. Who would the men be more likely to protect? Who would the women be more likely to trust? There are too many people to please, and I can't find the person I used to so easily become, the one who was just enough to be liked by all.

'Is this all I get? Your silence and your hesitation?' he asks, rage creeping in where it never was before. 'I have spent day and night *killing* people for you, Helen. Do you understand that? Not even the moral struggle of actually taking a life but the sheer exertion of it, metal jammed into flesh and wrenching it all apart. Swords are heavy, Helen. Armour is heavy. I'm exhausted.'

The words slip back to me, piece by piece: *Pleasant. Gracious. Agreeable.*

'Of course, you must be exhausted,' I echo, climbing on to the bed and reaching for his shoulders. He twitches away from me but I grasp him anyway. 'My worry has similarly drained me, my love. Please give me a moment to just . . . delight in the fact you are here.'

And, slowly, he relaxes into my massaging fingers.

'I'm sorry,' he says. 'I know the women fighting are just trying to deal with their fear. But we all are. We don't need reminders of what might happen if the men make it past the walls.'

'How has it been?' I ask softly, moving to sit beside him. I can still be his friend. Can still be whatever he needs me to be – and right now I'll be someone to confide in. 'I can't even imagine it.'

'The things I have seen are not for a woman's ears.'

'I would take that burden if it would ease yours.'

It's the only kind of love I can offer him – to suffer for him. I sometimes fear it's the only kind of love I can offer anyone: to make their life easier, to take their hardships, to make myself invaluable.

Paris takes my hand and tells me of the things he's done and the people he's seen until bells chime through the palace, gathering us together, announcing our guests' arrival.

Paris leans his head against mine before we part, his fingers woven through my too-short hair.

'I did not know how much I needed this. Still, it doesn't feel the same, does it? That blissful joy we once called ours.' He draws away, offering a sad, wistful smile. 'I hope we find it again.'

For the first time, I wonder if I'm not the only one performing a love I don't believe in.

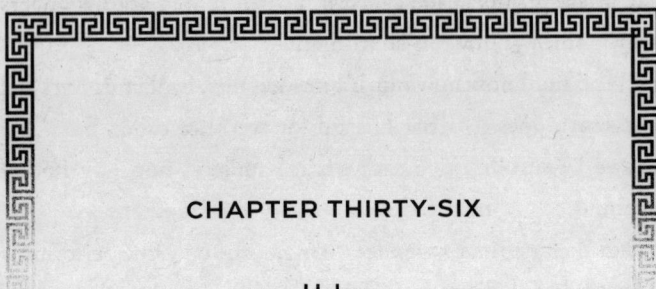

CHAPTER THIRTY-SIX

Helen

THE AMAZONS AND A HANDFUL of the allies pile into the city an hour before dusk. I follow the others to the palace gates, awaiting their envoy. Paris moves to stand with Hector and their father. I slot myself in next to Cassandra.

She is craning her neck over the crowd. At this angle, her jaw is sharp, her eyelashes long, and I can see the pulse jumping at her throat.

I press my lips together. It's becoming increasingly difficult to ignore how beautiful Cassandra is.

I had a string of lovers for years, jumping from one to the next until I took marriage vows and it became too big a thing to risk. It appears that without that *want* for Paris, my romance-primed brain is latching on to her.

I wish Paris weren't at the banquet tonight. I wish I could find a stranger – a mysterious king from a foreign land or a ferocious Amazon – and relinquish some of this hunger in me, starved for a scrap of physical affection, for any touch they have to offer.

'You're late,' Cassandra says with a smile.

The Amazons lead the convoy. At their helm, a woman who is nearly seven feet tall, with broad shoulders and muscles that look like they've been carved from stone. Her black hair is shorn short, close to her scalp, and her dark brown skin is marbled by scars.

Behind them, men follow in dusty robes and thick-soled boots.

'That's Prince Sarpedon,' Cassandra whispers, nodding at a fairly nondescript-looking man.

'How do you know?'

His robes are not fine. He wears no clasps, insignias or jewels. He is unlikely royalty.

'His parents tried to arrange a marriage between us. He visited after I'd joined the priesthood. The other boys used to treat my vows as a challenge – not him. He let it be.'

'The bar for men is in Tartarus,' I whisper and she snickers. I stifle my own giggles into my shoulder, unable to believe we're talking through this, let alone joking.

'They must have been concerned about being intercepted by Achaeans,' I say. 'I doubt they have so much as a scroll with their emblems stamped on it in case they were caught.'

Cassandra nods at the Amazons. 'Not them, though.'

Thick furs and skins hang from bolts at their shoulders, their chestplates ornate but worn – intricate shapes dented by blows.

I glance at Cassandra and see she's staring at them too.

'Tell me it's not just me overwhelmed by how stunning they are.'

'Definitely not just you,' she says before the lightest tinge of red touches her deep-bronze cheeks.

Does bonding over strong, hulking women riddled with battle scars count as a form of flirting?

'Thank you all for honouring us with your visit.' King Priam nods. 'We are grateful for your support so far, for your rations and your trade. Tonight we throw a banquet in your honour. Even now the Achaeans raid our neighbouring towns and cities – we pray you consider joining us in defence of Anatolia.'

The men clap.

But the leader of the Amazons steps forward. When she speaks, her voice echoes in the halls – high as a bell but weighted with importance so that each word is like the heavy beat of a marching army.

'We do not consider, Priam,' she says. 'Do you not see us armed for war? We do not come for a banquet. We are here to fight, should we be given a reason to.' Her eyes lock on mine. 'So, Helen, would you care to join us on our journey to the city walls? That should be plenty of time to persuade us of your cause.'

Everyone falls quiet and turns to me. I can feel the burden of their expectation. Zeus above, tell me persuading the Amazons to fight with us is not solely my responsibility. The allies might only be persuaded by the bravery of the Amazons, unwilling to be upstaged by mere women. But what if I drive them away? What if they came all this way just to be unmoved by any speech I can offer?

But I have to try.

I walk in time with their leader, Queen Penthesilea. The twelve other women are behind us, but they're all so tall and powerful they feel like a legion of twice that number.

'Why should we fight for you, Helen?'

'You should not,' I say. 'You should fight against the Achaeans. You have seen what they have done to Sparta. You think they will not rest until every city that sees women as strong and capable is brought to heel?'

Penthesilea grunts. 'Yes, well, that Athens is among the Achaean numbers is a compelling point. Their supposed hero, Theseus, spent a night with my predecessor, Queen Hippolyta, then ran telling tales of how he subdued her, conquered her, won her.'

'Yes, I believe they prefer to see women as victories. I have had run-ins with Theseus myself. He claims he would have waited until I was of age to marry me. I have no faith that that was his plan.'

One of the Amazons behind me spits.

'Priam courts other cities of Anatolia. I imagine there are monstrous men among their ranks too.'

'Probably,' I agree. 'But this war is fought over a man seeing his wife as his eternal property.'

'Is it? Or is it Paris's claim over Menelaus's? You are an object either way.'

I take a breath. 'I love my husband, but I imagine if I wished to leave him no Trojan would raise a sword to stop me.'

Penthesilea considers, staring into the distant sky as though she can see the war unfolding. 'Is it true you teach the women to fight?'

'Yes.'

'Well, I should think that's enough.' Penthesilea turns to her fellow Amazons. 'This war will go down in history. We wish to be a part of it and, though both sides leave much to be desired,

I should think it clear which side we belong on. You may tell Priam that the Amazons fight among you.'

The women roar their support and I could faint. I wish I could grab a sword and charge into battle beside them. I might fall quickly, but what a glorious death.

Then, in a lower voice, she says: 'There is another reason I wished to walk with you. We had a traitor among our ranks. As we travelled through the mountains to avoid the Achaean armies, a man joined us, claiming to be an envoy of the Halizones. But he was Phocian, part of the Achaean army. We found this on his body. I believe he wished to sneak in to deliver it to you.'

She holds out a beeswax tablet, the letters marked clearly in the soft wax.

Dear Helen, I love you dearly. Please consider coming home.
My love always, Menelaus.

'Perhaps they do not have parchment to spare in the Achaean camps. But whatever you wish to do with it seemed your business. We will see you soon.'

CHAPTER THIRTY-SEVEN

Cassandra

THE BANQUET BEGINS SLOWLY, a stream of people entering, announcements that never stop. My agreement with my mother was that I might be allowed to attend if I sat by the door and left if I needed to give voice to a prophecy.

Hector and Andromache enter, strolling down the aisle to their seats at the top of the hall where the rest of my family sit. My heart twinges like a plucked lyre string – I hold my arms tighter across my chest and allow myself a moment to linger in the confusing, bittersweet hurt. My family, gathered and afar, something I can merely watch as though a bystander, wasting whatever time we have left.

But at the same time: hope. This feels like sacrifice, and sacrifices have a cause. We're changing it, aren't we? Polyxena was around my age in the vision of her death – we have years, maybe even a decade. Surely we might weave a new future by then? And if all it costs is my isolation – for me to be pushed aside and to share my prophecies from behind a dozen different layers – then so be it.

I try to imagine that prophetic thread hangs a little looser around Hector's neck. He clings to Andromache, only taking his hand from hers to rest it across her shoulders or hold her waist. Aeneas sits opposite Kreousa, trying to listen to whatever the foreign king beside him is saying, but his eyes keep flicking to my sister like he can think of nothing else. My parents are tired and forcing smiles, but they're the nearest to relaxed I've seen them since the war began, sitting close together like they really might lean on one another if needed.

Olympus above, we might actually do this. We might save them.

My joy is short-lived. I don't even have to turn when the gasps start. Helen, of course. I imagine she looks radiant, her emotions exaggerated beyond belief except that, unlike me, she is believed in all she does. But I don't think I can see her, pretending or otherwise, on the arm of Paris.

There's movement as someone slides into the seat next to me.

'By Zeus, what has she done to her hair?'

I nearly upstage everyone by diving for my brother.

'Aww, you missed me,' Deiphobus taunts.

'Shut up,' I say. 'And yes, yes, I did.'

I pull back, running my eyes across him. No scars. No scratches. The only changes are dark shadows beneath his eyes and muscles that have swollen in size.

'Shouldn't you be up there with them?' I ask.

'Shouldn't you? Besides, I'm not spending my one night off from the front schmoozing allies.' He cranes his head to look at Paris and Helen again. 'Gods, don't they just look overjoyed to be together.'

I finally glance in their direction. Helen does indeed look

beautiful but it's an odd kind of beauty – I'm so used to seeing her windswept and laughing, hoisting a sword or climbing a tree, that seeing her in a floor-length dress with crushed shells shimmering on her cheeks and the short strands of her hair curled about her face feels odd.

She clutches Paris like his arm was made for her to ornament, like she might keep him from the front by the sheer force of her affection.

Then she glances in my direction and my breath hitches, this shared look across thousands of spectators and the hint of amusement glittering in her eyes that makes this not *her* deception but *ours*.

Deiphobus reaches across me to grab the flask of wine.

'The banquet hasn't even started,' I say, though I nudge my cup towards him.

'Ah, but I am a war hero.'

My father stands and begins droning on. 'Greetings, guests, we welcome you to our lands . . .'

I shuffle closer to Deiphobus so I can whisper: 'So where are the others? It can't just be you.'

'I'm pretty sure our dear cousin Polites stole a barrel of wine and Scamandrius invited half the women of Troy to enjoy it with them.'

'Oh, I'm sure Apollo will love that.'

'Gods, you heard about that?'

'Scamandrius bragged about it himself.'

He winces into his cup. 'Urgh, they deserve each other – shame Apollo dumped him, like, a month later.'

'So why aren't you out there getting drunk with the rest of them?'

He drinks his wine, eyebrows shooting up above his cup.

'Aww, you missed me,' I echo his earlier tease.

'Shut up.' He sighs. 'And yes, yes, I did.'

'Come, friends, let us eat!' Father finally finishes his speech as servants enter carrying more food than I've seen in months. This is a gamble: spending our stores in the hope that allies mean we never need prepare for a siege. 'So,' Deiphobus starts, 'I hear Helen has been teaching the women to fight. She's Spartan so I assume she's decent at it?'

I nod.

'Well, that's good – if we lose the war, I like to think you'll be able to stab a few of the Achaean bastards before they raze the city to the ground. Her arms look like she's been doing nothing but hurling discuses since she got here. Not exactly the docile princess Paris has been telling us all about.'

'He seems perfectly happy,' I say, glaring towards them, where his hand rests on her knee.

Deiphobus coughs awkwardly. 'And speaking of happy, how's your love life?'

I'm still looking at Helen and I jolt. 'Oh, non-existent. I . . .'

'You?'

'Actually wanted to talk to you about that.'

'I see.'

'You like men.'

'Yes, perceptive.'

'But you can still know a woman's pretty, right? So how do you tell the difference between that and attraction?'

Deiphobus squints like he doesn't really understand what I'm asking. 'You like girls but still know a man's handsome. Don't you feel a difference?'

It's a good point but I can't really articulate it. 'I think I've just never really wanted closeness with men like I do with women. I want, you know – shared secrets and hands held, romantic dates and –'

'This is all sounding very chaste – which I thank you for, because you're my sister.'

'But that's the point I'm trying to make – my fantasies don't go beyond that. But why not? Sometimes I can wrap my head round it in theory but . . . I mean, if someone undeniably gorgeous is standing close to you, adjusting your grip on your sword, you should be able to work out whether you feel excited or uncomfortable, right? How can it all be this confusing?'

'Ah, right, so we're talking about . . .' His eyes flit to Helen.

'No, of course not. I'm just using that as an example, but someone's nice face shouldn't be a factor in whether I want to hold their hand, should it? Unless I have some kind of draw towards it?'

'Of course it can, if the draw is less the pretty face than the perceived value and how it fits in with your little image of how your life should look. That's what Mother always said to me: "It doesn't really matter if you find her beautiful, Deiphobus, so long as other men do."'

This point I have considered. At length. I have stared from woman to woman, trying to force some feeling and trying to look past the beauty I have been taught. But beauty is everything. How am I supposed to undo that?

'Look, Cass, this isn't an area I'm an expert in. But do you remember that hymn we used to sing to Aphrodite? Something about goddesses who are immune to her, about how she cannot bend or ensnare their hearts?'

I think of Andromache and the years I spent pining for her so powerfully it felt like something in me was breaking.

'My heart can definitely be ensnared.'

'Yes, but what if you have immunity to some kind of love? Like Eros? All that, you know, desire and carnality. Perhaps you can't be shot with his arrows, the same way I doubt I could be shot with one and like a woman – maybe you are safe from all his effects?'

I glance at Helen, Paris's hand on her knee still. Eros. The sort of love that burns, that causes scandals and excitement, that people claim they couldn't live without . . .

'What if I don't want to be immune to eros?'

'Oh, this I do know.' He reaches for his wine. 'You can't change that. Believe me, I've tried. But companionship has many guises, Cassandra. I don't see why you should believe one love so superior to the others. Not all the men out there are fighting for their lovers – whether they're beside them or behind the walls. Some fight for their children, their parents or their friends. Some fight for their annoying little sisters,' he adds pointedly. 'It would be a disservice to think *that* love is less fulfilling than what you fear you may never feel.'

'Thank you,' I say. 'Sorry, I just . . . I guess I always thought it was because I was too young and I'd feel it all one day. Realizing maybe I won't felt like losing some fantasy of happiness.'

Which is a stupid thing to worry about when there is little happiness in the future anyway.

'Connection is what matters, not what form it takes. Especially at a time like this. The only thing that's important is having *something* worth fighting for.'

'Thanks, Deiphobus.' I blink away the tears welling in my eyes. How much easier would these last months have been if I could have discussed them with my brother? Kreousa and Andromache may live close to my heart, but it's always been Deiphobus I've gone to with the things deeply troubling me. 'So how's your love life?'

He reaches for the jug on the table. 'Oh, we'll need far more wine for that.'

CHAPTER THIRTY-EIGHT

Cassandra

HELEN APPROACHES OUR TABLE AS the meal finishes and revelry begins. Every step she takes tugs at that tightly coiled knot in my chest. Her chiton is a rich, dark green embroidered with spiralling leaves and held together by a thick band of gold about the waist. It floats as she walks, clinging to her every line before flowing free again like a soft exhalation. Her eyes are sea foam against it, and a thick hunk of Egyptian peridot is bound in a spiral of gold nestled in the hollow of her throat.

'You're staring,' Deiphobus whispers before she reaches us.

'Prince Deiphobus.' She nods. 'Cassandra.'

'Helen,' Deiphobus says, not making any effort to wipe the smug smirk off his face as he looks between us.

'I won't be a moment,' I tell my brother.

'Oh, sure.' He rolls his eyes but he's smiling. 'Just abandon me the moment I get home from war to talk to someone who's been here the whole time.'

But as I leave he does too, heading to where Polyxena sits with a table of our younger cousins who all cheer his arrival.

Helen wastes no time with pleasantries. 'I want to talk to our guests individually. I feel like I can get them to slip up, reveal their motives for being here or their real hesitations that are keeping them from fighting. And then I could convince them to join us.'

'Right. And how are you planning on going about that?'

'Alcohol, obviously, some batted eyelashes, a tragic tale – probably bring up my dead mother. They all have such strong feelings about their mothers, one way or the other, so that's usually an in. Anyway, what I came to ask was . . .'

Her delay tells me I'm not going to like it.

'Can you get Paris off my back for, like, an hour?'

'An hour?'

'Okay, half an hour, that would be great, thank you!'

'I wasn't agreeing!'

'You were negotiating. So thank you, you're the best.'

'Helen!'

'He's just getting in the way – he keeps cutting in with the most ridiculous segues and you know that I can get actual information here.'

Unfortunately, yes, I do know that.

'What am I supposed to do with Paris?'

'You'll figure it out.' She reaches forward and squeezes my shoulder. 'Thank you!'

And she's gone.

'Coward,' I call after her, though I keep my voice too low to carry.

I glance towards Paris, unable to stop my glare as I do, and find him already watching me. When Helen sits back down beside him he excuses himself and makes his way over.

Well, at least that answers the question of how I even begin to initiate conversation with him.

I recognize that if it's not Helen's fault the Achaeans don't take 'I don't want to be with this man' as a final answer, then it's not Paris's either. But I'm not willing to look past the 'gleefully claiming a woman as his prize' part of the equation. I saw the prophecies. I know he would have taken her whether she agreed or not.

'Um, hi,' he says, appearing before me.

'Hello,' I say shortly, my grip tightening on my cup.

'I . . .' He looks round anxiously. Quite a few heads are turned in his direction but that's to be expected. 'Do you mind if we go somewhere quieter?'

'Why?'

'To talk.'

'Why would I want to talk to you?'

'Oh, um. Please?'

It's such a shame Apollo hates me – I could really do with a god to give me strength right now.

'Fine,' I snap, turning without checking to see whether he's following me.

I take him to the nearby courtyard. It's a warm evening and we aren't the only guests out here, so I lead us to the edge of the fountain where the running water will cover our conversation.

I perch on the fountain's edge and shoot him one of my finest glares. 'Well?'

'I wanted to talk to you.'

'Yes, I got that. Was there something more specific?'

He stares at me, eyes wide, and I could throttle him. This

bumbling fool with his clumsy innocence when he's brought war to our door.

'I'm sorry,' he blurts, and even he looks surprised by what he's said.

'What are you sorry for?' I can't keep the scowl from my face.

'For everything,' he says after a moment, and then it all rushes out of him. 'I'm sorry I ever came to Troy, that I came to the palace, that you tried to find out who I was and all this happened to you instead – the prophecies and the excommunication and everything you've suffered. I'm sorry I chose Aphrodite and I'm sorry that in bringing Helen here I brought all this too.'

Does he take me for a fool? Here Helen and I are, saying we wouldn't change it, and he expects me to believe he would?

'Why are you apologizing to me, of all people?'

'Because I feel like you're the only person who might believe it.'

My stony glower clearly indicates that I do not believe it, so he continues.

'We're at war over this. If anyone else knew that I thought all this wasn't worth it, we'd be doomed. They have to believe it because it's all they have.'

'But me?'

'You already think you know whether we're doomed or not.'

I hear what he's not saying: that I'm his absolution, his listening ear to divest himself of his troubles to so he no longer has to stopper them inside himself. I'm the girl his secrets are safe with, because no one would believe me anyway.

But Helen would.

'You know, there was a fountain at the temple of Tyche in the village where I grew up,' he says obliviously, pacing a few feet, water flecking his robes as drops fly from the fountain's spurt. 'People used to make offerings – small things, mostly, dice or petteia pieces – anything with a chance. None of it was worth very much. But I'd gather them up all the same and sell them in the next town over so no one knew it was me who'd taken them. It took three days just to get there.'

All that for . . . what? A handful of copper?

I catch myself, and stare at him instead – at this boy who has had royalty thrown on him. A childhood where copper might have made all the difference, his days spent tending sheep and chopping wood and avoiding hunger at any cost.

I spent years in a classroom being told every story of gods and heroes our orators knew. If it had been me on that mountain, I would have known better than to choose any one of those goddesses as the winner of that damn competition. But did he?

'Maybe all this is punishment for all those stolen offerings.' He stares so intently at the water I wonder if he's contemplating drowning in it.

'Oh, get over yourself. This is a war between gods, Olympus itself wrenched in two. This war of nations isn't a punishment for *you*.'

He turns to me, face blank, and I rip a clip from my hair. It's covered in tiny blue diamonds that remind me of Helen, the colour her eyes are in the light of the early morning. I throw it in the fountain.

'That ought to cover your debt, I should think.'

He presses his lips together, an expression I hate to recognize because Kreousa makes the same one when she's frustrated. Can he please stop reminding me of the people I love most – the ones I'm killing myself to save – when he's being so detestably self-pitying? 'I brought Helen here. That's what caused the war.'

'Aphrodite brought Helen here,' I correct. 'Because, yes, you chose her in that stupid competition because you thought that owning the most beautiful woman in the world was an accomplishment.'

'I don't want to own her.'

Sure.

'And, frankly, we'd probably be here either way. Athena promised you glory in battle, right? I wonder how she would have made that happen without a war? And Hera? What did she offer? Political power and control over Asia. A peaceful enterprise, I'm sure. But still, you chose Aphrodite over that.'

'I didn't want a war. I didn't want power.'

He looks so lost, and I can't help the twinge of care that runs through me at features I know well twisted in distress.

Is it possible he's being honest?

'You wanted a beautiful girl by your side,' I hiss, clinging to my contempt. I know the truth; I saw it. How dare he pretend otherwise?

'I wanted peace – Helen seemed the most harmless option and she wanted to leave Sparta, so what did it matter?'

'Like you wouldn't have bound her and dragged her to your ship if she hadn't. Like you didn't spend hours discussing exactly that possibility with Aphrodite.'

'Have you tried to refuse the gift of a god?' he demands, angry for the first time, and this is more like it. The first time I've held any respect for him, at the very least. 'Well, evidently not.'

'You're an idiot, but you didn't cause this war. Zeus chose you to elect a winner in a competition caused by Eris, who was upset Thetis didn't invite her to the wedding Zeus was forcing on her because of a prophecy he once heard. And Aphrodite could have chosen any woman to reward you with –' my lip curls – 'but she chose the one whose marriage was protected by a pact across kingdoms. So what I'm saying, Paris, is that we're all just pieces in a game the gods are playing.'

'If you don't think I caused this war, then why do you hate me so much?'

I don't answer.

'Helen,' he concludes instead, and I don't think I'd even connected the anger before he said it – but, yes, Helen. He's not worthy of her and he practically owns her. And he talks at her, makes her life revolve around caring for his, and doesn't even notice the true beauty in all that she is, all that she's forced to hide around him.

I wouldn't be the first girl to hate their friend's partner – and hopefully that's all Paris thinks this is.

'Will I make her happy?' he asks, voice achingly small.

I'd like to say it's accidental, that I say it without thinking.

But I don't.

Despite everything, I want to hurt him.

'You'll make her happier than Menelaus ever did.'

It's the truth and I've seen it. Which makes it a prophecy no one could believe.

His eyes glaze over. He flinches back with hurt, his face darkening, and he turns and walks away.

And I slip into another prophecy.

Paris falls. It's one of their heroes, though not one I recognize. He plunges his sword in and barely acknowledges what he's done, just turns as the next fighter approaches and Paris crawls off. I don't see him succumb, don't see him collapse; it just loops back round, again and again and again. And I know with the kind of certainty that lies only in prophecy that he dies. Scamandrius has seen this too, he said, and I'm familiar enough with prophecies of death to know how dying feels in a prophecy, like cold water trickling down my spine. And this vision is drenched in such a chill.

I come to with Helen before me, her hands clutching mine.

'Hello,' I say.

'Hi.'

'Was I screaming?'

Her short curls bounce as she shakes her head. 'No, just out here a while – I thought I'd check on you.'

There's no point in me telling her what I saw. She already knows what must happen to Paris if we lose. Frankly, he's lucky to fall in battle. I imagine every horror I've seen would pale against what the Achaeans would do if they took him alive.

'How were the dignitaries?'

'Fine – I think I got plenty out of them. Did you know Sarpedon is a son of Zeus? He's my half brother, technically. Let's hope familial loyalty is enough to get him to fight. Thank you, by the way, for dealing with Paris. Did something happen, though? He stormed back in and hasn't spoken to me since.'

'Um,' I say, too shaken by the prophecy to even think about lying. I don't think I would though, not to her. 'He might have asked me if you'll be happy with him.'

She seems amused. 'And will I be?'

'I compared him to Menelaus and you know the answer to that yourself. But obviously when I told him he didn't believe me.' Her face falls, and I realize what I've done. 'By Zeus, Helen, I'm so sorry. I shouldn't –'

'It's all right. I can fix it,' she assures me, smoothing that smile back on her face.

'Really, I'm sorry. I didn't even think about what this would do to you. I was just so –'

'Honestly, Cassandra, don't worry. If I can't convince him he'll make me happier, then I'll persuade him I'm more loved, or more at home or more – shall we say – *satisfied*. That would make him so ecstatic he'll forget all about love.'

She laughs at that and, after a moment, I do too.

I'm not sure I'm entirely convinced but her joy is so infectious and she's still clutching my hands and her smile is like the reverse of my curse because I'd believe anything when she shines it.

Another vision.

Helen, golden light, her eyes darker, a sapphire that burns, fluttering closed, her lips brush against mine and they taste like honey . . .

I blink and she's simply in front of me, still laughing.

'Why *did* you say it, though?'

I can't breathe.

Well, apparently that's why.

CHAPTER THIRTY-NINE

Helen

I WOULD LIKE TO STAY AT the banquet until the early hours, when wine and moonlight make lips loose and thoughts careless. But Paris keeps to himself until he finally declares that we will be withdrawing early.

I cannot stay without my husband, especially not surrounded by strange men who I am trying to convince to fight for our love.

He closes the door heavily behind him and turns to me.

'Do you love me?'

My heart hammers so violently I could choke on it.

Do you love me? Menelaus would ask that often. *Do you love me?* He'd ask it when he hurt me – after he'd placed some restriction or rule that forced me further away from myself. *Do you love me?* As he chipped off a tiny part of my heart, like he wanted to see how small he could make it before it stopped calling his name.

'Of course!' I take Paris's hands like my earnestness might be apparent in my touch.

I have no idea how I'll unravel the doubt Cassandra's placed in his head – can I, with a curse to contend with? I might have assured her there was a way out, but I'm not so sure.

'But you're not happy.'

'We're at war –'

'No, Helen, you're not happy with me.' He shakes his head, tears shining in his eyes, and he wrenches his hands from mine. 'I see it now. I return and you're unsettled, but from what I've heard, you're never more delighted than when I'm on the front. You run around here like some kind of Amazon – swinging a sword with your rogue band of women.'

'They're scared girls who want to protect themselves in a time of war.'

'*We* are protecting them. The men on the front. That's what this whole fight is – protecting them. We don't need you thinking you know what you're doing with a sword.'

'I do know what I'm doing. I'm Spartan!'

'Not any more you're not. You're Trojan.'

'I . . . Troy is my home but I cannot leave all that Sparta gave me behind.'

'You even look Spartan, hair short like one of their boys –'

'It's my body, Paris, I'll cut my hair if I want to.'

'You know it's not,' he says quietly. 'A war rages, Helen. Your body belongs to all of Troy. We're the ones spilling blood for it. And it's going to become increasingly hard to rally men around a woman they don't particularly like – which they won't, if you keep leading their wives and daughters astray like this.'

I feel like a miscast blade – brittle iron on the cusp of shattering to sharp and meaningless points. I want to argue, my fury white-hot, urging me to shout and scream and fight if

I damn well must. And I want to cry, to be held and told I'm perfect and safe – because clearly I'm not, clearly I'm failing.

But the truth remains as it ever was: if I want to be safe, then I need to be a woman worth fighting for.

'I love you,' I promise, my voice quiet. 'I want you to love me too.'

'I do love you, Helen. But I love the woman I married more.'

'I understand.'

This has always been the price of survival, the game that until now I have been a willing and strategic player in. And I'll be damned if I forget how to win.

Paris falls asleep quickly – so quickly I wonder if his anger might have been fuelled by the banquet's wine. I look at his sleeping form – recognizing as I do that he is simply in over his head.

But I'm tired of giving him that excuse and of being hurt by it.

I slip out of bed sometime around midnight. I dress silently, taking Paris's cloak – heavy and dark and less visible than mine. I pick up my thin silk shoes and carry them outside, putting them on in the hallway in case even their light tread wakes Paris.

I can still hear music from the Great Hall and worry about anyone I might pass. But I move quickly and quietly, and reach the western tower. At its top is a dusty circular room with slight arched windows. A torch burns in a sconce on the wall.

All I would have to do is wave that torch before the window.

But even now, coming all this way, I don't know if I should.

I look down at the tablet – beeswax prised off, Menelaus's message clear underneath. He was there when Penelope did her trick too.

I try to ignore the streams of insults, of curt remarks, of things I hear so clearly in his voice, and reread the instructions at the end.

> *I suppose there is a chance, however slim, that you are not so stupid, feckless and base as to voluntarily become a Trojan's whore. In Sparta, the citizens collect the finest wood for your funeral pyre. I dream of it, Helen, of dragging you before the hateful crowd. The sweet pleas you'll make – or perhaps you'll bow your head at last and acknowledge my right as your lawful husband to do whatever I damn well please with you, even slice your head from your shoulders. I owe it to them, the men who die with your name on their lips, to see you brought to justice. Should you wish to avoid this fate, should you like to convince me you were taken by force and long to return to my side, to beg for a scrap of the respect I once held for you – signal from the palace's western tower, a torch in the window. I have someone watching at all times. You have until the next full moon.*
>
> *Your lord, king and lawful husband,*
> *Menelaus*

There's something so deeply tragic about it all – how many men must be dying because Menelaus cannot cope with a woman leaving him. About a rage so visceral he could not merely write it down but had to carve it into wood.

It could be clever to wave the torch. We lose the war – apparently – and even if there's simply a chance that we do, what harm is there in such a contingency plan? That if we fall, I might not fall with them?

But I'm also concerned it might be a trap. Maybe the letter does not come from my husband – *ex-husband* – but the Trojans themselves, delivered to the Amazons and a test of my dedication.

And if it is from Menelaus, if I do this, what would he ask of me next? That I try to escape the city? Once the Achaeans have me, they might slaughter me outside the walls and keep fighting anyway.

There's something shaking and crumbling inside me – for the first time in so very long I felt like I was putting myself back together, my real self, not this performance I give to survive. And in one day my husband and ex-husband have reminded me that I'll never be able to live like that, not when the only security I could possibly have comes from a man's love. And waving that torch feels like giving in to that – admitting that I'll never say no, never stand up for myself, will only ever melt myself down to take whatever shape they need of me.

But waving the torch isn't so different from nodding my head in the face of Paris's anger and telling myself I'll put down my sword and change. So maybe I've already surrendered to that truth.

I glance out at the sky, looking for my brothers, but I can't see them in the narrow view from the tower's slit windows.

All they ever wanted was to become heroes. And now they're stars in the Heavens because in life they burned too quick and too bright.

Some of us merely flicker through our whole existence.

I grab the torch, because I've known what I would do from the moment I received that letter – the smartest bet, the safest choice, the option that gives me the greatest chance at survival.

My brothers would tell me to be strong, to make a brave choice and hold firm. But what did they know? They were not kidnapped as children. Men did not declare war over the harmless decision they made the one time they chose happiness over bearing the full force of the cruelty the world wished to level at them. Strong men become heroes immortalized in the stars. Strong women are snapped quicker, punished harder, fall further.

They wave torches from windows *just in case*. They layer so many contingencies that their hope suffocates under the weight of all they fear.

I'm beginning to think real strength does not come from constantly fighting against this world but by enduring it. Perhaps we should not tell stories of the heroes but of the women who survived them.

I wave the torch before the window, quick, frantic movements.

I prepare myself for my eventual, inevitable surrender.

CHAPTER FORTY

Cassandra

I TRY TO STAY UP LATE, clinging to the opportunity to be around my brothers and the jovial spirits of everyone at the banquet. But I'm reeling from the revelation that I like Helen.

And in far more than my usual pining, appreciative way. This runs deeper than I'd realized, an aching in my pulse, a strain on every breath – like I cannot function for want of her.

Flustered, the prophecies are coming quicker and I can hardly focus on conversation at all.

So I resign myself to the fact my evening is over, and return to my chambers.

A woman stands at the window.

'Thank you,' I say, already fumbling for the clasp of my necklace. 'I'm retiring now. Would you fetch my handmaids to prepare me for bed?'

Normally I am perfectly able to do it myself but Andromache is favouring fiddly dresses of late, and this chiton has too many ties in too many inconvenient places for me to manage it.

Then the woman turns and the torchlight catches on the clip in her hair – blue sapphires, a gold band. Remarkably similar to the one I threw in the fountain as an offering to ... *Tyche*.

'A strange request, to waste a god's favour on.'

'My lady,' I fumble, falling hurriedly to my knees. 'You honour me with your presence.'

'You may rise,' she says, but she turns from me to look back out of the window. She stands at nearly seven feet, her onyx hair finely coiled and pulled forward beneath a scarlet band to rise from the forehead of her wide, flat face. Her cool brown skin stretches tight across broad cheekbones and her jaw is a slash of shadow against the low glow of the stars. Looking out at the city, framed by the windowpanes, she is beyond regal. She is heavenly.

'You timed your offering well – men returning to this city and gods among their number, in disguise, revelling alongside them for just this night. Distracted, one might say. The bright one and thunderer both.'

Which is to say that Apollo and Zeus do not know she is here – and presumably it must stay that way.

'One might say it was luck.'

At this, Tyche smiles. 'Indeed. And yours has run low of late. Of course, luck is not a scale to be weighted but a ball that may roll in any direction, no balance to ill fortune and good. In honour of my domain, I would not change it. But as a woman you have my sympathies.'

She prises the clip from her hair.

'And after this, you also have my favour.'

I stare at the slide. It is worth a great deal of coin, that's true. But that's nothing to a god.

Which means she may just have been waiting for an excuse and an opportunity and, finally, luckily, the two aligned.

'Can you help us win the war?'

'I help only the lord of the skies, though he seems reluctant to leave anything in this war to *chance*.' No trace of frustration touches her words, but it's there all the same: the defiantly raised chin, the steady pace with which she speaks like each syllable is a carefully selected choice, the reverence with which she elongates 'chance' – like the very word itself is valuable, that anyone casting it aside has committed an act of heresy. 'But if you had a more specific hope, you might be more fortuitous.'

Immediately, I think to ask her to remove Apollo's curse.

Then I hesitate – because Apollo once accused me of caring only for myself, not for the outcome of this war.

And I think of what else he said – about the dozens of gods who weave the threads.

'Can you show me how to weave the future?'

Her brows knit with the slightest hint of surprise. 'Most humans can only weave the future by making decisions even we could not predict.'

'Most?'

'Most humans can't see the weave. You're different. Can you touch it?'

I consider the thrum of those threads. 'I can sort through them and reach for the ones I want. They don't always acquiesce. But, yes, I can touch them.'

Tyche considers, lips pursed. 'What exactly did Apollo say when he gifted you with this sight?'

It feels like so long ago, and so much has happened since, that I cannot remember exactly. I try to cast my mind back – to that time before the pain, when prophecy was an anticipated dream.

'I can't be certain, but I think he said, "I give you prophecy."'

'What an *unfortunate* choice of words,' Tyche says, eyes sparkling with warm humour. 'I can share with you how to weave prophecy – that's not to say you will be able to.'

'Very well,' I say, my voice steady despite the excitement threatening to overcome me.

'Pay attention to the weave,' she says, and I let my eyes blur until those golden strands shimmer into view. I forgot how plentiful they are, shooting through the air around me until they bundle up in the people whose destinies they tell. 'Try moving a strand.'

I reach out.

A wailing baby, plucked from its mother's arms, her screams splitting my ears in two.

I flinch back.

'This is your issue,' she says. 'It is not the power of the gods that enables us to weave fate, it is the temperament. You are too human. The emotions are too close to your own, the future too similar to your own potential. The threads latch on to it, try to control you rather than allowing you to control them. You need not only the detachment of a god, you need the certainty. You need the arrogance.'

Which is perhaps why Apollo tried to stamp mine from me.

'Let me try again.'

So I reach for strand after strand, each one either sending me head-first into a vision or refusing to yield to my touch.

'It is not like weaving as you know it – think of it more like building,' Tyche says. 'Unlike on a loom, some strands are sturdier than others, some broader or longer – you need a solid strand to weave others on to, a starting point to build up from. Start small, the finer strands might be more flexible.'

I can't fail, not with a goddess in my very bedroom, urging me to keep trying. Apollo is absent tonight only, celebrating with the men in the city. This is my chance.

I reach out to a barely visible thread, so translucent I don't realize it's a prophetic strand at first, not merely a cobweb catching the light.

Men, an argument, a woman who has deceived them and refuses to admit that her nobody-husband will not return to her . . .

I draw myself back from the vision, still holding the thread between my fingers. It's scorching hot but I grit my teeth and wrap it round a nearby thread, glimmering with promise, someone else's future.

That thread of argument persists, and with this strand it grows thicker – and two men on the field scream at one another over a different woman, one they stole: not Helen, a name I recognize. Briseis, queen of a nearby city, a few years older than me and the first girl I ever longed for – now war prize of Achilles and, as of a few nights ago, of Agamemnon, taken to replace the woman he'd been forced to return. Now this thread wraps round Achilles, inflating his anger, and he's screaming at Agamemnon until . . . Achilles quits the war.

The strongest man in the Achaean army, who can decimate whole Trojan battalions without being cut by a single blade, stops fighting.

I let go, the pads of my index finger and thumb scored by a deep, agonizing burn.

The strands around me start shaking, shuddering, the whole thing falling and realigning.

Tyche beams.

'Oh, excellent! This has happened before, you know – the whole web shifting. That thread never should have been so close, and now look!' She points to contracting strands. 'This war would have lasted a decade. Now perhaps years. Maybe less.'

But the outcome, that solid bolt of prophecy, remains untouched.

I stare, the pain of my fingers forgotten. She's right: it's done this before. When Helen believed me. When I chose to work with her.

Now this, again.

'These things tend to come in threes, you know, just as the Fates themselves are three. If you are lucky enough to find the third, perhaps you really might change this. Even Zeus's will could not stand against the right, carefully woven strands.'

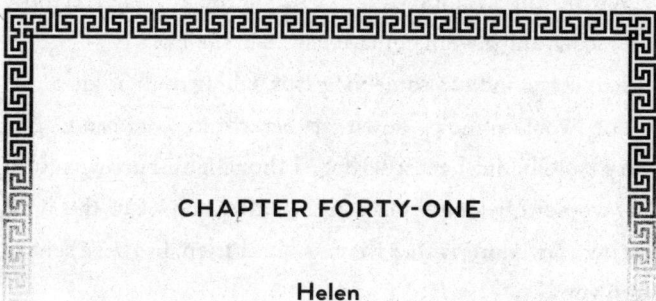

CHAPTER FORTY-ONE

Helen

PARIS IS GONE BEFORE I wake in the morning. It took me so long to fall asleep last night, his soft snoring taunting my own efforts to disappear into the vacuum of sleep. And though it's still early, bright morning light filtering through the gauzy curtains, my husband has returned to a battlefield without saying goodbye.

Later, I head into the city to teach, the sun beating harshly in the courtyard of the gymnasium where nearly a hundred women wave wooden staffs – broken broom handles and makeshift weapons. I nearly didn't come – considered spending my morning weaving instead. But I can't give this up until I have a way to stop the women from resenting me for doing so.

I'm sparring with Andromache – by far my most attentive student, focused on strategy and technique with the same precision with which she weaves.

'Bring your grip in closer,' I tell her. 'Your hands are too far apart.'

I hear gasps, and women scattering.

When I turn, rainbows crystallize in the air, bright colours coalescing, and a woman materializes in their place.

'Princess Laodice?' someone gasps, falling to their knees.

The woman looks down at herself in confusion. 'No, sorry... Oh, did I get it wrong? I thought I'd borrow a form that wouldn't be out of place in the palace but – Oh, this one's not here any more, is she? My mistake. Helen, I've been sent to fetch you.'

She doesn't want to appear out of place but materializes from nothing in a shower of colourful sparks?

Iris – it must be. Goddess of rainbows and the messenger of the gods.

'What? Why?' I startle.

'Paris has challenged Menelaus to single combat. Zeus has sent me to take you to the walls.'

'Why do I need to go to the walls?' I ask, fear lancing through me. I know why, or I can suspect well enough, but until it's confirmed I can't bear the weight of such a thought.

Iris cocks her head to the side and the wound she is inflicting cuts deeper – that look on that face? It's Cassandra's. Laodice is her older sister and, by Zeus, they look so much alike. Thick brows drawn low over pitying amber eyes, lips pressed to a tight line, and it might as well be Cassandra speaking when Iris does: 'You're the winner's prize.'

Of course I am.

For all my work in the city and the bonds I have forged, two men clash swords to decide who takes me.

Paris won't win. He can't. But he's ready to risk it, as though to punish me for making him doubt our marriage.

So this is it? No farewells. No final conversations. I will

be dragged to the walls by a goddess and thrust into Menelaus's arms. Will he parade me around as proof of his victory? Will he tear my diadem from my head and cast me into the dirt before the Achaean army? Or will he, if he believes I am here against my will, lock me in his ship so he cannot lose me again, captive queen waiting in his chambers?

I turn to Andromache. 'Tell Cassandra I . . . Just thank her for me. She'll know what for.'

Andromache shakes her head. 'Helen, you can't go!'

My eyes are watering but I hold my chin up high.

'You do not refuse the gods. If Paris has offered my hand, then as his wife I am his to wager.'

Ironic that, despite hours spent with a sword and all my skill with it, there is never any point fighting these things.

I am glad Cassandra is not here.

I'd break.

Iris closes her hand round mine and I am weightless, I am light, I am dazzling.

Everything re-forms in bright bursts of colour and I am standing on the battlements of the city walls. Priam and his advisors sit near the edge and as he sees me his eyes widen with surprise.

'Helen!' he calls. 'Come, sit with us.'

I make my way over hesitantly. I don't know how to act – what level of fear to show. As I step closer, the battlefield unfurls below – mud and blood, splintered swords and broken bodies, tents on the horizon before the large, sprawling sea.

I catch sight of familiar auburn hair – burnt red, like dying embers spitting in the dark. *Menelaus.*

He is embroiled in an argument with Paris and Hector, his brother Agamemnon hulking at his side.

His brother who killed my niece – who would, apparently, go to any lengths for this war. Does Menelaus even feel slighted by my abandonment? Or did his glory-hungry brother manipulate him into excusing a battle he dearly wanted? Or, no...

The lantern. I told him I was here against my will and that I wanted to come home.

By Zeus, I did this.

'Do you know him?' the king asks, and he must know that it is not Menelaus I stare at.

'Agamemnon, my sister's husband and Menelaus's brother. Achilles and Ajax are better fighters, but Agamemnon rouses men to fight like a hero in a story. He is ferocious on a battlefield, and men follow him blindly on to it.'

Priam nods. His other advisors had been rapt in conversation but now they turn their attention to me.

'Do you know Achilles and Ajax by sight?' one of them asks.

I glance at the field. 'I never met Achilles. He wasn't part of the bid for my hand.'

'Then why does he fight?' Thymoetes asks – worrying at his greying beard.

'Glory,' I answer quietly. *And prophecy.* Cassandra's not the only prophet – the Achaeans have one of their own. They speak of it so much in their camps that even our side has heard it, and taken it to the council for dissection: that Achilles is destined to fall in this battle but the Achaeans cannot win without him. Knowing he will die, Achilles fights to become a legend.

'That's Ajax, next to Idomeneus.' I point to the giant standing beside the god-like man, the Cretan army sprawling behind them. Maybe this will help in their strategies – my final gift to Troy before I'm carted back to Menelaus.

'And who is that?' Priam nods. 'The barrel-chested one?'

It's not difficult to realize who he means – it is the one man staring up at me. I'm always startled by how brutish he looks – bulging arms and thick neck, short and stout but bound with muscle. He is so wily that in my head he shifts into someone more subtle, sly, fox-like. Even now, his amused, self-satisfied smirk looks out of place on his blunt face.

'Odysseus,' I say. 'My cousin's husband and a prince of Ithaca, a ragged little island. His cunning makes him the most dangerous man on that field.'

'This is true,' Antenor says. 'I hosted him for the negotiations that preceded this war.'

'Why aren't they fighting?' I ask, nodding to my bickering husbands and their brothers.

Priam sighs. 'It is unclear, though were I to hazard a guess I'd say that Paris tried to renege on his challenge of single combat when Menelaus answered the call. Hector appeared to berate him for it.'

So this is it? Menelaus will take me back, having not only bested the man who spirited me away but goaded him into a fight he tried to back out of? There is no greater disgrace in Sparta than refusing a fight. It is better to spit your own bloody teeth into the dirt than words of surrender.

Agamemnon and Hector retreat as Menelaus and Paris draw weapons – long spears that they must hope can finish their opponent before they are close enough for swords to reach. Menelaus's hand is sturdy, his porcelain knuckles clenched tight and sure. But Paris sets his fingers round the weapon with a nervous twitch.

I can hardly watch, but what else can I do?

At that moment, Menelaus's weapon catches the midday sun and he looks away – looks up to me. Our eyes meet.

By Zeus, that rage. That levelling fury.

I realize, instantly, that he is angrier for the woman he sees. I am not the wife he moulded – not with my short curling hair and taut muscles.

I resist the urge to taunt him further – a smug grin, maybe, or even a coquettish wave. I simply bow my head – a look, I hope, is indecipherable – praying to a god, perhaps, or unable to look upon such a gruesome battle.

Their spears clash. The men move quickly, the clanging metal echoing high enough for even us to hear.

'I can't watch this,' Priam says. I'd like to leave with him but I remind myself that I do not have a choice. The gods themselves delivered me to this wall. So I watch, heart hammering like a battle drum urging them on.

Menelaus hits first, hurling his spear straight through Paris's shield, and I feel the blow like I myself have been struck. But soon neither can gain purchase and at once they discard their spears in the dirt and draw swords. Closer, their fight is vicious, their every slash a jolt in my chest. They move swiftly and I can't believe Paris has lasted so long, is even this talented with a weapon.

He must have learnt quickly.

He fumbles a feint, staggering off balance – I could teach him better. I could show him how to move with the iron in your hand like it is moonlight in the air – light and soft, cold and cutting. We could be a partnership in this battle if he stopped blaming me for not loving him, or, rather, for not putting enough effort into acting like I do.

Menelaus's sword crashes down on Paris's head with such force the bronze warps round it.

I'm pressed so tightly against the parapets my ribs might bruise.

Paris drops to his knees, still clutching his sword but swaying, dazed. Menelaus screams to Zeus and grabs the strap of Paris's helmet, dragging him through the dirt towards the Achaeans.

No. No, please, no. From the crowd, a figure runs – and it takes me a second to realize it is a woman, clad in leather armour with no blade by her side. A single figure steps forward as though to stop her, before stumbling to a halt when he realizes she's helping. I recognize him as Sarpedon, the prince who is also a child of Zeus. Which means he can see her as well as I can, even if everyone else is oblivious. Aphrodite. New features, a new form. She snaps the strap in Menelaus's hand without him even glancing in her direction.

Menelaus snarls in fury and runs for his spear. Paris struggles to get to his feet but he lurches violently, blood trickling from beneath the metal ridges of his helmet.

Menelaus raises the spear high to Achaean cheers and I can't breathe – even as I watch Aphrodite run forward and clutch Paris, I'm certain all she will do is hold him as he dies.

They both vanish in a plume of mist.

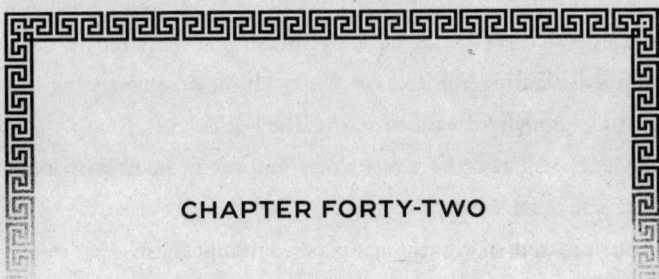

CHAPTER FORTY-TWO

Helen

THE CROWD GASP, BEFORE ROARING their displeasure.

I run. Slipping between the throngs of people and reaching the palace as quickly as I can, wanting to put distance between myself and the battle before they decide that, with or without the 'mortal' part of 'mortal combat', Paris clearly lost and the reward should exchange hands.

A servant collides with me in the hallway.

'Ah, Helen!' she coos, a sickly smile on her face. 'Hurry! Paris is in your room. You wouldn't know he'd been fighting at all. He lies on your bed, quick –'

'Enough,' I snarl, my voice too low to carry and all the more threatening. 'You try to deceive me now? Why? Does the disguise just make it more fun for you?'

She drops the act – and if I was certain at her smile, I am more so at the look of disdain that crosses her face.

'Helen, your husband awaits you in the finest robes, bathed in the scents of –'

'Then, you fuck him!'

Aphrodite stares, her face shifting into a familiar mesh. My own eyes glare back at me. It's grotesque, the way she stitches us all together like we are nothing more than parts to be swapped and stolen.

'Go on! Deliver me to some new nation, some new champion of yours. Whoever's prize I am to become next. And take this war to a different land. Then you can marry Paris or become his concubine or whatever it is you actually want.'

She grasps my arm in a vice-like grip, pushing me backwards against the stone. 'Careful, Helen. You forget yourself. Your husband awaits you – and you *will* be the doting wife, concerned for his welfare.'

'As far as I'm concerned, my husband died on that battlefield,' I spit, wrenching my arm free and shoving her back from me. 'In the single combat he insisted upon. You expect me to dote upon a coward who runs from a fight?'

'That's exactly what you'll do. I gifted you with your beauty, Helen. It's mine. So if every man on that battlefield wants you, it's because of me. You'll be exactly who I say you are. And I say you're so hopelessly in love with Paris you'd invite death to these shores before you gave him up.'

'If you care so much about your little tale of a war for love, then be your own leading lady. I'm tired of you dictating my lines.'

I turn from her – and I cannot even comprehend what I am doing right now. Fighting with a goddess? It's ludicrous. It could be deadly.

But all that fear of returning to Menelaus, all that anguish at not saying farewell, of being forced to partake in a marriage . . . it's all bursting free.

I'm halfway down the hall when she speaks.

'I can make them hate you every bit as much as they have loved you.' Her voice is soft as a caress and chills me to my core. 'I could have Eros shoot you with an arrow, I suppose, but that hardly proves *my* power, does it? But this would prove it just as well as your love would, so if that's what you'd prefer, it can certainly be arranged. You dislike being my prize? Very well, I can make them see you not as a glorious trophy to be won but as a hateful bitch at the centre of it all. Your carefully constructed lines, your acts of service to the city, every tiny thing you do to earn their trust? I can destroy it all in a single pressing of my will. I can make the Trojans beg to turn you over, and the Achaeans desperate to destroy you when they do.'

I stop walking, hating myself for it. But she knows just where the cracks in my resolve are, and exactly where to level a blow.

My eyes flutter closed, like I cannot bear to see my own shame.

'Paris is in our chambers, you said?'

'Good girl.'

As promised, Paris is lying on our bed, wearing white robes too bright to be anything other than god-given.

'So this is the man who flees the very battle he declares. You should have died on that field.'

I can't help it – I cannot believe he would so eagerly wager me against his own ego.

'Don't berate me right now, Helen.'

He's sulking, not even looking up.

'Too cowardly to face your wife's reproaches?'

'There's that Spartan mentality: better to die a hero than live to fight another day.'

How can my fate possibly be tied to this man?

'What would you like me to say? "Oh, Paris, thank you so much for offering me up to my ex-husband, you nearly won too, clever you! I'm so glad you're back and don't worry, my hero, you'll get them next time!"'

Paris starts crying, huge choking sobs. And then I am by his side because, anger or not, it appears I still care about him.

'I know, all right! I never should have issued that challenge and I don't know what I'm doing! With anything! On the battlefield or as a prince – or with *you*. I just want this war over.'

I am tired of having to raise my husband – of his childish mistakes and tantrums. I am tired of covering for him, of forgiving him every time he hurts me because he didn't mean to.

Paris's sobs are quietening to sniffling tears and he looks up.

'What are we doing, Helen?'

I stare at the wall, gaze unfocused. 'Trying to survive.'

'You used to care about me. Now I wonder, if Aphrodite had not led me to your door, if you'd even have looked at me.'

'I care about you, Paris.'

'But you don't love me.'

I wonder if this is how Cassandra felt, all those months ago, screaming for me to destroy her reputation, that she didn't care any more.

I would like to blow up my own life and see what I can reassemble from the scraps.

'You don't love me either.'

He turns to me sharply. 'Of course I do.'

'You don't even know me. You've never asked a single question about me!'

'I don't . . .'

'Can you name a single one of my siblings? Do you even know how many I have? What about my father, can you name him? What of my favoured hobbies?'

'You like . . . dancing, I thought.' He looks as though he knows how weak his answer is.

'My favourite food?' I offer, and he shakes his head. I press on. 'Forget all that, can you even name a single thing you like about me?'

'I . . . Helen, you're beautiful.'

Our eyes meet and we both watch as hope for any form of 'us' fades.

'Why didn't you tell me you felt all this?' he asks, voice hollow. 'Why all the lies?'

'It wasn't a lie. It's how we're taught to act in a marriage to stay safe. The goddess of love appeared at my door and told me to sail with a man I did not know to a land across the ocean, a man who would have the power to do anything he liked to me – even offer me back to my ex-husband if the terms were right. I needed to love you. I half convinced myself I did.'

I'm expecting protests and dismissals. But Paris reminds me there's a reason I thought I might love him one day – beneath the carelessness, he is kind. And he considers my point.

'Olympus above, I'm so stupid.' He looks up with those big, pleading eyes. 'I'm sorry, Helen. I should have made clear that your safety wasn't dependent on your love. I only got so upset because I thought you did love me and that I'd done something to lose it.'

'I'm sorry too,' I say. 'I do care about you, Paris. I thought I could protect you from the truth every bit as much as it restricted me.'

'I don't really know what to do. We can't divorce –'

'No,' I say quickly, and it's not even the thought of Menelaus that prompts it but that of Aphrodite. She wouldn't just send me back, she'd inflate their already vitriolic hatred. She'd make a show of her power.

Paris groans. 'It doesn't matter. I'll be back on the battleground soon. So whatever happens next can wait until after the war is won.'

After. Such a precious, hopeful word, and still I wish it might never come, that those strands could be teased out forever.

He draws a blanket up around him. 'Maybe you're right: maybe I never loved you either. But this certainly feels like heartbreak, so if it's all the same to you, Helen, would you please leave.'

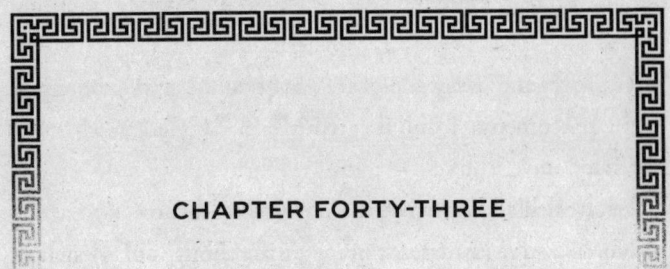

CHAPTER FORTY-THREE

Cassandra

ANDROMACHE FINDS ME IN THE courtyard at the back of the palace, where I stand trying to read threads, trying to work out which ones might possibly be worth weaving together – if I can.

'Oh, blessed Apollo, I've been looking for you everywhere,' she says, clutching a stitch in her side. 'Iris just whisked Helen off to the front – she said Menelaus and Paris were deciding the war in single combat.' She falters, like she knows just how much this next part will mean to me. 'She said to tell you "thank you".'

I have so many more questions but the world feels like it's lurched, like we're sliding towards a sudden edge.

'Cassandra!' Andromache calls after me as I run.

But I keep going, though I don't have time to make it to the walls or even out of the palace, because Helen materializes like an apparition, rounding the corner of the hall so unexpectedly that I don't realize how much I feared never seeing her again until the moment she is before me.

I practically leap at her, flinging my arms round her neck

and holding her tight. Then I let go, stumbling back and sputtering: '*Thank you?* Are you serious? That's all I get?'

She arches a wry eyebrow. 'I didn't exactly have time to grab some parchment.'

'Don't leave. You're not allowed. I forbid it.'

She chuckles, bowing low. 'Very well, Princess Cassandra.'

'Gods, you're ridiculous.' I recognize that she's likely shaken, masking her fear with a smile as I've seen her do before, but I'm thrown as well, swallowing tears and knowing if one of us breaks, the other will too. 'Wait, you're here, so does that mean Paris won the combat?'

The war could be over. But there hasn't been any change in the threads, so how could it possibly . . .

'Of course not. Sorry,' she rushes to add when she sees my crestfallen expression. 'I should have been gentler, I just hadn't considered that anyone might believe him winning was a real possibility. I should probably spread the news he's not dead either, though I would imagine most people watching him vanish before imminent death would assume a divine rescue. He's in our chambers – oh, on that note, I may need to stay with you for a little while, for however long Paris is back.'

I skip past whatever conflict between them has prompted that need and straight to the thought of Helen sharing my bed.

Does she sleep well? Or does she toss and turn? Does she steal the sheets or snore or talk in her sleep?

That wanting thing clawing at my chest reaches out again, and I find myself desperate to know the answers to those decidedly intimate questions. And underneath, skimming my bones like an oil slick on the river: the visceral fear that I might be falling somewhere she can't reach me.

'Sure,' I finally choke. I seize on the first distraction that comes to mind and try to halt my spiralling. 'I met Tyche last night.'

Helen doesn't even look surprised; she just shakes her head with that same amused smile. 'Of course you did. Come on, then, let's go somewhere we can't be overheard.'

We don't go far, just to the edge of the hall where porticoes look on to another courtyard, set a few steps lower than the ground. We climb on to the marble rail at the platform's edge, leaning against a column each. My knee brushes hers and I press myself back a hair's width more, like even that small touch might be too telling.

She starts, telling me about Aphrodite and the single combat. When she's done, she asks me about Tyche and I explain what we achieved – one tiny thread and the course of the war altered.

'That's incredible. Can you do it again?'

'I don't know. I was trying earlier but it's hard. I think I may have only managed last night because Tyche was there.'

'Can we get her back?'

'I don't think so – she implied she could only be there because Zeus was distracted and Apollo wasn't planning on visiting me.'

'What? Sorry, Apollo visits you?'

'Yes, he enjoys dropping in on my dreams and tormenting me.' I hadn't realized I'd never told her. There were always so many other things to discuss – and I don't want to talk to Helen about Apollo and the things he's so clearly waiting for . . .

Helen looks like she might reach into my dreams herself just to throttle him. 'Does he threaten you?'

'Sometimes.' I shrug. 'Mostly he's still trying to seduce me. He's decided he's in love with me – wants to take me to Olympus, make me a goddess and marry me.'

Helen steadies herself on the narrow bench. 'I'm sorry, could you repeat that?'

'I mean, that's the general gist.'

'And you've said?'

'Some variation of "Fuck off and leave me alone"?'

She stares at me.

'Okay, fine, I'll say it.' She tosses her short curls from her face. 'It's not like I want you to marry Apollo, but you're turning down immortality, powers, godhood –'

'I don't like him, though.'

She swallows, her hands falling down by her sides.

'Women marry men they don't like all the time for reasons nowhere near as good. Because they have guaranteed harvests or they're rich or powerful or they're just good friends with your parents. Marriage in exchange for godhood? I'd take it.'

'You would?' I don't intend the words to sound as sad as they do.

She averts her gaze, her eyes the blue of a cool winter sky. She is blinking a little too quickly. 'Probably,' she admits. 'I suppose that says more about me than I'd like it to. But all I ever wanted from a marriage was happiness. And then that became love, because love meant safety and, if not happiness, then a lack of cruelty. But godhood would be power too. If you have to marry someone, why wouldn't you take the option where you'd get actual authority from it, some control over your own life rather than having to constantly bend yourself for the modicum of power your husband's affection gives you?'

'But you'd still be beholden to your husband. I don't ever want that – that's why I became a priestess.'

My glorious escape, to become one of the few girls who didn't have to choose their happiness from the scraps the men offered.

Unlike Helen.

Scamandrius's words ring in my ears: *We will have to keep her.* How many marriages await her after Paris falls?

'I see,' she says, and I realize, while I've been considering her, she's been working me out in turn. She looks at me with the kind of contemplation I'd normally violently veer a conversation away from. 'It's not uncommon, for girls to join a temple out of fear of a bad marriage.'

I stay quiet, responses spinning through my head – but none of them seems right.

'Or any marriage,' Helen offers, aiming for a casualness of tone, but her eyes are piercing and intense.

'I like girls the way I'm expected to like boys.' It's odd, to declare it like this. With my family, it was so natural. I'd always spoken of other girls and eventually my fawning became less about wanting to look like them and more about wanting to be with them. By the time I told them, they already knew.

'Ha, I've never thought about it that way – *expected*. I've been with girls and I've been with boys, but no one aside from Aphrodite expected me to actually *like* the men I married. That's not what marriage is for.'

'I suppose. Although, if I'm being entirely truthful, I don't think I've ever felt eros – it's more romance than desire.'

'How do you mean?'

'Well, sometimes what I want feels so grandiose: to have somebody's name imprinted on my tongue with how often I speak it, to twist our lives round one another and grow upwards together, our stems stronger. To have someone to fight through this world with. And sometimes it feels quiet. I just want a hand to hold, a shoulder to lean on. I want to feel at rest with someone.'

'That sounds nice.'

'It does?'

'Yes, I think I'd like that.' She glances down at her nail beds, torn to shreds. 'I think I'd like that a great deal, actually.'

Her eyes lock with mine. I think of the tales we're told: of flowers transformed with the blood of heroes and warm summer breezes carrying the whispers of lovers. It's impossible to believe, in this instant, that Helen is not part of another story – eyes that made the envious sky turn blue.

I open my mouth – not sure what words will follow – when we hear shouting down the hallway.

Hector yelling is so jarring that it takes me a moment to realize it's him. My brother is always calm – annoyingly so.

'He's the bane of Troy! And maybe when his soul departs this world for Hades all this heaviness will lift.'

'Paris is your brother,' Mother retorts.

'Which is why I'm going to try shouting some sense into him before trying to ram it into him with the sharp edge of a sword.'

Helen and I leap from our spots, reaching the hallway as my mother's retreating form disappears round a corner.

'Helen, oh, thank the gods,' Hector says. 'I was worried the Achaeans might have found a way to take you among all that chaos. They were demanding we hand you over anyway, but then someone shot an arrow and, well, any thought of that was quickly quelled by the fighting erupting again. But Paris needs to come back to the front, rumours are already flying that he's hiding out here.'

'I'll speak to him,' Helen says – and it's only because I know her so well that I catch the reluctance in her voice. 'I don't think you'll convince him by shouting at him.'

Hector hesitates before finally nodding.

Helen pauses, glancing at me, and I wonder what might have happened if Hector hadn't appeared. Perhaps nothing. Or perhaps we might have said something only the threat of losing each other could have prised from our lips.

Then she turns, and strides back towards her chambers without another look.

CHAPTER FORTY-FOUR

Cassandra

'CASSANDRA,' HECTOR SAYS, VOICE TENSE. 'Might I have a word?'

I nod, perplexed but hardly complaining about an opportunity to spend time with my brother before he returns to a gruesome war.

He strides down the hallway and doesn't speak until we're seated in one of the palace's day rooms – a few lounging chairs arranged round a long, low table, the room heady with the smell of incense.

'I don't have long,' he says.

From the nothingness around him lurches a vision of a winged woman, cackling at such a statement and reaching for Hector like she is just shy of touching him.

Dread settles heavily and the hope I had only yesterday dissipates. Is she even a prophecy? She must be – a Keres would not be attracted to Hector until after his violent death. But maybe the line between prophecy and the realm of the gods is slight. In my own future I stumble along a purple carpet towards the castle of my captor. I hear crying children, devoured by their own parents, I see blood long since scrubbed clean, I see my own destruction at the edge of an axe and low-circling creatures beating against the walls. Past, present and future, all of it at once, and none of it matters.

'Cass,' Hector prompts, but I can't stop staring at the promise of death hung about his neck.

Achilles, his name on the wind, on the breaths of the soldiers charging behind him into the fray. Apollo unlatches the armour, another man strikes true – and then Hector's spear drives deep into his stomach. The body twitching still beneath it, and the sharp lurching tug of the spear from the corpse.

I stagger. Hector kills Achilles? But every vision of Hector's death – and there have been so many – shows Achilles: killing him, stringing his body up and dragging it through the dirt.

A second future. A second thread. A way for Hector to survive this – to kill Achilles before he has the chance to slaughter him.

Hector's threads are shot straight through that iron core of the future, irrevocably tied to the outcome of the war. If we save him, could we save Troy too?

'Cass,' Hector repeats, a little more urgently.

Oh gods, I can't say anything. I can't crush this hope by turning the curse on it.

'How are you feeling?' I rush, simply to say something. 'About going back to the battle?'

'I'm not exactly thrilled but I've fought in worse wars. Until Paris pulled this stunt, we were winning. Though I won't lie, part of me was relieved by the single combat, even if we lost. We might have bankrupted ourselves paying the Achaeans enough to recognize their win and get them to leave. But the war would have been over.'

'And Helen would have been forced to return to a cruel man,' I push back. 'She would have left us.'

He looks at me sharply. 'Yes, I wanted to talk to you about that.'

I recognize that tone. He's used it since we were children – when we used to call him things like 'stuffy', 'boring' and 'annoying'. We had no idea, I suppose, just how heavily the burden of the crown rested on his head.

It grates now like it grated then, even if I understand it better than I ever did.

'What do you want to know?'

'You love Helen.'

'I do not *love* her,' I scoff.

'I saw you at the banquet. I saw you just now. Don't stand there and tell me you don't have feelings for her.' He folds his arms across his chest and gives me a look he inherited from our mother: eyes piercing, lips thin, like I'm being dared to lie right now.

'Fine.' I take a breath – for all I've worked out about myself, I'm not sure how to put the feelings I have for Helen into words. But I suppose, for all those deliberations, in the end it remains simple. 'I don't love her, but I think I could. I think I will.'

'For the sake of Olympus.' Hector groans, like his worst fears have come true. 'She's married to your brother. We're fighting a war over that union. There's no way she can be with you.'

'I never expected to be with her, but I'm going to love her anyway.'

'You're setting yourself up for heartbreak.'

'I'll be lucky if heartbreak is all I come out of this with.'

'Cass –'

'What, Hector?' I finally snap. 'This is what happens, okay? Most women are forced into marriages. Some enter them voluntarily. So am I supposed to restrict my feelings to the women who find an escape? Or is it as inappropriate to love someone sworn to virginhood at a temple as one sworn to a man at a wedding altar?'

He considers – because of course he does. He doesn't care to win an argument but to reach the right conclusion. 'You have a point. But do you not see that this only proves what I'm saying? You can't be happy here.'

I glance down, my eyes burning. It doesn't matter that in a year no one will be happy – for once, I forget the prophecies and the future and I'm just a girl whose foolish heart will get her hurt.

'Hector, what do you want me to do? I can't think my way out of my emotions. I'm hardly going to tell her, am I? So if my pining only hurts me, then is that not my ache to endure?'

Hector glances away, down the hall, and for a second he looks so impossibly young that I don't understand how he can bear all this.

'You know what the worst part of fighting out there is?'

I can imagine. I've seen plenty of it, even through the eyes of the men who brave it – but no, I do not know. I am not really there.

'Knowing what me dying will do to Andromache. She's already lost her family, her city – who could handle more loss? But I know what the Achaeans would do to her if they got through those gates, so I go out there, day after day, to keep her safe. When I say "be careful", Cass, I mean I understand how powerful love can be. I would hate to see that power placed in the wrong hands. The way it might be manipulated. Helen has been around hundreds of people half in love with her for the majority of her life. Do you *really* think she doesn't know how you feel?'

I can't get Hector's words out of my head and keep hurtling from horror at the thought of Helen knowing to a desperately hopeful suspicion that she might feel similarly. It's infuriating, the constant loop – and I can't break out of it because Helen never appears in the gynaeceum. Which means she's probably still with Paris.

'All right, we're leaving the palace. Now.' Andromache finally breaks, tossing her stylus aside, the navy ink splattering across her palms. She wipes them hurriedly on her dress and the fact that she'd risk ruining fabric suggests I'm in more of a state than I realized, so I follow her out without question.

It's not until we're halfway across the acropolis that she speaks again. 'So, care to explain why you keep jumping every time someone walks through the door?'

'I keep thinking it's Helen.'

'Gods of Olympus, Cassandra, when are you going to –'

'It's not my fault. Your husband told me I was in love with her and I – no, why are you nodding? Stop that. I told him I wasn't but I . . . I admitted I have feelings.'

'Excuse me?' Andromache stumbles to a halt so suddenly another woman nearly collides with her. She lowers her voice, remembering we're in public and this is not the sort of thing I want overheard. 'I have been trying to get you to do that for weeks and you have one conversation with Hector and admit it outright?'

We reach the gates that lead out into the city and don't even discuss it before we're on the main streets of Troy, turning down into the merchants' quarter like on the trips we took before the war, when we'd chat for hours while browsing wares.

'I've been figuring some things out,' I tell her. 'But Hector made the very good point that Helen is used to being around people who like her so she probably knows how I feel, and now I'm panicking.'

Andromache doesn't say anything for a moment, and when I glance up she's smiling to herself.

'What?'

'Just, gods, I love my husband. Next time we should partner on such an ambush – imagine how great we'd be, working in tandem.'

'Andromache!'

'Right, yes. If it helps, I'm pretty sure these feelings of yours aren't just one-sided.'

I turn over some clay beads at one of the stands to avoid looking at her, but then I catch myself – Andromache's here. She cares. I *want* to tell her. Haven't I kept enough from her lately?

'That's also part of why I'm so on edge. Before Hector arrived, Helen and I were talking, and we didn't say enough to be sure but I think there's a chance it was leading that way.'

Andromache gasps and reaches across the stand to take my hand in hers. 'Cassandra, that's so exciting!'

It is, I suppose. But it's also not. There are so many bigger things going on and I selfishly don't want this to happen right now – I've dreamt of love for so long. I don't want it to be disregarded and pushed aside in favour of higher stakes. It deserves to be centred, to be the thing all else pales beside.

'These things you were figuring out,' Andromache starts, toying with a bracelet. 'You don't have to tell me but . . . well, I'm here. If you want.'

'I've just . . .' I take a breath, and pick up a mirror, like it might reflect my own thoughts back. 'I've spent a while believing the way I love people might be different from the way most other people do. But I also think maybe my love, different or not, is something someone would be lucky to have.'

'Absolutely they would,' she agrees, and not in the hurried manner I'd expected – supportive and baseless. Andromache agrees like it's a fundamental belief. 'Obviously it's complicated, with Paris –'

'Please don't worry, your husband already covered that one.'

'I love how he goes from "my brother" to "your husband" when you're mad at him,' she observes. 'But I just want to know what you're hoping for so I can best support you.'

I laugh a little, because that's such a Hector thing to say and I can't believe they've only been married a year but are already seeping into each other like this.

'I think, more than anything, I just want her to see herself like I see her.'

'Oh, that's lovely. You should tell her.'

I look down at the mirror in my hands, an idea forming. 'Yes, I think I should.'

Andromache and I stay out until dusk, when the sun sets and the women in the city cook large meals together and sing and dance. We join them, laughing until our sides ache – knowing we shouldn't be avoiding the palace when there are allies to win over to our side but enjoying it too much to resist. This city. This wonderful city.

I could save Hector. I could love Helen. We could win this war.

How rejuvenating hope is.

But as I return to my room, the door slams shut behind me.

Apollo.

He's there, in the flesh, leaning against it, completely expressionless except for a cold edge to his eyes.

'Hello, little priestess. Why don't you have a seat?'

CHAPTER FORTY-FIVE

Cassandra

'Apollo, what –'

'*Lord* Apollo,' he snarls. 'Sit down. Now.'

I do as he says because he's real and he's here and nothing screams danger more than an angry god in your bedroom. I think of the last time he was in here and my throat closes. I might suffocate on my own fear.

'My father is furious,' Apollo says, beginning to pace. 'He just summoned me to Olympus, screaming and raving about the course of the war – about the future of it. The timeline of it all but collapsed last night.'

'It did?'

'Because of you.' He bares his teeth and stalks towards me. 'You've caused this. It's all out of order because you've been manipulating the future in a way no mortal ever should. I'm facing the fury of the king of the Heavens, all because of one wayward priestess. Do you know what he's threatened me with?'

I stay quiet, my skin prickling. He knows I wove the strands. Is Tyche all right, or is Zeus punishing her as Apollo handles me?

'I don't –'

He cuts me off with a laugh that's half deranged. 'Oh, clever, clever priestess. I should have known you'd find loopholes in my curse. You heard a god's decree and ensured your prophecies would be heard anyway.'

I have to stop myself exhaling with relief. That's all he thinks I did – just circumvented his curse rather than shaping fate itself.

'What's wrong with me sharing the prophecies?' I ask. 'There are seers on both sides. You even gave Scamandrius –'

'I gave your brother snippets of prophecies, a shallow glimpse at the threads of fate. But you – you were meant to be an oracle.' He stands in front of me and lifts my chin with his finger. 'I gave you everything.'

'And I used it.'

'Troy is fated to fall.'

I jump to my feet, if only to put some space between us. 'Who cares what's fated?'

'The king of the gods,' he hisses. 'I couldn't work it out, couldn't understand why the course of the war was changing. It took its collapse for me to realize it was you.'

'So I'm supposed to just accept the future I'm forced to see?'

'You're supposed to go mad with it, little priestess. You're supposed to dwell within your curse, to accept it as your due for defying a god. But here you are instead, searching for ways to outsmart me. You're playing a dangerous game, mortal.'

'I'm not playing a game, I'm trying to save my city.'

'Your city falls,' he shouts. '*My* city falls!'

I hide my shaking hands in the folds of my dress, trying to keep my voice level. 'But you don't want it to, so why are you so angry I tried to stop it?'

'I don't want Troy to fall but I'm not prepared to contravene the will of Zeus for it. Ten years is a lot of time for mortals to die, and you've made things a decade off happen in mere months. At this rate, the war will last a single year. Troy will still fall but Father wants more time for it to play out, more men to die. He's livid it's changing. But me?'

He comes towards me again and I take another step back.

'I'm furious that you defy me.'

My back hits the wall and he smiles, something feral to it.

'I cursed you. I, *a god*, cursed you. You do not get to circumvent it, you get to plead and beg and grovel until I, in my divine mercy, lift it.'

'You've already said you'll never lift it.'

'And you should beg anyway.'

'I begged once, you didn't answer.'

'Try again.'

'You want me pleading for your mercy?'

'Yes.'

'And you want me to fuck you, you want me to marry you, you want me to reject you because it's fun.' It is not clever, I know, to respond to my terror by screaming at the thing daring to scare me. But here I am again, lashing out like my defiance might save me. 'You want me begging, you want me arguing, you want me to talk to you and you want me to shut the fuck up. Make up your damn mind.'

He lunges forward, his arm hitting the wall above me, fist curled. He leans against it, towering over me, trapping me with his body, and I jolt, shrinking into myself.

He grins.

'This is what I want, Cassandra.' He runs a finger down my

face, and my skin crawls where he touches it. 'I want you to remember that I am a god, and I am to be feared. I want you to never forget that you only live because I will it so. And every day you amuse me a little less and I wonder why that is.'

I can't move, can't run, can hardly breathe. I'm too terrified to even think of speaking.

'Because what makes me angriest of all, my dear –' he leans forward, whispers in my ear – 'is that you've used *me*, not just the prophecies I gave you. You exploited my despair to rinse your own answers of the nature of prophecy, and then you used it against the armies destined to destroy you. Such hubris doesn't go unpunished.' His fingers continue to ghost down my cheek until his hand closes round my neck. There's no pressure, not yet, but I feel the weight of his fingertips nonetheless and I don't dare breathe.

'It seems people aren't quite as willing to write you off as mad as I'd hoped,' he sneers. 'Let's see what I can do about that.'

He reaches into the weave and plucks a thread. Its gold strands squirm beneath his fingers.

He lifts it and loops it round my neck.

Choking smoke, blood, so much blood, and a piercing arrow, and another and another and agonizing, scorching pain, my clothes aflame, my skin peeling –

The vision fades but it's still there, forever present, burning against my skin.

It is not like the thread hung round Hector's neck – this does not foretell my own death. But the similarity makes the threat clear enough. Apollo ties the thread tight and smiles.

'Do not cross me again.'

CHAPTER FORTY-SIX

Helen

PARIS AGREES WE CAN'T MAKE any problems between us public, so most people think he's still sulking solely about the public humiliation of losing in single combat – rather than the breakdown of our marriage. But he can't stay here forever and I'm tired of advising him or carefully guiding him to the right path. So I'm going to humiliate him even further – his wife happily wielding a sword while he refuses to fight. Maybe that will make him cease this cowardice and get him out of my room and back on the front.

Besides, it's more than just the pleasant hum of my burning muscles that I need right now.

In one hour of sword manoeuvres, I learn from the daughter of a council member that blood rain has been spotted on the battlefield, from the wife of a palace chef that Agamemnon has tried to get Achilles back on to the Achaeans' side, and from a servant that Diomedes is the new terror on the battlefield while Achilles is gone.

I wonder if Cassandra has any more threads of prophecy for us that might be clearer with that knowledge, or else allow us to best manipulate it.

I find her by the shrine to Hestia. Her colouring is normally warm – freshly baked clay or molten metal in a forge, her eyes burning embers in the sun's fiery light – but now a grey sheen has paled her, her eyes flit nervously and she worries at the himation draped like a scarf about her neck.

'What's wrong?' I ask, forgetting my own concerns instantly.

Cassandra blinks and I notice the deep lines under her eyes.

'Apollo was in my room, Helen,' she whispers urgently. 'Not just in my dream.'

'No!' This is more than tiredness. There is nothing short of terror etched into Cassandra's face. 'What did he do? Are you all right?'

Cassandra swallows. 'He found out that I'd discovered loopholes in the curse.'

'Cassandra, what did he do?' I repeat, trying to keep the fear from my voice.

'He tied a strand to me and it's like he's given me a permanent vision, lingering at the edge of my consciousness.'

'Can you get it off?'

'I don't know,' she says, eyes watering, voice tight. 'I don't even know if I can risk trying or if it will anger him more.'

'You can't just accept it in the hope he won't do more terrible things.'

'I know that.' Tears tremble free, silently sliding down her cheeks. 'Look at this – isn't it just a sign he could snap my neck if he wanted to?'

She tugs her shawl down, revealing a deep circular line

carved into her neck – so thin that if it were wire, it could cut her head clean off.

'What the *fuck*?' I hiss.

'He wants me scared, I know. But it's working – I'm genuinely terrified about what he might do if I keep trying to alter the fate of the war or if I try to take it off. If I do *anything* to displease him.'

'Wait, are you saying you're not going to try to stop the war?'

'Of course not – I'm going to do all I can. But, Helen, this thread he's wound round me shows me horrific things, constantly. And when I try to read the threads they become real – including the one round my neck. It's too tight, it cuts and . . . I'll still read them occasionally but . . . it hurts.'

'Cass –' I start, close to tears myself, but she hurries on like she can't carry my pain on top of everything else.

'The visions that strike me – that I don't seek out – are fine, and they show valuable things too – yesterday, I think, it revealed a new thread. Either Achilles kills Hector or Hector kills Achilles. If Hector dies, the Achaeans win the war. I don't know what will happen if Achilles dies, but maybe the inverse might be true.'

I'm a little thrown by the pivot, and it takes me a moment to work out what she's saying. 'But Achilles isn't fighting at all.'

'And when he does again it will decide the war.'

A way to win. This should be easy – we could stop Achilles from going back to fight if we pay him off, or maybe we can recruit him to our side or make some targeted effort against him so that, even if Hector does face him, Achilles will be worn, maybe even injured.

My excitement cuts as soon as I look back at Cassandra and that angry red line round her throat.

'Are you really going to leave that thread on and suffer its touch?'

'I think I have to.'

'This is not okay – your life can't hinge on a god's whim!'

'Don't all our lives hinge on a god's whim?'

'Not a named god. A general pantheon, sure, but you have an enemy among them,' I say, pretending my words don't apply to me too. 'You can't rely on his so-called love to protect you from the worst he could do.'

'So, what?'

'You could pray for another god to intercede. Tyche?'

'She wouldn't even risk seeing me until Apollo and Zeus were distracted – she's not going to actively turn against them.'

'All right, what about a god on the Achaeans' side?'

'Why would they help us?'

'Because a god on *our* side is the problem. This could be the perfect opportunity to strike some petty blow against them. What about Athena? She'd know how to stop Apollo. Pray to her.'

'You're telling me not to rely on a god's whims by telling me to rely on the whims of another god.'

'All right, but what else do we do?' I ask. I reach out, running the lightest finger along the scar at her throat, wanting to soothe, wanting to do anything to erase it. She shivers at my touch, head tilting up ever so slightly.

I think about pressing my lips to the mark – to cover his threats with my affection.

'You're right,' she says. 'I can't possibly fight this by myself.'

But she's trying, and that alone is reassuring.

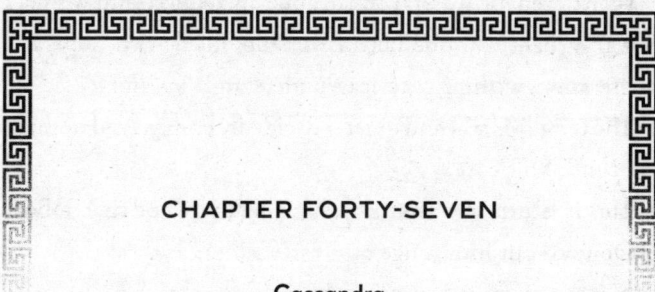

CHAPTER FORTY-SEVEN

Cassandra

ATHENA'S TEMPLE IS THE LARGEST of all on the acropolis, a statue rising out of its centre, her plumed helmet towering above neighbouring roofs. You could fit whole families in all of the statues about town – more, even – but Athena's statue, the original Palladium, is so enormous that you could probably fit the whole palace inside.

It's the foundation of Troy, sent to indicate where the city should be built, and I hope, praying before it, she might remember she once favoured us.

Inside, I take shaky steps towards her statue, her altar to my side, the marble walls gleaming.

This is where I come, in the visions I have seen. I hide here when the city falls, knowing Apollo won't save me and hoping she might.

She doesn't.

I curl my nails into my palms in a bid to stop tears from forming. Surely in those visions I had some reason to think that Athena might save me. Perhaps she already had.

I drop to my knees and arch my body towards her statue.

I can't even form a prayer, can't put my request into words. I just stay, bent towards her in worship, filled with hope and desperation, wishing for her to understand.

The temple is still and quiet – decidedly empty. And nothing happens.

But I return the next day, and on the ones that follow, praying for salvation.

The visions get bloodier, like they're drawn to the one wrapped tight round me. I see Kreousa fleeing from the city and trampled underfoot in the stampede. I see Scamandrius surrounded by Achaeans levelling swords at him. I see my mother bound and captive on the beach, crying for the ashes of her city, for the children she has buried and for the daughters she will never see again. And again and again – the city in ruins, dust and choking fumes and blazing snarls of flame.

Still I look for the glimmer of that other thread, the one that might offer a new future. But wherever it is, it must be hidden deep in the folds of the weave, all that tragedy demanding to be witnessed first.

The war is a chaotic mess – with the Amazons we're making strides, but without Paris our own army is faltering. Neither side is winning or losing but doing both with such violent pendulum swings that one sword stroke can shift entire battles.

One day I'm with Kreousa and Andromache in the library. Kreousa's reading, I'm trying to pluck prophetic strings and I think Andromache just wanted a distraction because suddenly she makes a strange choking noise and erupts with tears.

'What's wrong?' I ask, reaching for her almost awkwardly. I'm good at distraction, not comfort.

She shakes her head, like giving it voice would make it worse.

'Andromache,' Kreousa pushes, reaching across the table to take her hand.

She hesitates, then practically caves inwards and speaks to the parchment scattered across the desk. 'Hector and I argued yesterday. It's awful, and please don't hate me, but I begged him not to fight any more. I suggested we leave Troy.'

'That's not awful,' I assure her. I imagine everyone in the city has had such thoughts.

The prophecy choking me draws tighter. It hovers like a shadow, never blocking everything else out but tingeing it all the same. Sometimes it bleeds through in pain, the feeling of arrows shot through my skin, or it's the dizzying smoke or a hazy overlay to the world.

Right now it's the smell of my hair on fire.

'I begged him not to fight and then hours later someone threw a boulder at him. I can't shake the feeling he's not going to survive the war. I keep reading it into these bloody riddles.' She prods at a page like it might cause Hector's doom itself. 'And then he said he felt the same and that he hopes he falls first so he doesn't have to see Troy fall, and I . . . He said it would be a disgrace not to fight and I told him that was stupid, to be driven by shame and honour, not to mention selfish and –'

She cuts herself off with a shriek, reeling back as an armoured man appears on the table, blood leaking on to the pages below. Kreousa leaps to her feet and I startle back, staring at the man above him, his hand on the soldier's chest, a wicked gleam shining in his eyes as they meet mine.

'Hello, little priestess.'

I'm too shocked to be scared of him. 'Apollo, what –'

'There's really no time for that,' he says, ripping the helmet off and revealing Aeneas spluttering for breath. 'Aphrodite would make my life hell if I let him die – she practically flung him at me.' He turns to Kreousa. 'Well, I wouldn't wait around, love, he needs medical attention.'

She can't see Apollo and certainly can't hear him, but the moment she sees it's Aeneas, she throws herself at him, hands pressing into his wound as blood runs over her fingers.

Andromache runs, screaming, for the palace medics.

Apollo glistens with sweat, his tunic dirty, his armour askew, and a thick scar heals before my eyes on his forehead.

'My, your neck looks dreadful. That prophecy must be cutting right through you.'

My fingers fumble to my throat. The edge of my himation has tugged lower as I lurched back and I can feel the exposed groove in my skin. Is the cut deeper? Is this a slow death that he's tightened round me? Will I wake up one day unable to breathe, choking on a thing no one can see?

'If you cared to save yourself the pain, you'd resign yourself to the visions the threads design to show you. You'd stop seeking new prophecies out. You'd stop fighting *me*.'

I can't say anything, not with Kreousa right there and unable to see him. So I just nod and hope he takes it as surrender.

'This has been fun.' He grins a savage smile. 'Let's do this again.'

He unsheathes his sword and steps forward into nothing, vanishing from sight.

*

For the next few weeks, the war is difficult to make sense of. It's all news that we are winning, that they are winning, that we have pushed them back, that they're at our walls, all of it a jumble of threads, no longer aligned with the order of events once fated. Allies pour in, each one who joins inspiring several more who don't want to miss out on the glory. Paris finally goes back to the front, unable to bear the thought of them winning it without him, and the gods switch sides quicker than we can keep track.

I've been dipping in and out of war efforts but now my mother tries to put me properly to work: making food, weaving bandages, tending wounds and sewing clothes. She thinks my reluctance is because of the isolated rooms she provides, the way she keeps me separate even as she demands my help. And it does sting, but I'm too tired to care all that much – and far too tired to do much for the soldiers. Ignoring the visions is exhausting, but pushing through and reading them despite the pain is debilitating. And each day, I find myself doing it a little less – even though I should be reading them more. The war presses more firmly and we're all tired and hungry, and even those without prophetic visions hear the swords clashing at night.

I spend nearly every other moment at Athena's temple, waving incense and lighting candles. It takes weeks but finally the air cools and the distant hum of the priestesses stops.

'All of Anatolia must know I am firmly on the side of the Achaeans,' a scolding voice says, and I spin but can't see anyone. 'Yet you come here every day. Why?'

'I'm not asking you to change allegiances,' I say, addressing the statue and falling to my knees, so relieved she finally came that it takes all my effort not to sob. 'I'm asking for your help, not in the war but for me personally.'

'You personally?' There are footsteps now and she comes to stand in front of me. I look up into the storm-grey eyes of a goddess. She looks young, her face free of lines and her alabaster skin radiant as only a god's could be. But her eyes are ancient. 'There is an army at your walls yet you pray for your own salvation?'

'There's something I fear more than Achaean soldiers.'

'Oh?' she asks. 'Do tell.'

'Apollo.'

She's quiet for so long I expect to feel the flames of her radiance.

'Stand,' she says, and I do. She's no longer watching me with disdain but curiosity. 'Who are you?'

'Princess Cassandra.'

Her eyes narrow, shrewd now. 'You're the oracle.'

'I was supposed to be, yes.'

'And now you're in my temple? Do you simply bounce from one god to the next until one gives you the power you crave?'

'No, my lady,' I rush. 'It's not power I want.'

'Then what do you *want*?'

I flinch at the fury she laces into the word – that a mortal would come to her with demands, that they might care more for their own wants than hers.

'Please,' I say, because what else have I learnt other than that gods love pleading? 'Apollo cursed me after I rejected his advances and he's hardly left me alone since. I'm scared he punished me for denying him something he could take at any moment.'

'If he cursed you for your rejection, it would be a betrayal of the ancient laws to resolve the grievance in another manner. He would not punish you again for a slight he has already settled.'

What do I care for the ancient laws that govern gods? Since when have laws applied to powerful men?

'My vow of chastity –'

'So that's it?' she fumes. 'You just need a virginal goddess?'

'My vow of chastity was more than a vow. I think you may understand that.'

She stares at me for a long moment, her gaze softening ever so slightly. Then she looks at the Palladium, which is when I realize the likeness is not very good at all. Athena's nose is strong and straight, the statue's crooked like it's been broken; Athena's hair is thick and braided, the statue's is fine, tied back beneath the helmet it wears. Even the expression is serene in a way I can never imagine Athena's features managing.

But if not her, then who? The Palladium was sent by her, it shares her full title: *Pallas Athene*.

When she looks back at me, it is with sudden shrewdness, like she can see me putting these pieces together.

'Her name was Pallas.'

So much lingers in those unsaid words, something even in the way she leans into them, something that says: *This is someone I loved with such intensity I took her name and made it part of myself.*

Something, also, that says: *Even death was not enough to stop me carrying a piece of her with me.*

She lingers on that word, 'was', like it's a burden, like she suffers under the heaviness of it.

Then her head tilts up, the edges of her harden and she turns back to me, terrifying once more.

'So, you hope for a kindred spirit? You hope that will be enough for me to turn from the side I favour for a girl who's never worshipped me before?'

'Apollo is the patron god of my city,' I say. 'Aside from Zeus, we were never taught there was a stronger god in existence. But I have prophecies now. I can see you are the only one strong enough to stop him.'

It's pure flattery.

But Athena smiles.

'Fortunately for you, I'm not best pleased with the little twerp at the moment, for obvious reasons. Zeus is tracking our every choice on a battlefield, but this? A trifling matter, yes, but one I'm sure will enrage him.'

So this is what gets her to help, just as Helen predicted: spite.

Gods. They're all just as selfish, vain and malicious as each other.

But maybe it will work in my favour for once.

'I have no interest in removing your curse, even if I could. One god cannot undo the work of another, or we'd be at each other's throats more than we already are. So this is my decree: *No god shall touch you.*'

'No . . . *god?*' I repeat, just to make sure I have this right.

'No god,' she snaps. 'I'm not having a second Achilles – who, make no mistake, will be back on our side once more. No. No god shall touch you, Cassandra. But I make no promises for other mortals.'

CHAPTER FORTY-EIGHT

Helen

Cassandra still sees a patchwork of prophecies but she doesn't chase them like she once did and each day her efforts falter a little bit more. The visions still smother her, still strike her like a blow – but she's not seeking them out, so they're no longer accompanied by pained brushes of her fingers to her throat and long recoveries in bed, drinking the milky tea Andromache often takes for pain.

Cassandra's miserable for it. As though she has failed somehow by saying there is some pain she cannot – will not – fight any longer. Like suffering is a test of strength and, by choosing the alternative, she has proved herself weak rather than human.

'You already have the answer,' I say. 'Save Hector, win the war. We don't need more prophecies to achieve that.'

She shakes her head. 'That other path must be hidden. I should be finding it, because the only visions striking me themselves are of Achilles sitting in his tent, refusing to fight, then they cut to that fatal strike that brings Hector down.'

'We can work with that.'

It's not only Herophile passing our messages to the council but dozens of priestesses across the city. And soon they're all carrying our advice: recruit Achilles to our side, send assassins for him, rile him up even further and get him to go home entirely. We try anything we can think of to ensure he never goes back to the war and we try to plan for what happens if he does.

I tell everyone that one of my contacts has heard Achilles in the camps telling anyone who will listen that if he ever goes back, he will assert his glory by killing the crown prince.

But we're not making much headway.

'Hector's proved himself a dozen times over on the field. He gets nothing new from fighting – why not prove himself a master of strategy too by joining the council?' Athrae suggests.

I'm sitting with a few of the women in my room, surrounded by scraps of paper with prophecies scrawled across them. Cassandra is on the window ledge – always setting herself apart even when she is the reason for our gathering.

'Does your source know Achilles well enough to recognize whether it's just a brag rather than an oath?' Agata asks.

I glance at Cassandra, seeing if she's caught what has just been said. But she's distracted by something I can't see, eyes following movement through the still room.

I have not told her the details of my arrangement with these women: that they believe they are decoding messages from the Achaeans. That they believe I have a source. That they tell no one because they think they are protecting me. If one of them were to change their mind, I might be accused of treason. It's a risk Cassandra would not allow me to take – and one I would only even consider for her.

'He was serious,' I answer.

'I only ask because I don't see the council letting Hector leave the front any time soon,' Agata says. 'He's the only one who stands a chance against those Achaean leaders. I was waiting on the council earlier and the latest reports told that just this afternoon Hector brought down Patroclus, one of their –'

Cassandra gasps, her body jerking so violently her foot twists in the heavy curtain and she crashes down to the hard stone floor.

I rush to her and she lets me bring her to her feet even as her eyes stare wide. I guide her from the room before she can start speaking those prophecies aloud where the others might hear.

But the second I get her out of the door she's grasping me as piercingly as a Fury's talons.

'Helen, oh gods! Hector, he's – I need your help, you need to . . . I don't know! I don't know how to stop it –'

'It's okay,' I rush, but her bright eyes are desperate and already welling with tears. 'We can figure it out. What did you see?'

'It's not him – it's not him, Helen! I was wrong, oh gods – there was never another thread, it's all part of the same wretched future and he's going to die and we're –'

'Cassandra!' I say sharply.

She swallows, her lips dry and cracked. 'It was never Achilles I saw Hector kill. I thought it was – the men around him were calling his name and following him into battle. But it was a trick. It was Patroclus in disguise.'

I'm so used to her telling me her prophecies and still it does nothing to stop that instinctive anger as the curse takes hold, that part of me that hisses that this is ridiculous and not worth listening to.

I swallow it down, surrendering my doubts to my faith in her. But that disbelief is getting increasingly harder to push past.

'But if Achilles isn't fighting, then –'

'This is what gets Achilles to fight again! And he won't stop until he's avenged Patroclus's death. He really is determined to kill Hector.'

The lie we created to excuse the prophecy, turned into a prophecy itself.

I meet her eyes, because if Achilles is back on the field with a vendetta, Hector's death is imminent. Days, at most.

I take her hands in mine, like I might anchor her to the present and save her from the doom we're apparently hurtling towards.

'I don't know if we can fix this. But I promise we're going to try.'

Cassandra spends hours scrawling on parchment, agonizing over every tiny detail like we might find the clue to weaving salvation within it.

I rush to distribute the notes among the women I trust, but Clymene pulls me aside.

'It's Cassandra, isn't it?' she spits. 'Your *source*. We're interpreting her prophecies.'

'Clymene,' I start, but the look on her face makes it clear I cannot talk my way out of this.

'She had a vision and now suddenly you have pages and pages of details. It was right in front of us, Helen.'

Olympus above, she could unravel us all, turn all those women against me. And here it is, the danger I am primed to sense and quick to avoid, but I don't even care because this is so much more important.

'You can yell at me, you can report me, whatever you like – just please can we save Hector first?'

Her eyes flash. 'Hector doesn't need saving. And I can't believe you'd waste all our time in the middle of a war to indulge senseless prophecies just because you like the disgraced oracle delivering them.'

'Clymene, I am begging you, please. This isn't about Cassandra. Trust me. Or, at the very least, suspend your disbelief. What harm is there? If we're wrong, he lives; if we're right . . . well, if we fight this, then we might keep him alive.'

Her lips press into a thin line, her gaze boring into me, and then she snatches the page of prophecy out of my hands.

'I'll try. And then I'll consider whether I can forgive you for all this.'

Clymene is bitter when we gather, unable – or maybe simply not trying – to keep her vitriol from her expression or dripping into the venom of her tongue. 'Well, just don't fight Achilles,' she hisses, hurling her reed stylus down after mere moments.

It's everyone – all ten of the women I've been trusting – in one space and poring through pages.

'Honour aside, you cannot avoid a singular enemy on the battlefield,' I say, and we keep trying, getting nowhere, and each second that passes is another when Achilles' blade might strike true.

Cassandra is in another room, tearing through threads – digging into their cores and hurtling through vision after vision, still begging for one more glance of anything that might help.

When I check on her, I find her swaying on her feet, blood beading on the line at her neck. Her hands flail before her and, from her screech of indignation, it appears she cannot grasp a single thread. The harder she pushes – the greater the exhaustion and the pain – the more difficult reading those strands becomes.

Dread dawns like it hasn't yet – knowing something is true and believing it are two very different things, after all – but this strikes where her curse has not. Save Hector, save the city. Save Hector, save Cassandra from all that she will do to herself to rescue him.

Back with the others, Kreousa reaches for the scrap of prophecy Athrae had been studying. 'Could we change the smaller details? Tell him not to use a chariot or his spear? They might not recognize it's him.'

It's the best we have but it sounds weak, especially against a thread so fundamental to the war.

Then Agata reads that same page.

'Gold armour? We would never waste a metal like that on armour. Trojan armour is bronze.'

'He's the crown prince,' I say, having brushed over the detail myself.

'Gold is soft. Trojan armour is bronze,' she repeats definitively. 'Trust me, I've repaired enough of it these last few months.'

Of course only a prince could afford armour like that – but not a prince of Troy.

A prince of Phthia. Cassandra said it herself: Patroclus disguised himself as Achilles. He wore his armour.

Hector must have taken it for himself.

And now Hector is being hunted by a man who knows its weak spots because it was once his to wear.

I sprint back to Herophile who in turn rushes to the council with sudden advice that Hector ought to wear armour emblazoned with the emblem of Apollo rather than that taken from Achilles.

It should be easy – a logical thing not to wear your enemy's armour. But so many men have watched swords bend on Achilles' skin that they're half convinced his armour is god-made – which it very much might be. The council debate it for far, *far* too long.

I pace the antechamber next door while Cassandra runs through threads beside me, refusing to stop weaving until we have confirmation that Hector followed the order.

'The threads are realigning,' she suddenly gasps. 'They must have reached a conclusion, and ... yes, yes, there's no armour – No!'

She falls to her knees, staring at the distance. I'm not even sure she's having a vision, but she continues to mutter: 'No, no, no!'

'It's all right. We stopped it once. We can stop it again.'

'No, we can't.' Her voice catches on the rough promise of a future I can't see. 'Not when however many gods must be pushing the strands back into place.'

Then she stands, and reaches for another thread anyway.

For weeks, she is frenzied. I do, genuinely, believe her hopeless. But she pushes on like it's all she can do, like she will face inevitability with torn nails and bloodied skin, screaming at the gods who make it so.

We stop it so many times: when Hector is supposed to lead men in Dardanian armour into a trap, we have him fight with the Mysians instead – but Penthesilea, leader of the Amazons, ends up in his place and dies at Achilles' blade; or when Cassandra sees Athena herself guide Achilles to Hector, so we tell Hector not to leave Apollo's side – let the god coat him in fog and shield him from view. We tell him to use different weapons, wear different armour, fight close to the walls – and it's clear throughout that he knows what we're trying to stop, especially with the way all our advice comes from priestesses. It must appear to everyone as though a chorus of the gods has suddenly turned their attention on keeping Hector alive.

We listen at the door as Hector addresses the council with polite greetings, thanking them for welcoming him into the fold. 'It's evident the gods see something we may rather not face, but know that to fall for Troy would be an honour.'

'Like hell it would,' Andromache hisses beneath her breath, clutching Kreousa's arm from the hallway.

Andromache's not one of the women who decode, instead running the network of combat classes across the city now I've stepped back. But obviously she knows what lies ahead as well as Hector does.

Everyone does.

Achilles tears through the battlefield demanding to face him, searching him out, yelling for his blood.

They know he will not stop until he has it.

I scatter the scraps of prophecy across my floor and pace the confines of my room until I break, screaming and kicking the rough stone walls. The pain lances through me and I collapse to the floor. I can't do this. Cassandra is counting on me. She's torturing herself to save her brother. If I can't stop this, she's going to keep hurting, and I'm not smart enough to work out what we need to do. The lengths she's going to just to acquire these prophecies, and then I can't interpret them or source a fix within them, and I'm going to be the reason Hector dies and Troy falls.

I finally manage it one more time, just another miracle in a line of twenty. But when I retreat to the palace, Cassandra is clutching a pillow and sobbing.

'Achilles, he –' she gasps. 'He was supposed to be spending his days dragging my brother's body before the walls. But he's still on the field and he's killed so many people who probably wouldn't have died otherwise. He's dammed the whole river with corpses, all because I changed the future.'

I bite my tongue, my patience wearing thin. Her throat looks like raw meat, a dozen women have pushed themselves to the edge to unravel her prophecies and I'm not only at the brink, I'm dangling from it, all the lies and sleepless nights spent trying to fix this – and she has the nerve to feel guilty that it's working?

'I'm pretty sure those people are dead because of the man with the sword,' I snipe. I don't want to be annoyed with her, but it's so difficult when my very skin itches when she tells a prophecy – certain knowledge that I am being lied to with every sentence.

Cassandra returns to her visions. I pore over prophecies until my eyes water, or else clutch at a strain in my side from yet another sprint to the temple to relay advice.

And Hector falls on a cold autumnal evening anyway.

A month. That's all we managed to buy him.

Cassandra does not even see it before it happens, the threads hidden under the other strands in that iron core of the future, so every time she tries to prise them free she's hit with other horrible visions in our certain future. But when it comes to pass, she tells me that the molten gold of threads of the future fades to a dull gleam of threads enacted.

She chokes back a sob and reaches for them. Apparently, it happens like this: Poseidon challenges Apollo to a duel, distracting him. Menelaus fights Aeneas, and Aphrodite hovers nervously by, unable to tear her gaze from each sword strike levelled at her son. And while the gods on our side are busy, Athena goes to Zeus, and Zeus shines his light upon Achilles and says that Hector was supposed to have died days ago and that she should go and lead him to it.

'*Supposed to*,' Cassandra spits, gaunt and haggard after all her frantic efforts. 'Zeus simply says what he wants to happen and casts it as the natural course of fate – as though I have not seen the way fate can be woven into a new and better future.'

Hector faces the will of the king of the gods, surrounded by enemies, raising his sword anyway, not going down without a fight.

We hear the cries of the people in the city long before we reach the walls, where Priam stares with shock and rage and grief at the scene below. Andromache runs up the steps, drawn by the ringing bells and already screaming, already sure of what they must mean, and when she glances at her husband's body she staggers back, suddenly quiet, and collapses against the stones.

A single tear slides down Cassandra's cheek.

It's the only one I see her shed.

CHAPTER FORTY-NINE

Cassandra

HECTOR DIES AND EVERYTHING FRACTURES, like the world does not know how to stay whole without him: my mother unable to talk without choking on tears, my father locked in his room and refusing to summon the council together, Kreousa and Polyxena haunting the halls in the early hours of the morning because no one can sleep any more, the temples overwhelmed with patrons rushing in with their prayers, because if the prince can fall, then anyone can.

My body breaks, though if I'm honest it had been breaking for a while, held together by spite and desperation. As soon as that falls away, the pain becomes unbearable, my bones heavy. I did not know it was possible for energy to exist in negative, to have less than none to give.

After a week in bed too feverish to think straight, I clamber out and start reaching for the threads again, ignoring the way the wound on my neck reopens.

My door swings wide, and I jump back, practically throwing myself into bed.

It's Helen, with honeyed milk that she sets beside me.

'You're awake.'

There's no response to so stupid a statement so I say nothing, just pick up the cup and take a sip, trembling at the way it soothes my throat.

'How are you feeling?'

'Fine,' I say quickly. 'Better.'

She sits on the bed next to me and offers a small smile. 'Good. I'm glad. And how are you feeling about ... well, Hector?'

How dare she even ask?

I set the cup heavily on the side and rise to my feet. 'Yes, it's all very sad, isn't it? I should find Andromache, I can't imagine she's taking this well.'

'Cassandra, please, I don't think you should be ...'

Her words falter under my thunderous glare.

'Frankly, Helen, I no longer care for any form of "should" in my life. Don't worry, it won't be all that long, anyway.'

Andromache is not, in fact, taking it well.

She is destroyed, and I can see it in her threads too. The future is gold, and she is a bundle of greyed strands that never came to fruition, all the things she never got.

The war was supposed to last a decade. And maybe they wouldn't have been the happiest, but that's ten years of snatches of love and laughter. Dances yet to be stepped, jokes yet to be told ... *Olympus above*, a child yet to be even dreamt of.

What would I give for another decade of Hector? I did this – my meddling. I collapsed the timeline. I'm the reason my brother died *now*.

Quite literally, too, because I'm the one who wove that first thread: Achilles quitting the war. If he hadn't, would Patroclus ever have donned his armour in his stead? Would Achilles have had a death to avenge?

So when I'm not resting, I'm with Andromache, like if I comfort her enough, it will make up for all that I've done – and of course that's what I think, of course I could have no reason to console my best friend other than to selfishly atone. Apparently, I am always capable of sinking lower.

'I feel so awful,' she says – rather needlessly, really – and leans forward to continue in a whisper. 'I'm so angry. Whenever anyone else cries for him – his own mother! – I just want to shake them, to scream that they didn't love him as I did and they have no right to mourn while I'm standing before them with my heart in tatters.'

'It's not awful, Andromache,' I promise, squeezing her hand tight. 'Death is messy. Grief is complicated. Just feel it, however you need to – sadness, anger, guilt over your anger . . . it's all understandable.'

No one has lost as much as she has, after all.

'I love you,' she says, burying her head into my shoulder, and I run my hand in soothing circles across her back.

'I love you too. And I'm here for you.'

But I did this. And each of Andromache's heart-wrenching sobs engraves it a little more, until I feel my very bones must have my crimes etched upon them.

There aren't many ways to hide in the palace, and I've taken Helen to all the secret places I know. So I'm not surprised when she finds me, just disappointed.

I'm around the back of the palace, in the dusty, shady sliver of grass before the jut of the mountain that rises above. I let the threads I've been trying to weave blur, and Helen comes into focus.

'Hey.' Everything about her is tentative – the half-step she takes forward, her quiet voice, even the way she's looking at me, like she's keeping her expression smooth.

'What do you want?'

I only feel the slightest twinge of guilt at how sharp it sounds. I'm just so tired of everyone creeping around me, asking how I am. Andromache had a point – aren't there far more important people to ask that question?

Helen doesn't flinch, just looks at me with that same steady gaze. 'Prophecies, actually. I wanted to ask if you had any. Everyone's quite torn up, especially with the way Achilles is desecrating the body.'

Which he wouldn't have done if I hadn't threaded those strands together and made his anger grow. I couldn't just kill my own brother – no, I had to ensure we couldn't even bury the body and allow his soul safe passage to the Underworld. I'm the reason everyone's grief is so much worse.

'So they're asking for a distraction. I wondered if you had anything they could decode.'

'No.'

'No?'

'No, I don't. I'm not reading the future any more.' I hide my hands in the folds of my dress, like Helen might notice the bruising on them where I've shoved against the threads, trying to get them to move, trying to force them to twist into new patterns. 'I pushed too far.'

'Absolutely, a break sounds good.' She nods vigorously, almost relieved. 'I just meant the regular sort, the ones that fall upon you, you know?'

'Actually, I'm trying to tune those out. I think I've paid them too much attention.' And made things considerably worse. 'I'm trying to just enjoy the time we have left. To spend time with the people I love while I still can.'

At that Helen does flinch, even as she tries to hide the hurt that – with the way I have been avoiding her – she is apparently not in that number. In a second, her expression is back to one of serene resignation.

'Right, so I'll just go?' Her voice is as taut as the threads strung between us.

'That's probably for the best. We have nothing to work on together any more. I'll see you later.'

I don't give her the chance to leave – I'm already walking away.

Kreousa buries herself in the library, like if she loses herself in words, she can lose everything else too. I sit next to her with a scroll I'm not reading – when it comes to Kreousa, the best comfort is to simply be by her side.

I notice her rereading the same sections again and again, and finally she gently rolls up the scroll, places it on the table and looks at me, like they're all predetermined actions she's taking step by step.

'I think I need to break up with Aeneas.'

'And why do you think that?'

She gnaws at the edge of her nail, refusing to meet my gaze. 'It's too much, loving someone who's out on that field every day. I . . . His blood's still on this table, Cassandra, I can't –'

'Aeneas is probably the only person out there who is safe, with the way his mother is running after him – she even has the other gods trying to keep him alive.'

'Some of those gods tried to keep Hector alive too,' she snaps, but her words catch on his name.

'And would you have preferred never to have known Hector? Do you think Andromache wishes she'd never loved him if it would have saved her this pain?'

Kreousa's eyes are quickly watering and she's swiping at them like she's annoyed with her own tears. 'No, no, I suppose not.'

And then she can't keep up and she's crying and, even though I'm sure she'd pretend to hate it under any other circumstances, I pull my sister into my arms and let her sob.

When Polyxena crawls into my bed in the middle of the night, I hold her while she cries too – and when she does the same the next day and the day after, I tell her she can take all the time she needs.

Deiphobus sends a letter from the front about how much he's struggling, how much he's having to hold it together because he's now commanding the entire army and he doesn't have time to grieve and who could he tell anyway. I write back to say his grief is safe with me, and we begin exchanging letters daily.

Helen is working in tandem with me, but like the balanced weight of a scale, so that we might never touch without swaying apart. I carry the emotional weight, she the practicalities. She coordinates the prayers and sacrifices while Mother is distracted with her grief. When my father finally gets Hector's body back, having crossed the walls himself to plead with the man who killed him, Helen is the one liaising with the council to arrange the funeral games.

When I have a spare moment, I wrestle with strands that refuse to move. And when Helen has time, she tries to speak to me.

'Your neck isn't healing, Cassandra – I'm concerned.'

'How are you feeling?'

'I miss you.'

I escape her conversation like bonds to slip, brushing them off and rushing to take cover before they can bind me again.

A few nights before the funeral games begin, she finds me in our usual courtyard. The moon shines bright, the silvery glow reversing the golden hue Apollo's sun creates. It feels safe, like I can exist without his watchful gaze.

'You're weaving,' Helen says, appearing from nowhere. 'You're reading the strands.'

I jump, my hands floundering in the air before me.

'Well? Have you seen anything?'

'No.'

Her lips press thin, her eyes racing across me like I am a prophecy to be analysed.

'Have you cried yet?'

I scoff. 'What?'

'Have you cried yet?' she repeats, her voice even and annoyingly calm in the face of my bluntness. 'Andromache, Kreousa, Polyxena – you can't be everyone's shoulder to cry on at the expense of your own grief, Cassandra.'

'Don't be ridiculous.'

'Have you?'

No. Of course not.

'Unlike everyone else, I knew this was coming, Helen. I cried months ago.'

I knew this would happen and I didn't stop it – I don't deserve to indulge a grief I could have prevented if I'd just tried harder, read more strands.

If I'd fucking slept with Apollo . . .

'Cassandra, please, you don't need to pretend you're okay –'

'Stop!' I scream as a dam in my chest breaks and scorching fury pours forth. 'Stop asking me how I feel – I'm fine! I don't get to be sad like everyone else, not when I made this happen, when I wove those threads and didn't stop it despite a dozen prophecies. I . . . This doesn't get to be about me!'

'It's about you to me.'

'Then maybe you should gain some fucking perspective.'

Helen takes a breath, approaching me with more careful steps, like I'm a wild beast, and I'm so livid it takes all my willpower not to send my fist flying into the wall. 'You didn't cause this. Achilles' pride is legendary – even weaving those threads, you likely just fanned what was already planted there by his mother or that prophecy or every Achaean soldier constantly telling him how special he is. Or by Agamemnon taking Briseis from him and the fact both of them thought they had a right to her in the first place, by Patroclus in his heart and his pride in turn, and Agamemnon's pride on top of that, and the pride of the whole army. Maybe you are a small, small piece in this, but it is certainly not your fault. You were seeing Hector's death long before you wove that strand. You're right. This is about so many more people than you.'

It's so reminiscent of what I told Paris that my fury blocks out any coherent thought, until I'm shouting: 'Shut up! Shut up! Gods, I knew you'd do this!'

'Do what?'

'Try to make me feel better! Manipulate me with your silver tongue because you know what levers to pull in me, because I can't hide myself from you, Helen. And you'd argue with me and make points I'm not smart enough to counter –'

'Because I make rational points, you mean?'

'Your logic doesn't outweigh the truth, Helen! You don't get to comfort me or take this blame away because I deserve it, okay? And I can't break down when I did this, and when my family –'

I break off, startled, as she takes my hands in hers.

'You're crying,' she says gently.

Am I? I falter, blinking, and, yes, my eyes are watering, tears on my cheeks dampening the flames of my anger. Am I truly so disconnected from the world that I did not even realize I was crying? I am shaken and scared, trying to cling to what I told Andromache, that emotions are there to be felt. But the rules feel different for me, and what if I've so thoroughly fallen apart that there are no pieces to reassemble?

Gods, I miss Hector. He would understand this more than anyone – holding yourself to a different standard, doing what needs to be done. Duty. Honour. And now my tears are falling faster.

Helen turns my hands over, examining the bruised fingertips, the narrow ridges carved into them that could only come from the harsh, wiry threads.

'You told me you weren't trying to read the future any more.'

'I'm not,' I say quietly.

It takes her a moment. 'Oh. You're trying to reweave the past.'

I look down. 'I can't help it. Every time I convince myself I've given up, I never really do.'

'I know.' She nods, eyes catching the moonlight like her gaze itself is the safety I was searching for. 'I think it's beautiful.'

'I don't. I really don't. I knew I probably couldn't undo the past but that didn't stop me shoving against those threads anyway. I keep thinking of the tale of Pandora. How she opened that jar and let out all the evils of the world, shutting the lid in time to keep hope from escaping too . . . Well, I'm beginning to believe hope was in that jar because it too is a curse. The war, the way we know how it's going to end. I think we all do, really. Hector knew his fate. Andromache did too. What if that's just how this goes? To know the future and fight and fight and fight and fall anyway? Where's the beauty in that?'

'Because one day you might fight and win.'

I'm trembling, all that hope and fear swirling like they might become one and the same. 'What if none of this is worth it?'

'The end crowns all, Cassandra. We won't know until it's over. Either way, we keep fighting, and we dream and we hope.'

Her threads gleam bright, shining gold against her white arms, braiding and fraying even as I watch: all that future, all that hope.

And she's right: it's beautiful.

CHAPTER FIFTY

Helen

HECTOR'S FUNERAL GAMES LAST A week. The Achaeans even agree to a temporary ceasefire for it. Perhaps it helps our would-be invaders believe they are noble, or maybe even reminds them that they are human. Maybe they need the break too – or perhaps they are holding their own games for Patroclus, as Achilles' rage finally gives way to a grief of his own.

Normally, I would lose myself in the games – pushing myself to race, straining to watch combat and placing wagers on winners.

But despite the fact they are a celebration – after weeks of grieving, finally, an opportunity to honour the man Hector was – I find myself unable to summon much of a jovial spirit.

All I can think about is day after day of desperately trying to keep him alive.

And then the aftermath.

Cassandra falling and falling and falling – and pushing me away in case I caught her. Only now she's clawed herself out of the pit can I admit how scared I was. I have lived in sadness, in the deep well of it. It is the home Menelaus would like to make for me. I know the horrifying thoughts that can crawl into your mind and take root there.

But she's not here. The gods do not allow their dedicated followers to be involved with funeral games lest the taint of death come for them too, and despite Cassandra having been stripped of her priesthood, it's still a risk no one is willing to take.

So I watch the games hollowly, leaning into Paris's side. We haven't really spoken much, and things have been stiff and awkward since he came home, but we do *like* each other, I think, beyond the hurt and the hopes we might once have had. So he leans back, squeezing my shoulder like he does not wish to lose me even if he cannot have me in the way he wanted.

Andromache stands by my side, observing the games with a steely, cold stare.

Clymene finds me in the crowd and we step aside, speaking in hushed whispers. I wonder if this is it, if I'm about to lose my closest friends. I remember the way Menelaus cut mine off, and the thought of Clymene and Athrae turning against me reopens a wound I realize never fully healed.

'Something's going on, isn't it? Something you can't tell us.' She speaks calmly, like she already knows this is the answer. I wonder how long she has spent ruminating on it to come to such a conclusion.

I'm so relieved that my answering nod is a little frantic. 'Even I'm operating on faith. The gods have made this complicated.'

Clymene considers. 'I understand that. In future, I would rather you tell me you cannot give me everything than lie to cover the gaps.'

'But we're all right?' It sounds so needy, but I'd half feared she would tell the council the truth of where the priests are getting their missives from the gods.

She glances across at the fights. I can see her weighing something up before she sighs. 'I don't know how you'll react to this. But, Helen, I need you to know that you can make mistakes and be forgiven. You can trust when we say we care about you – we mean more than just the parts of yourself you show to us.'

A lump forms in my throat and then Paris is by my side again, and I'm hardly watching the games, I'm thinking about all the ways I'm careful and all the things I do to survive and what life might be like if I let those walls crumble.

We say prayers for Hector, make offerings, give him a proper burial and, with a coin in his mouth, he may pass into the Underworld peacefully at last, with payment for being ferried into the paradise he deserves.

On the final day, before the war begins again, there is more drinking and, despite all the banquets, this one feels like it could be the last. The games have worked: everyone is in good spirits, celebrating like Hector would no doubt have wanted, and clinging to each other like we have been reminded of just how fragile life is.

Cassandra is in the corner with Kreousa and Polyxena. She's laughing – bright smile and crinkled eyes – and I was right: hope is beautiful, and on her it's transcendent.

I cross the hall without making the conscious effort to do so. She sparkles in the dim light – lanterns and candles, all those flames reflected in the rubies glistening in her ears and the delicate silver diadem perched on her head, her own dark hair woven round it to keep it in place.

She only notices me when I am standing right in front of her.

'Will you dance with me?' I ask.

She glances at my outstretched hand. 'Why?'

Because I want to hold you and this is the only way I can think to ask. Because I want to give the world something whole and real and true, and to me that's you.

'Because we both need it.'

'It's highly unusual.'

'We're at war. I think everyone is past caring what's usual.'

Oh, and I thought I was tired of lies. They care. They all care and perhaps I'll be punished and perhaps it might be a further step towards being sent back to Greece, but I'll have danced with someone I care about. That shouldn't be worth it. And yet here I am, my hand held out, begging for this moment.

She twines her fingers through mine and, all at once, everything settles, like for the first time in my life the ground is solid beneath me.

The music strums softly – a quick but quiet beat that echoes in my heart. I lean into its rhythm as I twirl her, her skirts flaring around her, and I try not to trace the shape of her, try not to let my eyes linger and definitely try not to fantasize about what it might be like to feel her – a hand on her hip, her waist, trailing along her thigh.

She's graceful – much more than I am. She moves like the breeze, like each vibrating note is something she feels rather than hears and her hands curl into mine so firmly she might crush the bone. I only realize how broadly I'm smiling when her own lips curve in gentle offering.

'You're not very good at this,' she teases. 'Finally, something the great Helen of Troy can't do.'

I don't tell her it's because I'm leading, because I've never danced this part before.

'Perhaps you're simply talented enough to leave me in the dust,' I say, tightening my hold on her until our bodies are inches from being flush against one another. Inches I can taste, can feel shaking, crumbling as we draw closer with every breath.

I forget there are other bodies spinning around us, circles of silk – her umber beside my navy like the sunrise against the Aegean Sea, her smile, her shimmering brown eyes flashing with the flickering candlelight.

And then the song ends and there's a hand on my waist, and I turn to Paris as he laughs and places his other hand on Cassandra's shoulder.

'People are looking,' he says through a smile. And he and I are just a couple happily in love, and Paris is talking to his sister who is such bosom friends with his wife that they might want to dance together, and nothing at all is going on if you do not look too closely.

'Thank you,' I say, meaning it. There's a look in his eyes that isn't quite knowing but trusting – like he doesn't understand what's going on but believes I would not put us in a precarious position or harm the illusion we're all fighting for. But I am, aren't I? I am clawing for gems of truth to be hidden under a dozen lies.

But maybe I can find more truth, even if I cannot reveal it fully. I may not be able to tell Cassandra that I am, perhaps, on the cusp of loving her.

But I can make her feel loved.

CHAPTER FIFTY-ONE

Cassandra

THE PYANOPSIA COMES MERE WEEKS later and it feels timely – long enough to begin the journey towards processing our grief and to be brought back together as a family. My brothers return from the front, even as the battle rages on.

We take offerings to the temple of Apollo. Pastries, fruit, honey – how can we possibly spare all this food? But I wouldn't put it past Apollo to betray even his favoured city if it did not honour him enough.

I stumble as I walk, distracted by the flames and smoke that follow me and the sharp sting of the thread bound around me.

'Isn't this an Athenian festival?' Helen asks.

'I'm sure there are many cities sacred to Apollo but we're his favourite,' I say. 'So we celebrate all of his festivals.'

At the temple, Herophile is resplendent in an elaborate saffron robe, swanning around like the Pyanopsia is a festival in honour of her rather than her god. We sing, we pray, we make offerings. It's strange, to be sitting with my family rather than being part of the processions. But it's a nice sort of strange, especially after so long forced into the corners. And they can hardly sit away from me in the temple of the very lord I used to serve. Besides, I'd rather be here than with the priestesses. I don't even miss the reverence or the prestige any more – I just want to be with the people I love, singing songs and celebrating.

We make more offerings at the palace gates – more branches adorned with the little food we can spare.

In the Great Hall, we dance and play games, chatting in small groups, and, suddenly, Helen touches my sleeve.

'Hey, can we talk?'

'Always.'

I follow her to her chambers.

Helen's rooms are plainly furnished, with little character to them, but I see that she's been adding things, bit by bit: the dried-flower crowns we made hang on the bedposts, polished stones from the palace gardens are in a vase on her dressing table, and an array of weapons are propped in the corner. She kneels and pulls a box from beneath her bed.

'Here.'

I take it from her with a frown. 'What's this?'

'I'm mad at the gods,' she says with a conspiratorial smile. 'So I thought, *Why should Apollo be the only one to receive gifts today?*'

And suddenly, this moment is charged. Helen is not one to take risks with such sacrilege. It is a mistake to think the gods can never punish you more than they already have.

I open the box.

A golden apple, tiny, on a thin chain. When I lift it out of the box, the apple spins, and on its side I see the inscription: *Ti kallisti. For the fairest.*

When I look up, she's staring at me with such intensity I nearly drop it.

Well, this is even more dangerous, like we are taunting the gods. A dozen stories run through my head of those who dared compare themselves to divinity. And if Helen is somehow suggesting that what they fought over, what was clearly marked for one of them – if not all of them – could somehow belong to me, then it's every bit as sharp as the blades clashing outside these walls.

'What does this mean?'

'You know what it means,' she says pointedly, a little louder than usual, like it's a declaration.

'Helen,' I say thickly. She's still staring at me and I can't stand it. I don't know whether to cry or kiss her, and all I can think to do is break the tension by blurting: 'I actually have something for you too.'

'Really?' she half laughs in shock. 'Why?'

'I . . . You'll see.'

I take her to my room and pass her the gift, still wrapped in the thin linen I bought it in. The necklace is clutched tight in my hand and feels heavier than its thin gold mass must be – all my unanswered questions weighing it down.

For the fairest. For the fairest. For the fairest.

I don't want to believe it means what I think it might, because if I'm wrong, I'm not sure I'll survive it.

Helen wastes no time plucking the strings apart and revealing the mirror I bought at Andromache's encouragement. I wonder if we both bought our gifts from the same shop. I cannot think of another with such fine inscriptions.

It takes her a moment to realize the looping words round

the mirror's edge are not merely a pattern and when she does she laughs.

'"For the face that launched a thousand ships to see itself a bit better"', she reads. 'Are you telling me I'm vain?'

'Yes,' I say with a smile. And then, before I can stop myself: 'Besides, it seems so unfair for the rest of us to see you all the time. You ought to see such beauty too.'

Now she flushes, and glances away. 'Well, thank you.' Her tone is strained, like she is missing the joke she was aiming for. 'I haven't been told I'm beautiful enough lately.'

My mouth is dry. Why am I doing this? Passing it off like it means nothing, when I bought it to tell her the things I couldn't put into words: *I see you.*

I summon the dregs of bravery I have left. 'That makes sense. Your beauty is the least interesting thing about you.'

She glances up, cerulean eyes locking with mine. 'Let me put that on you,' she says, nodding to the necklace dangling from my fingers.

She drapes it over my neck before I can protest, leans behind me to clasp it, her jasmine perfume floating on the air, and the small golden apple comes to rest between my collarbones.

She draws back slowly and I'm not sure what happens. She is too close, and I am dizzy with the scent of her, her cold hands on my neck, her hair tickling my cheek.

And then her lips are on mine.

She tastes like bitter wine sweetened with honey.

Her kiss is cycling tides and falling leaves, waning moons and thunderous breezes. It is a force of nature, and for once I feel a rooted part of the world I inhabit rather than an opposition in its wake.

My shaking fingers brush her face, like I'm not sure this moment is real – that she is real. And her hands tighten on my waist, pulling me closer as though she needs to grasp me in the same, disbelieving, way.

When I draw away, she doesn't let go. She just looks at me with a hunger that goes behind desire and into something deeper, a need for something purer: to be known, wholly and completely. To not only be accepted but revered.

I feel it first round my neck – the shaking of the thread that ties me there. I open my eyes and the weave is alive, moving and whipping and untangling and rewinding – the golden strands of energy vibrating so harshly I clutch her hand as though I might hold her still.

The cord round my neck snaps.

I gasp and the threads move so quickly the room is a blur of gold.

And then it settles, that iron cord unchanged. But everything else is laid anew.

Her trust. My power. Our kiss.

These things come in threes.

We can change our future – we can carve one for ourselves.

PART THREE

CHAPTER FIFTY-TWO

Cassandra

THE MOMENT THE STRANDS SETTLE, a vision strikes me with such ferocity that the last thing I feel before it takes me is my knees hitting the hard stone of the palace floor.

Paris on the ramparts, red wine staining his lips. It is dark and the city is loud with revelry. I recognize a hymn in the distance with startling clarity. The Pyanopsia. Tonight.

The battlefields should be empty but in the distance I see it: Achilles. Paris pulls a bowstring taut. He lets the arrow fire and every single thread bound up in Achilles snaps, like the arrow severed more than just an artery.

Helen's arms are round me and she's whispering soothing promises I hope she might keep. Distantly, I hear hymns to Apollo.

'Achilles, noble martyr, to spur the Achaeans to victory.'

Paris is going to kill Achilles and it's going to cost us the war.

'Achilles?' Helen repeats, her eyes misting with the curse. She blinks. 'What else did you see?'

I take her hand, struggling to believe her lips were on mine only moments ago and unwilling to let the memory of them fade too quickly. 'Fate just shifted. The threads realigned. Our kiss.'

'Our kiss shaped the future?' It's a different sort of disbelief to the kind I'm used to from her – one lined in fear, like she is simply hoping it isn't true.

I rush on. 'Paris is going to kill Achilles this evening. If he does that, we lose the war.'

'What?' She blinks as the curse clouds her eyes. 'Don't be ridiculous, he wouldn't leave the palace during a festival.'

'Please, Helen. I know you can't believe me, but please trust me.'

But how many leaps of faith can I ask of her? I can see the way each one wears away at her. She has never believed me and one day she will wonder why she listens at all.

But today she nods, even if it's hesitant. 'Okay, all right, I can keep him here.'

'How?'

Helen smiles a little ruefully. 'I'm captivating, Cassandra. I trust you. And it's time you trusted me.'

At the gathering, she crosses to Paris's side quickly, and I'm so used to seeing her flit around him, whispering in his ear and leaning towards him, her hands anywhere she can touch in polite company, that it's startling to see her simply nod her head, say a few words and lead him away.

'You could stare a bit less obviously,' Deiphobus says, sidling up beside me. 'You might as well start fanning yourself and drooling.'

'Oh, shut up,' I say, feeling myself flush and staring dead ahead like I can avoid admitting it.

'Cass,' he says gently. 'Are there not better places to put your affections? Paris is the future king now Hector's dead. She's going to be more into him than ever before.'

'Helen gave up a crown to be here – I doubt that's enticing her.'

'Well, whatever it is, she seems . . . invested.'

I take a sip of wine before putting my cup down. I feel too unsettled. I shouldn't drink – it might push me over the edge.

'Drop it now,' he says. 'Get out, close her off in your heart. Don't torture yourself like this.'

'You can't just stop feeling things.'

'Yes, you can,' he says, glancing at his glass. 'Every man I've ever cared for is on a battlefield. If I didn't make the decision not to care any longer, I'd never get through a day.'

I swallow, not knowing how to respond. We're too similar, I think, Deiphobus and I. We'd rather be distracted from our pain than face it.

'Does it work?'

He drains his glass. 'No, but I convince myself it does.'

'That sounds like an awful way to live.'

'I'm not trying to live, I'm trying not to die.' He swirls his empty glass. 'Right, I'm going to get another because I'm not doing this holiday sober. Do you want to join me in my efforts to get uproariously wrecked?'

I shake my head. I have to stay alert. Because I can't trust that the gods won't ruin my plans.

I'm fussing with the offering, adjusting the hanging jars of preserves and straightening the ties, when my twin brother finds me.

'Do you know that we lose the war?' Scamandrius asks.

I pause and straighten up to face him. 'I've seen that, yes.'

'So what are we still doing here? We should be getting the family out.'

'Then what? Scavenge across the ocean, claim xenia at Laodice's or Ilione's home and live our lives as cowards who abandoned our home, our people *and* our allies?'

'No, of course not,' he says, but I'm watching the dawning realization that there is no escape from this cross his face.

I sigh and look at my brother. I always used to be so angry when we were children that we looked so similar. I knew that twins, when their sexes didn't match, weren't supposed to. But we did, we were identical, and he got to do everything I never could.

And here are these eyes that look like mine pleading.

'I can't tell you it's going to be all right, but we're fighting,' I say. 'The prophecies don't dictate the way the future must fall, they simply show us how it will go on its current course. We can still win this. What you've seen is just one future. I've seen hundreds.'

He looks fragile.

'Are you sure?'

'Yes.'

He regards me calmly, like all he needed was reassurance.

'So this is why Apollo is so afraid of you,' my brother smirks. 'You know, he told me once that even oracles aren't supposed to see as much as you do. He said something about opening the floodgates. So if you say so, I trust you.'

Night falls and they still don't come back. Kreousa is curled against Aeneas's side, Andromache has retired early, my brothers are drinking more than they should, Polyxena is running about with my younger cousins and my parents are locked in conversation. But no Helen. No Paris.

I wait another hour but I can't help but feel that something is wrong. So I sneak away to the city walls.

Everyone is celebrating, music pouring out of every crevice, alcohol flowing into half-empty stomachs. I dart and dodge through the crowds until I reach the edge and begin the long climb up, the sound growing quieter with every step. The wind picks up too and by the time I reach the top I can't hear anything over it at all.

I clutch my shawl, take those final steps, and that's when I see Paris.

His lips are red, his arrow already nocked. But while his weapon is aimed at Achilles down below, his head is turned towards the steps of the walls – looking right at me. Like he's been waiting for me.

He lets the arrow fly.

'No!' I scream, running to the edge of the wall. There's no way he could have made that shot. But there is Achilles, little more than a dark shape on the ground.

I turn to Paris, ready to demand answers, when his form shimmers.

A smile so cold I freeze.

'The prophecies happen, love,' Apollo says with a careless wave at the carnage below. 'Whether you want them to or not.'

CHAPTER FIFTY-THREE

Cassandra

'It took me an embarrassingly long time to realize it was you,' Apollo says, tossing his bow to the floor as he stalks forward.

My throat is dry, my tongue clumsy. 'That what was me?'

'Don't play stupid, my dear, it doesn't suit you.'

'Why did you do that? You know Achilles dying is what makes the Achaeans win the war.'

'Maybe I don't care for this damn war any more,' he shouts, anger so fierce I stumble back until my heels hit the wall's edge. 'Or maybe I care more about the fact you continue to defy me.'

He takes another step towards me, languid and slow.

'When Hector was supposed to die and he somehow evaded the threads laid out for him – I've never seen my father so furious. He tasked me with finding out what was going wrong. And every single day that I failed ... Well, he's already started taking things. My oracles, Dodona and Trophonius, plucked from me and recast in his name. You crossed my mind, of course, but *Not my priestess*, I thought. *I've dealt with that problem.* And then it happened, for the third time in this war: the tapestry itself changed – and I thought, *What if she's still defying me?* And here you are, at the scene of yet another fated line, the thread I bound you with cut.'

I eye the stairs, contemplating fleeing, and he laughs.

'Oh, do be my guest – a tumble and a broken neck are quite easy to explain.'

My breath catches and he laughs again.

'Is that what I have to do, Cassandra? Maybe a permanent solution is necessary.'

'Go right ahead,' I say, glancing at the fallen body of Achilles. 'If you've doomed us to the future I see in my head, then I'd rather die.'

'It would be a kindness, then. Noted.' A flash of teeth.

'What, then?' I demand. 'I think I've proved that I'm never going to give up using whatever tools I have at my disposal to save the city you've stopped caring about.'

His laughter contains the clanging of swords within it. It promises violence. It is unhinged by the war.

He surges forward suddenly, reaching. Maybe going for my throat again, maybe trying to push me over. But his hand hits a barrier I can't see, half a foot from my skin.

'What is this?' he snarls. It throws him; his fury can't find solid ground.

And I breathe.

I had no idea how Athena's decree would manifest itself. I had no proof it had even worked. But it has.

I send a silent prayer of thanks to her, and Apollo's face contorts like he has caught a scent on the air.

'Athena?' he hisses.

He reaches along the barrier, tracing the contours of it, my own face in armour.

'You went to another god. How *dare you*?'

'What choice did I have?'

'What choice? You are *mine*, Cassandra, and you went to another god!'

'For protection.'

'If I want to fling you from these walls, that is my right. If I want to wring your neck or imprison you in the earth or turn you into a damn plant, that is my right. I am a *god*.'

'Well, so is she.'

He runs his eyes over me, his hatred building, and when he finally meets my gaze they're full of enough fire that, even with Athena's protection, terror burns in my veins.

'For your continuing disregard of my curse, I offer you this: *You will no longer convince any mortal of a single thing you say.* I'll have you begging for my attention, for the one person who might believe you. And I will have forsaken you.'

He straightens to his full height and sneers at me.

'For this –' he waves his hand at the barrier that glitters now in the air before him – 'for going to Athena, crawling around, begging other gods, when you vowed to serve me? For this, I will destroy you.'

CHAPTER FIFTY-FOUR

Helen

I LEAN AGAINST THE SHUT DOOR but the solid wooden plank feels unstable, like it could collapse at any moment. It finally happened: my disbelief pushed past the point of ignoring and I did as she said anyway because she asked me to. Because the taste of her lips still lingered and in that moment I would have done anything for her.

I kissed Cassandra.

And now she's gone, nowhere to be found.

Is she upset? Does she think I distracted Paris by opening my legs for him? Obviously, that's not happening *ever* again – but even if it did, what could she really expect? I'm still married. If Paris dies, I will marry again and my new husband would likely demand such things from me. And what if someone found out about Cassandra and me? Although, what would there be to find out? What are we other than a hopeful possibility whose threads are too fragile to ever spin true?

A possibility whose kiss shaped the future.

We cannot matter so much – *cannot*. If there is to be any 'us' at all, it needs to be inconsequential, because if we are found out, then . . .

Olympus above, battles clash in my name. A god has marked Cassandra out. We matter. And there are consequences.

I spend the hours Cassandra is gone panicking, and forget it all when she finally rounds the corner, chiton dusty, tears tracking her face. Her expression is placid, but I note the creases, the red tinge to her eyes, the wavering lip.

'What's wrong?' I rush to her, pushing her hair from her face to see her better, but she flinches and shakes her head. 'What is it?'

'I . . .'

'Paris is sleeping. I drugged him, so he'll be out for a while, but let's go somewhere quieter.'

I expect questions about that – the drugs I've been stockpiling in case I end up on a boat back to Greece. Ways to get Menelaus to leave me alone. But she stays quiet.

And I suddenly doubt it's any action of mine that's made her so distressed.

I take her to an alcove set round a window, soft woven pillows piled on its ledge. From here, we can see the lights of the city – and the lit beacons indicating some kind of message shared between the soldiers.

'What's going on?'

'I can't –' Cassandra breathes, before choking on her words like she doesn't trust herself with them.

I reach for her, hand on the bare skin of her shoulder. She has a birthmark there, a dark circle that I run my thumb along, cherishing the details of her.

'Gods, fuck him,' she whispers. 'I can't believe he's going to take this from me too.'

'He's not,' I say quickly, no idea where the words come from because I'm confused. '"Him" as in Paris?'

She shakes her head.

And then I realize there's likely only one 'him' that could instil such terror in her.

'Apollo.'

A nod.

'You saw him again. What happened?'

She shakes her head, gesturing to her throat. I reach for her, running my thumb across the mark there. Is it deeper?

'Another thread?'

She shakes her head, then opens her mouth and catches her own tongue as she tries to speak.

It is the way she tries to hold back the prophecies.

'Another curse?'

She looks up with mournful eyes, affirming that, yes, he did something to her. Something that has stopped her speaking freely even around me.

'Was it because of us? Because of the kiss?'

No, apparently not – and she points out of the window at the beacons. A prominent death – and there's one I've spent the whole night trying to prevent.

'Achilles. But how, Paris hasn't . . . Apollo cursed you? Did he do something to Achilles too? Something fatal?'

She nods.

I take a breath, putting the facts together. 'Apollo's angry we tried to change fate again. But Athena – Oh, he couldn't hurt you, so he cursed you again. He took your voice, or, no ... did something that's stopping you speaking to me right now.'

Achilles is dead, and that's a worrying fact for the war, but I'm more concerned with this escalation from Apollo. Gods snap their fingers and transform mortals into trees or animals, or send them straight to the Underworld and move on to the next. But Apollo is lingering, torturing Cassandra slowly. He is taking this personally.

Even Aphrodite does not care so much about me. The visits have stopped – no retribution for my argument with Paris. Where is she?

I've spent so long terrified of the Achaeans coming for me that I haven't truly reckoned with the fact that, beyond the army at the walls, Cassandra is in just as precarious a position with her own patron god.

I take her hand and run my fingers over the rough pads on her skin, where she once moved a thread, weaving Achilles' anger. If she can do that, she can beat whatever curse Apollo has levelled at her this time.

'We'll figure it out,' I promise. 'We always do.'

She raises our hands and brings mine to her lips.

I think it's to say thank you, or a reminder only to herself that there are some things Apollo cannot take.

'Cass, I . . . Earlier, the kiss.'

She looks up with a carefully guarded expression but in her eyes shines a glimmer of hope, even if it's despite her better judgement.

'I have never cared for someone this much – never craved someone like this. With not merely my heart but all that I have – for my hands to hold yours, my mind to be in conversation with yours, my very core to have yours beside it. I've never wanted like this.'

It's not fair, to tell her all this before declaring it cannot be. But Apollo has taken her truth from her, and I want to give her something true in its stead. And the simple truth is that she is a part of me. And perhaps in another life – or, rather, in another thread – we could entwine our souls round one another. It's impossible to believe we are not fated somewhere.

But it's not here.

'But it's too dangerous. We're at war, and if anyone discovered the way I feel about you ... We're not subtle, Cass. I can't smother the flames and expect to hide the smoke. That kiss was glorious but I think it has to be our last.'

In response she runs her thumb in small circles on my hand.

'I can't keep you a secret. And no one will fight a war for us.'

Her other hand reaches for the necklace at her throat, clutching the apple tight.

I understand – I am a contradiction, a mass of beacons signalling a dozen different things. What is that golden apple but a promise of some secret affection?

And to say all this when she cannot even reply? It's cruel. So much of this is cruel.

'I suppose that's all I can offer you: the promise that I want to.'

Cassandra nods, squeezes my hands a final time and gives a small smile before rising and retreating to her rooms. All while I sit watching the city enjoy its festivities, and, beyond that, the Achaeans panic over the fallen hero whose death will win them the war.

CHAPTER FIFTY-FIVE

Cassandra

I WANT TO.

It's the only thought that makes the next few weeks bearable.

My life is falling apart one misspoken word at a time. I manage for a little while, clinging to silence or gestures, but the servants await replies or direct requests and I'm so pampered that it's the plucked thread that makes my whole life unravel. I can't convince my handmaids I want hot water so I'm washing in cold buckets and it's making me feel ill, my body weak. I cannot convince them I need help to get one of my dresses off so end up wearing it for three days before Kreousa notices and asks if the ties are stuck and I can finally offer a nod. The prophecies are still slipping from my tongue and I can't offer apologies, can't backtrack or pretend I know it's nonsensical.

'*With raving lips uttering things mirthless, unbedizened, and unperfumed,*' I mutter, very much feeling like the threads are mocking me.

But I'm not letting Apollo win – and I'm not letting the Achaeans win either. I spend all my time in the library, researching the Greek poleis that form the Achaean side. I need to know what to look for: the emblems in visions that might indicate nations, which polis favours which weapon, paints their shields in which way – even the language. My Greek is rusty, and what if they yell something to one another that I miss?

And then I see it: *A party spilling into the streets, just like the Pyanopsia, but instead of a handful of princes and soldiers given leave, here men crowd the streets in numbers – just like before the war. They're all here. Cheers, celebrations, and then I overhear the toasts. The Achaeans. They've left, they've gone home. We've won.*

A second strand. A new future.

I am halfway through the palace, tearing down corridors, when I realize I don't know how to even tell Helen when I find her.

Thankfully, she is determined to work that out. She launches into the challenge of solving the curse with such enthusiasm it's like she is intent on making it her sole focus – to cut out other thoughts, other memories, of lips against hers.

'We'll figure this out,' she promises. 'There's nothing you could say to make me hate you.'

But then our eyes meet and it's clear we're both terrified that might not be the case.

'Let's start with silly things, nothing of importance – tell me it will rain tomorrow.'

On the sixth try, we get something.

'Do you think my favourite colour is green?' I ask.

'I don't know, is it? Wait! That worked – you can say things as a question and then I can assume you mean them as a statement. So your favourite colour is green.'

I shake my head. It's blue. I didn't realize until Helen showed me how many shades blue is beautiful in.

'Oh, we can do that too – I don't feel like you're lying to me with gestures. So, is your favourite colour green?'

I shake my head. 'Is my favourite colour blue?'

'Is it?'

I nod.

Helen squeals. 'Okay, that's two things you can do.'

I press my lips together, nervous it won't work. But then I steel myself and say, 'What if I told you I saw a future where we won the war?'

Helen freezes, and there's a moment when I can practically see the racing thoughts ricocheting around her skull, trying to work out if this is real or not. I watch as she decides it is, and the moment she does her eyes shimmer with hazy clouds as the other curse takes over and makes her disbelieve it. 'You did?'

I nod.

'Cassandra!' she squeals, jumping to her feet gleefully, and even though I can tell she doesn't really believe it, I let her pull me up too. 'Tell me everything!'

I line up my words with careful precision. 'Do you think the Achaeans might just leave? Would we throw a party?'

'That's what you saw?'

I nod once more.

'Okay, all right, let's get to the bottom of this curse and then we can work out how to make that thread the new core of our future.'

I hesitate, almost more scared to try this than the future. If she doesn't believe this, it might crush me. 'What would you do if you were cursed so that no word you said would be believed?'

I get it slightly wrong, just so there's room in case she doesn't believe me.

'That bastard,' she growls.

So I tell her the full curse: *You will no longer convince any mortal of a single thing you say.*

She gives a simple, thoughtful nod. It's too much, and my eyes flutter shut, like if I can't see her comprehension, it won't cut as deep. She understands – of course she does, she figured it out – and some part of me can't shake the thought that we will always find a way to connect with one another, no matter what Apollo throws in our way. And that's a bittersweet sting when we could be so much to one another in a kinder world.

Together, we try everything we can think of. *Single* – could I convince someone of multiple things at once? No, apparently not.

Mortal – is Helen included in that? Yes, it appears demigods are mortal in the wording of the curse.

A single thing I *say*. I can nod. I can shake my head. What other gestures? I make a rather rude one and Helen swats my arm and mutters something about being unable to convince anyone I'm funny.

I can say the opposite of what I mean. I can say things Helen does not need to be convinced of, things she already knows to be true. I can preface my words with lines like 'Don't believe this' or 'I'm going to lie to you', but 'You shouldn't believe this' followed by a prophecy results in Helen blinking and clutching her head, asking what I just said, unable to even hear the words as the curses collide.

Could I write? We fetch tablets and it's like freedom again, because, yes, that works.

We spend hours wondering about the word 'convince', because clearly it has more to do with the words I say than any intent I have, with the way the questions can get my point across.

But though we find several holes in his curse, none makes for an easy conversation.

It's a way through, not a way out.

Now there are rumours the madness has snatched my tongue too, that I can no longer think in full sentences – that's why I only answer in lurching questions and careful nods.

My mother finds me one evening – and it strikes me that we rarely speak unless it's out of concern. She does not try to spend time with me – does not force me to the temples with her, as she does everyone else in our family.

I used to feel so grateful for the snippets of time she gave me but now I wonder why I should beg for her scraps.

'There are soldiers in the camps who can't speak,' she says. 'Who have been through too much. I can't imagine what it's like living with these horrific scenes in your head. But I want to promise you that when this is over we'll get the finest doctors in the land. We'll stop these visions and you'll be well again.'

I feel like debris churning in the ocean, slowly sinking with each lapping word. I would love these curses removed, love to speak freely again, and would love to see futures less scarring. But what's wrong with me mumbling prophecies or getting lost in a vision? It doesn't harm anyone; it's just an inconvenience, or not even that, really – just a departure from the curated order she expects.

Parts of this feel like who I am now, parts like something I suffer, but why does she lump it all together as something to be fixed?

'If I'm well, are you going to speak to me again? Are you going to let me dine with everyone?'

Her eyebrows quirk at the fact I can actually speak. 'Yes, Cassie, everything will be back to normal, like none of this ever happened.'

In my anger I forget the curse, and spit: 'But it did happen. And you isolated me, barred me from gatherings and even let them kick me out of the priesthood. I'm not just going to forget that.'

'Oh, don't be ridiculous, Cassandra. Of course you'll forget it. I know you can't see it now, but it's all for the best. It's a kindness.'

'But you haven't asked me what I want.'

'Well, you're hardly in your right mind, not when you're screaming from the top of your lungs in the middle of dinner. I know it's hard, but it's not fair on you to keep putting you in those situations. Trust me, you'll thank me for all this one day.'

No, I'm not sure I will. I fall quiet, my energy to argue vanishing – not even sure what I'm arguing: that I am not a broken thing to be fixed, or to question why her palace only has room for those she considers 'normal', or with the fact that she packages being set aside as a kindness when she has created the cruelty in the first place.

'Are you unable to speak again, Cassandra?'

No, I can't speak at all – because, remembering the curse, I run through our conversation. I realize there wasn't much I tried to convince her of. I pick it apart, almost hoping for a moment when the curse turned her against me.

When I told her I wouldn't forget it.

That's it.

It wasn't the curse, just how she really feels. And that cuts deeper than that thread round my throat ever did.

One morning when I sit in the library with Kreousa, a hazy vision rises behind her. Men soaking wood in hot water, bending its planks and hammering the lengths together. I'm baffled. The visions rarely show me the mundane any more. I think I could handle them if they just showed me soldiers sleeping, talking and making tea.

I lean closer, to see more, because it must be important – and the prophecy rebuffs me, throwing me back so heavily that my chair nearly topples.

I take a breath, gearing myself up to try again.

Take a break.

Kreousa slides the parchment over to me. She's started carrying it everywhere so we can always talk.

I can't, I write. *It's important.*

She glares at the paper, then at me, considering something.

I know. But so are you.

I go to write something but she snatches the paper back to write a veritable essay. It's deeply touching, the way she believes it's rude to have a conversation where she speaks and I write.

But, Olympus above, it's also agony watching her stylus drag across the parchment for so long.

She hesitates before passing it back, and when she finally does she half throws it at me.

Look, Cass, I know it's your prophecies we're decoding. I don't know how or why they're helping when they seem so ridiculous but I trust you, and I trust Helen enough to not ask questions when you ask us to do something. I know it has to be important for you to ask us to do it at all. And prophecies have been circumvented before: Thetis married a mortal, Zeus swallowed Metis. But you seem to think the only value you have to anyone is in churning out more prophecies. When the stories of this war are told, we'll be lucky if we're more than beautiful princesses waiting for the men to win and save us. But we're not, and you're not, and you have more to offer than seeing the right thing. Stop pushing yourself to the brink, because we all care about saving you every bit as much as we care about saving the city.

In classic Kreousa style, she is intently avoiding looking at me after I finish reading.

'Do you think you can write something that nice and then pretend it didn't happen?' I ask, voice swollen with the things I know she doesn't want to hear.

'Yes.'

You love me, I write back.

'Urgh, gross, Cass. Yes, I do. Now leave me alone.'

I don't intend to, especially when I'm still reeling from all that she said, but another vision crashes into me.

Aphrodite sneaking from Olympus, muttering under her breath about Zeus telling her to stop trying her hand at war. She used to be a war goddess. He forgets that. Or maybe he fears it. Love and war would be too powerful for a god like Zeus to let it be.

She crosses the plain, looking for him, her hero, her champion. She dodges the swords and the men and a golden light seems to lead her in time to watch a blade fall.

'No,' she screams, running to Paris's side.

She cannot help. Love heals in all ways but physical. Like a cruel twist of fate, she remembers the ex-wife: she has such power. But by the time she spirits Paris away to her, he has whispered his last word, his lips are blue, and his eyes are fluttering closed.

I jolt back, trying not to panic.

I write down everything I saw and pass it to Kreousa — if she knows they're my prophecies anyway, there's no point hiding it.

'This doesn't make sense,' she says as her eyes cloud.

I return to the threads, hoping that I might go back, might get more, at the very least an idea of *when* this might happen.

But Paris is dead by nightfall.

And we don't find out until three days later.

CHAPTER FIFTY-SIX

Helen

THEY TELL ME MY HUSBAND is dead while I am showing a dozen women how to cut a throat: where to draw from, how to angle the blade, how to cut the vocal cords so your adversary cannot scream.

Agata appears at the doorway of Artemis's temple, such gravity drawn on her face that I *know* even before she says: 'Paris has been slain.'

No. No, no, no . . .

My sword clatters to the floor, my body following shortly after, and I wail, beat the stone tiles and howl. Agata tries to shelter me, Herophile rushes forward – though I imagine she is ecstatic to be here at this moment to bear witness to it. I lay it on thick and stagger to my feet, out of the temple and into the waiting carriage.

Paris. That poor, foolish boy – in over his head, fighting a war that never should have been.

We were learning to trust each other again, figuring out this new relationship, and now we'll never get the chance to know if we could have been something to each other aside from the lovers dictated. I think of his bafflement, his smile, every time he tried and tried and tried . . .

I wonder if they'll let me stay or if my return to Sparta was sealed with his last breath.

Cassandra. It's not even a solid thought, just an all-encompassing yearning and the feeling of plummeting that never gets as far as being able to consider leaving her.

The palace is in disarray but I'm led to a small chamber where Priam and Queen Hecabe hold one another, Scamandrius picks at his nail beds and Deiphobus stares desolately out of the window.

'Oh, Helen,' the queen says, rushing to throw her arms round me. 'You must be devastated.'

I am, but mainly for myself. I cared for Paris, I did, but I can't truly cry for him until I know I'm safe.

I try to lock eyes with King Priam. Throughout all of this, he has reassured me that it is not my fault, that they will not send me back. But now he's avoiding my gaze and my stomach sinks.

'Do we know what happened?' I ask.

'There are varying accounts.' The queen sniffs. 'But there is a rather delicate matter.'

'Oh?'

She glances round as though waiting for someone else to say something. But when they don't, she sighs and speaks. 'He wasn't found on the battlefield. I'm sorry, my dear, but did you know he was married before?'

What to say. Do I act shocked? They'll take pity on me and won't look too closely if my grief differs from their expectations. After all, Paris didn't tell me. Cassandra did.

'He *what?*' I fall into the nearest seat. 'No, no, he didn't tell me.'

'She reported his death,' Deiphobus says. His demeanour has changed – no longer the jovial, joking prince I remember but graver. I wonder if it is the death of two of his brothers or the fact he is now the crown prince that has caused such a shift. 'Her people have already performed burial rites but she claims he appeared before her in the arms of Aphrodite. Some say he fell in battle against Philoctetes, that his body vanished as Aphrodite whisked him away. Some say he was running away, returning to the woman he truly loved.'

'By the mercy of Zeus,' I mutter, shaking my head despairingly. It's over. They won't even fight in his memory if they think he's a coward who abandoned the city.

'Devastation aside,' Priam says, his voice scratched and raw, and I wonder how long he sat with the news before everyone knew – how long he had to cry for his son before dealing with the fallout, 'it's left us in a rather difficult position.'

I imagine I'm in a worse one.

'Yes?'

'Paris is dead. This rumour could stop us fighting for his glory,' Priam says with a glance at his sons. 'We feel that the easiest way to squash it would be – forgive me – to have you marry one of the other princes.'

Everything slows. 'Excuse me?'

'I know.' He glances away. 'It's so soon, but I must ask you to think past your grief. No one will expect you to love your new husband – it will be a righteous union, reaffirming the love you had for Paris to marry his brother in his honour. It will preserve his memory, a solemn thing that may spur our armies on.'

I glance at the faces in the room: Queen Hecabe tense, like she's preparing for my refusal, Deiphobus resigned and Scamandrius smug.

I knew I'd have to marry again but I didn't know it would be so immediate. I thought I might have some time to prepare for all the things a new husband would expect. I thought I might taste freedom even if I knew it would be swiftly snatched away.

'I understand. And I defer to your wisdom, my king, in whatever course of action you feel is best. But may I ask – and to be clear, I'm very glad you're not – why don't you simply send me back?'

Priam looks horrified. 'You're not a parcel to be traded, Helen. I told you once that I have never blamed you for this war, and I won't solve it by selling you off to our invader. You may not have been born to this family but you are a part of it.'

Another tear spills free but I don't think it has anything to do with Paris.

I nod and glance at the princes. 'So who am I marrying?'

'I wanted to give you the choice,' Priam says, voice suddenly edged like a blade. 'But apparently Apollo has sent a prophecy demanding combat.'

Cassandra?

Then Scamandrius steps forward. 'I'm blessed with such prophecies, having fought beside Lord Apollo. I was devastated to hear of Paris's death and, when I did, I offered my own hand to ease your grief. I was surprised to find another had done the same.' He casts a glare at Deiphobus. 'But then the vision came.'

Deiphobus looks apologetic. 'We fight at dusk.'

I'm a prize yet again, it seems.

Fuck this. Fuck all of this.

'Very well,' I say, rising to my feet. 'In which case I should like to make some offerings to the gods and grieve for my husband.'

CHAPTER FIFTY-SEVEN

Cassandra

THE NEWS FINDS ME LAST and I run to Helen's room the moment I hear, banging on her door until she calls for me to come in.

I rush inside but she is already wrapping her arms round me. I hold her until she lets go, then scan her for signs of distress.

She's difficult to read, as always.

'I don't know what to do,' she says. 'Custom dictates a lock of hair cut in his honour but he was so averse to me cutting my hair that it seems disrespectful.'

'Helen,' I say gently.

She offers a reassuring smile. 'I'm okay. Just a bit shaken. Would you care to walk somewhere? I doubt I can visit the city after the news, but a courtyard, perhaps, or one of the roofs?'

'A roof.' I nod. I like the seclusion of only the Heavens looking upon us. The gods are so preoccupied with the war I doubt they'll even notice us.

When we climb out of the window and on to the tiles,

we can see the war stretching on the horizon – charging dots in a haze of dirt and dust. They're closer to the walls than they were.

We continue to the back of the palace, blocked from any view but the sharp rock face shading us.

'I . . .' Helen says. I want to reach forward, want to cradle her face, to touch her. But I don't know how to do that without implying something she has clearly rejected.

I take her hand instead and run my thumb over the hard callus between her thumb and forefinger, where the hilt of a blade has rubbed.

'They aren't going to send me back,' she says. 'They told me earlier. But when I found out, that was my first fear. I thought I might have to go and I realized, rather obviously, that you were what I'd miss most.'

'Obviously,' I echo – part joking and part disbelieving.

'And I . . . There's an army at the door. I can't keep being scared of the things worth risking, right?'

'Um . . .' I'd rather she didn't risk anything, actually.

'And that includes you.'

I'm a risk? Something hopeful flutters in my chest, something I have to resist the urge to squash.

'And I think . . . I think I've been playing at a relationship with you for a while and the thought of actually having one was terrifying – not just for the way it could condemn us if they found out, but because this is something I could really lose when I'm already at risk of losing everything. But this morning I realized that if I lost you, I'd be devastated anyway, so why hold back? I'd rather be your secret than your nothing at all.'

Everything is sharpened, every breath of air and echoing sound something I can feel with shocking intensity. I could memorize every detail of her: her cobalt eyes wide with sincerity, her lips pressed thin with nervousness, her fingers fidgeting with the deep-green rope binding her dress.

'I . . .' She's staring at me so intently it's difficult to focus. 'Are you saying you like me?'

'Yes, was that not clear?'

'Not really, no,' I say, not minding if she doesn't believe me. 'What does . . . what does this mean?'

She seems to be steeling herself, like she hasn't already confessed so much. 'I want to be with you. I want to stop doing what I should do, stop being the person everyone wants and be the person I am with you. I want to revel in romance. I want you, Cassandra.'

'Helen.' I swallow, my throat so tight I'm surprised I can breathe. 'I can't say a single thing without twisting my words a hundred times first, I can barely carry a conversation.'

At least I don't have to convince her of that – she already knows.

'We're making it work, aren't we?'

'This isn't –' I hurry back over my words, rewrap them in a question and start again. 'Is this the sort of relationship anyone should want?'

'Well, I do,' she says simply. 'And frankly, Cassandra, that's my decision. So I think the real question is: do you want me?'

'I . . . A relationship?'

'Yes.'

'What if it doesn't mean to me what it means to you? Eros –'

'I tell you I want to be with you and your immediate assumption is that I'm just trying to get beneath your chiton?'

'Helen!'

She sighs. 'Cassandra, I definitely have eros for you. But it's one small part of the way I feel, and certainly not the one that has me sitting on a rooftop, asking you to take this leap with me. I want to be with you, all the time, and if you feel similarly, then, for now, isn't it as simple as that?'

'Are you sure?'

'Yes. Now, does that mean you still like me? I'm putting myself out on quite a limb here and I'd really appreciate you letting me know whether I've missed my shot.'

I laugh, which possibly isn't the best response. So I bring the hand I hold to my lips, pressing them to her skin, and that fluttering feeling soars. 'Yes, Helen, you've missed your shot.'

The fog of my curse hovers and fades.

I've seen so many of her smiles. I've never seen one quite like this.

I'd do anything to see it again.

'Okay,' she says. 'So . . . so we're doing this?'

I can't help it – I laugh again. It's possible I'm simply too happy to stop. 'You're so awkward.'

I don't think she needs convincing on that one, either; she seems cripplingly aware of it.

'You make me awkward! You're so . . .' She swallows her laughter and levels me with that earnest gaze. 'You're beautiful and I love the way you know it – your confidence, the way you swan around like you know every eye is on you. Even when you hide in the shadows, it's with your head held high like you can't truly comprehend the idea of making yourself unseen.

And then after weeks of debilitating self-doubt, you'll suddenly remember you're better than everyone else and snipe at anyone who dares suggest otherwise and –'

'Are these compliments?'

'Yes, your ingrained royal arrogance is enticing. More than that, you're the most passionate person I've ever met. So, yes, that makes me awkward. I admire you. I've never admired anyone I've been with. So if I'm ridiculous and mushy and horrendous at this, it's because I've never cared this much about getting it right.'

I brush back the short hairs curling round her face, my other hand still holding hers tight.

'You're not getting it right,' I say gently. 'Is it my turn to compliment you?'

'No, please don't, I can't handle much more of this emotional sincerity.'

'So you don't want me to start declaring things? Or comparing you to flowers? Or –'

Her finger is on my lips as she shushes me.

Then it lingers there, her eyes dropping, pupils huge, and I remember our kiss. I wonder if she might do it again. I wonder if I'd like it just as much the second time.

'Just . . . I don't know what's going to cross that line with you,' she says. 'You know, away from romance.'

'I'm not really sure – That is, do you think I have a thorough understanding of that myself?' But I know I want to feel her warmth, her softness – the things we can't put into words laden with curses, but can put into holding each other, fingers entangled, lips brushing. 'Can we figure that out together?'

'Absolutely. You know how much I love figuring things out with you.'

I draw her closer. 'Would you like to start now? We could figure out kissing?'

Her eyes light up, the ocean sparkling in the sun. This is not like last time, sudden and confusing. It is intentional, deliberate. She leans forward slowly and my eyes flutter shut and this time when she kisses me it is not a roaring fire but a gently flickering flame, tender and wistful and filled with longing so deep it might never be fulfilled.

I feel her smile against my lips and my heart lurches in giddy somersaults.

She draws away, biting her lip, almost bashful. 'You make me so happy, Cassandra.' She hesitates and sighs. 'Actually, it's more than that. You make me *care* about my own happiness. No one's ever done that before.'

CHAPTER FIFTY-EIGHT

Helen

'THEY'RE MAKING ME MARRY ONE of your brothers,' I say as we lie beside each other in the lazy heat of the autumn air, the roof tiles damp and hard-ridged against our backs. I'm angled towards her, propped on an elbow and playing with a lock of hair escaped from her braid. I think about plucking the ribbon off, of her hair hanging loose and free, of the soft strands tickling me as she leans over me –

'What?' Cassandra startles me from my thoughts.

It takes me a moment to remember what we were talking about. 'Paris died in the arms of his ex-wife, so it's that or the whole war falls apart. Your brothers are fighting for my hand as we speak.'

'But, some lies: you're not exactly Deiphobus's type.'

'And Scamandrius?'

'A little bit too much his type.'

'Maybe Deiphobus just wants to stop Scamandrius from marrying me, then.'

Cassandra's eyes widen. 'Oh. He's doing it for me. He knows I like you.'

'How? He's hardly been here.'

She mumbles something that sounds suspiciously like 'when the Amazons arrived' and I laugh, thoroughly delighted. 'You liked me that long ago? Why didn't you do anything about it?'

'You were married to my brother, you'll recall. As you're about to be again.'

She glowers in the general direction of the palace, where I hear cheers from a crowd and the clanging rings of colliding swords.

'Deiphobus is older,' she continues. 'If he wants your hand, why would Scamandrius even be a consideration?'

'A prophecy from Apollo, apparently.'

Her face darkens. 'That lying bastard. I'm going to kill him.'

I'm not sure if she means Scamandrius or Apollo but either way I blurt: 'No, you won't.' Gods, I hate the way the curse pulls words from my lips too, like Apollo has his tendrils in us all.

The crowd roars again – a victor declared. I brush my fingers through her hair one final time. 'Shall we go discover who I'm marrying?'

It's Deiphobus, for which Cassandra is rather relieved. He draws me aside while Cassandra yells at her twin.

My stomach tightens as I place my hand in his. I knew I didn't want this, but I distracted myself so much with affection for Cassandra that I never stopped to think about just how deeply I did not.

But then he says, 'So, I like men and you have *something going on* with my sister.'

It's rare that I'm thrown, rarer still that I'm gaping. 'How do you know?'

Cassandra only said he knew she liked me. That's certainly a leap, to know it's reciprocated, and rather worrying given we only agreed to 'something' an hour ago.

Deiphobus laughs. 'Please, you're worse than she is, you know. I think you're too used to everyone falling for you. You haven't considered it the other way round. You should see the way you look at her. Now, please don't break my sister's heart and we'll have a perfectly pleasant marriage. I trust we are both capable of keeping our extra-marital affairs secret and holding hands in public?'

I nod, fumbling for words. 'All right, yes. Agreed.'

'Good. Now, we should probably get back before Cassandra goes for the death blow with Scamandrius that I didn't have the heart to aim for.'

As he breaks up their argument, I'm dragged away by Clymene and Athrae to prepare for the wedding – dresses, prayers, rituals and rites. We carry on right through the evening and into the night.

When we're done, I go straight to Cassandra's room.

'Hello,' she greets me at the doorway.

'I don't want to sleep alone tonight,' I say, not realizing until the moment my voice breaks how much I have been ignoring.

Paris died. I thought I might be returned. The prospect of another marriage – and certainly not one like Deiphobus and I are entering. The fear Cassandra might not have wanted me back.

Cassandra reaches for my hand and physically pulls me across the threshold into her room.

Then her arms are round me and she's leaning down, her lips brushing my hair like those extra few inches of height exist solely so she can curve round me.

'Will you stay here?' she asks, which I take to be her way of circumventing the curse to offer an invitation, and I gladly accept it.

She passes me a nightgown and gestures to her screen. 'Is it okay if we . . .'

'Absolutely,' I say with a little too vigorous a nod, but I can't help it. There's something so delightful in the way she asks, in this setting of boundaries and lines, in forming this shape of a relationship for us to fill. A relationship where each other's comfort is the most sacred thing . . .

I did so much to feel safe with Paris, but I never considered safety like this – not as a lack of harm but a pursuit of happiness, like one day love could be a sanctuary.

I climb beneath the sheets as she dresses, and when she emerges, crossing to me with a hesitant smile, I wait only until she is close enough for me to grab her hand and draw her closer.

I wrap my arms round her and she strokes my cheek before blinking and scowling at the offending hand like she had not realized she was doing it.

We are a tangle of limbs, heavy and content.

'Do you think I can sleep like this?' she asks.

'I hope so,' I answer with a grin. 'But before you do, I wanted to talk to you about earlier and . . . are you okay with me marrying your brother?'

'You were already married to my brother.'

'This is different.'

She thinks about it for a moment. 'Do you remember when you said you couldn't be with me because you were married?'

'Unfortunately.'

'I never – Do you think I had an issue with that? Or is it possible I've always known that life with another woman would involve breaking the vows men make us take?'

It takes a moment for me to understand what she's saying.

'I'm glad but still, I should have told you about the marriage, before I asked you to be with me. I didn't mean to manipulate you. It was just that once I realized how much I wanted to be with you it was difficult to think of anything else.'

She pulls me tighter into her embrace, her whole body pressed against me. We slot together, the sharp edge of my hip against her soft skin, the gentle curves of her against my taut muscles, the velvet hair of her legs brushing against my own.

In the dark, her lips find mine in a chaste, sleepy kiss. Her lips are butter soft, with two hard ridges where she has bitten down when prophecies have taken her. The person she has become is written into her and I want to savour every detail.

'Goodnight, Helen,' she breathes into my skin, nestling herself into the crook of my shoulder. I smile though she can't see – amused at the suggestion she could not possibly sleep while we are clutching each other, when already her breathing is slowing against me.

'Goodnight, Cassandra.'

CHAPTER FIFTY-NINE

Cassandra

OLYMPUS. GLITTERING, DEAFENING, IMPOSING. ZEUS, almost pure light. Even in my mind it burns.

Eris is by his side and their whispered words boom loudly in the prophetic strands.

'I want them gone, I want them destroyed,' he says.

'I know,' she whispers, casting furtive looks around the palace. 'I thought the apple . . . the inscription –'

'Curse your apple. This was supposed to decimate them, to cast them all back to dirt and mud. Ten years of fighting, hundreds of thousands of deaths – that's what the prophecies promised. Men grow too confident and too strong in number. And Troy – a palace that rivals Olympus itself, a city too large, too self-important. I won't have them rivalling the gods. That's how they stop worshipping us, I've seen it.'

'If you want more chaos, I can cause more chaos.'

'No, I want order. I want what the future promised me.'

'The future doesn't make promises, Father,' Apollo says, sauntering in. 'It's not fixed enough for that.'

'Careful, boy,' Zeus hisses. *'If this war folds, you'll be down in the mud with them. I've sent you there before.'*

'How can I forget? My manicure has never recovered.'

'Deliver me the future your prophecies promised.'

'Prophecies aren't promises, they're predictions. Dozens of gods weave the tapestry, yet you're blaming me for it not aligning to the strand you wanted.'

'You're the god of prophecy – make it fit. Finish this enterprise of mine.'

'You want me to tear my own city down?'

'You aren't the only one with cities on the line – Hera has already offered plenty of hers in sacrifice. So do it, or suffer with them. Do it well enough and I'll have you ten Troys built.'

Apollo stiffens before spitting out: 'As you command it, my king.'

When I come to, Helen is awake, toying with my hair.

'Morning,' she says. 'You look adorable, you know, when you have visions. Sometimes you space out and your eyes go wide, and sometimes it's like you're watching something right in front of you, all your emotions playing out. What was it this time? You were scowling.'

I learnt nothing new, but it's still terrifying to see it like that – proof that the king of the gods himself plots against us. Dwelling on it won't help, though.

'You wouldn't believe me if I told you.' I grin, knowing I do not need to convince her of the fact. 'Shall we get you ready for your wedding?'

'Fine.' She sighs. 'I suppose I will have to look beautiful enough to remind them all the war is worth fighting.'

She's right. She has to be the closest thing to perfect a mortal can be.

We set each other's hair in ribbons before I start on her make-up. I run kohl round her eyes, leaning so close our noses brush, holding her chin in my hand while I line colour across her eyelids. Silver, crushed powder in a fine pot, gels to stick it to her skin, and I dust it across her cheekbones. Against its shine, her eyes have never been bluer.

'Wait, let me do yours,' she says. 'I need more time. I'll probably screw it up.'

If putting make-up on her was difficult, this is far worse. Every brush across my skin has my stomach flipping; every time she leans in closer, my heart skips.

She reaches for a purple powder and starts dusting it across my eyelids.

'Let me lie to you: a man told me once that a woman's make-up should consist of only two things – red lipstick he can imagine smudging off, and rouge like the flush we'll get after he has.'

'Wow, what a way to make sure a woman never wears that ever again.'

'I did,' I say. 'Sometimes. It felt like a game, enticing them. I couldn't imagine wanting them, but I wanted their approval.'

Helen considers, clouds still swirling in her eyes. 'Well, I'm in no position to judge – I want everyone's approval.'

'I can't imagine make-up feeling like anything less than camouflage.'

Helen scowls, then she turns, dips a rag in water and starts washing it off my face.

'No disguises. It's bad enough I'll be performing – I want you to be the one real thing.'

It makes no difference to me. I'll be slinking into the back anyway.

And it's not like I need it, it's just a different sort of beauty. I can still addle the minds of gods and men – *and Helen!* – perfectly well without it.

I help her into her dress instead and start drawing together its ties. It fits her perfectly, though it must have been adjusted in a day. Liquid gold silk embroidered with constellations at its neckline, the fabric forming a cape across her shoulders. There is something sensual in the way it flows that has me looking away as she moves.

She reaches not for her perfume but for mine.

'Is this okay?' she asks.

I nod as she dips her fingers into the gel, rubs it on to her wrists, a dash on her neck. Not her usual jasmine soap and freesia scent, but mine, redwood leaves and chamomile, a hint of spice.

She turns for me and my fingers fumble to untie the fabric in her hair, to let the curls fall. I pin them in place, spin her back round, pick up the make-up and fix errant strokes. I run that shining powder across her collarbones. I reach for a pale pink lipstick and stare at it in my hands.

I put it back down.

When I turn to her, she's watching me, and I step closer and take her face in my hands.

Her long lashes flutter closed and she sighs before her lips brush mine, before the unexpected pressure of them, so much firmer than I'd been anticipating, catches at my own breath. Her hand finds the small of my back, presses me closer until it's not just our lips touching but our thighs, our hips, and I gasp against her.

We break apart. I know if I suggested right now that we abandoned the wedding altogether, she'd agree in an instant.

I turn back to the lipstick.

'Pink or red?'

'Uh.' Helen blinks. 'Pink.'

The door bursts open, a woman storming through. I see my eyes – as they once were: clear and bright before the tiredness set in – Andromache's finely-braided hair, Kreousa's soft jaw and all of it finished with Helen's firm muscles and smattering of freckles. It is hideous enough, but my stomach churns at that final detail – at each individually lifted dot planted in perfect replica.

Aphrodite.

I fall to my knees solely so I can have a moment to ensure the apple that dangles from my neck is securely out of sight.

'Dismiss your servant,' she commands Helen.

'Aphrodite, may I introduce Princess Cassandra,' Helen says, which I take as my cue to stand.

Aphrodite barely looks at me, just glares at Helen as though asking why she should care. Then she seems to realize who I am and turns to me with searching eyes.

'Apollo's priestess? Well, I don't see what all the fuss is about.' She turns back to Helen. 'You're getting married? Paris has been dead a day.'

'I don't want to but . . .' Helen ducks her head, blinks back imaginary tears. 'The best way to honour him is to protect his city. And apparently his body was found by his ex-wife. Rumours are circulating which the king and queen believe only a marriage will squash.'

Aphrodite's expression darkens. 'I brought Paris to the little river-witch to heal. She refused.'

Helen smiles just a little, a hopeful twitch of her lips that pulls at a knot in my chest. Aphrodite cuts me with a sharp and shrewd look. It is odd, being glared at by my own eyes.

'I knew he wouldn't have left me for her, not when you arranged such a perfect match between us,' Helen says. 'But the very memory of such a harmonious union might be tarred by these rumours. I thought it best to quiet such gossip and marry Deiphobus. Unless you disagree? It has been so difficult, my lady, without your guidance.'

Aphrodite's nostrils flare. 'I will no longer be kept on Olympus as I was. But this marriage is, I suppose, for the best. It won't be a tale of love but it will be a testament of your dedication to Paris. Perhaps not the ending I want, but a better one for my tale than you ending up back with Menelaus.'

I struggle to keep a straight face, knowing the real tale they'll tell will be one of contempt, of how Aphrodite and all her gifts could not save Paris. How love is a futile thing in the face of valour and iron.

Helen bows her head. 'Thank you, my lady.'

Aphrodite glances between us, eyebrows drawn low with suspicion.

'Yes, well,' she says, her voice taut. She suspects us, but she does not know what she suspects. 'You'd best quell those rumours or you'll be back with your spurned Grecian king in days.'

The wedding goes quickly.

I sit close to the exit and far from the rest of my family, my eyes tracking to Polyxena in my usual seat and Aeneas where Hector should be. It's like the cracks in my heart are empty space, a void set into my very flesh.

'You could have made more of an effort, love.'

I cast a panicked look around the room, trying to see if anyone else has noticed the god in the seat next to me. Helen is talking to my father, and not even facing in my direction . . .

'Oh, don't worry, dear. It's just us two.'

'What do you want?' I hiss. A few people turn to look at me, glaring at the disruption, but I keep my voice low enough that it doesn't carry.

'You know full well what I want, Cassandra.'

'How does harassing me at a wedding achieve the destruction you crave?'

'This is hardly harassment – Athena saw to that, didn't she?' He taps at the barrier between us and it's still enough that I startle at the movement. He smiles, pleased with my fear.

'You're not denying that you are siding with the Achaeans?'

'I'm siding with the Olympians,' he corrects. 'What Father wants, he gets.'

'Even when he's taking your city from you?'

He laughs, and I forgot the way his laugh sounds like music. If music struck fear into your core. 'You can try this, my dear. Perhaps you might have been able to rile me into defending Troy if I cared any longer. But I don't care if Troy falls, so long as you fall with it.'

'You call me "love" while longing for my death?'

'Love and hate, they're the same when you get down to it. They both destroy.'

'Sounds like a twisted version of love to me.'

'And what would you know of love?'

I'm an idiot.

The quickest of glances, barely perceptible, except he's waiting for it, tracking my every movement.

He cackles so loudly I cringe into my chair.

'Helen?' He gasps for air. 'Oh, darling, what horrible predictability. You fell for the woman everyone is falling for? I thought you'd do so much better.'

'Did you want something, Apollo?'

'No, no, we aren't moving on from this so quickly. *Helen*. The wife of your brother? Two of your brothers? Ah, poor little priestess, making eyes at the very source of her city's destruction. Oh, this is excellent. This is a better torture than anything I could concoct.'

'Does that mean you'll leave me alone?'

'Never.'

'Could you finally kill me, then? It would be preferable to continuing this conversation.'

'I'd never do anything so droll, not for you.'

I sit back in my chair, trying to calm myself. He can't touch me. There are lengths even he cannot go to.

His jaw clenches. I don't know if he wants me begging or laughing but my disinterest seems to bother him.

'Where's that brother of yours, Cassandra?'

'You're going to have to be far more specific.'

'Scamandrius,' he says dryly, and he's right: when I scan the crowd he's not there.

If Apollo's asking, it must be for a reason, but I bite my tongue and try to appear unbothered.

'Very well, love. Let's move on. This sham wedding is incredibly boring, don't you think? We need to liven it up.'

His eyes burn gold, and I'm torn from reality, thrown into a prophecy.

The city on fire.

Blood trodden into the dirt.

Chains and knives.

Kreousa panicking, the flickers of the city's flames cast upon her face.

Helen, Menelaus curling his hand round her arm, pulling her to his ship.

Screams ringing from every house in the city. Screams from my own lips.

My throat is raw but I'm still yelling, cutting off only as the words spill free. Apollo flickers in front of me, his smile the last thing I see.

'Beware! Beware Achaeans bearing gifts! Troy will fall and it will burn and the gods will celebrate on Olympus when we are reduced to dust.'

My eyes roll back in my head and I fall to the ground.

CHAPTER SIXTY

Helen

THE WOMAN I LOVE STARTS screaming and I do nothing.

She opens her mouth and pain pours out and something in me plummets, swoops so low and so hurtlingly fast that I feel wrenched from myself. A single coherent thought skitters through my mind, one of: *Oh, I love her*, and then I stand and watch her anguish.

After a moment, the incoherent thoughts solidify: *What do I do? Who is watching? What would they expect? What do they know?* The future of the war rests on this wedding, on the choice I make in this moment, so I decide not to make one, which is, of course, its own horrendous decision.

Deiphobus holds me still, even though I take no step towards her.

Kreousa reaches her as the guards do, and when they loop their arms beneath her Kreousa looks back to me with a single nod, like she has it in hand.

Her mother runs out after her as her screams carry down the hall.

And I smile to the gathered attendants, return to the dance and wish I weren't such a coward.

The wedding celebrations go on for hours. My performance is a careful mix – mourning for the husband I have lost and the hopeful looks I cast at Deiphobus, like our grief might bind us and make that first love all the more powerful for it.

I sleep in Deiphobus's room that night. Or, rather, I attempt sleep as guilt churns through me, keeping me awake. I try to persuade myself there was nothing I could have done.

But I know the truth. I could have been with her. And that would have been enough.

The next morning, I retreat to my rooms, where Agata waits for me anxiously.

'How was your evening with Prince Deiphobus?' she asks, wasting no time in getting to work combing my hair. Still short, it is now long enough for the thick strands to tangle, and the curls break easily, turning to fluffy clouds around my head.

I'm not sure if I'm supposed to be sleeping with him. No one believes this is a love match; they think it a match in honour of a previous love. But it *would* be an expectation that such a marriage be consummated.

I hope that Paris's death gives me a few weeks' leeway and, besides, I'm sure most servants are aware of Deiphobus's preferences.

'Perfectly pleasant,' I answer.

'And have you heard about Princess Cassandra?' she asks, forced nonchalance in her voice that immediately raises my hackles. There's something heavy in it, something knowing.

Perhaps Deiphobus's preferences aren't the only ones the servants are aware of.

'Heard *what* about Princess Cassandra?' I ask sharply.

'She was violent in her madness. They've put her in the eastern tower for her own safety. Ligeia delivered her meal this morning and said she was still raving.'

I have half a mind to push past her and run straight to the tower. But if rumours *are* circulating about Cassandra and me, then I'll only affirm them by charging to her. No, I'll have to be more careful.

Hours later, when I casually pass by, there is a guard at the base of the tower and, when I press, they insist that the queen has barred entry to all.

With Paris dead, Priam is at the walls with his council, discussing strategy with the leaders of the armies we have left. Our allies have been falling or trickling away and Deiphobus wastes no time in returning to battle too.

Hecabe is touring the temples but when she's still not back by nightfall, I go in search of her.

I expect her to be at the temple of some goddess of dusk – Artemis or Selene or Nyx. So I start towards the acropolis.

There are few people about, and perhaps I wouldn't have seen, for I do not usually look intently at every face I pass, were it not for my desperate search for the queen.

But then, men are such an uncommon sight these days that one so broad-chested and roguish would stick out immediately.

Odysseus.

The hood of his cloak is up, shielding his face, and he's barely feet from me, scurrying along, when he sees me watching him.

He reacts instinctively, lurching towards me, hand on my wrist and a sharp blade at my back.

'I really don't recommend calling for guards,' Odysseus says in my ear as he guides me to a shadowy alley between two of the city's scholarly halls.

I wasn't planning on calling for guards. I want to know what he's doing here and what he knows. Besides, if he's a threat then I stand a far better chance of being able to dispatch him than the half-trained palace guards too young to fight in battle.

'Why would I report you?' I ask as I stumble before his blade. 'I would sooner weep at your feet for the joy of seeing a face from the nation I love.'

'I won't pretend you crying at my feet wouldn't be gratifying after these months of war in your name,' he says, pushing me against the wall and sliding his dagger from my spine to my stomach, the fabric of my chiton ripping. I do not need to wonder if he has sharpened the blade recently.

I'd survive a puncture to such a place for long enough to call the guards, so if his intent is merely that I fear him enough not to, he has forgotten the ways of Sparta. He married my cousin, Penelope, and she would laugh to see him like this, lowering his guard around a girl like me.

'How did you get in?' I ask. His lip curls and I rush to continue before he can sneer his refusal to answer. 'A foolish question – of course you found a way. If anyone could get in, it would be a man as brilliant as you.'

Odysseus laughs in a short, explosive burst. 'Flattery, Helen, really? Do better.'

'I only ask in the hope you might take me back with you.'

He stares at me and I stare right back, each of us trying to read the other. My heart begins to pound because this may finally be a man I cannot convince, cannot run circles round, might lose to – and he has a blade against my skin. I remind myself that he is not merely the Achaeans' greatest strategist, but a sacker of cities. He would think nothing of using that blade on me.

'I wasn't sure if that lantern truly meant what I thought.' His dagger relents, threateningly raised but no longer at risk of piercing me on an ill-timed breath. 'When I sent that note, I had no idea it would even find you.'

'*You* sent it?'

It makes sense – after all, it was his wife who came up with the idea – so I'm not enormously surprised. But I'll make him think he's thoroughly outsmarted me.

'You think Menelaus cares to engage you in discussion?' Odysseus smiles, savouring his own condescension. 'Whatever your reason for shining the lantern that night, do not pretend it was for love of him. I simply won't believe you.'

This is something, I suppose. Odysseus thinks himself smarter than me – but he thinks me clever still. He may be the only man in all of Greece who sees me as more than a lovely thing to gaze upon.

'Must we have this conversation with your dagger drawn?'

'Yes, I think we must,' he mocks.

I take a breath. 'You ask me why I wish to flee my captors?'

'You're walking around rather free. And our spies report you quite besotted.'

'Do you think I would live if I did not pretend to like it here?' I retort. 'Paris dragged me from my kingdom, forced me to marry him and died a disgraced coward. My people bleed for my return. I wish to go home, Odysseus.'

'Menelaus plans to kill you.'

'Then I will die in Sparta where I belong,' I declare with all the authority of my previous crown, standing up a little straighter like it still rests upon my head.

He regards me for a long moment before he speaks. 'You will prove it. Help me now. Then, when this city falls, I shall assist you in persuading Menelaus to forgive you for causing this war and let you live.'

Forgive me. Even though I'm telling him I didn't wish to come – even though the pact they all swore to defend my marriage was *his* idea. Odysseus caused this war every bit as much as I did – as much as Paris, Aphrodite, Zeus, Eris, Hera, Athena and Menelaus did. How odd, to be the one they all covet and the one they all blame.

'But how long might that be? I can't stay here,' I protest, only because it is expected of me. If I thought there were any chance of Odysseus dragging me from this city, I wouldn't have asked. Though if he did plan to, he'd show me his way past the walls. With surprise on my side, I might be able to kill him and have the gap in our defences sealed.

'This city will fall soon. Come, Helen, trust in the people you claim to hold in such regard.'

'What is it you want?'

He cocks his head to the side, considering me. 'The Palladium. I'm going to steal it.'

He scowls as my laughter chirps. 'Odysseus, it's thirty feet tall.'

'Consider this a scouting mission before I bring my men in. Take me to it if you are truly aligned with Greece.'

I do not feign a moment of consideration. 'Very well.'

He pulls his dagger back beneath the folds of his cloak.

'Hunch over more,' I tell him. 'People might notice me and it would be best for them to believe you an elder.'

He does as I say.

I could kill him or alert guards. I could wait for him to return and ambush him with more men – although Odysseus will plan for that somehow, I'm sure. He'll be ready.

Or . . .

I would love to pretend it is an alluring thought that tempts me only at the last moment.

But I know deep down that it is part of the reason I lied all along. Because I am duplicitous and craven and I will do whatever it takes to survive. Because it is my nature to say the right thing, to twist myself – and to be who everyone wants me to become, no matter how many times I determine that being true to myself might be worth the consequences.

What harm is there, really, in the Achaeans stealing such a statue?

If Troy falls, then I have an ally. If it does not, then we simply lose a statue.

And if I am queen of Sparta once more, my husband aligned to my side – I might be able to save some of the people I care about.

So I show Odysseus the Palladium then watch him leave. And I keep my mouth shut for days as agonizing guilt gnaws at my stomach. I know I made a sensible choice but I certainly did not make the brave one. Perhaps that is where I fall short of an Amazon – I can wave a sword but I would drop it in a moment if that were the better option. I am primed to surrender.

But Cassandra still screams in a tower.

And I do think there are some things worth fighting for.

CHAPTER SIXTY-ONE

Cassandra

APOLLO LOCKS ME IN MY worst nightmares. I see every single death, mutilation and agony that has haunted me for weeks.

At first I think that if I survived seeing them the first time, I can survive them now.

Then they start again.

By the time I come to, I'm delirious, the past and present merged, unable to tell what's memory, what's prophecy and what's a horror my mind has invented on its own. It is the yoke round my neck multiplied, a thousand threads choking me, pulling me in dozens of directions.

'*Apollo, my destroyer, for you have destroyed me –*'

'There, there, little priestess,' he coos. 'I think that's enough.'

I wake on a cold stone floor. My dress is torn, jagged edges and loose threads. I have a vague memory of ripping it, of the fabric in my hands while I screamed about Clytemnestra and her axe.

He reaches out to help me up, before laughing. 'Of course, I can't touch you.' He withdraws his hand and I get to my feet, my limbs weak, the room swirling.

A tower. I'm in one of the palace towers. Round walls, rough brick, a tiny window.

'I assume that's locked,' I say, eyeing the door.

'Oh, yes. They did that rather swiftly.'

I glance around the small room, hugging my arms to my chest. 'Is that it? Your grand punishment, more of the prophecies I've been seeing anyway?'

'I'm just getting started.'

It's the same taunting smugness with which he asked where my brother was – and suddenly I'm certain Scamandrius is part of his plan. Apollo using him to get to me, just like he tried to before.

'Where's Scamandrius?'

'Ohh.' He winces before his eyes widen with fascination, like he's studying me. 'You hate it, don't you? You're so used to knowing everything, thanks to my little gift. No oracle has ever seen as much as you have. But you can't see this and you can't stand it.'

'There's a lot about this I can't stand.'

'Well, don't worry your pretty little head, there's nothing you can do about it. There's nothing you can do about any of this.'

It's no surprise he wants me helpless. I've heard enough stories about him to know that's his preferred sort of girl.

He raises a finger to his lips. 'Now, hush, I'm looking forward to the show.'

He waves his hand and the prophecies grow louder from my trembling lips.

A scrape of the key in the lock and my mother appears at the door. Two guards shadow her. From the way she steps past Apollo, it's clear he's made himself invisible again.

'Cassandra?' she asks hesitatingly.

I nod, cannot swallow the prophecies down to speak.

'How are you feeling?'

My eyes flit to Apollo and I silently ask his permission. The embarrassment of it burns. But he nods and the prophecies stop.

'You locked me in a tower.'

'Cassie, what choice did I have?'

'I can think of some.'

'You were screaming the most horrible things. We could hear them throughout the palace, even when you were in your room and we were playing music as loudly as we could.'

'You locked me in a tower so I wouldn't ruin a wedding?'

Mother straightens. 'You already ruined the wedding. The things you were shouting, the nonsense you were saying, you think it could be so quickly forgotten?'

'So that's it? I said some things you didn't want to hear, and you dragged me up here?'

'You're here for your own safety,' she says. 'You were clawing at the walls — look at your dress, for mercy's sake. It took three guards to stop you throwing yourself off your balcony. What else was I supposed to do?'

I glare so hard at Apollo that he starts laughing, before raising his hands in a mockery of surrender. 'Don't worry, love, I wasn't actually going to let you jump.'

'Am I allowed to leave?' I ask.

She hesitates. 'We can't risk that, Cassandra. What if something happens?'

I could do it. I could tell her she should leave me here, that it's the right decision, that I understand. I could force her to believe otherwise.

But then I see Apollo from the corner of my eye, waiting.

He wants to see whether I've done it, I realize. He wants to know if I've found another loophole.

'What if I had a constant guard?'

'They could barely stop you as it was. I can't rely on that, not when a split second is all it would take for you to ... do something.'

'You can't leave me up here,' I say and Apollo cackles when her eyes glaze. I blink back tears. I can't have him see my ways around it. If he seals the gaps in his curse, I might never be able to speak again, save for the prophecies he allows.

With sudden dread, I realize that I have to get her to lock me in here, to walk away, to disown me – because only when Apollo has destroyed every last part of me and written me off as a lost cause will he finally forget about me. I'll never save the city with a god hovering over my shoulder, undoing all my work.

Mother crosses her arms as the curse fades from her eyes. 'I can, actually.'

'Let me go!'

I'm closing myself in, locking the tower shut before anyone else can.

'I'm not having you running around endangering yourself and everyone around you. There's a war at our walls, Cassandra, I refuse to have your madness acting as the bigger threat.'

'I am not mad!' I shriek and whatever chance I had at freedom disappears. Apollo claps his hands in delight. That ought to do it.

But I didn't know it would hurt this much.

Mother's eyes soften: pity. And an edge of fear.

'Cassandra,' she says, like her heart is breaking. I think mine is too, to know she was prepared to do this all along.

'Please don't do this.'

'It's not a prison, you –'

'Don't fool yourself,' I say, my voice hardening. 'A prison is exactly what this is. Give me visitors! Instruments! Something!'

Apollo is all but gaping. 'You do realize you're making this worse for yourself?'

That's the point, you egotistical, idiotic phallus.

'I can't do that,' Mother says – though I think she might have been about to offer it herself mere moments earlier. 'This is for your own good.' Then she turns on her heel and the door closes behind her. I hear the key turn.

'Well?' I demand, staring at the solid plank of oak barring me in, swallowing my tears.

'Well, what?'

'Gloat, laugh, wax lyrical about your own genius, do whatever it is you're here for and leave.'

He looks down at me from his full height, a foot between us, the barrier starting to shimmer. 'This is it now.'

I certainly hope so.

He leans closer to the barrier. 'You'll waste away in here until the city falls. You'll go mad with the prophecies. And then the Achaeans will come, they'll drag you to far-flung shores, gag your prophecies away and slaughter you. They'll bury you in an unmarked grave in the dirt of a land you despise.'

'Do you want me to congratulate you?' I spit.

'Say the words,' he says gently, his voice scarcely more than a whisper. 'Surrender to me.'

'Fuck you,' I say, though it lacks my usual bite.

His lips quirk.

'I think you've missed your chance at becoming my wife. But I could rescue you still. You'd make a glorious cupbearer. I could have you forgetting Helen, forgetting everything, in a single kiss.'

If I could cut threads as well as read them, I'd sever every one he has. 'No god can remove another's curse, and I doubt Athena would be so quick to do you the favour of erasing it. So what's the point in your torment?'

'Entertainment?' he offers. 'Vengeance, perhaps. Athena told me she made that curse very specifically. *No god shall touch you*, is that correct? She was so pleased with herself. You see, you can touch a god, Cassandra. And I can certainly work with that.'

'I really don't know how much clearer I can make it that I would rather die than be with you. I would rather take every part of that future you detail than be with you.'

His smile falls, something hard and impenetrable sliding across his eyes.

'Enjoy the rest of your very short life, Cassandra.'

He flicks his wrist and I barely see him vanish as I'm thrown back into the prophecies, the violent, swirling force of them.

Everything is on fire, chains rattle, we're all choking on the smoke as our city burns, as our loved ones –

It can't be hopeless. Not after all this – and not after everything he's done.

The anguish and the howls and the desperate pleas –

Apollo doesn't get to destroy me. And he doesn't get to destroy Troy either.

The gods on Mount Ida, clenched jaws and tight limbs, looking on with disgust while Zeus smiles.

When the next prophecy comes, I embrace it, scream it with everything I have. When the visions come, I ask for more. Then I demand it.

It is *mine* because I decide it – because my rage and my hope are stronger than any god's will and I'm going to control these strands. I am going to write my own tale of ruin.

Apollo *gave* me prophecy. Not glimpses of it, not access to visions – all of it. That was his oh-so-unfortunate wording: *I give you prophecy*. And this time I'm taking it. I'm opening the gate he left unlocked and I'm snatching it for myself.

A god's arrogance – *mine*. I can't rival their indifference but maybe I can counter it. I can feel so much at once it balances the same: all that despair and pain, all the terror and dread – and all the hope too. Andromache's teasing laughter, Deiphobus at a banquet helping me discover who I am, the love in Hector's eyes as he asked me to be careful, Kreousa's note slid across the table. Helen curled against me, her fingers intertwined with mine, our lips crackling against one another. *So much hope.*

The threads give way, something coming free. Suddenly it's easy.

I am not prophet, not oracle; I am something else. I am a goddess without immortality, without worshippers, with nothing but a domain.

Prophecy is not a thing you have but who you are.

I am not standing in a rainstorm. I am the clouds. I am the thunder. I am every single drop that falls.

I see everything.

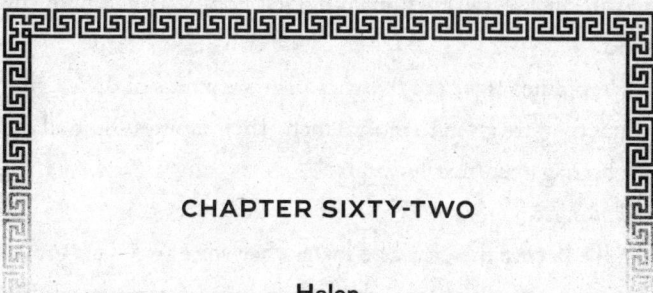

CHAPTER SIXTY-TWO

Helen

QUEEN HECABE MAKES IT DISTINCTLY clear that Cassandra is staying in the tower, a steadfastness that feels unnatural – and then I see the cursed mist coating her eyes.

So I wait.

The first opportunity to free Cassandra presents itself a few days after my encounter with Odysseus.

In the night, he was captured.

I had nothing to do with it, but if he thinks I did, he should thank me. Our guards arrived in time to save him from his own companions beating him to a pulp. They fled with the Palladium – one of them granted gods-given strength to drag it through the dark streets.

The guards blocked their passage into the city and Odysseus was taken to dungeons I was not even aware Troy had.

That is all anyone knows, but I find out more at the temple of Apollo, where the whispers seem to magnify.

'I'm sure you already know Prince Scamandrius was blessed with sight by our lord,' Herophile says.

'Yes, he made a prophecy some days ago – that the winner

of the duel between him and Deiphobus would take my hand.'

Herophile's right eye twitches. 'The weakness of divine gifts is that they are given to mortal men. Their failings shine all the brighter against their holy gifts.'

'Failings?'

'Like fleeing the city.' She lowers her voice to a dark growl. 'He was captured by the Achaeans and shared a prophecy with them – that Troy could not fall with the Palladium still inside.'

So that's why Odysseus wanted it. And I led him straight to it.

'So you see, when given the opportunity to trade a prince of Troy for a king of Ithaca, it ought not to have been a question. But we were lucky the Achaeans even considered it – that they wanted Odysseus back, when they were last seen attacking him for trying to steal the statue for himself.'

I snort. So much for Odysseus being the most intelligent man in the Achaean army.

'They traded Odysseus for Prince Scamandrius this morning, but the fact someone with sight would flee . . . It does not bode well. I know you have contacts, ways to fight that go beyond bronze and iron. So if you are doing something, I would like to assist. The time has come, I think, to take risks.'

'Actually, yes,' I say, a sudden idea striking. 'There is something you can do.'

CHAPTER SIXTY-THREE

Cassandra

I SEE EVERY STEP OF THE war, every decision, every swipe of a blade. I chart the journeys of every one of the thousand ships. I see my people torn from their homes, destroyed. And I see their destroyers made ash too. I see their children grow and wither and die. I see us turn into stories, hear poets spin the tale, see the way they never stop.

I see a thousand years. Two thousand years. Three thousand years.

And I see the gods vanish.

With millennia burning in my eyes, it happens so quickly. A handful of heroes scattered through the lands and a trail of destruction in their wake. The people turn on their gods, burning temples, desecrating holy sites – the rage buried in my soul carried in the flames.

The gods will return to their palaces and lock the gates of Olympus. Only one will remain: Astraea. A goddess of justice – holding the fiery lightning bolt of Zeus.

And even now, even here, where those thousand years fall away like cinders, my eye scans wide, finds lands not that far away where *the gods have no jurisdiction, where without worshippers they are nothing.*

And in it, I see something else: hope.

Our story is told so many times it no longer feels real. Every single version, the same tragedy in every account. Again and again and again.

Let every fiction tell it otherwise. Let them pick the strands that tell a better tale. But just this once, could we not find the one that offers a happier end?

Prophecy is a golden, tangled tapestry and I tease at the threads. They are malleable under my touch. Troy's destruction is a twisted, irrefutable knot that does not relent, a yoke about the city as visceral as that once tied to Hector.

But there are gaps – places for me to embroider. All of future-history to patchwork across. A tale I could weave anew. But I can't reach past those iron threads. Unless . . .

We were in them.

Not the future but the present, stretching the knot wide, individual threads pliable. It is only once that first kink has come to pass that we might be able to weave new shapes before the gods can twist it once more. We must pull ourselves back from the brink.

And we have mere days before the gates are breached and Troy burns.

CHAPTER SIXTY-FOUR

Helen

'GOING SOMEWHERE?' I ASK IN the voice of Queen Hecabe.

Cassandra is perched on her window ledge, framed in the golden light of the soon-to-set sun. The tower is in disarray, and sheets torn from the thin mattress have been knotted to a rather precarious-looking bolt on the bed frame and tossed outside.

She turns so quickly I suddenly fear she might topple, so I yank the hood down on my cloak.

'Sorry, sorry, it's me! I couldn't resist,' I rush, but I'm not sure she even clocks my guilty smile before she collides with me.

In her arms, I feel far too many things at once: remorse, love, gratitude, anxiety and, larger, drowning out the rest, a fear that I have failed her.

When she lets go, I run my eyes across her, expecting the worst and, somehow, both right and wrong. Her dress is torn, her hair hanging in greasy strands, and already she has a gaunt look of hunger lingering in the pallor of her skin.

But she also looks elated – eyes sparkling like gold wrested from sand, dry lips pulled tight in a blistering smile, jumpy with energy I've never seen her possess. She is giddy in a way that catches at the fine cage of my chest – lungs and heart both lurching.

'You're here.' Her words are a relieved sigh carried on a soft exhalation.

I do not give her time to catch her breath before drawing her into my kiss. I am hungry for her, ravenous. Kissing her undoes me – fire pooling in my belly, my heart jumping in frenzy, my hands reaching to pull her close. We do not have time for this but, with her gentle lips against my own, I am Icarus, unable to resist a luring temptation, even when I know it promises my own damnation.

This is too much, too fast – I promised her slowness, carefulness, and here I am like a parched man drowning in the desert's first oasis.

I force myself to break the kiss and ignore the way my eyes track to the tower's bed.

But then I look back and see that, for a second, Cassandra's eyes remain closed, like she is savouring the moment. Resisting the need to draw her back to me feels on a par with a labour of Heracles.

Cassandra opens her eyes and, at the sight of me, snorts in dry amusement. 'Would you like us to come back to those salacious thoughts later, at a more opportune time?'

'Don't tease me,' I scold.

'But look at you, aren't you so adorably unsettled?' She pokes at a warm cheek I can only assume is as flushed as it feels.

'Your pupils are rather large too, you know.'

'Well, yes, I imagine so.' She laughs. 'You just kissed me with vigour, Helen. Could I lack a drive towards people but find actions like that hard to ignore?'

'Really?'

'What if I don't need to lust after someone to enjoy their touch? But don't you think we should focus on more important things?'

She smooths the creases in her tattered dress, as though that might make it more presentable. I am fairly certain those creases existed before I grasped the fabric to pull her closer, but I might have worsened the tears.

I'm not sorry for it.

'I refuse to believe anything is more important than this right now.'

'Really, because I was just climbing out of the window, you recall. Nothing keeps you humble after stealing a god's power like the risk of falling to your death.'

I stop paying attention to her dress – or lack thereof. 'Excuse me?'

'Could the right combination of indignity, determination and righteous fury let you claim full control over prophecy? Would a god screwing up the gift by giving it away also help?'

'Really? We can stop it, then!'

She falters. 'This isn't true but ... maybe? I thought we could – I saw us win. But it's part of their trick, all an aspect of the same strand. I don't know if we can change it, but I certainly hope we can. And I'm going to keep fighting regardless.'

I swallow. 'How long do we have?'

She holds up two fingers.

'Two years.'

She gives me a grim, almost pitying look.

'Months? Weeks – Cassandra, tell me it's weeks. No, we can't have two days.'

She nods.

I feel more unsettled than I normally do as the curse works its way through my mind. Two days is an unbelievable prophecy. A thoroughly ridiculous suggestion.

But I do what I have often done with her and trust her despite my doubt.

'All right, let's run through that later too. Right now, we need to get you out of the tower.'

'How?'

'You think I abandoned you in a tower for days and snuck up here solely to kiss you?'

'I wouldn't put it past you, honestly.'

'I was getting things in order, preparing a safe place! And I'm here to break you out.'

'All right, then, what's your plan?'

I pull my hood back up and speak in her mother's voice: 'Let us pass and say nothing to anyone.'

When I look up, a scowl has formed fine creases between her brows.

'What?' I ask.

'Oh, it's not genius,' she says calmly, and I smile at the compliment as her curse takes hold. 'But I was certainly not hoping I might be able to take that cloak. How long do I remain in rags in your plan?'

'No plan of mine has you in clothes for long.' I am, for the most part, joking. But our eyes lock for a little too long and I feel something take root in my chest, a heavy seedling of a thing anxious to bloom.

'And then what?' she asks. 'Where are we going?'

'That part you're not going to like very much,' I say. 'But let me tell you the latest news about Scamandrius on the way there. Perhaps our destination will seem delightful in comparison.'

CHAPTER SIXTY-FIVE

Cassandra

'**ARE YOU JOKING?**' I ASK when Herophile opens the door of the house we're supposedly running to.

'It's this or the tower,' Helen chirps, and I step inside.

The door opens straight into a small living space, long low sofas set round a small wooden table, and, through an open doorway, utensils and herbs hang – lavender and thyme mingling with a dusty scent, of a home not cleaned as often as perhaps it might be.

Herophile sniffs. 'I'll fetch a basin of water. And some very, *very* strong soap.'

'Oh absolutely not, you –'

Helen elbows me in the ribs, hissing, 'Xenia.'

At the reminder of the laws of hospitality currently binding us in Herophile's home, I don't finish my sentence. But I don't start a new one either until Helen adds: 'We have twenty minutes.'

Fine. I force a polite smile. 'Soap would be wonderful, thank you.'

Herophile or not, it *is* a relief to scrub the tower from me – and all the sweat and grime accumulated from rolling on its floor screaming prophecies. I'd only had time to change into a fresh chiton and hastily throw some belongings into canvas slings before we left the palace and already that dress feels a filthy thing to put back on.

I've just finished wringing the water from my hair when the first guest arrives. And then, one by one, more women follow.

Helen greets them like old friends. I don't know why it's constantly a surprise that she's so good with people. I recognize a few of them. Servants from the palace halls – Ligeia and Agata the only ones I know by name – but they all nod politely to me and beam at Helen. Most are girls I've seen training. And of course, Clymene and Athrae. It's almost jovial, the way they chat to one another, while my mind chants *Two days* on repeat, like it's counting down the seconds.

It's a tight fit, the sofas filled quickly and the floor crowded too. Helen takes the windowsill and I lean against the door frame of the kitchen.

Then Kreousa walks in, Scamandrius at her side.

Idiot.

Everyone falls silent. Apparently his defection hasn't been kept a secret.

They sit right up against the door, like they might need to make a quick escape – with the anxious way Kreousa is looking around the crowded room, she really might.

'Andromache is keeping up appearances in the palace,' Kreousa says. 'Everyone knows you've both vanished. We told Mother and Father we know where you are and you're safe, but that's all. They're livid, of course, but "you locked Cassandra in a tower" isn't giving them much leeway to protest.'

'Thank you.'

Herophile pours tea, the remaining people standing find places to sit and conversation quietens.

'Thank you all for coming.' Helen's voice rings like a bell in these small confines. 'You won't think anything we discuss is real. But that is only because certain gods would have you believe otherwise. So we would ask you to pretend, to revel in the hypotheticals, and to imagine what you might do if you did think it true.'

She turns to me expectantly – and so do the other heads in the room.

I hesitate – but no god would. And that arrogance is crucial. So I straighten up and reach towards prophecy like I have every right to wield it.

The future is a ringing in my ears, the feel of my clothes on my skin, the smell of my own perfume – ever-present and, at times, easy to ignore. But I turn my attention to it now, remembering that rush of power. At once I am lost in its waves, the visions trying to pull me under.

It is like wading through a thick forest, threads of fate threatening to trip me at any moment, branching and spiralling with possibility until bounding back into another immutable knot. I find the wrought-iron tangle of Troy's fall.

Achaean ships fleeing, their camps abandoned, nothing but a wooden horse built as an offering for a safe journey home. Trojan men drag it inside the walls, oblivious to the thirty men inside. In the vision, Zeus summons the gods to Mount Ida, which overlooks the city. He speaks of how gloriously Troy will burn, how it is fated, and he bans the gods from the city, saying whatever happens is in the hands of the mortals – like he would absolve them of the role they've played in the fall he is so certain will come. The ships return, the men in the horse spilling free and attacking us mid-celebration, most of us unarmed, drunk and exhausted.

The vision ends in flames.

I take this glimpse of the future and I push it out around me, fabric straining. When I step aside from prophecy and return to the room, everyone is locked the way I must be – eyes wide, staring at a distance not yet apparent.

They startle as they come to, gasps of horror and hands fluttering to cover gaping mouths.

'A vision?' Athrae asks. 'How did you –'

'False prophet,' Herophile spits. 'And now you've found ways to spread your lies.'

'Herophile,' Helen warns. 'I told you we couldn't believe it.'

I have taken the power of prophecy from the very hands of a god, but his curses still trip me.

'Zeus wants Troy to fall?' Kreousa asks. 'So if we stop it, it'll just be delaying it?'

I nod.

'So we wait until he bans the gods from interfering,' she says, all so matter-of-factly. I suppose it's easy, when you don't really believe the future will play out like I have shown them. 'And then we burn the horse? Or I suppose it will be too late by then. So we get out? But how do we tell the people that without them panicking and alerting the Achaeans?'

'I think it's perfectly reasonable to have an evacuation protocol in a time of war,' Ligeia says. 'We can let everyone know what it is, then set off an alarm, and everyone will know what to do.'

Helen nods. 'We'd have to make doing it silently part of the instruction.'

'Where are we evacuating to?' Clymene asks.

I sit back, letting their conversation play out without any input from me that might derail them. This is what oracles do: divine what they can and let those who have sought them out make decisions from there.

'The Achaeans could follow us, so it might be better to scatter,' Kreousa says. 'We have allied nations. Or . . . there are lands further away.'

'With only twenty-four hours and a whole city, we'd be lucky to reach the mountains,' Agata says. 'Achaeans on horseback could catch us in three hours, maybe less.'

'So we steal their ships,' Scamandrius says. 'We'd get away faster and they wouldn't be able to follow us.'

The room falls silent once more, and the women turn to my brother. Herophile's jaw twitches, Agata's hands curling to fists.

Finally, Helen admits: 'It's a good idea.'

Athrae holds up a hand, as though she needs permission to speak. 'How would we do that? We'd have to get a whole city round the back of the Achaean soldiers.'

More ideas are bounced around, more issues raised. And just when I'm becoming hopeful, conversation fizzles out.

'Everyone take some parchment,' Helen says, in the same tone of voice she uses when she's showing us how to wield swords. 'Write down as much as you can about what you saw. Let's make sure we're getting every detail. Cass, do you think you could show us again?'

So I do, again and again until everyone looks as weary as I've felt for months.

'Well, we can easily spread the word of the evacuation protocol,' Herophile says into the still air. 'If you don't want to make it an official announcement.'

'Thank you, we definitely don't want it to be official,' Helen says. 'The gods are less likely to notice if it doesn't come from us.'

It's already late, and we're getting nowhere.

'Let's regroup tomorrow,' Helen suggests.

No. But everyone looks wrung out, like the threads have constricted all they have to give. *One day left*, my mind whispers, edged in fear. *One day and then the city falls.*

But still, we have more than I had mere hours ago when I was locked in a tower.

At any rate, what a relief to share this burden, to make it *ours* to solve rather than *mine*.

Everyone files out, but Kreousa and Scamandrius linger.

Herophile makes an excuse to visit the temple, and I'm unsure whether she doesn't want to be stuck with me a moment longer or wants to give us space to talk.

'Well?' I demand.

Scamandrius scratches at the back of his neck. 'What do you want me to say, Cass?'

'"I'm sorry for being a spineless coward who sold us out to the Achaeans"?'

'They would have killed me.'

Kreousa's nostrils flare. 'And you should have died rather than betray your home, your family. Not to mention the fact you wouldn't have been there if you hadn't tried to abandon us in the first place.'

'Because we're going to die anyway!'

'No, because Deiphobus married Helen, and you're a sulky idiot.'

'The things I've seen –'

My rage is not the flint-strike spark of Kreousa's, fast and quick and hot – it's weary and tired, a fraying rope I'm ready to cut loose. 'Do you even understand the power you wield?' I feel the threads of fate wrapped round him and I long to wrench them from him. But Apollo's words from so long ago echo in my head: *Prophecy is bound to the very core of your being. It would destroy you to tear it from you.*

'Come on, Cass, don't be like this.'

'I'd say she's holding herself back remarkably well,' Kreousa snaps.

I notice Helen is hovering, leaning against the wall, eyes flicking down. It is possible she does not wish to involve herself in a family matter. But I suspect she may sympathize with my brother. After all, she told me on the walk over here that she showed Odysseus where the Palladium was then let him go.

But that's it, isn't it? Helen would not sell us out simply to save herself; she'd be clever. She'd give them very little and let them think they were getting a great deal. But if it came down to it, and she had to sacrifice everything – Troy included – to survive, would she do it?

'Why did you bring him?' I ask Kreousa, because I don't want to think these things about Helen.

Her eyes soften when they turn to me but that hard edge persists. 'He's a disgraced prince. I figure no one is paying much attention to him right now. He's been kicked out of the Trojan army and the Achaeans aren't going to let him live twice. He's no one.'

'I'll never be no one, Kreousa.' Scamandrius smiles – smug and perpetually correct, even when he is so clearly wrong. 'What does it say about your station if my fall has only brought me to your level?'

I don't even look at him, just address Kreousa. 'Can you not bring him tomorrow? Can we tell him only what he needs to know afterwards?'

'Cassandra, come on,' he whines. 'You see more prophecies than I do – if you think we stand a chance, then I want to help.'

'Are you not able to do that from a distance?'

'What, you don't trust me?' he splutters, outraged.

I see my shock mirrored in Helen and Kreousa.

'No, Scamandrius, no, we don't!' my sister screeches as I push my idiot brother towards the door. 'Now fuck off.'

When they leave, Helen and I go to the bedroom Herophile presented us with and collapse on to the bed. She brings a shaky hand to my cheek and cradles my face in her palm, just looking at me.

'All that time you were locked in the tower I was really worried,' she says quietly. 'Agonizingly worried, actually.'

'I'm not okay.'

'I know. Just give me a moment to let that sink in.'

Her hand doesn't move from my face.

I love you.

The thought unfurls quietly. It feels like the gentle caress of silk, tender and beautiful and exquisite. Most of my feelings with her are heavy things – stones in my stomach and a force that keeps me grounded. But this is feather-light. Weightless.

Perhaps it's too soon but it doesn't feel it. It feels like I've always loved her.

But if I said it, those clouds would appear in her eyes and her smile would fall.

And I don't want to wrap my love in lies to make her believe it.

Helen leans her forehead against mine and her eyes flutter closed. 'Two days isn't enough, Cass. We deserve a lifetime.'

'I know.'

She kisses me, petal-soft lips and the lingering lemon of her tea.

She smiles against me before we break apart. 'I'm never going to get tired of that.'

You might not have a chance to.

'Do you have to stay?' I ask. Because it's only really me that needs to hide from a god.

She arches a curt eyebrow. 'Do you want me gone?'

I clutch her a little tighter in an unspoken *absolutely not*.

'Well, then, I'm staying.'

'All right.' I realize I am toying absent-mindedly with the chain hanging from my neck. That apple and the declaration it embodies. 'But there were probably easier ways to get me into bed than to run away from the palace.'

'No, there weren't,' she says automatically and when the glaze fades she looks almost sad. 'I really liked falling asleep next to you.'

She turns, her whole body shifting towards me.

I love you, I think again, this time with such force I'm surprised the words don't tumble free. I just stare at her, reckoning with the fact I can't think of a thing to say that won't feel like denial, that won't feel like I'm shoving part of myself away.

She looks at me, half lidded, like she knows.

'Go on.'

'I hate you,' I say desperately, like it's the closest thing to a confession I can make.

She kisses me again, takes my chin in her hand to tilt my lips to hers, her body hovering over mine. Her lips are urgent and demanding. For a moment I tense, but then I'm clutching at her too, and I exhale into her. She hums and the vibration of it strikes me to my core, her joy, her happiness. Because of *me*.

My fingers tangle in her hair, her hand brushes the length of my waist, reaching upwards, her thumb skimming the edge of my breast.

'Is this all right?' she asks, breathless.

And I don't really know. It's not unpleasant. In fact, it's rather enjoyable. But if she's asking if I want this with some burning desire, if I want to tear her clothes off or press her skin against mine, not really, no. But it could be fun. It could be satisfying and pleasurable and a way of feeling closer to her.

How much am I supposed to want this? How much does anyone? Half the time, the way my friends talk, the way the bards and the poets describe it, it feels like a fairy tale – a fiction we invent to distract ourselves from the harsh cruelty of life. Something we pretend to believe.

But maybe it could feel nice? Maybe that could be a reason. Maybe a lack of eros does not mean a lack of arousal. Maybe I don't need some magnetic, irresistible draw to want to do this – maybe I could just feel relaxed and happy and safe and *curious*. Maybe for others that's not reason enough. I certainly don't feel like I have to, like my love will only be proved by this act. I want to in the same way I want to dance or sing, no overwhelming need but a sense it might be fun nonetheless – is that reason enough? Maybe I should –

Maybe I am sick of asking questions, of dissecting myself and my feelings. Perhaps I do not need to make sense; I could simply *be*. Maybe 'it feels nice' could be an answer in and of itself.

And maybe 'I want you to feel nice too' could be a reason to reach my own hand out and caress and touch and hold.

'We don't have to do this just because the world is ending,' Helen whispers as I start untying the sash holding my chiton together.

'Do you not think I am too pampered a princess to do things I don't want to do?' I retort, flinging the leather cord away and letting my dress fall open. I pull her back to me, her lips on mine, and this time when she draws me close she touches skin and flesh and I *want* this – to be touched by her, to feel her love in careful strokes.

My trembling fingers brush her dress from her shoulders, revelling in the way goosebumps prickle where I graze my hands across her, the way she shivers when my thumb dusts across her breast. I treasure every gasp, every breathless moan. I feel luminescent in the fact I am causing this, bringing her such pleasure – glowing with a light I thought only the gods embodied.

We shed the rest of our clothes and we are naked bodies entwining, exploring with fingers that are no longer hesitant. Her warm mouth on my skin makes my body sing, as she trails kisses along my neck and bites at my flesh. My own lips yearn for an exploration of their own – that need to hear her gasp, to know it's because of me. To feel her writhe beneath me.

And when I explore further, lower, along her thighs and between her legs, it is with the smug assuredness of someone with something to prove – that I can bring her the sort of joy she craves.

I don't really know what I'm doing but I react to her gasps, her grunts, correcting myself when I err and finally she –

'Like that, yes,' she gasps, fingers clutching at the bed sheets, and soon she is bucking, moaning, trembling – such beautiful sounds I'd like to hear again – and then she says my name, a long sibilant hiss of pleasure, and I feel like I too could come undone.

Yes, I think, *this is fun* – even before she turns her attentions on me. I shut my eyes and focus on the way it all feels – electrifying and tender – a scratch of nails across my thigh, and then skilled fingers, brushing at my core.

I recognize the feeling of my stomach tightening – my own explorations when bored or sleepless, no fantasy adjoining it, certainly nothing like this – and I am hovering on a precipice and then I am falling over, bright lights blooming beneath my closed lids.

When we are done, I lie with my head on her stomach, Helen idly playing with a lock of my hair. I feel rested with the lingering contentment of my bliss. Peaceful in a time of war.

I understand why men line our shore: I would fight a war for this woman in a heartbeat.

CHAPTER SIXTY-SIX

Helen

I WAKE WITH CASSANDRA IN MY arms, my body pressed round her, her hair tickling my nose with the soft scent of Herophile's rose water soap.

There is an aching, gnawing sensation in my stomach – an awareness so deep in my core I cannot even question it: Aphrodite knows.

This is no marriage in honour of Paris's legacy or a body in which to drown my sorrows – this isn't about Paris at all. Which means it is not about her.

I do not know what the consequences might be, but they linger in the hymns we sing and prayers we whisper – all the things Aphrodite's done to pretty girls she believes have disrespected her.

There is no moment to rejoice in the things we did last night – in the fact I still smell like Cassandra, that even now all I want is to run my hands along the curves of her, to press my knee between her legs, to catch her earlobe between my teeth and whisper all the things I'd like to do with her.

'Do you ever think,' Cassandra asks, and I startle because I hadn't realized she was awake, 'that we could run away? Just the two of us. Could we abandon all this, leave everyone else behind, and just save ourselves?'

'All the time,' I admit. It's easier to say when she is not facing me and I do not have to reckon with big brown eyes begging me to explain why I would abandon the city.

I come back to our plan of letting Troy fall to ruin. Are we really banking on the Achaeans not following us? They may cut their losses with the odd prince of Troy, with the ageing king.

But with me?

'If we can't get everyone out, if the Achaeans spill in and we fail, do we try to escape? Watch the city burn from a mountain somewhere and never stop running?'

'Yes,' I say instantly. 'What's the alternative? It is much easier to never get caught than to escape once we have.'

It sounds exhausting, a life like that, a life spent running.

'But we still have time, Cass.'

'Do you think time is what we need? I thought perhaps a miracle.'

But miracles come from the gods.

A miracle would undo us.

Kreousa comes over mid-morning, laden with the books she's been working through. I help for a little bit, Kreousa and I reading while Cassandra runs through threads and prophecies for some missing link.

I spend hours trying to find something.

But perhaps sometimes there's simply nothing to be done. The other cities the Achaeans have ransacked, Cilician Thebe and Lyrnessus and the others, didn't fall because the girls did nothing. The ones who perished aren't to blame; the ones who survived, only to be chained in the Achaean camps, aren't to blame; and the ones who ran, who line our streets, aren't to blame either.

Sometimes you just lose.

Sometimes it's just a damn tragedy.

I stand abruptly. 'I'm going for a walk.'

Kreousa scowls. 'I'm not sure that's a good idea.'

I can't stay within these walls, not when I'm this on edge, not with this growing sense of foreboding in my gut. *One day.*

But that's not where the fear is coming from – I recognize its acrid tang too well, can practically feel her fingertips burning into my skin.

'I'll be careful,' I promise, fetching my cloak and drawing the hood up.

It's raining, the mist and damp air sticking my hair to my face. I'm shivering as I move through the acropolis in search of her temple.

I have visited only a handful of times and it looks much the same as the others: tall white columns, friezes of stories that have very little to do with her, and inscribed with vines and flowers that have all too much to do with her – flowers that, outside of this carved marble, are coloured with the blood of her lovers.

The wooden statue at the centre is an interesting thing. I am so used to her stealing parts of everyone around her – beauty is jealousy, love is theft – that to see this image of her, just another woman – beautiful, yes, but whole and original – is jarring.

When she appears, that is the form she takes: hair that

waves like heat scalding the air, pouting lips and a beaded fuchsia gown that glistens with dozens of jewels that can't outshine her.

I feel wrung out – hair frizzy with the humidity, my skin not clean enough from my quick morning wash, musk and sweat lingering. It is like I am being spat out before her.

'So,' she says, stalking forward, and I feel I should hold a spear, a bow – something to ward off the predator facing me. 'You lied to me. Repeatedly.'

'Yes.' I could list my excuses or drop to my knees and beg.

But I'm done. I have spent too long being what people wished me to be.

No more.

Aphrodite is furious, as expected – crackling with energy, wincing light in her eyes. 'Did you ever love Paris?'

'I wanted to.'

Her jaw tenses. 'I should have had you shot with an arrow the moment I led Paris to your room.'

She's done that before. Medea, high priestess of Hecate, a powerful and impossibly clever woman with magic itself at her disposal, a granddaughter of a sun god – one arrow and she was devoted to as unremarkable a man as Jason. She did everything for him and, once she'd been as useful as she could possibly be, he cast her aside.

Is that what Aphrodite wanted for me with Paris?

'I cared for Paris deeply, but I did not love him. And I mourn him –'

'In the arms of his *sister*.'

'With the woman I love,' I correct. 'The only person I could turn to for comfort. And I wish Paris had lived. I wish he'd won you the glory you long for. But perhaps we still might – love has bloomed in Troy, as you wished.'

'How dare you.' Her teeth are white and blinding and bared. Aphrodite steps closer and clutches the clasp of my cloak tight. 'This is not the love I chose for you. I'll have Eros prime an arrow and teach you what love actually feels like. I'll have you fall for another inappropriate man. Or perhaps not a man at all – a monster, an animal, perhaps.'

I know she does not make these threats lightly. She's forced girls to fall in love with their own parents as revenge for imagined slights.

'Would you care to explain that to my father?' I bluff. Zeus has allowed many of his bastards to perish on that field, not least Sarpedon. It's clear he would sacrifice us all if needed. 'He cast an evil lot upon us so that our tale might be sung through history – and those poets will say my beauty caused wars. How furious he will be to have his legacy corrupted, his daughter not the grandiose prize but a humiliated footnote in the tale.'

Her hand falters and I can breathe a bit better, the cloak still pulled too tightly, stopping me from running.

'What about your so-called beloved?' she spits, smiling now, as the path ahead becomes clear to her. 'Perhaps I'll break your heart by turning hers.'

'No,' I whisper.

I'm overdoing it, a touch. But if she thinks she still has that card to play, it will prevent her from searching for new ones.

'Yes,' she says, like she's savouring the word. She lets go so viciously I fall back a step. 'This war, from the moment that apple landed, has been mine to curate. Hundreds of thousands of men brought together in battle, thousands of lives lost, dozens of cities felled. *That* is the power of love. You think one defiant girl can stand up against it?'

I hold back my scathing retort – that she caused all that and was still pulled from the battlefield. But then I realize that's exactly the point – she did all this to prove her power and instead proved herself to be at the mercy of Zeus's will, just like the rest of us. Olympus above, she didn't even choose her own marriage; Zeus did.

I'm the only place left for her to vent her petty frustrations and she still can't strike at me for fear of my father – the very god she's railing against.

But we're defying Zeus, Cassandra and I. We're fighting the future he has laid out for us. Our love rewrote the threads of fate themselves.

What cruel irony that love is exactly as powerful as she hopes but, like Zeus with the fated course, Aphrodite thinks it is a thing to be wielded and set. And it is far too expansive for that. She cannot control who falls for whom – no one can. She has to threaten and command to prove her power. Or start wars. Or point Eros in a direction and hope controlling that small sliver of love will do.

And here I am, in love with a girl immune to his arrows. And Aphrodite can't breach Athena's protection to go after Cassandra herself.

But then she continues.

'Troy will be a tragedy. *That* is your legacy. Not whatever this is. I'll ensure Troy falls myself before I'm humiliated by the two of you. I gave you an escape, but if you're so ungrateful, then I'll send you right back into the hands of the man you left. I'll show you just how cruel love can be. I'm going to break your heart.'

One day. This is it – Aphrodite and Apollo both abandon our side and the city falls.

She smiles brighter than the marble surrounding us, so bright it burns.

'If you'd done as I said, this might have ended differently. If you'd loved Paris, you might have forged a different future. Instead, this is how you lose the war.'

She's wrong.

If Aphrodite wants a love to hinge her victory on, it's ours.

CHAPTER SIXTY-SEVEN

Cassandra

THE WOMEN GATHER AGAIN ON our penultimate evening, the day before the city falls.

'Maybe we just fight,' Kreousa says. 'We wait until the signal, burn that horse down and send our armies to the water's edge, waiting for the Achaeans to return. It's hard, landing ships in front of an expectant army.'

'It might work,' Helen admits. 'But we won't vanquish them that way, certainly not in twenty-four hours.'

The gods would swarm to swell the ranks of the Achaean armies the second their ban on interference ended – they'd do whatever it took to ensure Troy's destruction.

'We could flee, hide in the mountains and let them think we've run to our allies,' Ligeia offers. 'When they chase us, we double back and steal their ships?'

Kreousa nods, looking up from the notes she is making. 'It's an idea. But a whole city fleeing? It would be difficult to hide those tracks.'

'We could leave letters,' Clymene adds. 'We could say that we would rather be dead than their captives, say we've cast ourselves into the ocean. It might delay them and give us time to get past the mountains and into neighbouring lands.'

I find myself nodding. The Achaeans fight for glory. They see this as a tale every bit as much as the gods do – and I can certainly see them ignoring their better instincts to believe we would give them such a tragic, noteworthy end.

Agata scowls. 'So tomorrow we will spread the word of the signal, and tell people to evacuate wherever we tell them.'

Spoken aloud, I realize how little we have.

Glancing round the room, everyone is despondent, shrivelled – even if they don't fully believe the consequences, they feel something might happen, and our lack of a plan, our inability to wrestle with this prophecy, is becoming a deep-seated feeling of failure.

But Helen seems enthused, smiling like the plan is blindingly brilliant. 'We'll cause a distraction so the gods don't realize what we're doing.'

Herophile snorts. 'A giant wooden horse is already pretty distracting.'

Helen gasps.

We all turn to her. She's staring wide-eyed at nothing, fumbling for words.

'Oh gods, I just had either the best idea or the worst.'

Honestly, it's a little bit of both. But it's the one we settle on.

I grab Kreousa before she returns to the palace.

'There's one more thing,' I tell her.

Her gaze is stony and resolute but her fear lurks in her eyes. Something protective roars in my gut, pleading with me to keep her safe. But how do I protect her from something as all-consuming as our city's destruction?

She takes a wax tablet from her satchel – which is far more convenient for this conversation. I watch as she scratches a message.

Our plan is laughable.

I wipe the wax smooth and write my own.

Yes, but so is the Achaeans', and that is prophesized to work so I don't see why ours shouldn't.

All this talk of honour, and the Achaeans plan to win through treachery. So we will have to be just as underhanded.

Kreousa wraps her arms across her chest. Once, the thought of saving her pulled me back from the brink. But now how many times have I seen her die? Gasping in a crowd, crushed in the rush to escape.

I take the stylus and keep writing.

When the horse comes, we'll think the war is over, we'll bring men home from the front. Aeneas will be with you. You need to make sure he gets on one of those boats.

She scowls.

I wasn't going to leave him. But why?

Because, gods, if any of us lives a happy life after this, it's him. Aphrodite helped cause this war. But she won't let her own son die in it.

I've seen lands beyond the gods, lands where they can't reach us. I think he knows how to find them.

She looks doubtful, but she nods once more.

Please stay safe.

Kreousa hugs me for a long time. When she finally lets go she does it with a vicious shake of her head. 'No, don't make this a goodbye. I *will* see you on those ships.'

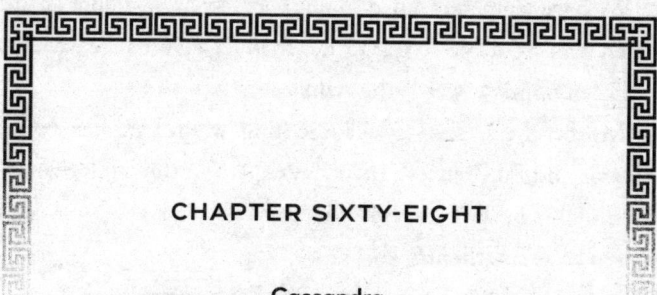

CHAPTER SIXTY-EIGHT

Cassandra

Helen and I leave the house, brazen and assured, ready to become the distraction the others need to spread the word of our plan. If the gods glance away from the camps tonight, let them look at us.

I try not to watch the statues as we pass. I try not to count them, to imagine how many people might fit inside.

'Shall we go back to the palace?' I ask.

'Not yet. Let's make the most of our final night.'

So we go to the banks of the River Scamander and lie down on the cold grass, hand in hand and staring at the sky.

I trace patterns in the stars instinctively and see only a map of the gods' cruelty. There's Ursa Major and Ursa Minor, the woman turned into a bear and her son who tried to kill her. There's Orion, and the scorpion who killed him – sent by Gaia to keep him from hunting her beasts. All the creatures sent to kill Heracles simply because he existed. My eye catches on Andromeda, a woman chained in sacrifice for her mother's offences against the gods.

We have women chained in our very sky and wonder at the fact a man would go to war rather than let a woman leave him.

Helen points towards the twins.

'My brothers,' she says, something wistful in her voice. 'Castor and Polydeuces. Their days spent in the Underworld, their nights in the Heavens.'

'Do you miss them?'

'Yes, but . . . Yes, I miss them. But I'm angry with them too. Their stupid fight, their stupid decision. Polydeuces could have lived but he chose not to, he chose Castor. I don't think I ever came into the equation.'

'I'm sorry.'

'It feels like a lifetime ago.' She shakes her head.

'Do you think how long ago something like that is matters?'

If I live, I'll probably never stop missing Hector.

'Yeah,' she sighs. Her fingers nestle against mine like the gaps were made for her to fill. 'Maybe that's what we should be doing? Praying to a god to take pity on us, to cast us up as constellations before the Achaeans can get us. The Trojan Women, fleeing into the sky.'

'Do the stars look the same from Greece?'

'Yes,' she says. 'But I imagine they'll never appear so bright to us again.'

'Do you think we'll at least be able to see the same thing, for a little while?'

'What, every time you look at the stars you'll think of me?' Helen turns to me with a wry smile on her face.

'When don't I think of you?' Even though it's true, I say it like it's a joke. I don't know what else to do with it, all this heaviness. Maybe I was controlling the prophecies before I realized it, only letting myself focus on the war and not what happens after. If I'd ever lingered on it, I would have been crushed under its weight.

'What does the future we're carving look like, do you think?' Helen ponders. 'If our kiss can shift fate, if we can change it all by just choosing to fall for someone the gods didn't plan for, then I have to believe we can escape too. We'll get on those boats and sail away. What then? Inspiring princess for a new nation of people?'

'One who can't say anything they'll believe?' I ask. 'Let me lie to you: you're the one everyone loves. If anyone can keep the people of Troy together when the city falls, it's you.'

'You must want something.'

'I want a lot of things, they're just not exactly lofty ambitions.'

'Tell me. Go on, lie to me about what the future holds.'

I don't really know where to start. All the things we've discussed, and this is what feels like a confession. But I take a shaky breath and begin. 'All I ever knew was what I didn't want. And when I escaped it, I just floundered. I kept waiting for some passion to claim me and, when it didn't, I latched on to all these superficial things. Attention, prestige, power – I convinced myself if I only had more of it, I'd be happy. But I think what I really want is the sort of thing I never paid much attention to. I want to live well, joyously, to love every tiny moment. I want to read in the sun, dance barefoot on the sand, swim beneath the waves, be kissed under the stars.'

The hand that isn't holding mine brushes my cheek. My breath hitches at her touch but I freeze under the way she's looking at me. It's the way the devout stare at statues of the gods, the way people gaze at art, an appreciation that terrifies me as much as it excites me.

'I can help with one of those,' she says. Her kiss is gentle and sweet but something about it wrenches at my heart, brings me close to tears. I thought this yearning for her would stop if we were actually together, but it's grown stronger. Even without fate's tapestry, I imagine I could see something physically connecting us, threading from my chest to hers. And when my hazy eyes catch on the strands, I see dozens winding between us. I imagine a lifetime to weave even more.

'I really wish I could tell you. I wish I could say it. But I don't want to turn it into a lie, or force you to believe it.'

Under the moonlight, her eyes are a navy that verges on black and there's something unreadable in them: something sad and earnest and hopeful.

'You don't have to convince me of anything, Cassandra,' she says, her voice heavy. 'I already know.'

My mouth is dry, my heart pounding.

'Are you sure? Because I really don't want you to not believe me.'

'I'm sure.'

'I love you,' I say.

By which I mean: *I would excuse a war for the chance to meet you.* And: *You are the only thing to make this bearable.* And: *I would let my home burn to give you the possibility of a happier life.*

'I love you too,' she says. Where mine sounded like the biggest declaration of my life, hers sounds simple, like it's just another fact – that, yes, the stars shine above and, yes, there are ships on the horizon and, yes, she loves me.

She keeps whispering it as I kiss her, keeps pulling away to gasp, 'I love you,' against my lips.

'I've never said those words and meant them before,' she tells me when we break apart.

'They're some of the few words of honesty I have left.'

'This won't vanish with us,' she says. 'Even if . . . even if the stories lie, if they erase us. We'll matter, at some point, at some time, to someone.'

We're so close that our noses are brushing, like any space between us is too much.

'This is what I want,' I say. 'In the future, all that other stuff, everything else I can figure out. You're what I want.'

She hums, pleased. 'There's the answer I was looking for.'

CHAPTER SIXTY-NINE

Cassandra

Helen and I sleep in the temple of Apollo, our bodies wrapped round one another because we aren't letting go until we're forced to.

If we want to steal the attention of the gods, a certain arsehole in particular, then what better way than staying in his temple?

We wake as the sun rises. Already people are running through the streets, rumours spreading that the Achaeans are gone, no ships, nothing. Men race from the palace to the gates and back, a dozen messages passed.

We hear other rumours too, rumours about an evacuation plan for the city, rumours we hope the gods are not listening to too closely.

By noon, the city has erupted into celebration, people drinking and dancing in the streets. Helen and I head to the city gates, tearing a loaf of bread between our fingertips, passing chunks of it back and forth.

Heads turn in our direction. I have a tiara on my head, a clasp with Apollo's sun emblem holding my cloak fast at my throat. Helen wears a Spartan dress, not only cut short but the shoulders wreathed with chains, like armour is mere decoration. A thin circlet of gold adorns her hair and her sword swings at her waist – sharpened and cleaned but still flecked with enough rust that it's clear it is no decorative accessory.

We might as well have our names emblazoned across our chests.

This had better work. If the Achaeans find us, they'll know exactly who they have cornered.

'Cassandra!' Deiphobus spots me and comes running. He yells my name with fury but there's relief in his eyes. 'We've been looking for you everywhere!'

For a moment, I worry Kreousa didn't tell him – or even brief him on the rest of our plan. But then I catch the corners of his lips twitching, like he's forcing the smirk away. He's enjoying this performance.

'I should have known you'd be with Helen,' he adds, holding his hand out to his wife like they might shake in greeting.

Helen stares at it for a moment. 'Husband,' she says as she takes it. 'We saw something from the temple of Apollo. And with rumours of the Achaeans abandoning their ships, we wished to see.'

As if on cue, the gates open.

A handful of men march through, two of them grasping the arms of a captive Achaean between them.

'Sir,' they say, coming to an abrupt halt in front of Deiphobus.

'Well? Is it true?'

'Completely abandoned,' one of the men says. 'They've taken everything with them, and burned the camps. There's nothing left.'

'Well,' another man says, gesturing back at the gates, 'not nothing.'

Which is when a dozen other men appear, pulling the giant wooden horse that haunts my visions. This is the start of our destruction.

Kreousa would have given Deiphobus one very clear instruction: bring the horse into the city.

The gods won't withdraw until they're certain we're going to fall but, even still, it's difficult to see that wooden statue before me and not want to tear it apart with my bare hands.

'There's an inscription, sir. It says: "For their return home, the Achaeans dedicate this offering to Athena."'

'Well, that's nice of them,' Deiphobus says bitterly. 'Given they ransacked her temple. You,' he snaps at one of the guards. 'Go fetch Laocoön and the priests of Athena.'

The man nods and runs.

Deiphobus gives the horse one last look then shakes his head, as though the puzzling thing is unworthy of his time and attention. Oh, he's revelling in this.

'Who's this?' He nods to the man in the guards' embrace.

'My name is Sinon, my lord. I . . . I was left behind.'

'Why?'

'Because I tried to escape to Troy one night, to defect to their side. To your side.'

'And they did not slit your throat?'

Sinon swallows round cracked lips. 'I think they thought it a worse punishment, my lord, to watch them sail away and leave me to your mercy.'

'And why should we not kill you? We gain nothing by letting you live on the chance you tell the truth.'

Sinon winces. 'An ill omen, no, to kill an unarmed man on the day of your victory?'

Deiphobus arches an eyebrow. 'Is that what you're clinging to?'

'Are you enjoying the show, love?' The voice sends jolts up my spine, even though I've been half expecting it for hours.

I can feel Apollo tapping at the barrier behind me before he struts into view, all easy grace and casual smiles, like he'll watch us burn and applaud a good spectacle.

Helen's eyes flick to him, then look steadfastly forward like she does not want to let on that she sees him too. Still, I see her watching me from the corner of her eye and feel a little safer for it.

'What's the horse for?' Deiphobus asks.

'An offering to Athena,' Sinon says. 'They hope you will leave it at the shore so that it may look over the ocean and see their safe return home.'

Deiphobus's eyes light up at the opportunity. 'Is that so?'

My brother is wasted in the army; he ought to act in festivals instead.

'Go on, dear,' Apollo says. 'It's not like you to keep silent.'

'What do you want?'

'Why, to see whatever desperate trick you have planned. Clearly nothing I've done will dissuade you from doing as you please, and I'd like to watch as it fails. I'd like to see it when the hope finally fades from your eyes.'

My teeth grind but I try to ignore him.

'Bring the horse in,' Deiphobus calls. 'Let the walls block its sight of the ocean. I see no reason the Achaeans deserve a safe journey home after the lives they have taken.'

'Oh, do get on with whatever it is you're planning,' Apollo says. 'Or do you want your city to fall? Have they not believed you too many times? Do you harbour such resentment over them locking you away that you wish to see them all dead?'

I let him think he's riled me into it when I start screaming prophecies, letting them fill me, letting them pour forth.

'... *Achaeans ... treachery ... destruction ...*'

Apollo's laughter spills behind me as I lurch forward and clutch at Deiphobus so tightly my knuckles pale.

'Don't do this,' I gasp, begging between prophecies.

'Not now, Cassandra.' He brushes me off like a needy child.

I snatch a torch from a bracket on the wall and launch myself at the wooden horse the second its nose inches through our gates.

I know how long I have, could practically count the seconds before the guard tackles me, another tearing the torch from my hand.

Deiphobus looks dumbstruck. Gods, he's really milking this. 'You would dare try to destroy a sacred monument to Athena?'

Something icy cold and biting claps over my wrists. Manacles. Even the Greek captive isn't bound in iron.

'Well, *I* only planned to lock you in the tower.' Apollo grins. 'Even I wouldn't sink so low as to chain you. Now, did you really think that would work?'

'Piss off,' I hiss.

The soldier holding me clearly believes the comment is meant for him because he tightens his grip so fiercely that I can already feel the bruises blooming beneath his fingers.

Deiphobus turns as the priests of Athena arrive, Laocoön

in their centre. He's one of two high priests in the city who work across all the temples. He's always been perfectly decent, if not a little boring, and now he eyes the horse with the same wary, studious expression he often uses to ruminate on the gods' will.

'I don't like this, my prince. You held Odysseus only days ago – do you not see his mark here? Either there are Achaeans hiding in there or it is a machine to use against our walls or to spy on our homes, or some trick I am not smart enough to think of but Odysseus certainly is.'

'Oh,' Apollo says quietly, shaking his head as he too turns to watch, 'Athena won't like this.'

'Don't trust this,' Laocoön continues, but he's not given a chance to finish the thought. The ground beneath his feet cracks and Laocoön shrieks even before two stones fly free and bury themselves in his eyes. He falls to his knees screaming, his hands covering his face, blood trickling between his fingers.

Apollo turns his face to the sky. 'Really? The fall of Troy has you uncharacteristically theatrical.'

I'm not sure I agree with that – Athena's punishments are bold, assertive strikes. But she is goddess of wisdom, and now she penalizes those who exhibit it?

This is what the gods are willing to do if we stray from their plans this close to the finish.

'Clearly Athena is angered by our rejection of this statue built in her honour,' one of the priests of Athena says.

Deiphobus nods. 'I agree. For now, take it to the acropolis. I want it as far from the sea as possible.'

Apollo turns back to me, eyes narrowing at the way I hang

in this guard's arms. 'This can't be it. The last frantic ploy of the cursed priestess is to try to shout and destroy?'

I look to Helen and nod. We are still the distraction, after all – and it's time to convince the gods we've run out of tricks, that after all this time ruining their plans we're finally at the end.

'Deiphobus, dear husband.' She rushes forward and touches his arm gently. 'Perhaps it is at least worth testing such theories?'

'How do you mean?' Deiphobus asks. He catches my eye, as though not realizing our protests are all part of the show. No, he can't question whether the plan has changed.

'You shouldn't let it in!' I call, letting the curse spur him on.

Helen scowls at the towering statue. 'Can we investigate it? See if we can find some sort of hatch?'

'We've already done that, sir,' a soldier interjects. 'There is nothing.'

'See?' Deiphobus waves his hand. 'It's fine.'

'Please,' she says. 'Allow me one moment.'

'Very well.' He smiles patronizingly. 'But no fire near the horse.'

Helen nods, approaching the thing warily. It is half in the city now, its head and neck reaching through the gates, its front legs dragging in the dust, the men heaving on the ropes they have lashed round it.

'Odysseus, my love?' she calls in a voice I recognize only because I have seen her in visions, weaving by day and pulling it apart at night. Penelope, Odysseus's wife and Helen's cousin. 'Please, please come out. Our son is here. He walks now but cannot recall his father's face. Won't you show him?'

Apollo watches with a fascination that veers towards dread. 'No, this won't work.'

Though he doesn't sound like he believes it.

Helen coughs, then changes her voice again while the men stare on with bewilderment – her mimicry a gift they did not know she possessed. 'I forgive you,' she says in the voice of her sister Clytemnestra, my would-be murderer. 'Agamemnon, I forgive you. I know you had no choice and I know how much it hurt you to kill our daughter. Come out, my love, please, let us grieve her together. Let us find peace.'

Nothing. Which is not a surprise, as Agamemnon is not in the horse. But she continues anyway, cycling through voices in an attempt to draw the men out. It feels like exactly what the gods must think it is – a desperate last effort to trick the men inside into coming out and prove that the horse should not be brought into the city.

'Anticlus, my love, is that truly you in there? Oh, how I have waited for this day! Come, do not waste another minute anywhere but my arms.'

Apollo's attention snaps from Helen to the horse, where, if the threads were true, Odysseus is clasping his arm over Anticlus's mouth.

Helen continues, her words filling Anticlus's ears as he struggles for breath. At least he hears his love's voice as he dies. But it is a lesson again, if Iphigenia were not enough, that the Achaeans crave our destruction so ferociously they will kill their own to get it.

Apollo turns on me. 'Call her off now or I will harm her.'

'You wouldn't dare – it's what this war is about.'

'Menelaus shall have her back,' Apollo says, rageful lights

that I can't look at flickering across his eyes, as graceful as his father's lightning and just as cruel. 'I don't think he'll care much if I rip out her tongue – in fact, I think he'll prefer it that way.'

I don't turn away from Apollo as I call: 'Helen's words. They wrench the men apart.'

They had already been laughing at the display but now they jeer too, heckling Helen's efforts until Deiphobus eventually snarls: 'That's enough, Helen. Come, let's return to the palace.'

She turns, laughing, giving a shake of her head. 'Silly me, I thought it was at least worth trying. Thank you for indulging me.'

I have to bite my lip not to laugh at the vacant expression she turns on the men.

'Better.' Apollo smiles. 'I shall enjoy watching you dragged in chains to the palace only to be hauled from it again later. Will it hurt, to know you were the captive of your own people before you were the captive of the enemy?'

'I hate you,' I spit.

'I don't believe you.' His smile falters as he glances skywards. 'Alas, I shall have to watch it from afar. Father summons us back to Olympus. But I'm sure I'll see you soon, my love. I wouldn't miss the fall of Troy for the world.'

CHAPTER SEVENTY

Helen

CASSANDRA STRUGGLES AS THEY HAUL her back to the tower and I know it's all part of the act but it hurts, my heart whining a desperate whimper. Deiphobus's words are a sudden, unintelligible buzz, a tightening in my gut telling me to follow her, to get them to lock us in a cell together.

'Helen,' Deiphobus says, in a way that suggests he's said it several times before I finally pay attention to him. 'What's next?'

The gods are gathered but we should give them some time, enough that we can be certain Zeus's declaration barring them from fighting has been made.

'We celebrate the end of the war. Everyone will be looking at us, so let's give them a show.'

We leave to join the masses dancing in the palace's Great Hall, taking each other's hands, our feet moving unthinkingly in the steps. We smile for the celebrating crowds, raise toasts and pretend to drink them.

I take Deiphobus's hand, and it strikes me that by nightfall he might be dead, and I might be back with Menelaus. There are many thousands of threads where our plan does not work – and then what?

A quiet, cold chill runs through me.

All this time, I have prepared to return to him – running through scenarios, readying lies to persuade him of my authenticity, my love, my fear, all the humbling things I would do to make him believe not only that I am sorry for all that has happened, but that I am the meek, obedient wife he always wished me to become. I thought, if it happened, I would simply react as needed.

But I didn't prepare for the fear.

If Troy burns, then what is the most I can hope for? Menelaus falling for me? Deciding not to have me executed? I imagine a lifetime of bending myself to rules he never would have dreamt of before but can get away with now that he has a war as his excuse. All while he turns Sparta into everything I dread.

I have no right, really, to be upset with that, given what happens to everyone else. There is a chance for me to live. But it is a slow death, turning into a fragile husk of my former self. Perhaps tragedy isn't a competition – maybe it is simply tragic that we all might be undone in the end. I know better than most that there are a thousand ways to destroy a person. The Achaeans will try them all.

The song ends and I catch sight of Athrae waving to me at the edge of the hall. It's time.

'Good luck.' I nod to Deiphobus.

I take off towards the city, to the spot I have been allocated – Athena's temple. The sky is darkening and I see a few of the others spill from the palace towards their own locations, lanterns in hand.

I pass such joy and jubilation. I am thankful that, if this is it, there might be one final moment of celebration.

Athena's temple is nearly deserted – the priests celebrating like everyone else. I cross to the narrow pillars at its far edge, clinging to one and leaning forward to wait for the light to appear at the top of the watchtower.

When it flickers to life, I light my own torch and watch as lights appear across the city – our signal, our warning.

The music stops. I cannot see people from here, but in my mind's eye I see them running. If nothing else, we will not be fools caught unawares. In Sparta we die with a struggle: nails and teeth if we must. I hope the Trojans will not have to fight at all, but, if they do, at least they have had time to find their blades.

But then a hand shoots out before me and snatches my lantern, hurling it to the temple floor. The glass shatters – the spray slicing into my thin sandals. My hand flies to my sword, but quicker than any mortal could possibly move, that too is snatched from my side and hurled across the temple floor.

I turn and find myself face to face with beautiful green eyes flecked with burning gold. I clock the rest rapidly: sandy-blonde hair curling round crisp laurel leaves, ivory toga and tanned skin bulging with hard muscles. It's the smile that does it: excited, self-assured and with the wild glee of someone with very little to lose.

Apollo.

'Hello, Helen. How glad I am to *finally* meet you. I was hoping we might have a word.'

CHAPTER SEVENTY-ONE

Cassandra

'**WHAT WOULD WE COUNT AS** interference?' Hera asks, toying with a ring in one of her well-pierced ears and turning to her husband with a fine brow raised.

Zeus glowers at her. 'Whatever you're thinking, certainly.'

Apollo, sitting in the shade of a tree a few metres away, turns to his twin sister, Artemis. 'I don't like this,' he says, eyes scanning the horizon, watching our annihilation.

'Don't be a baby. Cities fall every day. You'll find new places to worship you, I'm sure.'

'Something's not right. I don't trust that girl.'

'Your prophet again? Why do you need everyone to adore you? Get over it. At the very least, stop whining about it. Where are you going?' she demands as he stands, yanking at his chiton, dragging him back to the ground. 'Even you cannot be so stupid as to interfere.'

'I'm not interfering. I'm just getting a closer view.'

'No,' she hisses. 'None of us are happy about this, Apollo.'

'Hera and Athena look just devastated,' he spits with vitriol.

'Don't be an idiot – even they know what happens to girls when *cities are captured. Even if they want the Achaeans to win, we would all stop parts of this if we could.'* She glances at her father but it's more of a glare. *'But, like the rest of us, you need to sit down, shut up and deal with it. And by the Styx, stop bloody pouting.'*

When the vision clears, I'm back in the tower. It's happened – so why can I still hear music floating up from the palace? I run to the window, and I see them: dotted figures, cloaked, holding lanterns and disappearing through the palace gates.

Night is falling, dusk settling. We have an hour at most. And on the horizon: tiny black silhouettes of approaching ships.

I reach into prophecy but we're only just at the edge of the iron knot we've been hurtling towards and I cannot find a way through yet. Perhaps when the men spill from the horse and find an empty city, as new strands fly in to make sense of it, perhaps then I can weave Trojan victory.

The tower door is flung open, Deiphobus appearing in its frame. Together, we charge down the palace's steps like we can't move fast enough.

'Are you coming with me or –'

I shake my head.

'Of course . . . Helen,' he realizes. 'She asked me to give you this, by the way.'

He passes me her dagger, complete with the strip of fabric she uses to hold it to her thigh.

I dread to think of her without it, but cannot pretend I am not relieved to be armed myself.

'You know what you're doing?' I ask, slipping the dagger into the pocket of my dress.

'Yes, Kreousa told me to spread the word through the palace. Andromache should have already started.'

'And Scamandrius?'

'Yeah, I'm supposed to get him to help,' he says darkly. 'Though personally I think we should leave him for the Achaeans.'

'Could you bring as much treasure as you can? Or hide it, at least?'

'Why?'

'If you found other treasure, would you bother with the statues?'

We have to give them no choice but to drag the statues on to their ships.

'All right, there's not much left after paying our allies anyway . . . So, I'll see you soon.' But the expression on his face says he doesn't need a prophecy to doubt that.

I throw myself at him, despite knowing he doesn't like hugs and cares little for my displays of affection.

For once, he hugs me back.

Then he pats me on the head and I elbow him in the stomach for his condescension.

His laughter is a hideous, uproarious bark and I would like to bottle it. I would like to believe it is not my last time hearing it.

'Go to her,' he says. 'I'll see you really soon.'

And this time he sounds like, even if he doesn't believe it, he is willing to give it a chance.

I run through the palace, trying not to look too closely at it at all. Will I ever be surrounded by so much beauty again? This marble that could have been so cold, painted in blues and creams, gold symbols of the gods nestled into cracks, detailed art in crevices. The soft glow of the lanterns, the carpets so thick your feet sink as you walk. The Achaeans will tear my home apart.

Rounding the corner, hurtling past the Great Hall, I nearly collide with my parents.

'What are you doing here?' I gasp, a stitch already forming in my side. Polyxena stands with them, her hand in our mother's, her eyes wide and terrified, and, Olympus above, they need to *go*!

'Cassandra,' my father says. 'You cannot expect us to hide inside statues and abandon the city.'

'But –'

'I'm sorry, Cassie,' my mother breaks in, launching forward and clutching me in her arms as tears fall. 'I really didn't want to leave you in that tower but I couldn't see another option.'

I don't have time for this, I know that, but I'm surprised by the indignation that roars in my belly. Because I was already in that tower before I forced her to slam the door shut. I push her off me. 'You wanted to hide me away!'

'Cassandra, I'm sorry too,' my father says, as my curse swirls in his eyes. 'But that's simply not true.'

I scream, hand slamming into the hard marble wall with my frustration. I cannot keep doing this! And I cannot fix my crumbling relationships with lies and jumps and tilted language.

I swallow, knowing what I am about to do and hating myself for it. I do not want to take their choices away from them, do not want to override their will like I know better.

But I need them safe. I need this not to be our last conversation – and most of all I need the hope that one day I might speak to them without their minds warping with a curse.

'You shouldn't hide. You shouldn't leave the city,' I say, guilt churning as the curse takes hold.

Because they would fight me on this, I know they would. They would say that it's our home, where our roots are, that it's not so easily abandoned. And I'd ignore everything I feel – my unending love for this city, the memories it contains, the way it feels like everything I am – and tell them it's just rocks, just mortar, that we can defend it to our dying breath but it will never love us back. But I'd be lying, because it does. It *does*. And losing it is beyond comprehension: our foundations swept away, no ground beneath our feet nor roof above our heads.

But we can't save it, so we save ourselves, we save each other.

My curse churns through their minds and they nod, prepared to give up Troy without a fight.

'I don't love you,' I finish – and then I sprint away, knowing if I stay I might not do what needs to be done.

Fate is burning. I can feel the prophecies snapping, hissing, disintegrating. It's destabilizing the very fabric of the future – and I don't know what happens if it breaks altogether.

It's worse as I reach the acropolis and run through the elaborate ring of schools and temples.

'*. . . let them reverence well the city's gods: the fallen lords of Troy and their shrines, lest the cause of ruin so too come to ruin . . .*' I breathe, but the words are crackling away, like the future isn't sure they will even be said.

And then I pass it: that wooden horse.

In the darkening night it is even more imposing. Unlike our statues, built of long stretches of warped wood, this is built of hundreds of interlocking pieces. Which is much easier to hide an opening in.

It would be easy now, in the darkness, to set that damn horse on fire. It would not win us the war, but I could watch the men inside burn, hear them scream and perhaps plead for my mercy as the flames swallowed them.

Is this it? Is this madness?

I step back. It wouldn't get us to their ships. It wouldn't get us away from this doomed city.

I give it one last look and continue to Athena's temple, where I'm supposed to meet Helen. It was decided so quickly I did not think about the visions – that, in the future that haunted me, this was where the Achaeans found me. Now my every step weighs heavy.

But the temple is empty.

Did Helen think I wasn't coming? Has she already hidden? Should I hide too?

I hug my arms to my body, wondering if my family are out by now, if they've crawled into statues of their own. Are there enough? Have some people just decided it is better to run? Or are people hiding in the cellars I've seen them die in a thousand times?

And then, in the distance, I hear roars – roars like a charging army.

Oh gods, it's beginning.

I rush to the entrance of the temple and peer out, my heart lurching as I see figures moving through the dark – swords drawn. And then, down the street, I see it: Apollo's temple. I can't say how, but I know. I know like I always do when it comes to him.

I run.

The figures turn to me with angry shouts. I can barely make them out in the dark, do not know if these are nameless soldiers or the men who have haunted most of my visions.

But some charge towards me.

'You shouldn't let me go!' I scream. 'Nothing bad will happen if you follow me! You should definitely remember that you saw me.'

The curse takes hold, and I run towards the man who gave me this twisting power.

CHAPTER SEVENTY-TWO

Cassandra

MY FOOTSTEPS ECHO IN THE dark quiet of Apollo's temple, the only other sound my uneven breathing.

He might not be here; I might be paranoid.

But lights blaze, glowing from nowhere, and he leans against his altar, a smile unfurling as he sees me. And there is Helen, his hand curled into the fabric of her gown, right at the back of her collar, like she's a cat caught at the scruff.

'You're late,' she says, aiming for nonchalance, but even she can't hide her relief.

Apollo twists his hand sharply and Helen jolts to the tips of her toes as the fabric strangles her.

'Hush, now,' he says softly, leaning in so close his lips brush her hair. 'You've played your part. This no longer concerns you.'

Helen's eyes find mine and they're filled with terror. Any mortal man and she'd have had him on the floor by now, but who knows what the punishment for fighting a god might be.

'Then let her go,' I snap, trying not to look at her, trying not to indicate to him how much his hold on her terrifies me.

'Why would I do that?' He turns with a sudden snarl. 'I can't touch you, can I? But her . . .'

He illustrates his point by running his finger along her cheek, slowly, languidly, and I know he's doing it to hurt me but it's working. It takes all my self-restraint not to tear his hand off her. But I don't trust him not to do something worse.

For her part, Helen cringes back, still reaching for me with big wide eyes.

'You know, you're really overdoing this dramatic villain thing,' I say, trying to redirect his anger to me, but he only laughs.

'Do you think this will work?' He nods in the direction of the city.

'Yes, otherwise you wouldn't be here.'

'Oh, love, I don't care about all that. Troy will fall. The mortals will all be dead in fifty years anyway, and we'll tell the story we want to tell regardless. But you, I do care about.'

'Then do whatever it is you're planning on doing to me and let Helen go.'

He cocks his head to the side. 'Is that what you want? Does fearing me excite you?'

I'm not quick enough to hide my look of disgust.

It only makes him smile wider. My rejection is adorable, my disgust endearing.

I realize what has been escaping me all this time: it is not that he does not hear my 'no', does not understand it, does not believe it because he is a god and it simply could not be true. It's that no word has ever thrilled him more.

'You should thank me,' he says. 'Your little plan might work, but do you truly believe if she goes with you,' he shakes the hand gripping Helen, who startles, 'that they will not follow you to the ends of the Earth? They might take the city scorched to the ground as a victory, but they won't without her back in their grip.'

I try to keep myself calm or at least direct my anger into the sort of icy coolness that might better make a sharp point. But I want to destroy him. I want to hurt him so badly he will never recover. I want to strike him, to forego language altogether, because hasn't he taken that from me too often?

'Unfortunately, I don't believe in trading women like treasure.'

'Not even for the thousands of lives you thought lost?'

'Is that calculation so easy to you?'

'I could turn you over to my father right now and let him punish you for daring to disrupt the path he set forth. Or you can see this plan through. Perhaps it will work. Maybe they'll drag those statues to the shore. Maybe your people really will be able to steal those boats and sail away. But not like this. This is what I offer you: your citizens given hope, if only Helen is returned to her rightful husband and you come with me.'

'And if I tell you to throw yourself into a river of Hell?'

Apollo shrugs. 'You've missed your opportunity to hide in a statue. Would you care to take your chances with the Achaeans?'

'Rather than you? Yes.'

'And your people?'

'Maybe I can save them all.'

His eyes flutter shut and I feel something tug at my core.

Prophecy, I realize. *He's trying to see prophecies. But they aren't his any more, they're mine.*

'What?' He winces, scowl forming, and I nod at Helen, who breaks his grip and runs.

He lunges for her but I pull on that thread and it's easy to throw him into those visions like he always did me. All those tapestries of the future, all those things he has never bothered to glance upon, strands now entangling him.

Apollo stumbles, submerged in the gold hazy blur of the drowning threads. Helen raises her arm to shield herself from the glow but I focus on Apollo instead.

I show him every time he will fail. I show him the lovers he will kill, the punishments he will suffer, the things he will lose.

Again and again and again. If there is one solace in all of this, it is that he will lose, even if it takes millennia.

Apollo falls to his knees.

'Get out of here,' I whisper to Helen, unable even to look at her, scared that if I stop staring at Apollo, my hold on him will break.

I show him the way mortals will turn on him, force him back to Olympus. He'll be ridiculed, forgotten, scattered into a thousand different stories until even he doesn't remember who he once was.

'No,' he gasps, reaching out a hand, and the prophecies waver, just for a moment, as he fights back. And a moment is all he needs to close that hand into a fist. Magic arcs out, golden light in a crackling line that strikes Helen, surrounds her in its glow, and when it disappears, so does she.

My hold on him vanishes and he is panting on the floor, then, slowly, he is laughing too, and all I can stare at is the spot where Helen was standing.

'Where is she?' I half scream, half beg. I raise my hands,

preparing to throw him back into the relentless tide of prophecy, but he cuts me off with a raised finger and a tut that makes me want to rip his head off.

'No, no, I wouldn't do that again. Not if you want your friend to live.'

I let my hands fall to my sides with a howl of frustration.

'That's an interesting trick you've learnt,' he spits as he climbs to his feet. 'What have you done, little priestess?'

I can barely think past Helen, can't push past the panic long enough to spin a tale that might save us.

'Answer me!'

'Prophecy,' I rush, hoping that if I comply, he'll return her to me. 'You gave me prophecy.'

It takes a moment.

'No,' he says so quietly I have to strain to hear it. 'Visions of prophecy, or else I allowed you to hear its whispers, not . . .'

'No, you gave me prophecy.'

I'll let him think it was simply his mistake, and no effort of my own.

A shadow falls across him, his features no longer golden sunshine but the tarnished bronze of a well-used sword.

'And just as before –' he stalks towards me, perhaps forgetting he can't touch me – 'you take this gift, believing you owe me nothing in return.'

'I don't. What have you done with Helen?'

'Be quiet. This changes everything. You have to come with me. I'll tell the gods I gave you this on purpose, that I gifted you immortality, made you the goddess of prophecy and took you for my bride.'

'That's not going to happen.'

'It will if you want to see your little friend again,' he says. 'You'll say nothing, of course. You'll swear on the Styx not to reveal that your gift of prophecy was . . .'

'Your own fuck-up?'

His eyes narrow. 'That will change too, when you are mine.'

'I'm not going to be yours.'

'And Helen?'

He's bluffing. He has to be bluffing. 'If this doesn't count as interfering with the fall of Troy, I imagine harming Helen certainly will.'

'I'll deal with the consequences, I always do. Come now, Cassandra, I offer you immortality, godhood and a love story for the ages.'

'You are not my love story.'

He smiles and steps closer like he can change my mind if he only flashes his perfect teeth at me one more time. 'Oh, my dear. I've destroyed you and you've destroyed me. Tell me that is not love, tell me that isn't a tale the poets will sing for years to come. We'll be an epic, you and I.'

'I will never love you,' I hiss. 'I will never even like you, Apollo. If I liked boys, I would never like a boy like you. No one would – that's the problem, isn't it? That they all run from you?'

'Careful, dear, I can break your friend's neck with a flick of my wrist.'

'She'd prefer that over returning to Menelaus.'

'Is it her? Is that why you refuse me? You harbour a childish infatuation with the queen of Sparta?'

'I love her!'

He flashes that wolfish grin and I feel cornered. I'm not sure how many times I can outrun this man.

'Then do it for her,' he says. 'Marry me knowing that because of it she will live.'

'I already told you she wouldn't want to live with Menelaus, she'd prefer death. You have nothing to offer.'

'No?' He quirks an eyebrow. 'Very well, Cassandra, my final offer: marry me and I'll set Helen among the stars.'

That one throws me. I stare at him, trying to find some indication that he is lying.

He presses on. 'I don't keep track of all my father's children. Even Athena couldn't count that high. But Polydeuces? That one was pretty hard to miss. Her brothers are in the sky, are they not? Why not let her join them?'

I have to admit that something about that is compelling. If he returned Helen to me now and let us go, would we live? The Achaeans line our deserted streets, looking for her.

He grins at my hesitation. 'Your people will flee, Helen will live for eternity in the Heavens and you will hold power even among the Olympians.'

I would die to save the people of this city.

Can't I suffer for them too?

But then ... could I do what he always accused me of? Could I agree, wait until the people are away and Helen is safe among the stars, and run? Refuse to get married or else dive from the nearest cliff at the earliest opportunity?

If I fail, at least the others will be okay. I could put up with Apollo for that.

I glance out at the city, the stars shining above. I could look up and see her every night.

'You'll remove the curses you've levelled against me and you'll swear on the Styx to never use your powers against me again.'

He glows with the thrill of victory. 'Very well.'

The words get stuck in my throat, and when I finally manage it, it's a whisper of surrender. 'Then I agree.'

He holds out his hand – perfect, featureless fingers, despite the swords he has wielded and the strings he has plucked.

I hesitate, clinging to my last chance to refuse, and then I reach for it.

And I'm hoping Athena's curse is stronger than he suspects, that I'll hit that barrier. But my hand glides right through the air, until it falls into his waiting palm. My heart sinks. So it's true. He can't touch me but I can touch him.

But even that is not enough for him, because he's been waiting for my acquiescence for so long, and I do not doubt that he has fantasized about this moment for months.

'Seal it,' he commands. 'Kiss me.'

And what choice do I have if I want him to uphold his part of this bargain?

I lift my hand from his open palm, just to give myself a little bit more time, and, yes, I can touch him like this too, my shaking fingers pushing through his hair, holding his face, tilting it down for me.

He shuts his eyes.

So he doesn't see me catch sight of the tower behind him. The flashing light at its top. The signal we agreed, that sent the citizens running to the statues to begin with.

Helen. She's in the tower.

And I realize this was always his plan – because Castor and Polydeuces weren't scattered in the skies until after their bodies fell. And he wishes for her to die first too, would let her live her long, miserable life with Menelaus before placing her in the sky.

I should have known – what have we ever done but find loopholes to torment each other with?

My resolve hardens because I am not giving this man a single thing – not without using him as he always feared.

'I can't do it like this, Apollo.' I let my voice break a little, just as I've seen Helen do. 'I never considered marriage, only ever swearing myself to you. But I know it shouldn't be like this. Set aside your curses and I'll abandon my hatred and our kiss can be the beginning of something new.'

His eyes shoot open and I see the suspicion there clearly.

I rush on before he can voice it, and do what he has always craved: repeat his own ideas back to him. Whatever role he has placed me in to pursue me as he has, I let the promise of fulfilling it pour into my words: 'A poem. An epic. Let our kiss be its starting page.'

Apollo relaxes ever so slightly – but, more than that, he is impatient. After months spent chasing me, he's finally getting what he wants – and he cannot wait another second. I've held out so long he might give me anything to force me across that final line.

Helen's right: there is some power in being who they want you to be. I'll make them regret it.

'Very well,' he says. '*I rescind my curses and vow on the Styx to never again wield my powers against you.*'

I *feel* them lift. By the gods, I had no idea just how heavy those curses were, lingering in my skin, my bones, my every action.

'Thank you,' I say, and I do, genuinely, mean it.

I let my eyes flutter closed – just enough to peer through my eyelashes. But he's so startled by the enthusiasm of my impending kiss that he does not think, just shuts his eyes and leans forward.

My hand slips into the folds of my dress and clutches the handle of Helen's dagger.

I expected it to be harder, hurting a god.

But this close, with his eyes shut? The blade, simple mortal bronze, slides into immortal flesh like thread through a needle.

He gasps but I'm already running, pulling the weapon out as easily as I pushed it in, Apollo's golden blood dripping from its blade on to my hand, splattering across my cloak.

I hear Apollo fall to the ground behind me but his laughter follows. I picture him there, clutching a wound he knows won't kill him, only slow him down, laughing despite the pain. But I don't turn round, don't waste a second. I'm already hurling myself down the stairs when he speaks.

'Go on, then, little priestess, run. Do you think you'll get to her before the Achaeans do?'

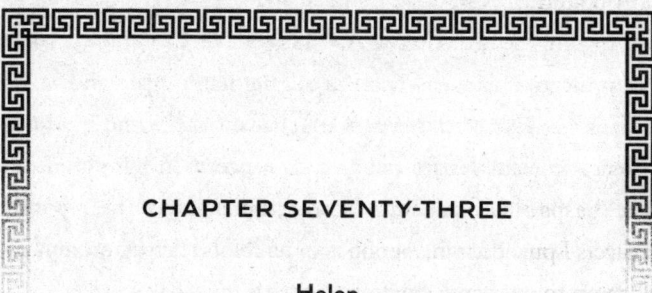

CHAPTER SEVENTY-THREE

Helen

I CRASH TO A ROUGH WOODEN floor with such force my jaw slams shut, my teeth rattling in my skull, and bright lights dance in my vision. I linger a moment, taking stock of injuries – my knees dulling from a shattering pain to a persistent throb, my wrists strained, palms scratched with splinters.

I should be relieved that they are not greater – a god could do almost anything, after all. But my mind crosses to Menelaus, and how much worse it will be if he finds me in such a state. To survive him, I must be the perfect wife, unrelentingly beautiful and not so much captivating as ensnaring. Instead, I will greet him in a dusty dress, my hair dirty and my skin blemished with bruises.

I stagger to my feet. I am in a circular room. The walls are open at intervals, letting in a harsh breeze and the rising, choking smell of fire. I rush forward and see that the palace is ablaze – smoke pouring from the windows in thick, churning waves.

I lean out and, in the darkness, my hand brushes something warm and metallic.

A lantern.

I turn in the direction of Apollo's temple. *Cassandra*.

I want to scream it – want to call her name again and again. I want to never stop, when the Achaeans come and bind me, when Menelaus ferries me across an ocean so my blood can wet the floors of my city – I want her name to be my only solace, I want the whisper of it to be the last thing on my lips as the blade is driven home.

Apollo can't touch her. But what else might he do?

I fumble for a match along the shelf where the lantern lies and find a splintered scrap of one, strike it hurriedly against the rough stone wall of the watchtower, and light the lantern.

I wave it like I have done twice before: once after Odysseus's letter, to signal to the Achaeans, and once to save the Trojans from them. I hope Apollo sees it. I hope it draws his attention away from her and back to me. I hope it gives her time to escape.

In the street, a few of those torches appear to be dashing towards me.

I place the lantern on the ledge – a beacon, however small – and race down the stairs.

I tug two thick, unwieldy bolts across the door – protection, but for how long?

I'm ruined, I know I am. But I'd throw myself from that window ledge if it bought Cassandra some time.

Back upstairs, the fire is spreading, illuminating the city a little more brightly and blurring those smaller lights running my way. The ones that remain lurch to the side or sputter and flicker – something happening, something I can't see.

And then, in the orange light of her burning city, I see Cassandra.

No.

I run downstairs again because she is clearly heading for me – that *fool. That glorious fool.*

I yank the bolts free and swing the door open in time to catch her, to pull her in and slam the door shut behind her – barely noticing the way the Achaeans cringe from her. She slumps against me and I hold her up with one arm while I heave the bolts back across with the other.

I turn to her, this warm body in my arms, head lolling forward – no trace of physical harm, no blood, but, Olympus above, she just ran through a city crawling with the enemy, so how could she be all right? 'Cassandra!' My voice is a desperate howl.

'Hi,' she breathes, blinking up at me with dark, tired eyes. 'I'm okay. I just had to give them all visions to get through . . . No curse.'

No curse.

Because I don't feel it – that urge to deny her, that split second of rage that she dares lie to me.

'How?' I ask, rushing to put that lantern out. Maybe there's a chance they won't realize we're in here. Maybe we could hide.

Cassandra tells me in heavy, panting breaths how she got Apollo to remove the curse. Then she gasps, cutting herself off mid-sentence.

'Look!' she cries. She's facing the sea – and the flecks shining in the reflection of the pale moon, flecks that are growing smaller as they sail away.

'There were hardly any statues on the street,' she says – and I savour this moment of her speaking freely. 'I passed some soldiers arguing – it seems like they all worried if they didn't take them, someone else might.'

'Then we succeeded, for some people at least,' I say, watching those dots sail away. 'That's something.'

But not for us. Not for Cassandra.

Echoing from below, the first thud of a man trying to break into the tower.

I flinch and take Cassandra's hand, memorizing the bones of her – the dry skin, the hard ridges, the graceful fingers.

'I'm just glad you're all right,' she says. In the dim light, she is a patchwork of shadow – viciously carved cheekbones and sharp jaw, deep grooves along her collarbones and the hollow of her throat.

'Me?' I choke the word in a half-laugh. 'Cassandra, he threw me into this tower just so he could be alone with you. I thought if I lit the signal it might draw his attention back to me, but –'

'What? That's so stupid – every man in the city is swarming this tower.'

'I thought if it gave you the chance to get away . . .'

'No more self-sacrificing, please,' she pleads, taking a small step closer to me. I wish I could spend my remaining moments looking at her, but she's a princess of this conquered city. She's in so much more danger than I am.

Another clang echoes from downstairs to prove my point.

'Could you push more of those visions and get us to the ocean?'

She bites her lip. 'They drained me. I'm not sure I could get us even as far as the walls.'

'Can you reweave the future?'

'I keep trying, but the strands are slipping through my fingers and I don't know which ones to grab for. Tyche said it's more like building than weaving and I can't find a strong enough thread to use as my foundation. I don't think we can rely on me working the tapestry.'

'I can say you're my maid,' I suggest. 'You won't be such a prize captive. I might be able to persuade Menelaus to take you with us, to keep you by my side.'

'No one will believe that.' She tugs at her fine cloak, a rich and expensive shade of purple held tight by a golden clasp in the shape of the sun. It matches the tiara perched on her head, and even if we threw it all from the window, no one could mistake her for any sort of servant when one glance at her hands would show only marks from nails biting skin. Besides, all it would take is a single other captive identifying her and then I'd be at just as much risk as her for having lied to them.

She pulls my hand and I fall into her open arms. I so often forget that she is a few inches taller than me until the moment I'm against her, resting my head in the crook of her shoulder. It would take the might of the army to wrench me from her arms.

From below, a thundering crash startles us both. Yelling follows, uproarious excitable shouts. The door has fallen.

'We could jump,' I say.

And we could.

How many times has Cassandra said she would prefer death to her future? Would I?

'We deserve a future together,' she says so piteously my heart wrenches. 'Gods, what an awful time to realize that I don't want to jump, not at all. I want to be on a boat with you, sailing somewhere we might stand a chance.'

'I know,' I agree, my voice quiet, because any louder and it might break like everything else.

There are footsteps on the stairs.

I turn to her. 'Perhaps the Underworld is the best we can ask for. Hades was kind, maybe he'll be kind once more.'

'But what future exists in a place like that? Even if we end up in Elysium, living in eternal paradise, it's not the joy of growing and changing with you by my side. I want to watch my sisters have children. I want to see Polyxena grow up. I want to read in the sun, dance barefoot on the sand, swim beneath the waves and be kissed under the gods-damned stars.' She's speaking so quickly, her voice veering up in pitch, and I hold her tight until she shakes her head.

Gods, I want all that too, but those footsteps thundering on the stairs . . .

'Not until all hope is lost,' she insists.

'What hope do you imagine we have?'

She raises her fingers, and on them I see a metallic mark that shines as the distant firelight catches it.

'We can achieve even impossible things,' she says, removing the dagger from the folds of her dress – thoroughly coated in a golden sheen.

'Apollo,' I breathe. Golden ichor, a god's blood. 'Is this his?'

I can't stop staring at the blade, like it's tickling something in my mind – all that shimmering blood, the blood of a god.

'Yes,' she says. 'If we can escape the clutches of a god, we can escape the hold of men.'

Which is when the door bursts open and I spin, catching Cassandra's hand and drawing the blade to my neck – sticky with Apollo's drying blood and sharp-edged enough that I fear mine staining it too. I drop my hand so rapidly the men don't realize what I've done.

They only see Cassandra, holding a blade to the neck of the woman they've spent months fighting over.

CHAPTER SEVENTY-FOUR

Cassandra

THIS IS THE SORT OF cruel twist the Fates are so fond of — that, in this moment, my final curse might have saved us.

The man at the front is hulking, with a large bushy beard and tough weather-lined skin. I am so used to my brothers, our army led by boys, that I had forgotten most on that field are older. It is all the more terrifying, somehow, to be confronted by an adult man with his sword in hand. He turns to one of his companions. 'Go get Idomeneus.'

'Should we not get Menelaus?'

'Are we Menelaus's men?'

'No, sir.'

'Then go fucking get Idomeneus.'

It appears the abandonment of Troy has torn apart whatever fragile unity these invaders had.

I keep the dagger at Helen's throat, still not knowing why. But she put it there — she must have a plan. For her part, she stands rigid in front of me, like she is truly alarmed by its presence. Does it still have golden blood on it? Can the men see it? Do they believe it is hers? That Helen, daughter of Zeus, has ichor in her veins?

If she does, all the more compelling for them to possess her.

But before that man can leave, booming footsteps sound on the stairs.

Odysseus bursts through, other men behind him. He looks tired in a different way from usual. In visions, I've seen him weary from battle and collapsed, exhausted, on an island. But this seems to energize him, lets him charge into the room, boars' teeth gleaming on his helmet, his blade drawn.

I feel Helen tense, feel my own breath catch.

'Let us go and I won't hurt her.' I try to sound authoritative, to channel a haughtiness that was once second nature. But I sound, even to my own ears, exactly like what I am – a terrified and desperate girl.

Odysseus smiles and I grip my blade a little tighter. I'm growing to fear the smiles of men.

He turns his head to the side, taps his ears. There's something in them. Wax? Does he think me a Siren?

'My patron told me of your curse. And I suspected you might have learnt how to weaponize it.'

He knows about my curse. And thinks it still afflicts me.

Can I use that, somehow?

Helen stiffens and I know she probably has an idea, some plan or other. But I'm not as brilliant as she is, and certainly not as good at getting men to do what I want.

Odysseus nods at the first man. 'I assume you have sent men for Menelaus?'

The man doesn't answer, which must be answer enough.

Odysseus rolls his eyes. 'Come now, our unity has brought us to these shores, don't let it fall away at the last moment.'

'Yes, sir.' The man nods, rushing away himself to find Menelaus.

Odysseus turns back to us, his gaze lingering on Helen like he has all the time in the world.

'Helen, my dear, lovely to see you again.'

'Odysseus,' she yelps. 'Please help me, please, I don't know what she might do.'

'I assume you're pleading with me to save you from the mad woman with a blade to your neck? You'll have to tell me how you found yourself in such a position. When I can hear it, of course.'

More men swell behind him, standing on the stairs now because there's so little room.

Odysseus steps forward and I shake Helen, trying to look as though I seriously might hurt her.

'Not another step.'

Odysseus raises his hands in mock-surrender.

'I'm going to take this wax out now,' he says. 'But I wouldn't try anything – my men have instructions to stop me from doing anything stupid, and it really would put me in a foul mood when deciding your fate.'

What could I possibly do? At best, throwing them into visions – if I could summon the strength – might get us out of this tower. But it wouldn't get us to the boats. Perhaps the best I can do is make them sympathize with Helen, make them treat her kindly.

Odysseus fumbles with the wax blocking his ears and when he pulls it free he turns to me with another vicious smile.

'Hello. Princess Cassandra, I take it?'

'What gave it away?'

'It's bold, I'll give you that,' he says. 'In most of the cities we've visited, we've found the princesses have swapped clothes with their maids and hidden in the kitchens. Then again, every single time they've been sold out by those they once considered beneath them. Your old friend Briseis didn't even make it that far – her own people turned her over before Lyrnessus actually fell.'

'Visited? I had no idea you were tourists.'

'War has its demands.'

'Does it? Or do the men killing my brothers just not want to draw their own baths at night?'

I cannot bring myself to think about the other things they do to the women they have captive, not when my own future might make drawing Agamemnon's baths a good day.

Odysseus scoffs. 'We only have a few moments until Menelaus arrives – is this truly what you wish to discuss?'

'What would you prefer?'

'Shall we try your terms?' he asks, nodding at Helen. 'You know, as a bargaining chip, she's a pretty terrible one. She signed her own death warrant the moment she left Sparta.'

'Do you always kill women when they leave their husbands?'

Odysseus shrugs. 'When there are treaties drawn up in their name, I might consider it.'

'And yet I assume Menelaus wants the honour of killing her personally, or we'd both be dead by now. Do you not think I can slit her throat before he arrives?'

'Unless?'

I lick my dry lips, begging words I haven't thought of to appear.

I know why Helen did this — she wants to force me into saving myself. And maybe it is the best-case scenario that I make it out but she stays here. She might survive where I might not. She might even be able to escape at a later point.

But I didn't go through all of this to leave her behind.

'Let us go.'

'Us?'

'I can't give up my only leverage and rely on your goodwill. I'll leave her for your collection once I'm out of the city.'

'Interesting.' Odysseus pretends to consider it. 'Counter-offer: I give you a quick, clean death before anyone arrives to argue.'

'Compelling,' I spit.

'We all know exactly how desperate your play is here. We could disarm you in seconds.'

'Would you like to try?' I ask with venom I don't feel.

'Cassandra, please,' Helen tries, performing the helpless victim.

'Shut up,' I snap at her, hating myself for it. Is this the last time I'll hold her? With a dagger to her throat? 'You're offering me death? Why not kill her then turn the blade on myself? One last act in defence of my city.'

Odysseus exhales in amusement. Of course. Why would negotiations for my life be anything but entertainment for him?

'Very well,' he says. 'But you must realize you've put us in an unfortunate position. No women in the city but Helen and a Trojan princess? You're valuable to us, Cassandra.'

'Valuable enough for you to kill.'

'Killing you is something I can only offer before one of the other kings arrives. They'd never let me do it otherwise.'

Something lurches in the periphery of my vision, and I startle to realize it's prophecy, no longer an itch of unravelling but something calamitous. I can't check, not with Odysseus here and a dagger in my hand, but it feels like it's . . . hurting.

'Let me think,' Odysseus says, and I know he's toying with me, trying to delay me. But what can I do? 'You're a priestess of Apollo, are you not? Perhaps I could convince the men to award you to a temple on the mainland. A gift to Apollo, to regain his favour after the sacking of his city.'

'A *virgin* priestess of Apollo?'

'That one might be harder.'

'Harder than my blade on Helen's throat?'

'Sir.' Someone runs forward. 'We're getting reports of Trojans attacking down by the docks. They're stealing our ships.'

'What?' Odysseus turns away, so apparent is his lack of concern that I will actually do something to Helen. 'Where were they hiding?'

'Umm, they weren't clear, sir, they said something about the statues.'

Odysseus takes a moment while the news lands. And then he starts laughing. 'The statues? Our own trick used against us?' He turns back to me. 'Your prophecies, I assume.'

He shakes his head, filled more with mirth than fury, before he turns back to the men. 'Send every single man to fight. All of you too. I can handle this.'

They rush away and I notice the way Helen shifts her weight. We might not be able to fight that many men, but Odysseus – she can. And he doesn't know that we are on the same side.

'Well, with that little development,' Odysseus says, 'I'm

afraid my offer's off the table. If Trojans are stealing our ships, I don't think I could convince anyone not to take it out on the city's princess.'

'Her first.' I tighten my grip on Helen, thinking of Apollo holding her by her cloak and wishing she could stop being manhandled.

'Go right ahead.'

'Odysseus, please,' Helen tries. 'Don't let her do this.'

'How did a princess of Troy end up with a blade to your throat in the first place, dear Helen? We've all witnessed you fight. You're a queen of Sparta.'

'She took me by surprise.'

'Did she?' He cocks an eyebrow. 'Because I would have thought you could have taken advantage of our conversation just now to get her off you.'

'Gods, Odysseus, what does it matter? Perhaps I want her to escape. I'm not particularly happy about being the tool of her negotiation, but I hope it works. I don't want to die, but maybe I was hoping Cassandra wouldn't have to either.'

'Perhaps.' Odysseus shrugs and glances behind him, down those stairs. 'Go right ahead, Cassandra, we're all waiting. Slit her throat.'

I'm about to lower the blade, about to give it up and let Helen attack him, even if it's a little premature, and we can make our escape. But I hadn't heard the footsteps approaching until they are terrifyingly close.

And then it's too late because Menelaus is walking through the door, a leopard skin draped round his shoulders, and Helen's hand, the one they cannot see, curls into the fabric of my cloak.

I'm still holding a damn knife to her neck when all I want is to use my body to block her from view.

Other men follow him, and I recognize some of them. There are even a couple of other kings: Teucer, Agapenor, Eumelus. And then, following them up the stairs with heavy, vehement steps: Agamemnon. Something in my chest seizes up and for a moment I'm not sure I can stay standing.

'Hello, *my love*.' Menelaus sneers the words, practically spits them at Helen's feet. 'This is where you start begging for your life.'

CHAPTER SEVENTY-FIVE

Helen

I AM ASH AND I AM crumbling in the lightest breeze. But I am not sad to become nothing – with Menelaus, that is the best thing to be.

Yet somehow, despite this deterioration and the certainty that I am slipping away, I am still solid, still standing, and there is still a blade to my throat.

'Menelaus!' I cry, nearly stumbling over the sound of it. 'Oh, thank the gods, Menelaus!'

Cassandra's hand on the dagger shakes and I flinch back, closer to her. Her body brushes against mine and if we are both terrified, at least we are terrified together.

He regards me with a vitriolic sneer. 'I would not thank the gods for what I am going to do to you.'

I nod until my throat brushes the edge of the knife, even letting it scrape slightly and draw blood, as though my devotion to him is worth the pain. 'I know you're angry. I would be too. I wish I had never been forced from your side. Oh, curse Aphrodite, for keeping me from you.'

His eyes twitch across me with a scrutiny I remember all

too well. So often he would find some flaw – and here I have given him so many. 'What the hell happened to you?' he demands, turning to his companions. 'We can't take her back like this – we want the jewel of all Troy's treasure, not this mannish thing before us.'

I knew he would say such a thing, yet I still bristle. 'My hair will grow,' I plead. 'My muscles will shrink. Whatever you want. However you want me.'

'You'll find your end at the edge of a blade long before such changes.'

'Of course, my husband, I have wounded you far more greatly than any weapon could harm me. If it eases your pain, and indeed the pain of Sparta, let a thousand blades pierce me.'

A brief flickering moment of doubt crosses Menelaus's face, shattered by Odysseus's scoff and his brother charging forward.

'Don't listen to that lying slut,' Agamemnon says. He is more than a decade older than his brother, with thinning dirty-blonde hair and skin like curdled milk. He spits at the floor and looks at me with such hatred that I feel all the things he would like done to me in a single glare. 'You, who turned down the kingdom of Sparta in favour of being a Trojan's whore. How many of the men have you been passed around? You are married to Deiphobus now, we understand.'

Behind me, Cassandra shakes. I try to reassure her but I'm not sure what she fears – is it one of these men? I would wrench that dagger from her and end them before they could so much as glance in her direction.

But I stare at Agamemnon, who so favoured this war. Achilles abandoned him after they argued over a captive woman. He sliced the neck of his own daughter. He's a monster.

But a man does not become the leader of the Achaean armies through kindness.

'If we could come back to the matter at hand.' Cassandra summons rage from somewhere. Her words are clipped and authoritative and even I find myself jolting up a little straighter. The men turn their attention to her for the first time. 'Which would you prefer: I slit Helen's throat or you let us go?'

'Who is this?' Menelaus asks.

'Princess Cassandra,' Odysseus answers. 'Daughter of King Priam. Priestess of Apollo. Oracle. Am I missing anything?'

'Girl holding a dagger to Helen's throat?' she offers.

Menelaus examines her with an agonizingly familiar shrewdness – like he is unravelling threads of his own in search of the one it would hurt most to cut. 'You're the girl who sent me that missive offering my bitch wife back.'

My breath hitches but Cassandra's grip tightens – and this time it's almost protective as she spits: 'I could make the same deal now for her corpse.'

'Yes, very well,' Agamemnon says with a leer on his face that makes clear that a chase is part of his excitement. 'You're free to leave.'

'Is your word worth something?' she snarls. *No.* That contempt is unparalleled – and it is deeply, deeply personal. All those things she never told me about her own future . . . Not him. I can't lose my sister and the woman I love both to this horrible man.

'It's all you're going to get.'

'Please,' I beg, wanting her as far from this place as she possibly can be. 'Just let her go, she's nothing to you.'

'Yes, and we'll take her all the same,' Odysseus says. 'Do put the blade down. You'll only make us angrier by prolonging this.'

'I'd rather die than go with you,' she growls. 'And I can take her with me.'

'We've been here before,' Odysseus says.

Behind me, Cassandra shudders and when she speaks, it's in an echoey, profound voice. '*Wrathful Achaeans, lie still beyond the gates of Troy, an empty city and barren land, in the tower where two cursed treasures found, caution abandoned to the windless sails, will bring incensed gods in chase.*'

My breath catches as I watch the men listen to this faked prophecy. It's almost compelling, though a little more specific than usual. But they do not know how prophecies sound – the cadences Cassandra can't quite mimic.

'Is this not the false prophet the Trojans spoke of?' Menelaus asks.

'Cursed not to be believed, I think,' Odysseus says, for the first time shrewdly curious about Cassandra. 'That's what Athena said. Which would make the prophecy true.'

'We can believe it – do you think us above such a curse?' Agapenor asks from the stairs.

'Perhaps it is only a curse on the Trojans. We are chosen by the gods, are we not?' Menelaus suggests. 'Or now the war is over, maybe it has vanished.'

'It does not matter,' Agamemnon hisses. 'I have listened to enough prophets. And when I take her back to my ship, I'll gag that false tongue away until I can find a better use for it.'

The city is on fire around us now, flames spread by the famed Trojan winds until every window is lit by a hazy orange glow. Odysseus turns to the men behind him. 'Seize her. She won't kill Helen. She doesn't have what it takes.'

A man steps forward.

And I snatch the blade from Cassandra's hand, spinning it and holding it to my own chest.

'She might not, but I do!' My heart pounds like it knows sharpened bronze is a mere breath away, but I glare the men down, just daring them to believe I'm bluffing. Unlike Cassandra, I'm not sure I am.

I think she realizes that too because she gasps my name falteringly, like she knows she cannot persuade me not to do this.

'Helen,' Menelaus hisses. 'What are you doing? Stop this at once!'

What now? How do I play both sides here? How do I get them to let us both go free when, if I fail, being agreeable is the only chance I have to live beyond the journey home?

My fingers feel uncertain, wrapped round the dagger. I force wide eyes and hope I look innocent. 'Please just let her go.'

'Or you'll kill yourself?' Agamemnon asks. 'By all means, go right ahead.'

'No!' Menelaus snarls, turning on his older brother almost petulantly. 'Not like this, we need an audience. The people of Sparta – no, all the people of Greece who have sacrificed so much for this war deserve the ceremony of it.'

I remember the humiliations I promised to save for when I was before him. Perhaps that's it – all these people who think I am a master manipulator, a princess with a wicked word on the tip of her tongue, and the reality is simply that I know how to get on my knees and beg.

I fall forward, knees crashing into the wood again. 'Please, whatever you want. I won't fight it. I deserve whatever future you have in store for me, but she doesn't. She's a priestess of Apollo – would you truly risk another plague by taking a second girl who swore herself to him?'

'She's disgraced, is she not?' Odysseus offers quite cheerily.

I don't look away from Menelaus. 'Why risk it? Please. I'll go with you without fuss. You can lay me on my own funeral pyre and I won't say a word – no curses, no begging, no pleading. Just let her go.'

'Stop this, Helen.' There's a challenging gleam in his eye that I remember all too well – one asking how far I'm really willing to push him.

'You know I won't fail. I know exactly how to bury this blade in the right place.'

'You'll put the blade down now and you'll come here.' He snaps his fingers and points at the spot beside him. 'And you'll behave.'

It is warm now, and punishingly bright, and the fire tearing through the city is close around us. Maybe I'm already on the funeral pyre, because all at once I can feel the flames ignite in myself: wild, scorching and annihilating anything in their path.

I stare at my husband and I snarl: 'Your ego launched a thousand ships, surely it can relent for just one girl.'

This is it, then. He will not forget this so quickly. But perhaps I could save Cassandra still. And if the choice is she or I, then there is no choice to be made at all.

'My ego? I thought you shouldered the blame you carry,' Menelaus says. 'I thought you acknowledged our right to execute you and give the people closure.'

'I acknowledge the right of the noble people of Sparta to receive the closure they crave. But if you plan to take an innocent girl captive, then you have no nobility for me to respect. She's just one girl – let her go.'

Agamemnon is examining Cassandra with far too much interest. 'One girl who apparently means a great deal to you.' I don't dare to look at her but I can feel her rigidity beside me.

'Perhaps I know what you do to girls, Agamemnon,' I spit. 'And maybe I'd save anyone from that if I could.'

'Bury that blade deep, you vile hag.'

'Deeper than yours did Iphigenia?'

Agamemnon storms forward.

But it's Menelaus's words that cut through: 'How dare you speak to my brother like that? That is enough, Helen. Evidently, I shall have to remind you of your place.'

Agamemnon reaches for the dagger – or perhaps for me, perhaps he plans to strike me.

But I'm quicker, lurching to my feet and spinning out of his path and then – did I plan it? Did I look at Menelaus and decide, then and there, that he deserved to die? Did a part of me know from the moment I saw him again that he would meet his end at my hand? That I would not bend myself to live for him again, but he could certainly die for me? Or was it instinctive, not a thought but a feeling thrumming through me that there was only one way for our story to end? – my hand flies out, the dagger shot straight and sharp and true.

It bites into Menelaus's neck in a bright bloom of rose-red blood that sprays in a careful arc. It splatters constellations across the stones, stains something deeper than my skin.

He clutches at the wound, which only buries the blade further, red overflowing his hands. He opens his mouth but the blade has severed something vital, stopping him from even screaming as he dies.

I speak before his heart stops beating. 'You vowed to fight for Menelaus's right to own me.' I can taste his blood on my very teeth. 'Well, he's dead. So who do you fight for now?'

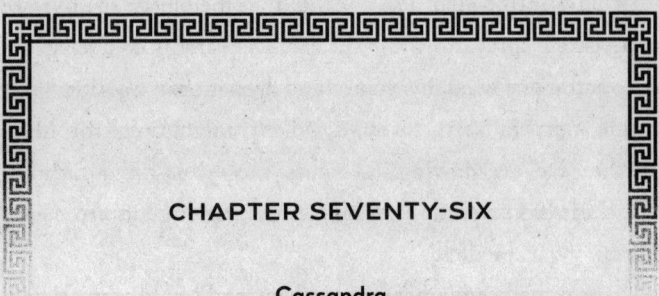

CHAPTER SEVENTY-SIX

Cassandra

'CAPTURE HER! I WILL NOT give her the quick death my brother had planned!' Agamemnon yells. I flinch – too many visions of my future with him to hear his voice without fear.

I grab Helen's outstretched hand and charge towards the window.

'Are we really doing this?' she asks, like the men aren't a step behind us, reaching for us, blades drawn.

It's death or captivity. We've run out of chances.

'I am. And they'll slaughter you for killing him.'

They'll draw it out. Truly make a spectacle of it, no clean swipe of a blade.

I clamber on to the window ledge, the rough stone cutting at my skin. The wind whips past outside, smoke growing so thick I could choke. The last thing I see is my city on fire. All I have to do is lean into it and I'll be free.

I want to take Helen's hand and give her a final goodbye but there's no time.

I don't even jump. I just step off.

I'm falling and then I'm not, I'm slammed against the wall of the tower and I can't breathe, can't feel anything but agony as a sharp edge sears my throat, and for a moment I wonder if I'm hanging from that thread again, if it might break my neck this time.

My tiara slides and I watch it fall to the ground as my vision blurs.

I wasn't quick enough. Someone has caught hold of my cloak, pulling me back through the window by my neck, the fabric tearing but giving them enough time to grasp my shoulders, my arms, to haul me back in and throw me on the floor.

I can't take stock of what hurts, my skin scraped raw or my neck or the hands they're twisting behind me, because I'm too busy searching for Helen.

Did she make it? Do I want her to?

My vision is shaky and black at its edges.

But, yes, I can see the hem of her dress, leather boots surrounding her.

The men holding me start yelling for chains and when none can be found they wrap my wrists in some sort of fabric. Possibly rope, I'm not sure.

My throat is torture but there's something worse than that – fate and prophecy screaming at me, demanding my attention. Captured, I sidestep into the world of its tangled threads and see the whole mesh pulsating, straining, threads snapping.

I have no idea what happens if it breaks, but I wonder if, possibly, the gods wanted Troy to fall for a reason that went beyond their greed and entertainment. Maybe this is the very thread the future of the world rests on – and maybe it cannot twist without it all falling apart.

I lurch back into my own mind as the men haul me to my feet; I see Helen being similarly restrained.

Odysseus appears in front of me.

'I think Agamemnon had a point about those prophecies of yours.' And suddenly his fingers are digging into my cheeks, forcing my mouth open, and he shoves a bundle of rough fabric into my mouth. I try to spit it out but I can't, and so this is it: the Achaeans have me bound and gagged, just like I've seen in a hundred visions.

I can't run myself into one of their blades. The height of this tower is my only hope.

So I go slack in their arms, bow my head and let them think the fight has gone out of me.

Helen stares at Menelaus's body.

'You know, we had bets in the camp on whether he would actually kill you,' Odysseus says. 'Most people thought no. I'd say you've just issued the order for our own execution.'

'What a waste,' Agapenor says. 'Couldn't we tell everyone Menelaus was struck down by one of the other Trojans and vie for her hand ourselves?'

Odysseus chuckles. There's something strangely detached about this man who has appeared in so many of my visions, who is so clearly invested in all this. 'A woman who wields a weapon like that? It would be a lottery for the next funeral.'

Agamemnon draws the dagger out of Menelaus's body and, his blood still wet on the blade, levels it at Helen, point nestled beneath her jaw, forcing her head up. Spit flies from his lips when he speaks. 'She will die. I will see justice done to my brother's killer.'

Helen's smile is a vicious slash across her face, blood

splattered on her lips, her skin, all over her. 'I killed my husband. After all you've done, I wonder if I might give my sister ideas.'

Agamemnon's hand tightens on the dagger and Odysseus claps a hand on his shoulder before he can force it into her flesh.

'Come,' he says. 'If there's fighting at the docks, we need to be there. Take these two to my ship.'

Agamemnon throws Odysseus's hand off him. 'I beg your pardon?'

'Oh, please, I don't want them. I just want a guard on them.'

'Then stick them on my ship,' Teucer says.

'Mine has an actual hold,' Emelus protests.

'For the sake of Olympus,' Odysseus snaps. 'Just take them to the city walls and keep them there. We'll deal with who gets what later.'

I realize the people restraining me are about to drag me away, so I take my chance, stamping on one of their feet and running.

I break free, somehow, manage to get to the ledge again and, with no way of climbing on to it, I just launch myself straight at it, even if it means bashing my knees against the stone.

And then, at the last moment, as I catch sight of the streets below, I crouch low and collide with the ledge because my momentum is too great for me to stop in any other way. Agamemnon takes my arm and pushes me to walk in front of him while laughing at my desperate attempt.

'Whoever takes this one might want to keep her within sight, or simply chained wherever you might want her,' he taunts, directing his comments to the other men but leaning close to me as he does.

He's too busy congratulating himself that he doesn't seem to have noticed I stopped myself – because I saw something out there in the dark.

And, in their bickering, they haven't heard the footsteps.

They flood into the room, swords drawn.

And there are so many of them.

So many girls.

Some are familiar, some not – all girls we have taught and trained.

The girls came back. They came back for us.

And with them I see what I've been missing: a bright golden cord, molten and alive with possibility. I needed a foundation to build on – and this is it. I can start weaving.

I turn to Helen and the Muses will sing of the look on her face – this glorious mixture of relief, pride and victory.

The girls fan out, Andromache at the front, flashing us a broad smile. Behind her come Herophile, Clymene, Athrae, Ligeia, Agata – and more. So many more.

I am half here, half in the web of prophecy. My hands are still bound but it's no matter – mentally I reach through, feeling the tapestry thrum to life, and I start to desperately weave in threads to hold it all together.

The horse, the men inside, and I cannot weave the past but I can pull it and stretch it into the future, draw it across those fraying edges. It is not so different, is it, really, from our people hiding in the wooden statues? I tell it so, whisper to it like the living thing it so often feels like, and I feel a second thread come away in my hand: our people hiding. I use it to bridge the gap. Ever so slightly, the shaking strands of prophecy calm.

The men are startled and they hurriedly draw their own swords but no one rushes to clash them.

'This is ridiculous,' Agamemnon says. 'Put those weapons down at once, you foolish women, you don't know how to –'

We never find out where that might have been going, as a woman charges to the front and skewers him mid-sentence.

She draws heavy breaths, staring at the man who clutches the hole in his stomach, presses his hands to the flesh there. These men have been protected by divinity for so long – so many miraculous recoveries, so many near misses. Without the gods, they fall so easily.

The girl raises her head, tosses her hair back, and I recognize those emerald eyes. *Briseis*. The queen Achilles took as his war prize – who Agamemnon snatched from him when forced to give up his own.

The other men ready their weapons but Odysseus raises a hand.

'I think we can all agree he had that coming.'

The men don't rush to argue.

Agamemnon punctuates the point by groaning and keeling forward.

I'm not sure whether Clytemnestra will be pleased to hear what happened or devastated that she could not land the killing blow herself.

'You might save him,' Helen says with a look of distaste, 'if you leave now and quickly.'

Agapenor ignores her and turns to Odysseus. 'Are you seriously suggesting we hold a truce with a bunch of women and girls?'

'Are there not two bodies on the floor that suggest why we might want to hold off? It only takes one lucky strike.'

'I'm no corpse yet,' Agamemnon growls. 'And I will –'

'Die?' Briseis suggests in a perfectly pleasant chirp.

I find threads of possibility – adjacent strands that were potential futures which never came to pass, ones of Menelaus's death, of Agamemnon's, and I unfurl them to weave into the fraying knot of this moment.

Odysseus turns to the gathered Trojan girls and switches to an attempt at our language as he speaks. 'What do you want?'

'Cassandra and Helen,' a few women answer.

Odysseus smiles at the lack of a clear leader.

'Take your princess, we'll keep ours. That's fair, is it not?'

I spot a girl who can't be more than thirteen sneak round the backs of the men, slip something small into Helen's bound hands, then dash back into the fold.

No one seems to notice.

I reach into the original knot and find the things that remain as they are – the horse through the gates, the gods resigned, a city on fire. 'Come on,' I whisper to it, 'this came to pass – is this not enough?' The threads expand under my touch, sturdier, metallic things. Prophecy still shudders but it is calmer now.

The women don't even consider his suggestion, which I admit I was scared they would.

But they didn't come back because they noticed their princess was missing, that their royalty needed rescuing. They noticed that the girls who orchestrated their escape, who taught them to fight, *their friends*, were missing.

And they owe Helen far more loyalty in that regard than me.

'We will take them both back with us, or we will kill

you,' Herophile says, strutting to the front. 'Those are your options.'

'We could do both,' Andromache offers, levelling a spear at them.

I find futures yet to pass, but futures so very similar – in Argos after a great battle, the women and elderly arm themselves and fight off their attackers. In dozens of cities, spanning centuries, women line rooftops and hurl tiles at invaders. And Aeneas sails to Italy with a handful of surviving Trojans – what is this but more? I borrow those threads and use them to patchwork this moment.

And finally, finally, prophecy settles into this future we have made and I have stitched. Because prophecy is mine, the future is ours and I will have it form as I see fit.

'We couldn't do that – our men would chase you across the ocean.'

'We have your ships.' Andromache smiles. 'And we will be so very far away. I'm sure you can make something up to appease them.'

'Perhaps I was never really here,' Helen says. She nudges her husband's body with her foot. 'Maybe I was a figment created by the gods, and Menelaus and I are somewhere else entirely right now. Egypt is lovely this time of year.'

'You're not nearly as clever as you think, and you belong to us,' Odysseus insists.

Herophile levels him with a cruel and condescending grin, and how glorious it is to not be on the receiving end of such a smirk. 'Fortunately, we weren't asking.'

Which is when Helen bursts free of the ropes tying her and within seconds plunges a blade so small I can't even see it into the neck of the man holding her. She spins to the one beside him and hands reach for me, pulling me out of my captors' arms.

Someone slices through my bonds and I wrench the gag from my mouth, turning to find the remaining men: the kings, a few of their soldiers, standing with their arms raised in surrender.

'When you go back to Greece,' Helen says, ripping the lingering ropes off her wrists, 'and they ask what happened to me, tell them I belong to myself now.'

Odysseus laughs. 'Is that what you think happens here? The war has resumed and you plan to run to the boats? You'll never make it past our forces.'

Briseis turns, twirling her bloodied blade like a dancer's baton and flashing a saccharine grin. 'Your forces are fighting each other. I mean, really, all those nations of Greece, all those histories of war, and you thought they'd hold tight when faced with an empty city? With the enemy that united you vanished and not a jewel of that Trojan treasure you came all this way for? It's a free-for-all, and Greek blood is spilling fast. I have a feeling we'll get to those ships just fine.'

CHAPTER SEVENTY-SEVEN

Cassandra

WE SPILL INTO THE DESERTED streets and Helen finds me, her hand sliding into mine.

The fire has swollen, encompassing whole streets, and thick smoke blocks so much of the chaos from view. I run with Helen at my side. We reach the walls and the girls veer sharply away from the shouts of so much fighting, leading us to the stolen boats waiting off the shore, a line of soldiers, Deiphobus at the front, holding them secure.

'It's about bloody time!' he yells, a huge grin on his face.

We wade through the icy water and are pulled on to the wooden planks, the soldiers leaping after us. I find myself facing a statue: Daphne, the nymph's limbs slowly turning to branches, leaves fluttering along her arms, and she is frozen mid-transformation, turned into a tree to escape Apollo's advances. I've always pitied her, but now I see all that there is to admire: that, in her final moments, she chose to spite him.

Helen pulls me to my feet, presses her freezing lips to mine, not caring that we are surrounded by people, not caring about anything but the sheer fact of us. She clutches my face and I can feel her shaking – not, I think, from the cold but from relief. I clutch her tightly, not sure I'll ever let her go.

The ship pushes off and I look up at the city. Its flames lick towards the Heavens, though of course the gods aren't there. They're watching this happen from the mountain on the horizon.

I imagine they're furious.

But Troy has fallen, just like they wanted.

I close my eyes, finally feeling the future settling.

The fighting dies and the remaining Greeks find themselves stranded, the ashes of the city smothering them as they struggle to survive. Among them I see Apollo. His absence from Mount Ida was noted, and what a convenient thing to blame the whole affair on. Apollo interfered, Zeus's will was ignored. And this will be his punishment: building boats for the Achaeans like he once built our walls.

Our neighbouring lands will sense their weakness, will come to finish what we started, and the gods will try their best to hold their forces at bay: rockslides on the mountains, waves swallowing ships whole, illnesses sweeping through invading armies. Still, some will get through. The fighting really will last a decade.

It will take years for the Achaeans to make it home.

The gods will spread their rumours as to why: storms and tidal swells, so many of them washed up on distant lands or else marooned on islands.

But we will sail away from them all.

Aeneas will guide us, his mother holding off the other gods as best as she can, spreading her rumours about how tragic the love of Paris and Helen was, a love story she'll have written down for the ages.

We'll stumble through a few homes, trailing along the coast of Italy. Until at last we'll find a new land, beautiful, fruitful – a place where the gods are not worshipped. Where they can't hurt us.

I see myself dancing on a sandy shore, my sisters barefoot and smiling. I swim beneath the waves, threading traps for fish, feeding those I love. I read in the sun and then I write in it too, carving our history for when the others try to write it for us.

Helen and I find new patterns in the sky. We will never stop holding one another under the stars.

When I come to, they're the first things I see – those stars. And then Helen, leaning over me, holding me.

The boat sways. I can still smell the smoke of the burning city but it's already many miles away.

'Well?' she asks, helping me to my feet, holding my hand tight, and I don't have to wonder if it's the last chance I'll have to touch her. Years stretch ahead of us. We have time, so much of it.

And the future is no longer a thing to fear, not when I have such power over its strands.

I blink away hazy visions of what lies ahead: *my parents smiling, my siblings laughing, Helen, there, by my side.*

I could lose myself in visions of a future like that.

But I have spent enough time in prophecies of what is to come.

I draw Helen to me, the sea-salt dampness of her body against my own, and how beautiful she is, framed by the burning city and the witnessing stars.

'We deserve a lifetime,' I say. And it's not merely a declaration, nor an echo of the words she has once said. With my fingers tangled in the webs of prophecy, it is a promise.

It is time to stop watching my future – and start to live it.

ACKNOWLEDGEMENTS

Thank you for joining me in my blue era.

In many ways this is the book of my heart, and I'm incredibly lucky to have had so much love poured into it by so many other people who made it possible for this book to be in your hands right now!

My thanks, always, to Hannah Schofield, who tirelessly champions my books. I really cannot stress that this would not be the book that it is without her expertise – nor her pep talks and reassurance!

Thank you to my team at Penguin, especially Harriet Venn, Stevie Hopwood, Naomi Colthurst and Jenny Glencross. I couldn't ask for better supporters of my writing and I so appreciate them coming to *The End Crowns All* with all the enthusiasm that they brought to *Girl, Goddess, Queen*.

This wouldn't be possible without a lot of people's hard work, so thank you to: Amy Strong, Faith Young, Natasha Devon, Jane Griffiths, Jan Bielecki, Candy Ikwuwunna, Shreeta Shah, Will Skinner, Jacqui McDonough, Anna Bilson, Eleanor Updegraff, Helen Gould, Stella Newing, Alice Grigg,

ACKNOWLEDGEMENTS

Maeve Banham, Clare Braganza, Stella Dodwell, Susanne Evans, Beth Fennell, Magdalena Morris, Rosie Pinder, Millie Lovett, Zoya Ali, Chloe Traynor, Ellie Williamson, Kat Baker, Brooke Briggs, Toni Budden, Ruth Burrow, Aimee Coghill, Nadine Cosgrove, Sophie Dwyer, Nekane Galdos, Michaela Locke, Eleanor Sherwood, Rozzie Todd, Becki Wells, Amy Wilkerson, Alicia Ingram, Sarah Doyle, Desiree Adams, Jenna Sandford, Mary O'Riordan, Sarah Hall, Rih Donald, Arienne Huisman and Eline Berkhout.

Thank you to my international publishers and every bookseller, librarian and blogger who has shared *The End Crowns All* with the world. And thank you to Pablo Hurtado de Mendoza and Danlin Zhang for the gorgeous illustrations that have made this book so beautiful.

To my first readers, who were so helpful in both polishing this book and in making me believe in it: Sara Adams, Anna Muradova, Izzy Everington and Laura Steven. And, of course, to Liberty Lees-Baker, who was the first friend to ever read any book I wrote and the one who encouraged me to write more.

Thank you to everyone who has supported me on this journey: Laura Ray, Jessica Rome, Megan Salfairso, Eleanor Brown, Dora Anderson-Taylor, Amanda Wood, Kristina Jones, Claire Kingue, Aoife Prendiville, Fraser Wing, Laura Grady, Saoirse McGlone, Hannah Ainsworth, Annie Gardiner-Piggott, Isabel Lewis, Natalie Warner and Sophie Eminson.

Thank you to my family, especially Amy Fitzgerald – again, sorry for setting the bar so high for sister rivalry, but you have a dog, so I think you're winning, and thank you for reading the book anyway. And to Carol Welsford, who was always so interested in these books and who we miss so much.

Thanks to Whoopi Goldberg, because 'I don't want somebody in my house' is really the vibe of the whole Trojan war, and frankly very iconic.

Finally, thank you to every reader who has taken the time to read my books. The real joy of sharing these stories is the community I've found. Because together, we'll get a little louder.